SPRING SURPRISES

Book Six of the Joe Beck Series

C.J. PETIT

Copyright © 2022 by C.J. Petit
All rights reserved. This book or any portion thereof may not be reproduced or used in any manner whatsoever without the express written permission of the publisher except for the use of brief quotations in a book review.

Printed in the United States of America

First Printing 2022

ISBN: 9798838983206

CONTENTS

CHAPTER 1 1
CHAPTER 2 67
CHAPTER 3 111
CHAPTER 4 142
CHAPTER 5 187
CHAPTER 6 215
CHAPTER 7 246
CHAPTER 8 265
CHAPTER 9 291
CHAPTER 10 315
CHAPTER 11 349
CHAPTER 12 382
TRANSITION 443

CHAPTER 1

February 23, 1864
Idaho City

Joe smiled at Faith as he said, "I'll be fine. It's not even a two-hour ride to Centreville and the snow isn't that deep."

Faith exclaimed, "But it's so damned cold! *Why can't Tap find any more deputies?*"

Joe kissed her on her forehead before replying, "You know why, Faith. It was hard enough before but after Ezra was gunned down last month, it's become almost impossible."

"But why can't Tap go to Centreville?"

"Because he's the sheriff and I'm his deputy. Besides, even though I'm an old man of seventeen now, I can handle the cold better than he can."

"That's a terrible excuse."

Joe smiled as he said, "I know, but it was the only one that popped into my head."

Faith sighed before saying, "I suppose I'm just having one of my moods again. I hope I'll return to normal after Kathleen Maureen arrives in April."

"You're not moody at all, Faith. It's just that we're still adjusting to our new life. If I had to guess, I'll bet that Marigold is driving Chuck crazy by now."

"I'd almost forgotten about her. I wonder how they're all doing in Oregon."

"Maybe we'll get a letter from someone before spring arrives."

"Do you think so?"

"Yes, ma'am. They all know where we are, so they'd just have to mail it to the sheriff's office."

"I hope you're right. You've been right about most things since I met you."

"Do I have to show you my ugly chest scar to prove otherwise?"

Faith laughed before saying, "You can show me tonight, Mister Beck."

Joe said, "And you can let me feel Kathleen Maureen trying to kick her way into the cold world," then wrapped her in his arms and kissed her.

SPRING SURPRISES

After their lips parted and Joe released her from his grip, Faith said, "When do you think you'll get back?"

"If I'm lucky, I'll return late this afternoon. But it's more likely that I won't leave Centreville before tomorrow morning."

"Promise me you'll be careful."

"I made you that promise months ago and haven't broken it yet."

Faith nodded then watched as Joe pulled on his fur-lined hat and tied the straps under his chin. After pulling on his heavy gloves, he kissed her again then left the warm kitchen for the devastating cold.

Once outside, he walked through the six inches of snow to the barn then tugged the door open and entered. He'd already saddled Duke, so he just took his reins and led his stallion through the door, pushed it closed then mounted.

He didn't see Faith through the kitchen window's frosted glass, but still waved before he rode down the drive. After reaching Third Street, he turned left and headed to Main Street. Five minutes later, he left Idaho City and began the lonely ride to Centreville. He'd only been to the town twice before and while it had been cold for both trips, it wasn't nearly as bad as it was now.

Tap wouldn't have asked him to make the ride in this weather if it wasn't for a serious problem. The trouble had started as most of them did, in a saloon fueled by liquor. In one of the town's six drinking establishments, two sets of partners had been squabbling over the border between their adjacent claims.

It had quickly escalated when friends of one of the pairs added their support. Then the other pair of miners had solicited help from their drinking partners and the squabble developed into a full-fledged barroom brawl. When one of them pulled his pistol and fired, it had ignited more gunfire. One prospector had been killed before the horrified saloon owner dispatched a rider to Idaho City to inform Sheriff Fulmer. After notifying Tap, he'd immediately headed back to collect the five dollars the bartender had promised to pay him for making the frigid journey. What would make Joe's job more difficult was that the man didn't know any of the shooters, including the dead man.

As Duke carried him to Centreville, Joe hoped that the cold weather had forced a resolution to the situation but suspected it was more likely to have gotten worse. His biggest concern was that the prospectors who were in the wrong wouldn't appreciate his arrival. At least the frigid temperatures would make an ambush extremely unlikely.

When the cold began to turn his cheeks red, Joe pulled his heavy scarf higher until only his eyes were left unprotected. He knew it could be worse. The sun was keeping his back warmer and there wasn't much wind which would make him even more miserable. But it was still cold enough that even his

SPRING SURPRISES

thick wool socks and boots didn't keep his toes from becoming numb. As uncomfortable as he was, he knew that Duke suffered even more, despite his heavy winter coat.

Through his thick wool muffler, he said, "Spring is going to be here soon, Duke," then patted his stallion on the side of his neck.

He was more than halfway to Centreville when he spotted a prospector's cabin about a mile ahead and just to the left of the snow-covered road. The tendril of smoke spiraling into the sky from chimney tempted him to take a break but decided to keep riding because it wouldn't be fair to Duke. The cabin probably wouldn't be that warm anyway and nothing like their house in Idaho City. He'd been lucky enough to buy two heat stoves in December to keep Faith warmer, but now he wished they were more portable.

He didn't think the prospector who built the cabin cared too much about his comfort as long as he found gold. His biggest worry, other than claim jumpers, should be the deep blankets of snow on the mountain behind his cabin. Avalanches were common, and a big one could smash his cabin into kindling and bury the prospector.

Joe studied the terrain behind the cabin and soon realized that the prospector must have understood the risk when he chose the site. There was a deep crevice behind the cabin that would minimize the danger of his home being smothered in an avalanche of frozen water. He then let his eyes climb the mountain to predict the path the tsunami of snow would follow if gravity had its way. Joe scanned the deep drifts and soon realized that the tons of snow would end its thunderous journey somewhere on the road ahead.

Even though he knew it was highly unlikely for an avalanche to begin without provocation, Joe still nudged Duke into a slightly faster pace. As his black stallion accelerated, Joe felt a bit foolish. But even as he laughed at his unnecessary concerns, his enhanced mode suddenly emerged. He didn't ask why it had but began to scan for the danger which had triggered its arrival.

He stared at the cabin but didn't see anything moving against the white blanket. But his eagle eyes soon spotted a narrow, string-like shadowed path that left the cabin and climbed diagonally up the side of the mountain. But the direction the climber had taken made no sense to him. Shortly after leaving the cabin, he would have to either fight his way through the deep drifts or cross the bare spots and hope the rock wasn't covered in black ice.

Joe followed the prospector's broken, angled path until it disappeared behind a small, sharp ridge that was almost six hundred yards from his cabin and around four hundred yards higher on the mountainside. He knew that there was only one reason for the prospector to leave his cabin in this weather. Joe had learned enough about the gold hunters to assume that the prospector had found some specks of gold behind the ridge and even the frigid weather wouldn't keep him from searching for the mother lode.

As he stared at the ridge that was just ahead, he didn't understand why he'd been elevated into his enhanced mode. He had his answer just seconds later when he saw a small cloud of smoke appear at the edge of the ridge. When the smoke began moving quickly across the white blanket of snow, Joe instantly recognized it as a fuse.

Just as he slammed his heels into Duke's flanks, the fuse ignited a small pack of black powder. The blast sent shock waves through the snow which made it release its grip on the rock underneath.

As he'd already identified the likely path of the avalanche, now that he was in his enhanced mode, Joe was able to quickly calculate how much time he had before the tons of snow buried him.

As Duke charged along the road, the enormous wall of snow was building mass and momentum as it raced down the side of the mountain. Joe needed to reach the cabin before the avalanche struck the road and knew it would be close. Even if he wasn't swamped by the massive flood of snow, Duke could be knocked to the frozen ground by the edge of the avalanche.

He looked back just as the white wave reached level ground and created its own snowstorm. The cloud of snow was all that reached him, so he slowed Duke knowing they'd narrowly escaped a frozen grave. He figured that the prospector was using the powder to blast away rock to start a new dig and didn't even bother checking for road traffic in this weather.

Joe may have survived the avalanche but now the road back to Idaho City was probably blocked and might not be able to return for at least two days. So, there was no way for him to let Faith know he was safe. Despite her assurances, he knew she still worried whenever he had to leave Idaho City to resolve a dispute. The delay caused by the prospector's carelessness would give Faith more reason to worry and that irritated him.

When Joe looked back at the enormous snow cloud, he decided to visit the cabin just to give the prospector a piece of his mind. When he reached the cabin, he'd probably have to announce his arrival with a gunshot and didn't care if it angered the prospector for interrupting his hunt for gold.

As Joe approached the cabin, the enormous, glittering white cloud still drifted in the cold air behind him. So, when the man who lit the fuse looked down at the road and saw the impact of his blast, he wasn't able see Joe. He soon left the ridge to return to his cabin but still didn't spot Joe. His eyes were focused the ground as he made his way down the slippery slope.

SPRING SURPRISES

Joe when turned off the road and headed to the cabin without even looking for the prospector because he assumed he'd be looking for gold in the newly exposed rock. But when he was close to the sorry structure, he looked toward the ridge and was surprised to see the prospector already making his way back down the side of the mountain. He pulled up before the cabin, dismounted and tied Duke's reins to a stubby branch that jutted a few inches out of one of the cabin's logs.

He was tempted to enter the cabin to wait for the prospector but didn't want to trespass. Besides, he probably kept his mule inside, and Joe didn't want to step in one of the mule's malodorous gifts.

He patted his stallion's neck and said, "I'll just let that prospector know I'm not happy that he blocked the road, Duke. Then we'll head to Centreville where I'll stable you in a warm barn. I just hope those boys have all calmed down before I find and arrest the killer."

Joe then walked to the edge of the cabin and stared at the prospector as he continued his slow, careful trek through the deep snow. As he focused on the man, he noticed that his gloved hands were empty which seemed strange. *If the prospector had gone to the ridge to dig for gold, where were his tools?* Even if he had only gone to the ridge to blast a hole in the rock, he would have brought a pickaxe or shovel to do a quick search. He wouldn't have abandoned them in the snow, either.

If he was returning just to protect his cabin from a trespassing stranger, Joe thought he'd be moving much faster. He was puzzled by the prospector's behavior as he continued watching his descent. As he drew closer, Joe noticed his head was down as he followed the path he's already carved in the snow and began to believe that he hadn't spotted him and Duke yet. *If he hadn't, then why did he leave the ridge so soon after setting off the powder?*

Joe then settled on the most reasonable explanation. The prospector had seen him after starting the avalanche and was returning to apologize for his carelessness.

The man was just thirty yards away when he raised his eyes and spotted Joe standing at the corner of his cabin. The unexpected sight stunned him into a sudden stop before he turned then started to hurry back up the slope.

Joe was surprised when he saw the prospector's reaction. While he didn't understand what had sparked it, Joe quickly chased after him. He may have had longer strides, but he still had to avoid falling when he reached the snowy path that angled up the side of the mountain.

He was still slowly gaining on the prospector and suspected that it was his badge that had spooked the man. He probably had a criminal past, which wasn't uncommon among the men searching for gold.

SPRING SURPRISES

The man was climbing as quickly as he dared when he looked back to see if he was being followed. But he never even caught a glimpse of Joe before his left foot slipped.

Joe was still moving as he watched the prospector tumble into the deep snow on the downslope then slide a few feet before coming to a stop. He was face down as he struggled to push himself onto his feet and almost looked as if he was trying to swim down the mountainside.

Joe reached the spot where the prospector had involuntarily left his path, then sat down and used his behind as a sled to slide downhill.

When he was close, he grabbed the flailing prospector's jacket and helped him to his feet. When the man finally stood and turned to face him, Joe thought he looked familiar. It took him four seconds to mentally stripped away his beard and was stunned when he recognized Eddie Pascal. His belief that the avalanche was just a careless accident was instantly replaced with a deep suspicion that Eddie was trying to use a mountainside of snow to kill him.

He still gripped Eddie's coat as he exclaimed, *"What the hell are you doing here, Eddie?"*

Eddie stammered, "I…I…I was just…I was looking for gold, Joe. Honest."

Seeing the terror in Eddie's eyes lowered Joe's fury to a simmering anger before he asked, "When did you become a prospector?"

"Right after I left Idaho City."

Joe let go of his anger as it wasn't serving any purpose then let go of Eddie's coat before he asked, "And that's your cabin?"

Eddie nodded and replied, "Yeah. I didn't build it though. It was already there when I bought the claim. It ain't much, but my horse likes it. I had to keep him inside last night or he mighta froze to death."

"Let's go visit your cabin, Eddie. There's no reason to climb straight up, so just make a new path through the snow and I'll follow you."

Eddie was obviously relieved and said, "Okay," before he turned and began plowing his way back to the cabin.

As Joe followed, he was certain that Eddie had lied about everything he'd already told him. As long as he'd known him, Eddie had been the very definition of a spendthrift. Despite his large salary, Eddie would be down to his last few dollars by the end of the month. He'd even asked Joe for a small loan before July's payday which he'd never repaid. Maybe he'd changed after leaving Idaho City, but Joe found it hard to believe, at least in how he handled money.

SPRING SURPRISES

While the beard had altered his appearance, his personality seemed to have undergone a transformation as well. He used to be irritatingly subservient, pompous and sneaky. While Eddie had yet to grow a backbone and was still sneaky, he was definitely more confident in his lies.

However, none of those observations helped him to understand why Eddie had started the avalanche. If he hadn't run away, Joe might have even believed Eddie's lies. But as they approached the cabin, Joe faced a dilemma. He needed to get to Centreville to deal with the killing, so he might have to pretend to accept Eddie's explanation and continue his freezing ride. What bothered Joe was that there was a good chance that he wouldn't find Eddie when he returned to Idaho City.

When they reached the cabin, Eddie turned and said, "Sorry for starting that avalanche, Joe. I guess you've got to be getting to Centreville pretty soon to find out who killed that feller in the saloon."

Joe stared at Eddie and asked, "How did you know about it if you were in your cabin with your horse?"

Eddie knew he'd blundered and immediately employed what he believed was his best defense. He'd lie his way out of trouble.

He smiled as he said, "That feller who was on his way to tell Tap about the shooting stopped by to warm up. He told me what happened before he left."

Maybe if Eddie had worked with Joe a little longer, he might have realized that he was just wasting his time. But he was satisfied that Joe Beck would swallow it hook, line and sinker.

Joe didn't even nibble at the baited hook before he said, "Then maybe you can help me, Eddie. Tap told me the dead man's name, but all I can recall is that it was Jack something or other. Do you remember his last name?"

Eddie hesitated as he knew he hadn't included any names in the story he'd created for Clark to give Tap. But what if Clark decided to make up a name for the dead man when Tap had asked him. He should have asked Clark exactly what he'd told Tap when he stopped by on his way back to Centreville.

Joe knew he'd thrown Eddie off balance and could almost hear the gears grinding inside Eddie's head as he searched for a new lie.

Eddie finally chose what he thought would be the safest answer and replied, "Sorry, Joe. I wish I could help you, but that's all he told me, too."

Joe was almost disappointed in the quality of Eddie's lie but didn't want to continue the interrogation outside, so he asked, "Can I warm up a bit before I head to Centreville?"

SPRING SURPRISES

Eddie glanced at the cabin's door before saying, "It ain't much warmer inside, Joe."

Joe put an end to the verbal standoff when he sharply said, "I'm tired of your lies, Eddie. Let's go inside where you'll tell me the truth for a change."

Eddie nodded then opened the door and entered the cabin before Joe followed him inside and closed the door.

Joe ignored the horse standing on the dirt floor near the fire as he said, "Before I decide what to do with you, Eddie, I want you to tell me why you tried to kill me."

Eddie shook his head then said, "I wasn't trying to kill…"

Joe interrupted him when he exclaimed, "I told you I didn't want to hear another lie, Eddie!"

Eddie took a step back and briefly thought of trying to pull his pistol but knew Joe was much better with his Colt. He had no choice other than to come clean and depend on Joe's compassionate nature.

"I'm sorry, Joe. I was just afraid you might shoot me if I admitted it. You ain't gonna shoot me, are you?"

"You should have known I wasn't about to shoot you before you told your last lie. Now tell me why you started that avalanche."

"I was doing okay as a deputy until you showed up. Tap started bragging about you like you were General Grant, and everybody started looking down their noses at me. It got so bad I hated going to the jail every day. Regular folks thought it was okay to make fun of me and I blamed it on you. The final straw was when those rebel lovers started telling me that even a sixteen-year-old kid was more of a man than I was. That's why I left town."

Joe knew that Eddie had exaggerated about the final straw incident as he'd spoken to one of the men who'd driven him out of town. But he was surprised that Eddie genuinely seemed to believe he hadn't been a subject of ridicule long before he and Faith arrived. Joe still thought that Eddie's hatred was not only real, but powerful enough to make him design and execute what was almost a perfect assassination.

Joe then asked, "So, you had someone report a fictitious murder to Tap knowing he'd send me to Centreville, is that right?"

Eddie sighed then quietly replied, "Yeah."

"So, there's no reason for me to ride to Centreville."

"No."

"Is this your cabin?"

"No. It was abandoned."

SPRING SURPRISES

"What do you do to make a living in Centreville?"

Eddie quietly replied, "I help out in The Big Nugget saloon. They let me sleep in one of the rooms upstairs."

As he looked at the ex-deputy, Joe wondered what he should do with him. Despite his attempt to dump a mountain of snow on top of him, Joe felt somewhat responsible for Eddie's situation. While he never teased Eddie, he hadn't stopped others from taunting him. He was sure that Eddie had noticed his smile a few times as well.

Joe didn't want to keep Duke standing in the cold any longer, so he said, "Eddie, the reason people made fun of you had nothing to do with me. It was the way you acted. You tried too hard to make people like and respect you. You even went as far as to dress and speak like President Lincoln. I'm surprised that alone didn't get you shot. There are a lot of men, including a fair number of Yankees, who aren't very fond of Mister Lincoln. If you wanted their respect, all you needed to do was to be a good lawman.

"Now I'm willing to forget about what you did because I didn't stick up for you as I should have. So, you can return to Centreville, and I'm going to see if I can plow my way back to Idaho City."

"You're not gonna arrest me?"

"Not unless you try to kill me again. I've got to get going."

As Joe turned to leave, Eddie quickly asked, "Do you think Tap will let me be a deputy again?"

Joe turned and just stared at Eddie while he imagined what Tap would think. They were desperate for help, but Joe wasn't sure that rehiring Eddie was a good idea. At his best, he had been a below average lawman until the day he'd quit. And if he didn't change his behavior, it wouldn't be long before he quit again. Even if he stopped trying to impress everyone, a lot of the men in town would still mock him for his Lincoln impersonation.

After almost a minute of deliberation, Joe said, "I have to tell Tap what happened when I see him, so I don't know if he'll take you back, Eddie. But if he does, you'll have to work hard at being a good lawman. And for a while, you'll still be taunted for the way you acted before you quit. When that happens, you need to just smile and take it. You can't let them get to you."

Eddie grinned as he said, "I'll try, Joe. I'll try really hard. But I gotta go back to Centreville and pack my belongings."

Joe nodded and said, "Don't shave your beard, Eddie," then turned, opened the door and left the cabin.

After pulling the door closed behind him, Joe untied Duke's reins, mounted and turned his stallion away from the cabin. He wasn't sure he should have let Eddie believe Tap would rehire him, but it wasn't his call. If Ezra hadn't been killed, he was sure that Tap wouldn't take Eddie back. But they were so shorthanded that there was a good chance Tap might give Eddie a second chance. They could use three or four more deputies as the population was still skyrocketing.

After he turned onto the roadway, Joe wasn't sure if even Duke could force his way through the deep snow. But as he approached the edge of the white blockade, he noticed that the avalanche had laid bare much of the side of the mountain. He dismounted, took Duke's reins then led him off the road and started to climb just high enough to avoid the deep drifts. When he reached that level, Joe carefully led Duke along a meandering, treacherous path along the side of the mountain. It took him almost thirty minutes to cover the same distance that had only taken him two minutes on his way to Centreville. He came close to falling twice before he saw the other edge of the avalanche and began his descent.

Joe blew out a long breath in relief when he reached the road, then said, "Let's go home, Duke."

He mounted his tall black stallion and didn't feel nearly as cold as he had on his way to Centreville. It was partly due to the morning sun was now warming his face but mostly because he knew Faith would be surprised when he returned much sooner than expected.

He knew she'd be happy and relieved when he entered the house, but her mood would quickly change when he told her about Eddie's avalanche ambush. Faith would be understandably angry just hearing about the assassination attempt but might be furious to learn that he hadn't arrested Eddie. He couldn't imagine her reaction when she learned that Eddie was not only going to return to Idaho City, but also hoped to be a deputy again.

Joe would tell Sheriff Fulmer the story before he faced Faith, so maybe Tap wouldn't even consider taking Eddie back. But he knew that how he portrayed Eddie would heavily influence Tap's decision. As he drew closer to Idaho City, Joe was still undecided which direction his report would take.

It wasn't even noon when he entered Main Street and as he passed Third Street, he looked at his home and saw the smoke rising from the chimneys and the cookstove pipe. Knowing that Faith was warm made him smile beneath his wool scarf before he turned his eyes to the jail a few blocks away. He hoped Tap hadn't gone home for lunch but if he had, it would give him more time to decide how to tell him about Eddie.

Joe soon pulled up before the jail, dismounted and looped his reins around the hitchrail before stepping across the icy boardwalk and entering the warm office.

Tap was reading the morning copy of *The Idaho City Bugle* and was surprised to see Joe. He just watched as Joe stomped the snow off his boots then began to peel off layers of cloth protection.

SPRING SURPRISES

When Joe freed his head from his fur-lined hat, Tap asked, "How'd you get that mess cleaned up so fast, Joe?"

Joe was pulling off his gloves as he replied, "I never made it to Centreville, Tap. Nobody was killed and there wasn't even a gunfight."

Joe stuffed his gloves into his coat pocket and was hurrying to the heat stove when the sheriff asked, "That feller rode all the way from Centreville in the cold just to tell a made-up story?"

Joe had his palms close to the heat stove as he said, "It was just a way to lure me into an ambush."

Tap exclaimed, "*Somebody took a shot at you? Did you kill the sneaky bastard?*"

Joe looked at Tap and replied, "Nope. Instead of throwing lead at me, the ambusher tried to bury me in an avalanche. Fortunately, I spotted the smoke from his fuse and managed to get far enough down the road before the powder charge went off and started the avalanche. I thought some prospector was just blasting away some rocks to look for gold and didn't see me.

"So, I was still planning to continue on to Centreville but decided to stop at the prospector's cabin and let him know he needed to be more careful. I wasn't going to wait very long because it was so cold. And if the man had stayed put behind the ridge that he'd hidden behind to light the fuse, he might have gotten away with it."

"So, how'd you find out he was tryin' to drop a mountain of snow on top of ya?"

Joe stepped back to the desk and sat down before answering, "I saw him coming back to the cabin but when he was close, he looked at me then suddenly turned and hurried back up the mountain. I figured he was wanted and was spooked when he saw my badge, so I chased after him. After a minute or so, he slipped and fell into the snow. When I caught him, I was about to ask him his name when I realized that I already knew him. It was Eddie Pascal."

Joe paused as he expected Sheriff Fulmer wouldn't hear anything as he loudly expressed his shock and fury. He wasn't wrong.

Tap's brow furrowed, his eyebrows shot upwards, and his eyes bulged as he exclaimed, *"Eddie tried to kill you? Did he go crazy after he quit?"*

"Yes, he intended to kill me, but no, it wasn't because he lost his mind. Let me tell you what drove him to do it."

As Joe began to tell Tap about Eddie's motive, he wasn't sure he could adequately explain why he had been so lenient. But after he did his best to describe the odd confrontation, he waited to see Tap's reaction before he mentioned Eddie's desire to resume his role as a deputy.

After Tap asked, "He blamed you for everybody makin' fun of him? He was dressin' like Abe Lincoln before you even showed up."

"I know. I just made it worse because he's three years older than me, but everybody treated him like the kid."

Tap leaned back and said, "I reckon I didn't help none, either."

Joe nodded then said, "I felt pretty guilty myself because I didn't stop anyone from teasing him. That's why I didn't arrest him."

Tap sighed then asked, "Did he say what he's doin' in Centreville?"

"Yes, sir. He's working in a saloon and living in a room on the second floor."

"I reckon that's why we haven't seen him around."

Joe decided it was time, so he said, "Just before I left the cabin, Eddie asked me if he could come back and be a deputy again."

Sheriff Fulmer stared at Joe for a few seconds before asking, "What did you tell him?"

"I told him it was up to you. Then I said if you gave him back his badge, he'd have to change the way he behaved. He had to stop trying to impress everybody and just work really hard at being a good lawman."

"Do you reckon he can do that?"

"I'm not sure. But we could use the help, even if he's not much better than he was before."

"You're right about that. We could use another three or four deputies, but after we lost Ezra, I don't see that happenin'."

"I thought Tom Walker was interested."

"He just asked about the pay, but his folks talked him out of it. I think it was just a way to get his pa to give him a raise."

"He probably wouldn't have lasted very long anyway."

"I reckon you gotta go home and tell Faith what happened. After you do that, you gotta ask her really nice not to shoot Eddie when she sees him."

Joe grinned as he said, "I'll ask, but I think it'll be better if I hide her pistol."

Tap snickered then stood and said, "You might as well head home and get it over with. I'll lock up and get some lunch after you're out the door."

Joe nodded before he stood, pulled on his hat and gloves, then left the jail. After mounting Duke, he headed down Main Street on his way to Third Street. He may not need to hide

Faith's Colt, but he was sure that she would make Eddie regret his decision to return to Idaho City. Maybe by the time she did see him again, she'd be too busy with Kathleen Maureen to unleash her fury. Yet even as Duke carried him home, he had no way of knowing that Faith would never meet Eddie Pascal again.

———

Because he didn't have to get around or through his avalanche deposit, Eddie had returned to Centreville almost an hour before Joe entered Idaho City.

When he entered The Big Nugget, Clark Kingsley looked past his full house, spotted him and shouted, "C'mon over, Eddie! Did you get it done?"

Eddie walked across the barroom floor then saw the other poker players all turn to look at him. Before takin his second step, the old Eddie Pascal returned in spades.

He pulled off his hat, grinned and exclaimed, "You're damned right I got it done! You shoulda seen it!"

The four men at the table whooped before Clark loudly said, "Pull up a chair and tell us about it, Eddie."

Eddie slid a chair from a neighboring table then sat down and said, "Beck was so wrapped up to keep warm that I coulda been standing up and waving a flag and he wouldn't have spotted me. I lit the fuse and watched it burn across the snow until…BLAM!"

All four men jerked when Eddie shouted, so Eddie laughed, then continued his fairy tale, saying, "Then it was like the sky was falling when that wall of snow broke loose and kept growing as it roared down the mountain. Beck was so surprised by the powder going off that he stopped moving to see what happened. He was still looking up at the mountain when the snow hit him. That big stallion of his was knocked over and Beck fell out of the saddle just before he got buried by snow."

Clark quickly asked, "Are you sure he didn't dig his way out?"

Eddie shook his head as he replied, "Yeah, I'm sure. I watched where he got buried for ten minutes. His frozen body won't be found for a few days."

Blue Bill Bradley smacked Eddie on the back then said, "I didn't figger you had it in ya, Eddie. But you sure proved me wrong."

Eddie grinned then said, "I ain't had anything to eat today, so I'm gonna head over to Jack's to get some chow."

Blue Bill said, "I reckon killing lawmen takes a strong stomach that needs feedin'."

SPRING SURPRISES

Eddie nodded, then stood and headed for the door. He knew it wouldn't be long before everyone knew that Joe Beck was still alive, and he'd become an even bigger laughingstock than he'd been in Idaho City. He wasn't about to try to kill Joe because he was at least honest enough to admit he wouldn't survive a second attempt. He couldn't return to Idaho City, either. He had to clear out as soon as the weather improved and would need to leave the county, too.

As he headed to Jack's Eatery, Eddie wished he'd never heard of Joe Beck.

―――

After stripping Duke, Joe patted him on his flank and said, "Thanks, Duke. It's not as warm in here as it is in the house, but your ladies and Bernie are keeping some of the cold away. And after I tell Faith what happened, I think the temperature in the house will climb a degree or two."

Joe didn't even smile at his attempt at levity as he left the small barn then closed the door. As he walked to the house, he looked at the kitchen window and wasn't surprised to see Faith's face behind the frosted glass. Despite the frigid air, he yanked off his fur-lined hat and waved it three times overhead. He didn't bother pulling it back on before he climbed the porch steps and crossed the icy porch.

He was reaching for the doorknob when the door flew open and his smiling wife said, "I didn't expect to see you back so soon, Joe."

Joe passed through the doorway and as Faith shut the door, he replied, "I was halfway to Centreville when I learned that there hadn't been a murder or a gunfight."

As he began hanging his outerwear on the brass hooks along the kitchen wall, Faith asked, "Why would someone ride all the way from Centreville in this weather if it wasn't true?"

Before he replied, Joe gently scooped her into his arms and kissed her.

When the long kiss ended, Faith smiled and said, "You feel like an icicle, Mister Beck."

"You sit down while I get some coffee. Then I'll explain everything."

Faith didn't need any encouragement to get off her feet, so she quickly took a seat and watched Joe pour a cup of reasonably warm coffee before he sat beside her at the kitchen table.

After taking his first sip, Joe said, "Before I tell you what happened this morning, remember you're carrying Kathleen Maureen and you need to stay calm. Okay?"

SPRING SURPRISES

Faith had been enormously relieved when she'd seen Joe ride to the barn but after hearing his caution, she began to worry about what he was preparing to tell her. Regardless of how bad it was, she didn't believe it would harm their baby if she flew into a rage.

So, she said, "I'm not making any promises, but I'll do the best I can to stay calm."

"That's fine. Anyway, I was about halfway to Centreville when I saw a crude prospector's cabin. Then I noticed a deep path that left the cabin and angled up the side of the mountain. I was looking at this ridge when I noticed a small column of smoke…"

As Joe told her about the explosion and the avalanche, Faith managed to remain reasonably tranquil because she believed it had been caused by the prospector's carelessness. It was only when she heard him say that the prospector suddenly ran away that her temper began to simmer. It wasn't much longer before it reached the boiling point.

The moment Joe named the man he believed to be a prospector, she exclaimed, *"Eddie Pascal tried to kill you?"*

"You can imagine what a shock that was. After we returned to the cabin, it didn't take long for me to see through his lies. We went inside and I asked him why he'd tried to bury me in snow, and he said…"

Faith thought she couldn't grow any angrier at Eddie Pascal until Joe said that Eddie had blamed him for the way people treated him. She clenched her hands into tight fists and hoped that Joe would soon tell her that he'd beaten Eddie into a quivering, bloody mess before taking him to jail.

Joe could see the fury growing behind Faith's blue eyes before she turned her soft hands into hard fists. Now he only hoped she didn't punch him when he told her that Eddie might be returning to reclaim his badge.

He wrapped his big hands around her fists and waited until her fingernails reappeared before saying, "Just before I left, Eddie asked me if Tap would let him have his job back. And…"

Faith snapped, "You must be joking! *He asked if he could come back here and expect everyone to pretend that he didn't try to kill you?*"

Joe took a deep breath and replied, "I told him it was Tap's decision. Then I said he'd have to change his behavior if Tap gave him a second chance."

"So, that…that sniveling, cowardly weasel might be walking the streets of Idaho City wearing a badge he doesn't deserve when he should be walking up the gallows steps for trying to kill you. You don't think Tap will agree to it, do you?"

Joe was about to confess that it was a done deal when he had an epiphany that provided the only argument that might mollify Faith.

He quietly replied, "We're really shorthanded, so he doesn't have a choice, Faith. But look at it this way. If he does get his badge back, he can be sent out of town instead of me."

Joe knew his last-second argument had served its purpose when he saw the fire in Faith's eyes settle into smoldering embers and felt her hands relax.

Faith sighed then said, "That's the only good thing to come of this. But how can you work with him knowing that he tried to bury you under a mountain of snow? Aren't you worried that he might try it again?"

"No, I'm not. I warned him that I'd keep an eye on him and wouldn't hesitate to shoot him if he tried. He knows I'm a much better shot than he is, too."

Joe could tell that Faith was still worried about having an armed Eddie Pascal in Idaho City, so he said, "To be honest, I wouldn't be surprised if he doesn't even show up. It was common for him to say he'd do something, but if it was even remotely difficult, he'd find a way to avoid doing it. And returning to Idaho City would be very trying for Eddie. So, unless he really grows a backbone, we probably won't see him again."

"You aren't just saying that to calm me down, are you?"

Even though that had been his motive, after he'd offered the suggestion, Joe recognized that it was not only possible, but it was very probable that Eddie might remain in Centreville.

So, he was able to honestly answer her question by saying, "I did hope to soothe your concerns, but I also believe that it's more likely that Eddie won't show up."

Faith smiled before she said, "Let me fix you something to eat before you go back to work."

Joe stood, said, "I'll feed myself, Mrs. Beck," then walked to the cold room.

As Joe began assembling his lunch, Faith said, "I forgot to mention that Doctor Taylor wants Sarah to stay with me more now that I'm getting close."

Joe looked at Faith and asked, "Is he worried about something?"

"No. Everything's fine. It's just that Kathleen Maureen is a very active baby, and he doesn't want me to be alone if I go into labor earlier than expected."

Joe let out a long breath before he smiled and said, "So, he's just being cautious. I agree that Kathleen Maureen is a busy girl, but I hope he doesn't expect Sarah to be a midwife."

"She's just going to stay with me whenever you're not here. If I do go into labor while you're gone, she'll fetch Doctor Taylor."

Joe finished making his sandwich, then returned to his seat and said, "I thought all soon-to-be mothers intentionally delayed going into labor until late at night. Then they could disturb their husbands' sleep as a small measure of retribution for putting them in that condition."

Faith laughed and rubbed her rounded bump as she said, "I think that's a small price to pay."

Joe smiled then began to wolf down his sandwich. He'd been relieved when Faith told him that Doctor Taylor wasn't worried about her or their baby. But knowing that Sarah Walker would be spending more time at their home did create a measure of consternation.

Sarah was the only daughter of the Walkers of Walker & Sons Dry Goods. He'd first met Sarah at her parents' store just after they'd arrived in town. She was a very pretty girl with a Marigold-like figure but without a hint of Marigold's vivaciousness.

Yet despite her demure, almost shy personality, for some reason, Sarah made him uncomfortable. He didn't understand why he felt that way because she never came close to flirting with him. She'd even befriended Faith, which was understandable as they were almost the same age. Yet whenever she was nearby, he felt inexplicably nervous. He'd never mentioned it to Faith because he didn't want to damage their friendship.

His only hope was for Jimmy Pritchard to finally get the nerve to propose. Jimmy was tall and not bad looking, but he had a bad stuttering problem, which may have been the reason for his hesitation. Sarah had been seeing the butcher's son since she was fifteen, but it wasn't anything like the powerful attraction he and Faith shared from almost the first time they met.

Joe finished his sandwich then forgot all about Sarah Walker when he looked at his perfect wife and quietly said, "I love you, Faith."

Faith softly replied, "You know that I love you too, Joe. What inspired you to tell me?"

"I can never tell you too often, sweetheart. I just wish I didn't worry you so much."

"I don't worry nearly as much as you seem to believe. As you've told me many times before, life is difficult for each of us, especially out here. I may worry a little when you're gone, but I'm also very proud that you make people's lives safer."

Joe smiled as he stood and said, "I've always been proud of you, my love. But now I've got to leave you for a few hours. Duke had a hard morning, so I'll just walk to the office."

Faith slowly rose to her feet and said, "Now that I know you're safe, I'm going to take a short nap."

Joe hugged her again then kissed her before saying, "That's a good idea."

SPRING SURPRISES

After her husband released her, Faith waved then walked down the hallway and turned into their bedroom.

Ten minutes later, Joe was taking off his heavy coat when Tap entered the jail, grinned and asked, "Back so soon? I figgered you'd spend another hour just holdin' a towel full of snow against a big bump Faith put on your noggin."

Joe hung his coat and replied, "I hate to disappoint you, Sheriff Fulmer, but Faith took the news very well."

The sheriff hung his coat next to his hat then said, "Then it was probably better than how Mary behaved when I told her the story."

Joe sat down and waited for his boss to sit behind the desk before saying, "The reason Faith wasn't so angry was that I told her I didn't think that Eddie would come back. I only mentioned it to calm her down, but as soon as I said it, I realized that it was probably true."

Tap nodded and said, "I was wonderin' about that myself. I knew Eddie a lot longer than you did, and I could never count on him to do somethin' that needed muscle or plain old guts. I just can't see him changin'."

"I guess all we can do is wait to see if he shows up. If he does, then I may have to hide Faith's Colt after all."

Tap snickered before he said, "Even if he comes back, we still could use another four deputies, Joe. I was kinda hopin' the gold would begin dryin' up by now and make some of those gold-hunting crazies leave. But they're still pourin' in, and it's gonna get worse, too. The cold is keepin' things quiet for now, but it's gonna get really busy when the weather warms up."

"At least it's not the commissioners' fault. They even pushed our salaries up another twenty dollars a month in January hoping it would be enough to get us some help."

"It's too bad that the only ones who want the badge ain't gonna be any help at all. They'd just be well-paid hoodlums. I ain't gonna hire any of those prospectors who came up empty, either. I ain't gonna give 'em a badge 'cause they'd most likely disappear after their first payday."

Joe understood Tap's dilemma but said, "You didn't know me from Adam when you offered me a job."

"That was different. As soon we started talkin', I knew there was somethin' special about you. And don't forget, you didn't take the job 'til after you caught those bank robbers."

Joe grinned and said, "I can't tell you how relieved I was when Bo Ferguson told me to leave the wagon train."

"Do you still miss some of the friends you made along the way?"

"I think about them sometimes. I know Faith does, too. I guess the ones we miss the most are Herm and Becky Berger,

SPRING SURPRISES

Will Boone and his family, and of course, Bo Ferguson and his new family."

"Maybe you'll get a letter from 'em after they're all settled in Oregon."

"I hope so. I'm anxious to hear from Mrs. Chalmers, too. Her husband is a Union captain but was captured by the rebels."

"He's the one who gave you the Henry, ain't he?"

"Yes, sir. He also gave me everything I needed to leave my small shelter in Missouri."

"Those repeaters sure are hard to come by. You've got the only one in town and D.M. says he might not be gettin' any 'til this blasted war ends even though he has a whole case of the ammunition.

"You do know that I have two Henrys, don't you?"

"Of course, I do. You got the second one after you shot those gunrunners."

"I'm pretty sure that Faith doesn't need it anymore, so would you like to have hers?"

Tap grinned as he replied, "I sure wouldn't mind as long as Faith says it's okay."

"I think she's dangerous enough with her Colt."

"Tell her I'll do the saloon stroll all of March if she's willin' to part with it."

"That won't be necessary, Tap. It's my job too, and Mary wouldn't be very happy about when you tell her about it."

"I reckon she'd be more'n unhappy. But seein' as how we'll be usin' those Henrys on the job; I can have the county buy a few boxes of cartridges."

"It's a lot cheaper than hiring a few more deputies."

"One of these days, Joe. One of these days."

Joe said, "Maybe…" when the door opened, and Father Burns entered the jail.

Tap and Joe both stood before Tap asked, "What can we do for you, Father?"

The priest replied, "I was entering the church and was knocked over by a man who had just stolen the poor box. By the time I recovered, he'd disappeared."

As Joe quickly walked to the pegs to put on his coat, Tap asked, "Do you know him?"

"No. All I can tell you is that he was short and wore a dark blue coat and a gray wool cap."

As Joe was pulling on his furry hat, Tap asked, "Which direction did he go?"

SPRING SURPRISES

"I saw his tracks go down the alley between the church and the convent but didn't follow it. I thought it would be better to let you and Joe find him."

Joe pulled on his gloves and asked, "Was he armed, Father?"

Father Pat looked at Joe and answered, "I don't know. He could have had a pistol under his coat."

Joe nodded then said, "I'll find him."

Father Burns began unbuttoning his heavy wool coat and said, "I'll wait until you return, Joe."

Joe nodded then quickly left the jail and turned right.

As he trotted along the slippery boardwalk, Joe couldn't imagine a man could be so desperate that he'd stoop to taking the church's poor box. The most it probably contained would be around a dollar in pennies and nickels. But as he hurried toward Second Street, he suspected that the thief had only grabbed the poor box on the way out of the church. He could have already collected much more valuable loot. There was probably about ten pounds of gold in the religious artifacts on the altar and in the sacristy.

Joe turned onto Second Street and focused on the church with its adjoining school and convent. To complete the convent before winter arrived, Father Burns had the builders lengthen the school and create living quarters for the nuns. The construction was completed just in time for the six Dominican nuns to be welcomed to Idaho City by the winter's first blizzard.

The extension createdan eight-foot-wide alley between the convent and the church that the thief had used as an escape tunnel.

But as Joe hurried down Second Street, he pictured the area behind the church and tried to predict which direction the thief had gone. If he had his horse waiting for him, he could already be on his way to Boise City. But if he decided to head to Centreville, he'd run into Eddie's deep white roadblock.

He wasn't about to use the narrow alley to begin his search, so Joe angled to his left and headed for the back of the church. Just before he reached the western wall, he slowed to a walk to catch his breath.

Thirty seconds later, he looked behind the church but didn't see anyone. He started trotting to the alley and after just a few steps, Joe spotted an already frozen pile of horse dung. He didn't stop at the alley but followed the wide path the thief's horse had created in the snow.

Less than a minute later, he felt his stomach twist when the trail turned toward Third Street. He knew the thief wasn't about to use his home as a hideout, but he was still on edge after Eddie's bizarre avalanche assassination attempt.

SPRING SURPRISES

But before he reached his barn, the thief's path curved to the left then blended into the tracks left by the traffic on Third Street. Tracking him would be much more difficult now, and if he had only stolen the poor box, Joe probably would have just returned to the jail. But he had already convinced himself that the thief hadn't just run off with some nickels and pennies. so he entered his small barn and began saddling Duke.

A few minutes later, as he led Duke out of the barn, he was going to tell Faith that he might be late but remembered she was going to take a nap. So, he mounted his big black equine friend and rode past the house before turning onto the street.

After he reached Main Street, he saw a rider and two wagons on the road but recognized the man on horseback. He hadn't seen any fast-moving riders pass the jail, so he turned right on Main Street and headed north. He guessed the thief had decided to take the road to Centreville. Joe didn't think he was taking much of a gamble with his decision because he'd probably never find the thief if he'd ridden to Boise City. There was another good reason for the man to go to Centreville. If he had stolen the gold objects from the church, he'd wouldn't be able to have them melted down in Boise City. That wouldn't be a problem in Centreville.

Ten minutes after he turned onto the road to Centreville, Joe spotted a short line of steaming horse dung. While it wasn't nearly as frigid as it was this morning, it was still cold enough to freeze the dung after ten or fifteen minutes. That meant that he was less than two miles behind the rider but couldn't see him because of the curve about a mile ahead. He recognized the possibility that he could be someone other than the thief, but whether he was innocent or criminal, he'd soon discover Eddie's barricade. He might try to climb over it along the mountainside, but Joe thought it was more likely that the thief wouldn't risk falling. He had probably already turned around. so Joe kept riding toward the curve.

While he may not have been wearing a pistol when he ran out of the church, Joe was sure he was well-armed now. He wanted to get close without spooking him into a gunfight, so he removed his badge and slipped it into his coat pocket. Joe wished Duke wasn't so easily identified, but he no longer had a choice in mounts as all of the mares had swollen bellies and Bernie was enjoying his retirement.

As he entered the curve, time slowed to a crawl and his already incredible vision sharpened, revealing even the tiniest detail. He was halfway through the curve when he and the returning rider spotted each other across eighty yards of snow. The suspected thief was surprised to see Joe and quickly pulled his chocolate brown gelding to a stop.

While Joe didn't recognize the horse or its rider, he did match the vague description Father Pat had provided. But he began to have doubts about the rider's guilt when he just sat in his saddle. He expected him to either pull his pistol or wheel his horse around and race away.

SPRING SURPRISES

As he drew closer, Joe began examining the rider. His face was mostly hidden by his heavy wool cap and a thick scarf, but it was his eyes that convinced Joe he was the thief. They should have been focused back on him, but they weren't. They were furtively shifting back and forth as if searching for an escape route. Joe suspected the last place the stranger wanted to go was back to Idaho City. He might be thinking of a way to convince him to turn Duke around and ride back alone, or he was planning to add to his day's haul.

Joe slowed Duke to a walk then pulled up a few feet away before the stranger said, "The road's blocked ahead, mister, so there ain't any way of makin' it to Centreville."

Joe nodded then said, "Thanks for warning me. I reckon I'll just head back to Idaho City. I haven't seen you around before. What's your name?"

"Joe Smith. What's yours?"

Joe grinned before saying, "I'm a Joe, too. Joe Goodchild."

After passing their phony names, Joe Smith asked, "What do you do in Idaho City, Joe?"

Joe Goodchild replied, "I work with D.M. Elliott, and he's teaching me to be a gunsmith."

"I reckon that's why you got a Henry repeater."

Joe said, "I'm damned lucky to have it," then turned Duke around and waited for the thief to start moving.

As they began riding side-by-side back to Idaho City, Joe Smith asked, "Why were you headin' to Centreville, Joe?"

"I was supposed to deliver four boxes of Spencer cartridges to John Quimby. I reckon he's just gonna have to wait 'til that snow melts. Why were you going that way?"

Joe Smith hesitated before replying, "Um…I'd rather not say 'cause it's kinda private."

"That's alright. It's none of my business anyway."

After they'd ridden another twenty yards or so, Joe Smith asked, "You must do a lot of shootin', don't ya?"

"Probably more than anyone else I know, even D.M."

"Did you ever shoot anybody?"

When Joe looked him, he noticed that despite the sub-freezing temperature, Joe Smith was sweating and suspected it wouldn't be much longer before he panicked.

Joe laughed then said, "Nope. I don't figure I'd be able to shoot anybody. I feel bad enough after I kill a deer."

His reply was meant to relieve the thief, but Joe soon realized he'd made a mistake. Joe Smith now believed he had an advantage. And as they were just two miles or so from Idaho City, the thief would have to act soon.

Joe Smith slowed his gelding a bit, but Joe expected that he might try to give himself another advantage, so as soon as Duke began to pull slightly ahead, he leaned back until his stallion was again alongside the shorter horse. To an observer, the horse dance was almost unnoticeable. But one of the two Joes was frustrated when he saw other Joe react so quickly.

Deputy Joe could almost feel Joe Smith's anxiety kick up a notch, so he prepared for the thief's next and probably much more dramatic move. It was just a question of what form it would take.

Joe Smith suddenly pulled up and exclaimed, "Damn! I think my horse just tossed a shoe!"

Duke was already twenty feet away when the thief dismounted, so Joe turned Duke around and was pulling his Henry from its scabbard when Joe Smith yanked off his right glove, threw open his coat and grabbed his pistol.

Joe was levering a cartridge into the repeater's breech as Joe Smith whipped his Colt out of his holster. The standing Joe saw the mounted Joe readying his Henry as he lifted his revolver to his target and knew he only had a slight time advantage. He was near panic as he set his sights on his target then cocked his hammer with the palm of his left hand as he always did. But when his gloved hand reached the protruding tab of steel, the thick leather just slipped across the hammer. He still automatically pulled his trigger but already knew it wasn't going to fire. He'd been close to panic before he'd set his sights on the other Joe, but knowing he was about to die made him freeze in utter fear.

Joe didn't know why the thief hadn't fired, but as he settled his Henry's sights on Joe Smith's chest, he noticed that the man wasn't moving. He still had his finger on his trigger but didn't fire as he waited for the other Joe to give him justification for pulling his trigger.

For ten long seconds Joe kept his sights steady as he waited for the thief to so much as twitch before he decided to force the issue.

He shouted, "I'm Deputy Sheriff Joe Beck. I don't want to kill you, Joe, so just drop your pistol."

Joe Smith blinked before he released his grip then after his Colt spun on his index finger, he let it fall into the snow.

Joe loudly said, "Now take a dozen steps away from your horse."

After his prisoner shuffled backwards until he was a safe distance away, Joe lowered his Henry's muzzle then released the hammer before dismounting. He kept the repeater pointed in Joe Smith's direction as he walked to his horse then recovered his snow-encrusted Colt.

He slid the revolver into his left coat pocket, then lowered his Henry and asked, "Is Joe Smith your real name?"

The man slowly shook his head before replying, "It's Matt Feldman."

"Did you rob Saint Joseph's Church?"

Matt snapped, "It's a church! They didn't need all that gold!"

After Matt had confirmed Joe's suspicion that the thief hadn't settled for the poor box, he said, "Alright, Matt. We'll mount up and head back to Idaho City. Before you do, I want you to understand that I didn't tell the truth when I said I'd never shot anyone. In the past two years, I've had to kill almost two dozen men."

Matt had been staring into Joe's piercing blue eyes as he spoke and shuddered when he realized the young deputy was telling the truth.

Joe turned, then walked back to Duke and stepped into his saddle. He waited for Matt to mount before they started riding.

Because he only suspected Matt had stolen more than just the poor box, Joe simply asked, "Why did you steal from the church?"

"I needed a stake to buy a claim and figgered they didn't need all that gold."

His suspicions confirmed, Joe then asked, "But why did you take the poor box?"

"Well, I was poor, and it was sittin' right there. With all those rich people in town, I figgered there musta been over a hundred dollars in there."

Joe rolled his eyes before saying, "You must not go to church, Matt. If you did, you'd know that most folks who attend services aren't rich. And almost all of the money they donate is put on offering plates and in baskets on Sundays. I'd be surprised if there was a dollar's worth of nickels and pennies in that poor box.

"If you hadn't grabbed it before you knocked down the priest, I think Father Burns would have just brushed himself off and entered the church to pray. He might not have reported the missing gold items for a couple of days."

Matt looked at Joe and sharply asked, "You mean if I didn't snatch that poor box, I mighta got away?"

Joe nodded as he replied, "Probably. Sunset is just an hour away, and once the sun was down, it would have been almost impossible for me to find you."

As Matt quietly cursed himself for his mistake, Joe asked, "I don't remember seeing you before, so when did you get into town?"

SPRING SURPRISES

"Last night. I was workin' in Boise City for a few months hopin' to make enough money for a claim. But I wasn't even close to havin' enough when I heard about that Catholic church. Then I just waited 'til the weather was so bad that nobody would come after me."

Joe looked at Matt and knew he wasn't the sharpest tool in the shed, but didn't believe he was a hardened criminal, either. He seemed to be more pathetic than dangerous. But as they approached Idaho City, Joe hoped that Matt's almost innocent demeanor didn't convince Father Pat to forgive Matt and refuse to press charges.

He might even ask him not to arrest Matt for trying to shoot him. But even if Father Burns pleaded for him not to charge Matt, Joe wasn't about to let him off with a stern warning. After telling Faith that he'd let Eddie Pascal go after trying to kill him this morning, Joe wasn't about to perform an encore.

Shadows covered most of Main Street when they entered Idaho City and soon pulled up before the jail.

Joe pulled Matt's Colt from his coat pocket then said, "Go ahead and step down, Matt. I want you to take your saddlebags with you before we go inside."

Matt just nodded then slowly dismounted, tied off his brown gelding's reins and began to unstrap his saddlebags

Joe quickly stepped to the ground and tossed Duke's reins over the hitchrail before he pointed the Colt at his prisoner.

Matt slid his bulging and obviously heavy saddlebags from his horse, stepped onto the boardwalk and opened the jail door.

Joe followed him inside, and as soon as he closed the door, he heard Father Burns exclaim, "You caught him!"

Joe didn't see Tap, so he asked, "Where's Sheriff Fulmer?"

Father Burns had been sitting behind the desk when they'd entered the room, so he stood before replying, "He's looking for Bobby and Tommy O'Connor. Charles Lambert claimed that they stole half a dozen sweet cakes from his bakery."

Joe nodded then said, "Matt, set your saddlebags on the floor, then I'll get you into your cell. You can have the first one."

Matt looked at Father Burns but didn't say anything before he lowered his saddlebags onto the pine floor and started walking to the cells.

After Matt entered the cell, Joe said, "I need you to take off your coat and your gunbelt."

When Matt removed his gloves, he glared at them for a few seconds as if they were to blame for his predicament before he shoved them into his pockets and unbuttoned his coat. After handing his coat and gunbelt to Joe, he sat on the cot and stared at the floor when he heard the sharp clang as the cell door closed.

SPRING SURPRISES

Joe laid Matt's pistol on the desk then walked to the pegged wall and hung Matt's coat and gunbelt before he began to strip off his own outerwear.

As Joe was hanging his hat, Father Burns said, "Sheriff Fulmer and I expected you to return within a few minutes, so I stayed and talked to the sheriff. After an hour, I was surprised when you still hadn't returned, but the sheriff said you probably were tracking the thief. I couldn't understand why you would spend so much time trying to recover the poor box. It never has more than fifty cents inside."

Joe didn't say anything before he hung his coat on a peg then stepped to Matt's saddlebags, lifted them from the floor and set them on the desk next to his pistol before sitting down.

Father Burns took a seat on one of the three other chairs before asking, "Is the poor box in his saddlebags?"

Joe was releasing the straps on one of them as he replied, "I'm sure it's in one of them, and so are the other things he stole from the church."

The priest's eyelids spread wider as he exclaimed, "*He stole more than just the poor box?*"

Joe opened the first saddlebag, and Father Burns was stunned when Joe pulled out a gold candlestick. After setting it on the desk, he removed a second and stood it beside its twin. Then he extracted a gold serving plate before releasing the straps on the other saddlebag.

As the priest stared wide-eyed at the desk, Joe took a gold communion wafer cup from the saddlebag and set it onto the desktop. Then he slid the last gold object from Matt's saddlebag and gently placed it onto the desk.

Father Burns whispered, "My parents gave me that chalice when I was ordained. It had cost them almost all of their life savings," then slowly lifted the chalice from the desk.

As Joe removed the small, wooden poor box and added it to the desktop collection, he still wasn't sure if Father Pat would press charges. He lowered the saddlebags to the floor and was about to ask that question when the door opened, and Sheriff Fulmer stepped inside.

After Tap closed the door, he glanced at Matt before saying, "When I saw Duke out front with another horse, I figgered you musta caught the lowlife who stole the poor box."

As the sheriff pulled off his gloves, Joe said, "His name is Matt Feldman, and he just got in town yesterday. He stole a lot more than just the poor box, Tap."

Tap's view was blocked by Father Burns, so as he hung his coat on a peg, he asked, "What else did he steal?"

Before Joe could speak, Father Burns turned, held out his chalice and said, "He took many of the church's valuables as well as my chalice, Sheriff."

SPRING SURPRISES

Tap stepped closer then saw the golden display on the desktop before he asked, "Did he come quiet, Joe?"

"No, sir. He behaved himself at first because I had my badge in my pocket and gave him a false name. But when we were a couple of miles out, he said his horse threw a shoe and pulled up. After he dismounted, he pulled his Colt. I was expecting him to try something, so I already had my Henry in my hands. I had to bring a live round into the firing chamber and that gave him the advantage."

Sheriff Fulmer quickly asked, "Did he get a shot off?"

"No, sir. His gloved left hand slipped over his hammer when he tried to cock it."

"Then why ain't his body hung over his saddle?"

Joe shrugged before replying, "When he realized his hammer hadn't budged, he just froze, so I held my fire."

"Lordy, Joe! You told me how everything slows down for you when things get hairy, but are you tellin' me you could see all that and still keep from pullin' your trigger?"

"I think he was going to miss anyway, Tap. He was rushing to get a shot off and his muzzle was pointed above my head."

Tap shook his head as he said, "Sometimes I get to thinkin' that you ain't human, Joe."

Father Burns then answered Joe's unasked question when he said, "Jesus said, 'Render therefore unto Caesar the things which are Caesar's; and unto God the things that are God's'. I will forgive Mister Feldman for his sins but understand that he must be punished for violating man's law."

Tap said, "I was gonna have Mister Blanton charge him with attempted murder, but I reckon he'll be more'n happy to add a charge of theft, Father."

Father Burns asked, "May I take what he stole back to the church, Sheriff?"

"That'll be alright, Father."

Joe opened the bottom drawer, pulled out a canvas sack and handed it to Father Burns.

The priest smiled, set his chalice on the desktop and said, "Thank you, Joe," then began carefully moving the stolen items from the desk into the sack.

When he finished, he lowered the weighty sack to the floor then stood and walked to the pegs to dress for the cold walk back to the church.

Tap looked at Joe and said, "It's gettin' late, so you can write your report tomorrow before you visit Mister Blanton."

Joe nodded then smiled as he asked, "Did you catch those two brazen bakery bandits before they struck again?"

SPRING SURPRISES

Tap snickered before he replied, "I nabbed 'em then marched 'em to Judge Bob O'Connor who sentenced 'em to doin' their mama's laundry for a month. He gave me a quarter to give to Charlie Lambert to pay for the sweet cakes, too."

"So, I guess your report will be a lot shorter than mine."

Before Tap could give an appropriate response, Father Burns stepped close to the desk, smiled at Joe and offered his hand.

As they shook hands, he said, "I cannot thank you enough, Joe. If it hadn't been for your skills and dedication, I would have lost my parents' precious gift. It means much more to me than all the gold God buried in these mountains."

Joe simply replied, "You're welcome, Father," before the priest pulled on his gloves, picked up the heavy sack and left the jail.

Tap smiled and said, "I reckon you'll be in his prayers for a long time now."

Joe glanced at their prisoner before saying, "I'll bring Matt supper and let him use the privy after I finish the saloon stroll."

"You spent most of the day in the saddle, Joe. I'll do the stroll and get him some chow."

"I appreciate the offer, Tap, but I'm okay."

"Are you sure you don't want me to take the stroll?"

"I'm sure. After we lock up, I'll bring his horse with me and stable him with Duke for the night."

"Okay. Let's get outta here."

As they removed their heavy coats, Joe grinned and said, "I haven't forgotten about the Henry, either."

Tap was relieved that he hadn't had to mention Joe's offer and just chuckled.

―――

Fifteen minutes later, Joe left his small barn and walked quickly through the moonlit snow. He could already smell the wonderful scents of whatever Faith had prepared for their supper, but it was the still overpowering need to see his wife that made him hurry.

He may have been anxious to see Faith, but he still slowed when he started up the icy porch steps. After avoiding two nearly fatal situations, Joe wasn't about to fall and break a bone or two in front of his pregnant wife.

Joe was smiling when he opened the kitchen door and stepped inside. He was closing the door when he saw Sarah Walker at the cookstove and Faith sitting at the table smiling at him.

SPRING SURPRISES

He pulled off his fur-lined hat then said, "I'm sorry I'm late, sweetheart. Just after I returned to the jail, I had to leave town again to chase down a man who'd robbed Saint Joseph's."

Faith said, "You can tell us about it during supper. Sarah heard you'd gone to Centreville before she came to visit but didn't know about the avalanche until I told her."

Joe was unbuttoning his coat as he smiled at Sarah and said, "It's nice to see you again, Sarah. I hope you don't think I was ignoring you."

Sarah laughed lightly before saying, "I know you weren't ignoring me, Joe. I hope you had less trouble catching the thief than you did this morning."

Joe removed and hung his gunbelt before saying, "It wasn't hard finding him and it wasn't as cold as my earlier ride, either."

He focused on Faith's smiling face as he walked to the table and before he took a seat, he leaned over and kissed his precious wife. It wasn't a quick smooch, either. He just didn't know why he felt as if he needed to reassure Faith.

After their lips parted, he smiled and said, "I missed you, Faith."

Faith laughed before she said, "Not that I don't appreciate your passionate greeting, Mister Beck, but you've only been gone six hours."

"It's always too long when I'm not with you, sweetheart."

Faith looked at her husband and wondered why he seemed so maudlin.

Joe said, "I can't stay long. I'll be doing the saloon stroll, and I have a prisoner to feed. So, I'll help Sarah set the table then tell you about the church thief."

As Joe turned to start filling their plates, Faith said, "If you're leaving so quickly, you should start telling us what happened before you take a seat."

"Yes, ma'am. Father Burns came to the office and reported that a man had stolen the poor box, so I left the jail…"

After they were seated, Joe interrupted his story to say grace.

He returned to his verbal report and was about to cut into his fried beefsteak when Faith exclaimed, "*He had a misfire, and you didn't shoot him?*"

Joe made his cut, then stabbed the piece of meat with his fork before saying, "I was in my enhanced state and after his hand slid over his hammer, I felt as if I had plenty of time to pull my trigger. If he'd tried to cock it again, I would have shot him."

Sarah quickly asked, "What do you mean by your enhanced state?"

SPRING SURPRISES

Joe glanced at his steak-loaded fork and before he could answer Sarah's question, Faith replied, "Whenever Joe is in a dangerous situation, his mind reaches a much higher level. Time slows down and he can see and hear even the tiniest details. It appears even if he's unaware of the danger, but he's learned how to summon it when he believes it's necessary. Even though I know about it, I'm still shaken when he tells me things like that."

Joe swallowed and said, "Anyway, after I disarmed him, we returned, and I locked him in a cell. Father Pat was surprised when he realized that Matt had stolen much more than the poor box. He was close to tears when I took his chalice out of the saddlebag."

As Joe rammed another piece of steak into his mouth and began chewing, Faith asked, "Do you think he'll hang for trying to shoot you?"

Joe quickly masticated his meat then after swallowing, he replied, "I don't know what Judge Oliver will decide, but I think it's more likely that he'll sentence him to ten years of hard labor."

Faith said, "Then you'll need to escort him to Fort Boise."

Joe just nodded as he continued to clear his plate.

———

Twenty minutes later, Joe left the house carrying the sealed pot he'd used to transport his sour pickles across the plains. He had a large jar of his tangy tubes in the pantry, so now it was just an odd pot. Tonight, it was particularly convenient, as Joe was using the pot to bring Matt Feldman his supper. It still would be cold by the time Joe reached the jail because he had to make a side trip.

As he was preparing to leave, Faith had asked him to escort Sarah to her home. While he wasn't comfortable with the idea, it was a perfectly reasonable request. And even if it wasn't, Joe could never refuse anything Faith asked of him.

As they walked down Third Street with the full moon lighting their way, Sarah asked, "Were you afraid when the thief aimed his pistol at you?"

"I wasn't, but it's not because I'm brave or foolish. When I'm in my enhanced state, it's as if I'm a spectator. I'm watching the action from afar and figuring out what will happen. I can't describe it any better than that."

"After all the stories that Faith told me, I still think you're the bravest man I'll ever meet."

"I could tell you just as many stories about Faith. Like how she left the wagon train on her own to search for me without even being armed. I think Faith is braver than I am and probably smarter than me, too."

"I'm very lucky to have her as my friend. And I'll do all I can to help her even after the baby is born."

As they turned onto Main Street, Joe said, "I know she enjoys your company and we both appreciate your help, but don't abandon your social life, Sarah. I wouldn't be surprised if Jimmy Pritchard wasn't worried that you might be avoiding him."

"Jimmy is far from being worried, Joe. In fact, whenever I see him, the first thing he asks is if Faith told me any more stories about you. You're like a legendary hero to him."

Joe looked at Sarah as he said, "I'm not legendary or any other kind of hero. Besides, isn't Jimmy almost two years older than I am?"

"You look much older than he does, but age has nothing to do with it. You've done things that could fill a dozen dime novels. Even today, you've already accomplished more than most men would in their entire lives. Jimmy isn't the only one who thinks of you that way, either."

"I was just lucky when I found myself in those situations, Sarah. I just hope by luck doesn't run out."

"I don't think it will and neither does Faith."

Joe was relieved when they turned onto Fifth Street. The Walkers' home was the first house behind their store, so in another minute, his escort duty would end.

When they stepped onto the porch, Joe said, "Goodnight, Sarah."

Sarah smiled and said, "Goodnight, Joe."

As she reached for the doorknob, Joe quickly turned and without worrying about the icy steps, hurried down from the porch carrying his pot. He soon reached Main Street and headed for the jail still wondering why Sarah made him so nervous.

———

After feeding Matt his cold supper then letting him use the privy, Joe returned him to his cell. He washed out the pot, left it on the desktop then grabbed one of the two twelve-gauge shotguns from the rack. He checked the load before leaving the jail to do the nightly saloon stroll, which they sometimes called the whiskey walk.

Even though it was a Tuesday night, he knew that most of the saloons would still have raucous crowds. It was because a good portion of their clientele didn't have regular paydays. They'd bring their gold dust and nuggets to the assayers then rush to their favorite saloons to spend every dime on liquor or painted ladies. While most of the men were simply noisy, there were a few who were regular troublemakers. He'd learned who they were after just a couple of weeks and focused on their favored haunts. Tap had taught him how to deal with the bad boys without locking them up, but tonight, Joe hoped they just behaved themselves.

Joe had the shotgun's twin barrels leaning on his right shoulder as he walked along the boardwalk past the first line of saloons. He listened to the noise coming from each establishment as he passed by but would only step inside if he heard trouble. The outer doors were all closed but they wouldn't block the sounds of a loud argument.

It took him almost twenty minutes before he returned to the jail. He'd only had to enter one of the saloons, The Red Sunset Gambling House. It was one of the seedier stops on the saloon stroll, but when he entered the place with his shotgun, the shouting match died before anyone pulled his pistol.

After returning the shotgun to the rack, Joe glanced at his sleeping prisoner, took the pot from the desk then left the jail and locked the door. As he hurried along the boardwalk, he thought Faith would already be sleeping by the time he returned, but knew he'd have to add wood to the heat stoves and fireplaces before he could join her.

Thirty minutes later, after adding fuel to the hungry fires, Joe quietly stepped into their bedroom and sat on the chair near the window. The bright moonlight filled the room as he tugged off his boots and studied Faith's peaceful face. He couldn't imagine what his life would be like without her and still believed that it wasn't just chance that brought them together.

God had put him on this earth to love and protect Faith Hope Charity Virtue Goodchild Beck.

He managed to undress without disturbing Faith but was now hesitant to join her under their blankets and quilt. He knew that just one touch from his cold feet would brutally interrupt her dreams. Joe was still debating about using the bedroom next door which was now a nursery when Faith's eyes opened.

She smiled and softly asked, "Aren't you coming to bed, Joe?"

Joe smiled as replied, "I didn't want to wake you, Faith," then managed to slip under the covers without letting any of his icy skin contact his toasty warm wife.

He rolled onto his left side and said, "I'm not going to touch you until I'm warmer."

"Thank you, my considerate husband."

"How are you and Kathleen Maureen?"

"We're both perfectly fine. You shouldn't treat me as if I was an invalid, Joe."

"I suppose I do go a bit too far, but it's because you're so precious to me. And after she's born, so will our baby girl."

"You do know that it could be Sam who's trying to kick his way out, don't you?"

SPRING SURPRISES

"Of course, I do. But after I convinced you that you were pregnant with Kathleen Maureen, I'd hate to lose my status as a clairvoyant."

Faith laughed before asking, "If we do meet Kathleen Maureen, we won't be addressing her with her full name, will we?"

"That would take too many syllables. I think Katie would work best with Beck."

"I like it, too. And I think you're warm enough now."

Joe wasn't sure about his feet, so he bent his knees slightly before wrapping Faith in his arms and kissing her.

When their kiss ended, Joe whispered, "May I ask you something, sweetheart?"

Faith smiled as she quietly replied, "Doctor Taylor said it won't hurt Katie if we make love, Joe."

Joe grinned before saying, "I was going to ask you if it's alright if I give your Henry to Tap."

Faith laughed before she said, "And here I was hoping you were inspired by my enlarged bosoms."

Joe caressed her left breast as he said, "I'm very inspired, my newly well-endowed wife."

Faith breathlessly said, "I don't need the Henry, Joe. I only need you."

By the time they fell asleep, the heat they generated made Joe completely forget his long, frigid day.

CHAPTER 2

The temperature was noticeably warmer as Joe walked to the office the next morning. It was as if Mother Nature was apologizing for the past week of bone-chilling cold. Joe appreciated the gesture but suspected that it was just a temporary reprieve.

After presenting Sheriff Fulmer with Faith's Henry and Matt Feldman with his breakfast, Joe sat at the desk and begin writing his report,

Tap was admiring his new Henry as he said, "I'm really grateful, Joe. But you didn't have to give me a box of cartridges. I'll pay a visit to D.M. and pick up a few boxes at the county's expense."

Joe looked up from his report and said, "I think that one's fired fewer than a dozen rounds."

"How many have you fired with yours?"

"Probably around forty. But I keep them both clean and well-oiled."

Tap grinned and said, "Maybe you didn't shoot Feldman 'cause you didn't wanna clean your Henry after one shot."

Joe chuckled then resumed working on his report.

When he finished writing, Joe opened the desk's center drawer and pulled out a ledger. He slid his finger down the list of names and said, "It looks like Mister William B. Dillingham, Esquire is next up."

Tap pried his eyes from his repeater and said, "He paid Chester Long to take his slot. I'm sure Chester will be grateful for the ten dollars the county will pay him."

Joe nodded then marked an open column on Chester's row before closing the ledger and returning it to the drawer.

Because Matt Feldman couldn't afford the twenty dollars to pay for a lawyer, the county had to foot the bill. Even though there were almost as many lawyers in town as there were saloons, none wanted the position of public defender. They made more money by settling claim disputes and other lucrative civil cases.

As Judge Oliver heard all of their cases, they couldn't complain when he set up the system of rotating the assignments of defending destitute prisoners. As almost all of the criminal defendants were unable to afford a lawyer, it wasn't long before the successful attorneys began paying the less talented lawyers to replace them in the courtroom. Chester Long was one of those lesser skilled barristers but wasn't nearly as shady as his more successful colleagues.

SPRING SURPRISES

Joe said, "I'll let him know after I talk to Mister Blanton. It's already above freezing, so I wonder if Eddie Pascal is going to show up."

"Even if he does, we could still use another two deputies before spring shows up for real."

Joe said "Yup," then stood, walked to the peg wall and removed his coat.

After leaving the jail, Joe turned left and headed to the county courthouse. He knew he wouldn't need to spend much time with the prosecutor. Mister Blanton was a bigger gossip than any of the town's old biddies, so Joe would be surprised if he didn't already know most of the story.

He soon entered the large brick building and after crossing the foyer, turned into Duke Blanton's office and approached his clerk's desk.

Ed Royster grinned at him and said, "Mister Blanton is anxious to hear all about your arrest of the church thief. Go on in."

Joe replied, "I won't be long, Ed," then slipped his report from his inner coat pocket and walked to the prosecutor's office.

As he passed through the open doorway, Duke Blanton said, "Have a seat, Joe. Is that your report?"

Joe replied, "Yes, sir," then handed him the report before taking a seat.

Mister Blanton didn't even unfold the two sheets of papers before he leaned forward and asked, "Go ahead and tell me what happened after Father Burns reported the crime."

Joe thought he'd just have to deliver his report and answer a few questions but didn't hesitate before telling the story. As he gave the oral version of the report he'd just written, he was surprised by the prosecutor's intense interest. Joe didn't think the story was that intriguing. He could understand it if Mister Blanton was Catholic and wanted to unleash holy vengeance on Feldman. But as a practicing Lutheran, he wasn't overly fond of Catholics.

When he described the silent Colt-Henry standoff, Mister Blanton interrupted him when he excitedly asked, "You didn't fire your rifle because you saw his gloved left hand slip over his pistol's hammer?"

Joe replied, "Yes, sir. But I would have fired if he tried to cock it a second time."

Duke Blanton grinned as he said, "When I first heard about it, I didn't believe it was possible. But you really did it, didn't you?"

Joe nodded then replied, "After he lowered his pistol…"

SPRING SURPRISES

Duke Blanton interrupted him again when he said, "I just wanted to hear if that part of the story was true, Joe. I'll read your report for the rest."

"That's fine, Mister Blanton. I'm going to notify Mister Long that he'll be the public defender in the case."

Mister Blanton snickered then said, "I hope he doesn't get his client hanged."

Joe replied, "No, sir," then stood and walked out of the prosecutor's office.

He waved to Ed as he passed by and headed for the hallway. At least now Joe understood what had prompted the lawyer's interest. He probably just wanted corroboration of the almost unbelievable non-shooting part of the arrest. Now he'd be able to include the tidbit to his link in the town's gossip chain. His motive for asking about the non-gunfight didn't matter, but Joe seriously disliked wasting the time it took to tell him.

Joe left the county courthouse to visit the less impressive office of Mister Chester Long. It wasn't a long walk as his office was just three blocks away on Wells Street. But there weren't any boardwalks he Wells Street, and the break in the freezing weather had already turned the streets into a town-wide muddy swamp.

After mucking his way to the two-story building that housed Mister Long's office, Joe climbed the steps along the outside wall then opened the door to the second-floor hallway.

Unlike the prosecutor and the prosperous attorneys, Mister Long didn't have a clerk. So, when he entered the one-room office, he found the lawyer sitting at his desk reading a newspaper.

Chester looked up, saw Joe and asked, "Am I getting the church robbery case, Deputy?"

Joe nodded as he replied, "Yes, sir. I just dropped off my report with Mister Blanton."

"Okay. I'll visit my client in a little while. Before you leave, can you tell me what he's like?"

Joe knew he wasn't asking for a physical description, so he replied, "He's a typical bad luck prospector who wasn't able to earn enough money in Boise City to buy a claim. I don't believe he's a hardened criminal, either. I believe he was just another desperate victim of gold fever. But I could be wrong because he didn't hesitate to pull his Colt. And if he'd been less panicked, he would have shot me."

"Oh. Tell him I'll stop by in a few minutes. After I talk to him, I'll go visit Mister Blanton. Maybe he'll agree to a plea bargain if my client agrees to plead guilty."

"That's between you and your client then Mister Blanton and Judge Oliver, sir. I'll let Matt Feldman know you're coming."

"Thank you, Deputy."

Joe gave the lawyer a short wave before leaving his small office then trotting down the outside stairs to the blanket of thick mud.

When Joe ended his return sloppy stroll and entered the jail, he grinned when he saw Tap sitting at the desk and still fondling his Henry.

He hung his hat on a peg and as he began unbuttoning his coat, he loudly said, "Matt, your lawyer will be stopping by shortly."

Matt replied, "I heard you and the sheriff talkin', and it sounds like he ain't a good lawyer."

Joe hung his coat before saying, "At least in our great nation you get a lawyer. A lot of other places in the world don't bother with a trial at all. They just hang you or cut off your head."

Just as Joe started walking to the heat stove to have a cup of coffee, the door opened, and Jimmy Pritchard stepped inside. Joe didn't think he'd come to report the theft of a calf's liver, and hoped Jimmy wasn't going to throw a punch at him for escorting Sarah home last night.

But Jimmy just glanced at Joe before he yanked off his hat then looked at Tap and said, "I…I heard you needed dep-dep-deputies."

Joe understood why Jimmy had suddenly decided to apply for the job but didn't want to tell Tap until after Jimmy left.

He could see the look of astonishment on the sheriff's face before Tap asked, "You've been workin' with your pa since you were ten, Jimmy. So, what made you want to be a deputy?"

Jimmy stepped closer to the desk before replying, "I want to b-b-be one. Th-th-that's all."

As much as they needed help, Tap wasn't about to hire Jimmy. Eddie Pascal quit because of the ribbing he took for his outlandish behavior, and Tap knew Jimmy would be subjected to even more taunting for his stuttering. He didn't believe that Jimmy would last long enough to quit, either. If he was a newcomer without a family, Tap might have let him take that risk. But Jimmy wasn't a newcomer, and the Pritchards were an important part of the community.

He leaned back and said, "Jimmy, this is a dangerous job. Sometimes we run into trouble without even lookin' for it. Just yesterday, two fellers tried to kill Joe. Do you even know how to shoot?"

Jimmy finally acknowledged Joe's presence with a short glance before he replied, "I c-c-can learn."

SPRING SURPRISES

Tap said, "Tell Jimmy what happened yesterday afternoon, Joe."

Joe stepped closer, looked at Jimmy and said, "We were a couple of miles out of town when the prisoner suddenly pulled up. Even though I was expecting him to try something, he was still able to draw his pistol before I was ready. If his hand didn't slip over his Colt's hammer, I wouldn't be standing here, and Matt Feldman wouldn't be in our jail."

Jimmy was looking at Matt as he slowly said, "W-w-were you s-s-scared?"

Joe wasn't trying to impress Jimmy but understood that Tap wanted to dissuade him from the notion of wearing a badge.

So, he replied, "We can't afford to be scared, Jimmy. Fear leads to panic and panic can get you killed."

Jimmy turned his eyes to Joe and said, "I w-w-wouldn't be a good d-d-deputy," then turned to leave the jail.

Joe saw the disappointment in Jimmy's eyes, so before Jimmy took his second step, Joe said, "You don't have to be a deputy to visit my house, Jimmy. With Sarah spending so much time with Faith, I'd like having a guy around, so I can talk about things that are of no interest to ladies."

Jimmy stopped, looked back at Joe and asked, "Really?"

"Sure. Stop by whenever you feel like it."

Jimmy smiled, said, "Okay, Joe," then waved to Tap and hurried out of the jail.

After he was gone, Joe took a seat in front of the desk and Tap said, "I didn't expect Jimmy to ask to be a deputy. He's too gentle-minded to wear a badge. I appreciate your help in makin' him change his mind."

Joe was about to explain the reason for Jimmy's request when Chester Long arrived to talk to his client.

As the lawyer removed his hat, Tap said, "He's all yours, Mister Long."

Chester replied, "I'll let you know when we're finished, Sheriff."

Tap nodded then he and Joe stood and walked past the cells to the sheriff's small, private office.

After closing the door to let the lawyer and his client converse in privacy, Tap took his seat behind his desk.

Joe sat on one of the two other chairs and said, "I think I know why Jimmy asked to be a deputy, Tap."

"I was wonderin'."

"You know Sarah Walker has become Faith's friend and visits the house a lot. Well, as I was escorting her home last night…"

SPRING SURPRISES

Tap exclaimed, "You didn't!"

Joe rapidly shook his head before saying, "No, no, of course not. But she told me that Jimmy thinks I'm some sort of hero, and he probably believed that if he was a deputy, he could become her hero. They've been seeing each other for a long time and she's beginning to believe he'll never have the courage to propose. I want to help him get up the nerve to ask her, which is why I invited him to visit our house."

Tap asked, "Are you tryin' to be a matchmaker?"

"No, sir. I just want to help Jimmy gain some confidence. Maybe it'll help with his stuttering, too."

"Well, good luck with that. How's Faith doin'? Mary thinks she looks further along than you figgered."

"Faith is doing very well, and Kathleen Maureen is kicking up a storm. I think she's going to be a strong baby girl."

"Maybe that's 'cause she's Sam Grant Beck."

Joe grinned as he said, "I suppose there's a fifty percent chance that I'm wrong, but we'll find out if I am early in April. At least I didn't suggest naming him Ulysses or Hiram."

Tap laughed then said, "I reckon that's why Faith is happy with Sam."

Joe smiled as he said, "And Sam isn't even one of the general's given names. We can thank the U.S. Army for giving him that moniker."

While they waited for Chester to finish talking to his client, Tap began giving Joe advice about how to adjust to life as a father. As Joe listened, he heard much of the same guidance his father had given to his older brothers before they all died.

He had been so focused on Faith, his new job and their new home that he hadn't spent much time thinking about his family. But despite the almost seven years that had passed since he'd lost them, Joe was still able to remember their faces. His mother's image was particularly vivid as he pictured her singing Kathleen Mavourneen at his bedside. That vision made him smile knowing that Faith would be singing it to their children.

Joe was so distracted by his memories that he was startled when Chester Long loudly knocked on the door, opened it and said, "I'm leaving to talk to Mister Blanton."

After the lawyer walked away, Tap and Joe stood then left his private office. As they passed Matt's cell, Joe noticed that he seemed unusually calm. He assumed it was because Mister Long had told him that he'd be able to convince a jury to find him not guilty. If Matt had been a resident of Idaho City for more than a month, he'd know better.

SPRING SURPRISES

When they entered the front office, Tap said, "I'm gonna head on down to D.M.'s and get some more ammunition for our Henrys."

Joe sat behind the desk and asked, "Did you already ask the county commissioners?"

Tap grinned, grabbed his hat and replied, "Kinda."

Joe chuckled knowing that the 'kinda' meant that Sheriff Fulmer would let them know after the ammunition was stored in the jail's gun cabinet. He was curious how many boxes he'd bring back from D.M.'s shop.

As soon as Tap left the office, Joe turned and said, "You seem to be in a good mood after talking to Mister Long, Matt."

Matt said, "He said not to tell anybody what we talked about."

"I know you can't. I was just surprised that you seemed almost cheerful after you talked to him."

"I reckon I can tell ya that he's a better lawyer than you and the sheriff think he is. But I ain't tellin' you what he said."

"What the sheriff and I think doesn't matter anyway. What's important to you is what the jury thinks."

Matt quickly said, "There ain't gonna be a jury," then exclaimed, "Damn it!" and laid down on his cot.

Joe knew the conversation was over, so he turned around, opened the bottom drawer and pulled out Matt's Colt Dragoon. The rifling was pretty worn down, so a lot of .44 slugs of lead must have passed through its barrel. Joe suspected that Matt wasn't the original owner and just picked it up recently at a bargain price. But he did appreciate the old Colt's smooth steel hammer. If it had the etched grip of later models, maybe Matt would have made that shot.

Joe returned the pistol to the drawer and thought about how he could help Jimmy Pritchard gain enough confidence to propose to Sarah. Joe's problem was that he'd never had a lack of confidence. Even when he was a young boy, he always believed he could do whatever task lay before him.

But as he recalled those early years, he began to understand why he was so self-assured. It was because of his father. Even though he was his youngest son, his father always took time to guide him, to point out his mistakes without demeaning him and to praise him when he did well. By the time he was six years old, Joe did his best just to keep from disappointing his father.

Joe didn't know Jimmy's father very well but doubted if he was anything like his own father because very few men were. If he was like selfish, domineering John Quimby then Jimmy would either have to revolt like Ed and Jeremy Quimby or meekly submit. Maybe that's why he was so shy and was also the cause of his stuttering. Of course, it simply could be that he was just born that way.

SPRING SURPRISES

Either way, Joe began to believe if he just befriended Jimmy and gave him a pat on the back every now and then, it might give him a boost in confidence. He'd ask Faith for her opinion when he went home for lunch.

Joe put thoughts of Jimmy Pritchard aside and focused on their almost dangerous lack of deputies. When the commissioners had boosted deputy's pay to an incredible hundred dollars a month, he thought they'd be flooded with candidates. But of the eight who'd applied, not one had come close to meeting Tap's minimal standards.

Even during the harsh winter weather, a trickle of newcomers had arrived in town. When spring arrived, it would become a flood. The only saving grace was that most of them wouldn't live in town. They'd take a few days searching the mountain valleys then hurry to the land office, stake their claim and rush back to start panning or digging for gold. The lucky few who struck it rich would either stay in Idaho City and buy a mail order bride or pull up stakes and head to California.

The violence that was common in the mining camps was usually solved with even more violence by the prospectors. It was when the gold hunters descended into town that they became his and Tap's problem. And if they didn't get more help soon, Idaho City could be overwhelmed with lawlessness. And that was something he'd couldn't allow to happen. He wanted Faith and their baby to feel safe.

Joe knew a few good men who could do the job of keeping the town safe, but all of them were two hundred miles away in Oregon, including the one who had planned to stay. He was certain that if Chuck hadn't shot himself in the butt, he would have been more than willing to take the high-paying job by now.

The thought of Chuck's embarrassing wound made Joe smile just as the door opened and the county prosecutor's clerk entered the jail.

After he closed the door, Ed Royster said, "My boss wants you to talk to Judge Oliver."

Joe quickly asked, "Do you know what it's about, Ed?"

Ed looked past Joe to Matt Feldman as he replied, "I have an idea, but I'm not allowed to tell you."

"Okay. I'll head over there as soon as Tap gets back."

Ed nodded, then turned and quickly left the jail.

Joe hadn't needed Ed's subtle hint to understand that the judge wanted to talk to him about Matt Feldman. It was just a question of why Judge Oliver needed to talk to him instead of Mister Blanton. When Ed entered the jail, Joe thought the prosecutor needed him to clarify something in his report. Being summoned by Judge Oliver was unexpected and very unusual. But even though this would be the first time he'd spoken to the judge outside of the courtroom, Joe wasn't nervous about the meeting. But he was definitely curious.

He began to think of possible reasons for the judge's request when he heard a loud thump outside the door. He popped to his feet just before Sheriff Fulmer swung it open then grunted as he lifted a crate from the boardwalk and lugged it inside.

After setting it on the floor, he closed the door then grinned and said, "D.M. only took eight boxes. The county's gonna pay for the sixteen he left inside the crate."

As Tap pulled off his gloves, Joe picked up the heavy crate and carried it to the gun cabinet where he set it down.

He began transferring the boxes of cartridges to the shelves and said, "Ed Royster stopped by a few minutes ago. Mister Blanton wants me to talk to Judge Oliver."

"That's kinda different. What does he wanna talk to you about?"

"I don't know, but I'll find out what it is soon enough."

Tap hung up his coat and said, "Well, you'd better get over there to see what he wants."

Joe stacked one more box of .44 Henry ammunition onto the shelf before saying, "Yes, sir," then stepping away from the crate to put on his hat and coat.

Tap had already emptied the crate by the time Joe left the jail and three minutes later, he entered Judge Oliver's outer office.

As soon as he stepped inside, the judge's clerk said, "Judge Oliver is expecting you, Deputy Beck. Just wait here for a moment and I'll let him know you're here."

Joe nodded and watched the young clerk who was probably five years older than he was, stand, tap on the judge's door and open it.

He just leaned inside and said, "Deputy Beck is here, Your Honor."

Joe didn't hear the judge's reply before the clerk waved him in. The clerk closed the door immediately after Joe entered and found Judge Oliver sitting behind his surprisingly average-looking desk.

Judge Oliver said, "Please have a seat, Deputy."

Joe nodded then slowly sat in one of the two chairs set before his desk then waited for the judge to reveal the purpose of the visit.

"You've only been a deputy for a few months, so I know this must be somewhat unusual for you. A little while ago, I was visited by Mister Blanton and Mister Long about a possible plea agreement for Matt Feldman."

Joe's surprise was evident, so the judge held up his palm before saying, "Before I approved the agreement, I wanted to talk to you. I wouldn't have any objections to the plea bargain if it was just for the theft. But the attempted murder of a law officer is a much more serious charge. I'll only sign the agreement if you agree to its stipulations."

"What are those stipulations, Your Honor?"

"Matt Feldman will be taken to Fort Boise where he'll sign three-year enlistment papers. I know it's nowhere close to the severe punishment he deserves for his crimes, but I'd like to hear your opinion."

Joe thought about it for a minute or so before asking, "What if the war ends before his enlistment expires?"

"He'll continue to serve his enlistment, probably at Fort Boise."

Joe nodded then said, "I didn't think he was a hardened criminal, so I don't have a problem with the plea bargain, Your Honor."

Judge Oliver smiled then said, "I'm not surprised by your decision, Deputy Beck. I imagine you must be tired of hearing people tell you that you look older than you are. But what's more impressive to me is that you think and behave like a man closer to my age. Yet despite your youth, you've already earned a remarkable reputation in the short time you've been in Idaho City."

Joe avoided blushing as he asked, "When will I be escorting Mister Feldman to Fort Boise, sir?"

"It'll probably be Friday. I'll sign the agreement then notify Mister Blanton and Mister Long. You can tell Sheriff Fulmer when you return to the jail, but let Mister Long give the news to his client."

"Yes, sir. Is there anything else I need to know before I leave?"

"Only that I stipulated that his horse and saddle be given to you. The army wouldn't let him have his own horse, and I suspect that you'd treat the animal better than the county would."

Joe was anxious to leave, so he didn't argue about the chocolate brown gelding that was still in his barn with Duke, Bernie and the ladies.

So, he just stood and said, "I'll tell the sheriff about the arrangement in his private office, Your Honor."

Judge Oliver surprised him when he rose, shook Joe's hand and said, "I'm glad that I had a chance to talk to you, Joe."

Joe replied, "It was honored…sir," narrowly avoiding using the judge's Christian name.

After leaving the county courthouse, Joe was surprised that Mister Blanton had agreed to the plea bargain so quickly when he hadn't even met Matt Feldman. But in his report, he'd honestly depicted Matt as more desperate than evil. Maybe after the prosecutor read it, he was more susceptible to Mister Long's offer of a plea bargain. When he'd notified Mister Long that he'd been chosen to be Matt's defense attorney, his only question had been about Matt's character.

He soon entered the jail and as he was taking off his hat, Tap asked, "What did the judge want?"

Joe hung his hat and began unbuttoning his coat as he replied, "It's kind of personal, so I'll tell you in your office."

Tap nodded, then stood and anxiously waited for Joe. He still hadn't figured out why the judge needed to see Joe and hoped it wasn't because some disgruntled citizen had filed a fictitious complaint.

After Joe hung his coat, he stepped across the front office then he and Tap continued past the cells and entered the sheriff's private office. Joe closed the door but neither of them took a seat.

Joe said, "Mister Blanton and Mister Long arranged a plea bargain for Matt Feldman."

Tap snapped, "*A plea bargain?* He tried to shoot you!"

"That's why the judge wanted to talk to me before he approved it. He would deny the agreement if I wanted him charged with attempted murder of a law officer."

"Did you let him off the hook?"

Joe sighed before he replied, "Matt doesn't impress me as a criminal sort, Tap. After the judge told me what was in the plea deal, I figured it was the right way to go."

"What is it?"

"Matt needs enlist for three years and won't be mustered out even if the war ends. I'll be taking him down to Fort Boise on Friday."

"I can live with that. Are you gonna tell him?"

"No, sir. The judge said Mister Long will let him know. But because the army won't let him keep his horse, the judge is giving him and Matt's tack to me. I don't really need another horse, so do you want him?"

Tap grinned as he shook his head and said, "Nope. I ain't got any place to put him and besides, you already gave me Faith's Henry. I reckon Chester Long's gonna show up soon, so we'd better get back out front."

Joe opened the door and as he walked past the cells, he noticed a slight smile on Matt's face. It was as if he already knew he was going to join the army instead of facing a much more severe penalty. Joe was sure that Matt didn't know the plea bargain had been approved, so he figured Mister Long had made it sound like a done deal.

SPRING SURPRISES

When he returned to the front desk, Tap asked, "Do you wanna get some chow?"

Joe replied, "You go ahead, Sheriff. I'll head home to have lunch when you get back."

Tap said, "Us old folks don't eat a lot, so I'll be back soon enough."

Joe chuckled and wasn't surprised when after the sheriff donned his coat and hat, he snatched his new Henry before leaving the jail.

After he'd gone, Matt asked, "Why'd you hafta see the judge? Was it about me?"

Joe turned, then answered, "It was about a horse."

"A horse? A judge wanted to talk to you about a horse?"

Joe replied, "Yup," without saying it was Matt's chocolate brown gelding.

———

Twenty minutes later, Chester Long threw open the door and marched toward the cells without bothering to close it behind him.

Joe stood to close the door when Mister Long said, "I need to talk to my client, Deputy."

Joe walked to the door and closed it before saying, "I didn't think you were here to talk to me, Mister Long."

When Joe returned to the desk and sat down, Chester asked, "Aren't you going to the sheriff's office in back?"

"No, sir. I know why you're here and what you're going to tell your client, so it's unnecessary."

Mister Long quietly said, "I suppose it is unnecessary," then stepped past the desk.

Matt was tightly gripping the cell's bars and before his defense lawyer reached him, Matt exclaimed, "*Are you gonna tell him to let me outta here now?*"

Mister Long replied, "Perhaps I didn't fully explain how a plea bargain works, Mister Feldman. First, I had to convince the prosecuting attorney to agree to the deal. I told him you weren't a violent man then reminded him that a plea arrangement would save the county the time and cost of a trial. After he agreed to the plea bargain, it had to be approved by Judge Oliver."

Matt snapped, "You didn't tell me that!"

"And I apologize for that omission. After we met the judge, he said he'd only approve the plea bargain if Deputy Beck didn't charge you with attempted murder."

"*Attempted murder?* I didn't even get a shot off!"

SPRING SURPRISES

Chester sighed then said, "But you pulled your pistol with intent to kill Deputy Beck. So, if the deputy hadn't agreed to drop the charge, you could have been hanged."

Matt placed his right hand across his throat as he said, "So, what you told me before didn't mean nothin' if Beck didn't let it go."

"I'm afraid so. But he did agree to drop the charge, and the judge approved the plea arrangement. So, on Friday, you'll be escorted to Fort Boise to sign your three-year enlistment papers."

"What's gonna happen to Barney?"

Chester blinked before asking, "Who's Barney?"

"My gelding. I don't want somebody turnin' him into a plow horse."

"The judge awarded your horse and tack to Deputy Beck, and I don't think he's going to be plowing any furrows."

Matt looked at Joe and asked, "Is that why you let it go?"

Joe replied, "The judge told me of his decision after I agreed to drop the charge. Besides, I already have a stallion, four mares and a donkey in my barn."

"You ain't gonna sell Barney, are ya?"

Joe would have been surprised if he ever saw Matt Feldman again but still replied, "No, I'll take good care of him. You can have him back after you muster out."

Matt instantly confirmed Joe's belief when he said, "I ain't ever comin' back here."

Chester then said, "My work is done, Mister Feldman. Good luck in the army,' then turned and quickly headed to the door.

As he watched his lawyer leave the jail, Matt said, "He didn't even shake my hand. He musta thought I was gonna kiss him or somethin'."

Joe snickered before saying, "He's probably just in a rush to get his ten dollars from the county."

Matt walked to the cot, sat down and said, "I appreciate you not chargin' me for tryin' to kill ya."

"Just don't try to shoot anyone else who doesn't need a bullet. Okay?"

Before Matt could comment, Sheriff Fulmer entered the jail and immediately said, "I saw Mister Long headin' to the courthouse. I reckon he just told our prisoner what you told me."

Joe replied, "Yes, sir," then stood, left the desk and as Tap hung his coat, he took his down from its peg.

SPRING SURPRISES

After leaving the jail, Joe turned right then stepped quickly along the boardwalk. He hoped that Sarah wasn't visiting so he could tell Faith about Jimmy Pritchard. If Sarah was there, he'd still need to tell Faith about his visit with Judge Oliver. He didn't think she'd be upset with his decision not to press charges. Faith may not be happy about it, but she shouldn't be as angry as she was when he told her he'd let Eddie Pascal go. Of course, in her motherly condition, it was more difficult for him to predict how she'd react.

He soon left the boardwalk and stepped into the mud before he turned onto Third Street. The sudden warmth which had melted the snow and created the muck was now turning some of the water into vapor. The shimmering dark ground seemed more like a swamp than a road. It reminded him of the chilly autumn mornings when he fished in the big pond near his family farm.

Joe turned onto his home's walkway and used the gravel to scrape most of the mud from his boots before he stepped onto the porch. He still used the heavy, bristled doormat to remove the last of the muck before entering.

As he hung his hat on the coat rack, Joe loudly asked, "Are you prepared to serve sustenance to your husband and master, woman?"

He was unbuttoning his coat when he heard Faith laugh then just as loudly answer, "I will feed you, lord master, but alas, your taster is unavailable."

Joe chuckled, hung his coat then hurried across the parlor and entered the hallway. When he stepped into the kitchen, he was relieved to find Faith alone. Joe quickly wrapped his arms around his wife and kissed her.

When Faith was released from his gentle embrace, she asked, "Did you manage to go the entire morning without anyone trying to make me a widow?"

Joe smiled and said, "I did. I'll help you to get our lunch on the table while I tell you about the two surprising things that did happen this morning."

Faith said, "Go ahead," before they began walking to the cold room.

"Jimmy Pritchard showed up and asked Tap if he could be a deputy."

Faith's eyes widened as she asked, "Jimmy wants to be a deputy?"

"I think Tap was a surprised as you were. Even though we're desperate for help, Tap wasn't about to hire him. He knew that Jimmy wouldn't last long if he pinned on a badge. I think he only asked because he wanted to impress Sarah."

As Faith took a small ham from the shelf, she asked, "Why would he need to impress her? He just needs to work up the courage to propose."

SPRING SURPRISES

Joe pulled one of his sour pickles from the large jar before saying, "Maybe impress was the wrong word. He seemed to believe that he wasn't good enough for Sarah and being a deputy would make him more worthy."

Joe took a big bite of his pickle as they left the cold room and Faith set the ham on the counter. He took down two plates and set his pickle on one while Faith opened the bread box and took out the loaf of dark bread.

As Faith began slicing the bread, she said, "I can't believe Jimmy would think like that after all the time he and Sarah had been together."

Joe shrugged then said, "It was the only thing that came to mind. But after Tap turned him down, I noticed how disappointed he was, so I tried to make him feel better by asking him to come to visit us. Is that alright?"

"Of course, it is. Besides, now that Sarah is planning to spend more time here, I might be able to get him to propose to her in our parlor."

Joe grinned as he said, "If anyone can, it would be you, Faith Hope Charity Virtue Goodchild Beck."

Faith smiled as she continued slicing the bread when Joe asked, "Has Sarah ever talked about Jimmy's folks?"

"She talks more about his father than his mother and doesn't like him very much. She says he treats Jimmy like a stupid little boy even though Jimmy's as good a butcher as he is. His mother doesn't challenge him, either. Why did you ask?"

"When I watched Jimmy almost beg Tap to make him a deputy, I noticed his lack of confidence. I never had that problem because of how I was raised by my own father. I know I'm younger than Jimmy, but I thought if I became his friend, I could make him feel better about himself. Then he might be able to propose to Sarah."

Faith looked at him and said, "I'm still amazed when you say things like that. I know you've been hearing it for a long time, but even though you just turned seventeen, you sound and behave as if you're much older."

"That's what Judge Oliver told me this morning. That's because of my parents. Then having no one to depend on for a few years, you think and behave that way, too. So, wise and intelligent wife, what is your opinion?"

Faith put down the knife, then put her hands behind his neck and said, "I think it's a wonderful idea."

Joe gave her a quick kiss then after she began slicing the ham, Faith asked, "So, what was the other item of interest you wanted to tell me?"

Joe smiled as he said, "I'll wait until you don't have that sharp knife in your hand."

SPRING SURPRISES

Faith didn't reply as she continued using the sharp knife and hoped that whatever he needed to tell her wasn't too troublesome.

When they sat down to have their lunch, Joe said, "Judge Oliver's clerk stopped by and told me the judge wanted to see me. When I met him, he told me…"

Faith's anxiety had surged when Joe told her he'd been summoned by the judge, but when she realized Joe wasn't in trouble, she breathed easier.

Joe decided it might be wiser to inform Faith of his decision to drop the charge in the form of a question, so he said, "After the judge explained the plea agreement, he told me that he'd only approve it if I didn't charge him with attempted murder. I told you that I believed Matt Feldman was just desperate and wasn't a dangerous man. So, would you be upset if I agreed to the conditions in the plea bargain and just let him spend the next three years in the army?"

"It's up to you, Joe. It's not the same as it was with Eddie Pascal. He used to work with you then planned to kill you for no reason at all."

Joe nodded but before he could say anything, Faith asked, "Am I right in assuming that you've agreed drop the charge before the judge told you that you spoke and behaved like a much older man?"

Joe chuckled before replying, "Yes, ma'am. I'll be escorting him to Fort Boise on Friday, and we get to keep his horse and tack."

"The barn is getting pretty crowded, Joe."

"I know. When spring gets here, I'll have it expanded to give them more room. I offered the gelding to Tap, but he didn't have any place to keep him. But after I thought about it, I realized he'd be a good addition to our small herd. With all of the ladies unavailable, the gelding will be handy when I need to give Duke a break.

"I don't have to give him a new name him, either. We have Bernie, Betty, and Bessie in the barn, so do you want to guess what Matt named him?"

Faith thought about it for twenty-one seconds before she smiled and said, "I'm going to guess that it's either Bennie or Barney."

Joe laughed, leaned over and kissed her before saying, "It's Barney. And as much as I'd like to spend the afternoon with you, I need to finish my lunch and get back to work."

―――――

On his way back to the jail, Joe stopped at Jack's Diner to pick up Matt's lunch. After transferring the tray with its large bowl of warm stew, two biscuits and one spoon to Tap, he hung his hat then began removing his coat.

SPRING SURPRISES

He had just hung his coat when Father Burns entered the jail. Joe hoped that when the priest heard about the plea arrangement, he hadn't told Judge Oliver he wasn't pressing charges for the theft. He didn't care about losing Barney, but thought Matt was already getting off pretty easy with having to serve three years in the army.

Father Burns closed the door and said, "I was just visited by Mister Blanton's clerk. I was surprised when he explained the terms of the plea bargain."

Joe said, "The sentence was probably less than he deserved, but I didn't believe Mister Feldman should hang for what he did."

Joe was relieved when the priest replied, "I agree with you completely. I can't tell you how astonished I was when I learned you had dropped the charge. Very few men would forgive a man who had tried to kill him, Joe."

"I didn't forgive him, Father. I just didn't think he should hang for failing to shoot me."

"Whatever your reason, it was still a mark of your compassionate nature. And it wasn't even the first time this week you've displayed concern for your fellow man. The clerk told me that Eddie Pascal had started an avalanche in an attempt to murder you earlier in the day, yet you didn't arrest him, either."

"Eddie was out of his head, Father. Besides, he used to be a deputy."

"Well, I just stopped by to tell you that I'm proud of you and very happy that you and Faith are members of my parish."

Joe replied, "Thank you, Father," and hoped that the priest didn't bless him with Tap and Matt Feldman watching.

Much to Joe's relief, Father Pat just patted Joe on his right shoulder before turning and leaving the jail.

As Joe walked to the desk, Tap said, "I was kinda worried that Father Burns mighta told the judge to let Feldman go."

Joe sat down and said, "So, was I. But then I realized, if the judge tossed out the plea bargain, I could charge Matt with attempted murder. Is that right?"

Tap took his seat behind the desk and replied, "I reckon so, but I hope it doesn't come up again. Anyway, I got a favor to ask ya, Joe."

"You don't have to ask, Tap. Just tell me what you need."

"Can you do the saloon stroll again tonight? Joseph is runnin' a fever and Mary's pretty worried."

"Of course, I will. Why did you even come back after lunch? If his fever gets worse, you don't want Mary leaving to fetch the doctor. You should head home."

SPRING SURPRISES

Tap popped to his feet, said, "Thanks, Joe," then hurried away from the desk.

As Joe moved to the chair behind the desk, Sheriff Fulmer quickly pulled on his coat and hat, then waved and left the jail.

Joe hoped young Joseph just had a mild case of the flu and would get better soon. But he knew that some types of flu can be deadly and could quickly devastate a family or even a town. That thought made him shift his concern to Faith. He knew she was strong and their baby was doing well, but the thought of Faith coming down with the flu was frightening. He had a sudden urge to run home to protect her but knew it was irrational.

Joe was almost ashamed of himself for letting his emotions overwhelm his common sense. Especially after the many conversations he and Faith shared about the risks everyone faced almost daily.

He smiled at his purposeless concerns then looked at Matt and noticed he'd finished eating. So, he stood then walked to the cell to retrieve the tray.

As he took it from his prisoner, Matt asked, "Did I hear that right? That avalanche that kept me from goin' to Centreville was there 'cause one of your pals tried to kill ya?"

"Yup. That's how that mountain of snow became a roadblock to your escape."

Joe was walking away when Matt snickered before saying, "And you let him off, too? Maybe you oughta trade in your badge for a Bible and start preachin'."

Joe set the tray on the desktop and sat down before replying, "If everyone lived by the Good Book, then we wouldn't need lawmen at all."

After Matt stopped talking and laid down on the cot, Joe thought about the Bible stored in their desk drawer with Faith's journals. Just after the arrival of spring, she'd be adding Kathleen Maureen's name to the line below the entry of their marriage. He smiled knowing that she might be writing the name Sam Grant Beck but still believed Katie would enter the world with the coming of spring.

―――

The rest of the afternoon was uneventful, so just as the sun began to set, Joe locked up and headed home. He'd make a detour to the Fulmers' home to see how Joseph was doing, then just cut across the empty lot east of St. Joseph's church, convent and school.

When he turned onto Second Street, he saw a buggy parked in front of Tap's house and suspected it was Doctor Wallace's rig. He picked up his pace and soon turned onto the walkway. After he stepped onto the porch, he wiped his boots on the doormat then knocked on the door.

SPRING SURPRISES

Just seconds later, the door opened, and Tap said, "I was hopin' you'd stop by, Joe. The doc just finished checkin' our boy and said he needs to take out his appendix. Mary and I are gonna stay with Joseph 'til the operation is done. So, can Grace stay with you and Faith?"

"Of course, she can."

"Come on in, and I'll get Grace dressed."

Tap turned before Joe entered, closed the door then followed the sheriff into the parlor. When he saw six-year-old Grace sitting on the couch, she looked as if she was attending a funeral.

When her father picked up her coat, Grace stood, stretched out her arms and focused her sad eyes on Joe.

Joe took off his hat, smiled and said, "Hello, Grace. Your papa told me that Joseph has a bad tummy ache. While the doctor is making him feel better, you'll be staying with me and your Aunt Faith. Okay?"

Grace's sad expression didn't change as she simply nodded while her father buttoned her coat.

After he tugged on her thick woolen hat, Tap kissed her on her forehead and said, "I'm sure Joey will be back before you know it, Gracie."

Grace softly replied, "Okay, Papa," before her father picked up her small travel bag and handed it to Joe.

Joe took Grace's hand then followed Tap to the foyer.

Tap opened the door and said, "I'll see you in the mornin', Joe."

Joe replied, "Yes, sir," then he and Grace stepped out of the house into the cold evening air.

As they stepped along the walkway, Grace asked, "Is Joey gonna die, Uncle Joe?"

Joe knew what he should say, but replied, "I won't lie to you, Grace. There is a chance he may die, but there's also a chance we could be eaten by a giant grizzly bear before we reach my house."

Grace quickly scanned the shadowed street before she anxiously asked, "Are there really grizzly bears out there?"

They were crossing the frozen mud of Second Street when Joe said, "Bears are almost everywhere, but most of them sleep in the winter. I was just trying to tell you that even though Joey might die, he probably won't. Just like we won't be surprised by a hungry, scary grizzly bear."

"Oh. When will Joey come back home?"

"That's up to the doctor. He has to cut a hole in Joey's tummy to take out his appendix then sew him back up again.

So, don't be afraid if he doesn't come home for a few days. Okay?"

"Alright. Does it hurt not to have a 'pendix?"

Joe smiled as he replied, "Not at all. The doctors don't even know why we have one. It looks like a little worm and just sits in your tummy without even wiggling."

As they crossed the shadowed empty lot, Grace giggled before she asked, "Do I have one?"

"We all have them. I still have mine and so does your Aunt Faith. They don't give most people any trouble, but sometimes they get mad and make our tummies hurt."

Grace rubbed her stomach as she said, "I hope mine doesn't get mad."

"So, do I."

After successfully navigating the lot without meeting a grizzly bear or any other fearsome creatures, Joe and Grace climbed the back porch's steps.

Faith was preparing their supper when she heard Joe's footsteps on the porch, so she smiled and dropped her spatula onto the cookstove. As she turned to embrace her husband, the door opened, and she realized he wasn't alone.

Joe closed the door before saying, "Joseph has appendicitis and Doctor Wallace is going to operate. So, Grace will be our guest for a while."

Faith said, "I'm sure your brother will be fine, Grace."

As Faith removed her hat, Grace said, "Uncle Joe told me all about the 'pendix. And bears, too."

Faith laughed as she began unbuttoning Grace's coat. After they went to bed, she'd ask Joe how he'd managed to include bears and appendicitis in the same conversation.

———

Just twenty minutes later, Joe left the house to bring Matt his dinner and make his nightly saloon stroll. After he'd gone, Faith took Grace to the nursery which would now serve as her temporary bedroom to prepare her for sleep.

Joe's biggest hazard as he trekked to Jack's Diner were the ice-covered ruts left by the wheeled traffic. Some were more than eight inches deep and a misstep could break an ankle. While it wasn't a potentially fatal danger, his enhanced level still emerged, which assured him that he wouldn't place his boot into one of the man-made miniature canyons.

After delivering his prisoner's supper, Joe grabbed a shotgun then left the jail leaving Matt to eat in the dark. He hoped he wouldn't have to enter any of the saloons but didn't believe he'd be that lucky. He'd made more than fifty whiskey walks and only three had been clean tours.

Joe was beginning to believe this would be his fourth when he reached Pete Parker's Palace and heard a man shout followed by the sound of glass shattering. He yanked open one of the double outer doors, stepped inside, then stopped to find the trouble. It didn't take long before he identified the problem. He saw a tall, unkempt older man jabbing his index finger at a smaller, equally filthy drinker while he loudly and profanely described the other man's ancestors.

Joe gripped the shotgun with both hands, and as he strode across the barroom floor, the background noise faded, but the shouting and jabbing man didn't notice.

The man being insulted had yet to move when Joe stopped just six feet away and shouted, "That's enough!"

The angry man finally ended his tirade, looked at Joe and snarled, "This ain't none of your business, Deputy. This is between me and him."

Joe didn't even look at 'him' as he stared at the loud troublemaker who had obviously had a few too many and said, "If you two had taken your fight outside, I might agree with you. But you made it my business by having it in here. What's your name?"

The man was still seething as he replied, "Floyd. Floyd Abernathy."

Joe looked at the silent partner in the barroom argument and asked, "What's your name?"

The sober, smaller man never took his eyes from the loud jabber as he said, "Walt Lawrence."

"What happened, Walt?"

Walt pointed at Floyd as he said, "I just sat down when that bastard showed up and grabbed my whiskey. He tossed it down his gullet then threw the glass at me. He woulda hit me if I didn't duck. You gotta…look out!"

Even though Joe had been facing Walt, he'd been using his peripheral vision to monitor Floyd. So, before Walt shouted his warning, he'd seen Floyd's right hand start to move. When Floyd's fingers wrapped around his Colt's grip, Joe just rotated the shotgun until the left barrel introduced itself to Floyd's hat. Floyd was still gripping his pistol when he crumpled to the saloon's floor.

Joe looked at the barkeeper and said, "He should be out for a while. If he gives you any more trouble, send someone to my house. It's 15 Third Street."

The barkeep nodded before Joe turned and left the saloon. As he walked past the remaining establishments along the saloon stroll, he didn't dwell on the incident. It was typical of the majority of alcohol-infused confrontations. Most of them were nipped in the bud by the bartender's scattergun. If it wasn't, by the time he or Tap showed up, most of them had escalated to a fist or knife fight. Surprisingly, even the biggest brawls rarely turned into a gunfight. What made this one different was that he'd arrived just as it started.

Joe finished the whiskey walk with no more incidents then turned for home. As he crossed Main Street, he thought about visiting Doctor Wallace's house, but figured the doctor might still be in surgery while his parents prayed for their son. As he walked along the moonlit street, Joe added his own prayers for Tap's son.

When he entered his foyer, he removed both shotgun shells and slid them into his coat's pocket before hanging his hat and coat on the coat rack. He leaned the unloaded shotgun against the wall then quietly walked to the hallway. When Faith hadn't greeted him, he wasn't the least bit concerned. With Kathleen Maureen sharing her mother's energy, he would have been surprised if she'd been able to stay awake. It was just a question of where she was sleeping.

Joe entered the dark hallway and noticed that Grace's bedroom door had been left open. When he looked inside, he smiled and tiptoed to the bed. Grace was peacefully sleeping beneath the covers while fully clothed Faith slept on top of the quilt. He wished he could let her rest, but one of the other effects of her condition made it necessary. If he didn't wake her, she'd soon need to use the bedpan in their bedroom.

He leaned close to her left ear and whispered, "Faith, sweetheart, I'm home."

Faith's eyelids slowly opened before she yawned, rolled onto her back and quietly asked, "Is it late?"

"No. You've probably only been asleep a couple of hours."

Faith covered her mouth as she yawned again, then sat up and slid her feet to the floor. Joe helped her to stand before they left the room and walked to their own bedroom.

Joe smiled as he opened the door and said, "I'll empty the bedpan when you're finished."

Faith kissed him then entered their bedroom and closed the door as Joe walked to the kitchen.

―――

Thirty minutes later, Faith had already returned to dreamland when Joe slipped beneath the covers. She'd hadn't remained awake long enough to ask him anything, including how he'd managed to link appendicitis to grizzly bears.

Joe closed his eyes and silently said another prayer for Joseph before asking God to protect Faith and Kathleen Maureen.

CHAPTER 3

Joe was returning to the desk after giving Matt his breakfast when Sheriff Fulmer arrived. When Joe saw Tap's tired but relieved expression, he knew that Joseph's surgery had been successful.

Tap took off his hat before saying, "Joey is already home and sleepin' in his own bed. Doc Wallace will be visitin' to check for infection for a few days but said he should be okay."

Joe grinned and said, "That's great news, Tap. You should keep your coat on and go tell Grace."

"That ain't necessary. Mary was gonna fetch her right after I left."

Joe let the sheriff take the chair behind the desk before he said, "Grace was pretty worried about her big brother, so she'll be really happy when Mary gives her the good news."

Tap yawned before saying, "Just like Mary and I were when the doc told us."

"You look pretty tired, boss. Why don't you take a nap on one of the cots?"

"I'm alright. How'd things go on the stroll?"

"Just one loud argument in Parker's that I ended by popping a drunk on the noggin with the shotgun."

"You get the name of the feller you dropped?"

"Floyd Abernathy. The other guy's name was Walt Lawrence."

"I haven't heard of either of 'em. Did they look like prospectors?"

"That would be my guess."

"I reckon we're gonna see a lot more of 'em in the next few months, too. If I can't find some good deputies soon, I might hafta hire some of those fellers I already turned down."

"At least they'd have to work for a month to collect their pay before they hurried back to their claims."

Tap grunted just before the door opened and the judge's clerk stepped inside.

He walked to Joe, handed him an envelope and said, "This is Judge Oliver's court order to carry out the plea bargain. You need to give this to Colonel Funderburk when you arrive at Fort Boise."

Joe nodded before the clerk turned and quickly left the jail.

After the door closed, he looked at Tap and asked, "What is his name, anyway?"

SPRING SURPRISES

Sheriff Fulmer replied, "It's Maurice Lemond. And he doesn't like bein' called Mo, either."

Joe pulled the judge's order from the envelope as he said, "I reckon he wants to be a judge himself."

The order didn't even fill half the page and simply informed the colonel that Matthew Feldman was to enlist for three years and could not be mustered out before the term of enlistment expired. In the remote chance that the army refused to accept him, Matt was to be escorted back to Idaho City for trial.

Joe handed it to Tap then looked at Matt and said, "We'll be leaving tomorrow morning to make the ride to Fort Boise. If the army doesn't want you, you'll be returning to face trial."

Matt looked up from his breakfast and said, "I ain't comin' back here even if the army doesn't want me."

"With all that killing going on back east, I think the Union army would still take you even if you couldn't see ten feet in front of your face."

"I don't mind killin' Injuns, but I ain't gonna go back there and kill any Southerners. If they send me into that war, I'll change sides."

Tap gave the order back to Joe and as he slipped it back into the envelope, he asked, "Were you born in the South, Matt?"

"Not the deep South. I grew up in outside of Sedalia in Missouri."

Joe's eyebrows rose as he said, "I've been to Sedalia a couple of times. My family had a farm just north of Warrensburg."

"How'd you get out here? Did you run off to keep the army from takin' ya?"

"I wasn't old enough to be conscripted when I left. I joined a wagon train and ended up in Idaho City."

Matt quickly asked, "You ain't old enough? How old are you?"

"I turned seventeen last month."

"You're joshing me! I can't believe I got caught by a kid. So, you musta been lyin' when you said you killed all those fellers."

"It doesn't matter to me what you believe, Matt. After I leave you at Fort Boise, you'll never see me again."

Matt ended the conversation when he resumed eating, so Joe began debating whether or not he should mention Matt's Southern sympathies to Colonel Funderburk. If he did, he might be returning to Idaho City with Matt. That possibility made him quickly decide to let the army learn about it after Matt had signed the enlistment papers.

SPRING SURPRISES

Thursday soon turned out to be more hectic than usual as Joe and Tap had to respond to a succession of calls. While none of them took very long to resolve, the sheer volume kept them constantly on the move. Lunch wasn't possible for either of them, but Joe managed to get some food to their prisoner by early afternoon.

It was mid-afternoon before Tap and Joe were reunited in the jail. As soon as they sat down, Joe said, "You're ready to fall over, boss. Why don't you either lay down or head home?"

"I can hang on another couple of hours, Joe."

"Maybe so, but you'll be dead on your feet when you leave. I'll make the walk tonight. Okay?"

Tap hated the idea of saddling Joe with the duty three nights in a row but knew Joe was right, so he replied, "Alright. But I'll owe ya a couple of nights off."

"You won't owe me anything, Tap."

"Like hell, I don't. If you didn't show up when you did, I'd either be on my own or still stuck with Eddie Pascal."

"Speaking of Eddie. If he is coming back, he should ride into town today or tomorrow."

Tap grinned as he said, "Maybe he'll be sittin' behind the desk when you get back from Fort Boise tomorrow."

"Then he can take Friday's saloon stroll, hopefully without his stovetop hat."

They both laughed knowing that they'd probably never see Eddie with or without his tall, black beaver chapeau.

―――

Joe was wearing his fur-lined hat when he turned onto the vacant lot and saw the light coming from his kitchen window. He hoped that Sarah wasn't visiting Faith because she'd probably expect to be escorted home again.

He made a small side trip when he entered the barn to check on their small herd. His monthly hay order would arrive tomorrow, but he needed to buy a couple of bushels of oats pretty soon. While he was adding hay to their stalls, he estimated how much bigger it should be now that Barney would be a member of the equine family.

Joe dumped the last armload of hay in Bernie's stall then rubbed his donkey's nose as he said, "How about if I bring you along tomorrow? You won't have to carry anything, but you need the exercise, mister."

Joe patted Bernie on the neck then left the barn. He hadn't seen anyone through the window before he opened the door and stepped into the kitchen. He was relieved when he only found Faith waiting for him.

SPRING SURPRISES

As he removed his hat, Faith smiled and said, "When Mary told Grace that Joseph was sleeping in his own bed, she danced around the kitchen for almost a minute."

"I'm surprised Mary didn't join her. I guess it was because she was just as tired as Tap was. I suggested he take a nap in one of the cells, but we were too busy. I figured he'd be worse by the time we locked up, so I'll be doing tonight's stroll."

"I thought you might."

Joe hung his coat and gunbelt then stepped behind Faith, wrapped his arms around her then slid his right hand across her bulging middle.

He kissed her cheek and asked, "How are you and Kathleen Maureen getting along, sweetheart?"

"We haven't had any serious arguments today, but she still has frequent tantrums."

Joe snickered before saying, "I hope she's calmer after she arrives," then began kissing the back of Faith's neck.

Faith sighed before she quickly said, "You have to stop doing that, Mister Beck. We have to get you fed and out of the house."

Joe kissed her once more before releasing her and saying, "I suppose duty comes first."

As he helped Faith set the table, Joe asked, "Didn't Sarah visit today?"

"No. She's doing the store's end of the month bookkeeping. But she'll be spending most of the day with me tomorrow while you're gone."

"I should be back before sunset. I just told Bernie that I'd bring him along just to give him some exercise."

After sitting down, Joe said, "Tap said that if he doesn't find any good deputies before spring, he'll start hiring some of those failed prospectors. They may not last longer than a month, but they could handle some of the routine work."

"I still can't understand why it's so hard to find deputies when the pay is a hundred dollars a month."

"Tap can find plenty of men willing to take the pay, but they're all unwilling to do the job as it needs to be done. Speaking of doing the job, I've got to get going."

Faith nodded before Joe said grace. As they began eating, Joe told Faith about the more titillating problems he and Tap had resolved during the busy day.

———

It was still above freezing as Joe headed home after his fourth quiet saloon stroll. He knew this false spring wouldn't last long but hoped winter didn't return with a vengeance before Saturday.

If the frigid cold didn't return tomorrow, Joe thought about visiting the small canyon that had attracted his attention when he and Faith first came to Idaho City. He'd never had the time to explore it before but wanted to see if the stream was a good candidate for his long-postponed feather fishing expedition.

But even if the stream was too shallow for fishing, Joe still might want to buy a quarter section of the canyon. He wouldn't have to homestead the property, either. Their savings were more than sufficient to buy it outright. If he still thought it was a good idea after exploring the property, he'd ask Faith about it after he returned tomorrow night.

―――

The false spring was still hovering over Idaho City when Joe rode Duke down Third Street early on Friday morning trailing Barney and Bernie. As he was saddling Barney, Joe decided to put the pack saddle on Bernie. He wasn't planning on buying anything in Boise City but didn't want anyone to think he was trying to sell his donkey.

After dismounting, Joe tied off Duke then detached Barney from the trail rope and knotted the gelding's reins to the hitchrail. When he entered the jail, he wasn't surprised to find Sheriff Fulmer sitting behind the desk.

Tap grinned and said, "Your prisoner already had his breakfast and used the privy, Deputy Beck. He's even got his coat and hat on. So, you just gotta open his cell and take him to Fort Boise."

Joe snickered as walked to the cells and said, "It sounds as if you want to get rid of me, Sheriff Fulmer."

"I wanted you to get back quicker, so you could welcome Eddie Pascal."

Joe was grinning as he took down the big key ring, unlocked Matt's cell and asked, "How's Joseph?"

"He's doin' really good, but he's already hungry 'cause the doc said we can only give him soup for a few days."

"That's good news. When I get back, I'll pay him a visit."

"I'm sure he'll be happy to see ya, Joe."

Joe nodded then waved before he and Matt left the jail. Five minutes later, they left Idaho City behind and began the long, descending ride to Fort Boise.

Matt hadn't said a word since leaving his cell until he asked, "Why'd you bring the jackass? Are you gonna buy somethin' in Boise City?"

"Nope. I only brought him along because he needed the exercise."

"If you got all of them horses, then why did you buy a donkey?"

"I didn't buy him. When I left Missouri, I was pulling a hand cart until I found him in a burned-out barn in Kansas."

"If you didn't find him, you were gonna pull that cart yourself after you joined a wagon train?"

"I'd pulled the cart to towns more than ten miles away and figured I'd be able to keep up with a wagon train. By the time I realized how difficult it would be, I found Bernie."

"How'd you get all the horses?"

Joe figured telling the story would help pass the time but would avoid mentioning Faith almost as if he needed to protect her.

He began the tale by saying, "The wagon master gave me the first one, a mare he called Bessie when…"

Joe was about to tell Matt about the Mort Jones shooting when the canyon came into view. He stopped talking as he focused on the stream flowing out of the tall pine forest. He followed the rippling water before it disappeared from view then tried to estimate the canyon's depth.

He was still studying the canyon when Matt loudly asked, "Why'd you stop talkin'?"

Joe pulled his eyes from the canyon then looked at Matt and said, "I was distracted. Anyway, I was sitting on my heels near at the creek's bank when…"

Matt didn't ask another question until Joe described in detail how he'd cauterized the wound. The gruesome image also elicited a grimace before he asked his question.

Joe continued his long narration which included having to answer Matt's frequent questions as they made their way along the muddy, twisting roadway. He had to pause when they greeted a few prospective prospectors heading to Idaho City leading their pack animals. He had a longer break when they passed a small convoy of three heavily loaded freight wagons.

Joe was close to telling how he'd set the plains ablaze when they spotted Boise City. Then less than a minute later, Fort Boise appeared to the west of the new town.

Joe ended his tale when Matt pointed at the large fort and said, "I guess it's better than gettin' hanged."

"I reckon the army will just keep you at Fort Boise for the next three years. Just don't do something that will get you thrown into the stockade."

Matt just grunted as he stared at the fort, and Joe figured it wouldn't be long before Private Feldman found himself behind bars again. He had a feeling that even with the court order, Colonel Funderburk might see Matt as a problem and refuse to take him. NCOs were less concerned about soldiers with bad attitudes, so he decided to seek out the top sergeant in the hope that he would take custody of Matt.

As they approached Boise City, Joe noticed how much it had grown in the since he'd first seen the town. More buildings were under construction, and Joe figured it would be bigger than Idaho City when the gold rush ended in a few years.

Matt remained silent as they angled to the west to bypass the town and soon entered the outer buildings of Fort Boise. When they reached the guarded gate in the high walls of the protected part of expansive fort, they pulled up and dismounted.

Joe stepped closer to one of the guards and said, "I'm Deputy Sheriff Joe Beck. I'd like to speak to your top sergeant."

The short private looked up at Joe and replied, "Sergeant Nicholson's office is next to the command building."

Joe nodded then said, "Let's go visit the sergeant, Matt."

Matt just tied Barney's reins to Bernie's pack saddle before he began walking through the wide gates. Joe quickly followed leading Duke, Barney and Bernie.

They had to avoid the formations of soldiers as they crossed the open parade grounds but soon reached the office of the post's top sergeant. Joe tied off Duke then he and Matt stepped onto the stone walk before entering the sergeant's office. Joe expected the highest-ranking enlisted man to have a private acting as his assistant, but soon learned he was mistaken. Aside from Sergeant Nicholson, the only other soldier in the office was a young corporal.

As the visiting NCO turned to see who'd entered, Sergeant Nicholson snapped, "You know better…" then stopped when he realized Joe and Matt weren't in uniform.

Joe smiled as he took the court order from his pocket and said, "Sorry for not knocking, Sergeant. I'm Boise County Deputy Sheriff Joe Beck. His name is Matthew Feldman. This is a court order from Judge Oliver which requires Mister Feldman to enlist for three years."

After Joe gave him the court order, Sergeant Nicholson took just a minute to read the short document before asking, "What did he do to earn this?"

"He stole some gold artifacts from St. Joseph's church."

Sergeant Nicholson looked at Matt as he said, "I reckon you got off easy, Feldman. Let's head over to the admin building and get you signed up."

As Sergeant Nicholson stood, he said, "You coming along, Rock? You gotta pick up your paperwork anyway."

Corporal Aubrey Roche quietly replied, "Might as well."

SPRING SURPRISES

The four men left the top sergeant's office and turned left. As they walked along the stone walk, Joe wondered why the other NCO seemed so dispirited by having to visit the administration building.

When they entered the large office, Sergeant Nicholson said, "I'll take charge of Mister Feldman, Deputy."

Joe nodded as he said, "He's all yours, Sergeant."

Joe stayed put as Sergeant Nicholson led Matt down a hallway then disappeared into another office. He watched as the corporal stepped to the front of nearby desk and just stopped.

The private sitting behind the desk, stood and shook his hand as he said, "We're all gonna miss you, Corporal Rock."

Corporal Rock quietly said, "I shoulda kept my temper, Tom. But I meant every word I said. So, just give me my papers and I'll get outta here."

The private reluctantly reached into a flat box filled with papers, extracted a thick envelope and handed it him.

He shook his hand again as he said, "Good luck, Rock."

Joe noticed the absence of 'corporal' and suspected that the corporal had just been mustered out of the army. It wouldn't have made sense to him if he hadn't been part of Sergeant Will Boone's conversion to Mister Will Boone.

Joe followed Mister Rock out the door, and once outside, he said, "Excuse me, Corporal. May I talk to you for a few minutes?"

Mister Roche turned and replied, "What do you wanna talk about, Deputy?"

"It seems as if you were just mustered out of the army. Is that right?"

"It isn't a big secret. If you hang around the post for ten minutes, you'd hear somebody talking about it."

"I need some chow before I head back to Idaho City. You can tell me about it while we're eating, and I'll buy."

Rock smiled and said, "You've got a deal, Deputy."

"Before we fill our stomachs, I've got to collect my horses and donkey."

As they headed back to the top sergeant's office, Rock said, "That's one mighty handsome stallion, Deputy."

"His name is Duke and mine is Joe. The gelding is named Barney, and he used to be the prisoner's horse, but the judge awarded him to me. The donkey's name is Bernie."

"The name on my enlistment papers is Aubrey Roche, but ever since I started wearing long pants, everybody calls me Rock."

SPRING SURPRISES

As Joe untied Duke's reins, he said, "One of my best friends was a sergeant who was mustered out against his will. He just had a bad company commander who happened to be the nephew of an even worse post commander."

They started walking across the parade grounds before Rock said, "My company commander is a good officer, but I can't say the same about Colonel Funderburk."

As they approached the front gate, Joe asked, "What did you do that was so bad to make him decide to muster you out of the army?"

"It was my big mouth that got me in trouble. In a few days, it'll be six months since we got paid. I told Lieutenant Williams that if the boys didn't get paid soon, they'd start to desert and start looking for gold. I said the colonel oughta wire headquarters and tell them he was sending a heavily armed detail to collect our back pay.

"When the lieutenant told the colonel what I said, he had Lieutenant Williams bring me into his office. After I got there, he asked me to repeat what I said. I told him exactly what I told the lieutenant, and I didn't leave out my cuss words, either. When I finished, he turned red then stood up and started yelling. He said I was insubordinate, and we oughta be happy that the army was still feeding us. I know that I shoulda just apologized and let it go, but I kinda lost my temper."

They stopped before Ryerson's Sutler Store and Diner, and Joe tied Duke's reins at the long hitchrail. After entering, they turned to the diner section of the large building. As they headed to a table, Rock held up two fingers to a short, older man behind the counter. The man nodded then turned and disappeared through a doorway.

After they removed their hats and coats, they sat at the table, and Rock said, "I just ordered a couple of regular lunches. I don't know what it'll be though."

"That's okay. I assume that your colonel didn't just grin and tell you he was just kidding."

Rock replied, "I don't reckon Colonel Funderburk knows how to grin. When he said he was gonna bust me to private, I figured I didn't have anything else to lose, so I told him he wasn't good enough to be a private in an army of ants."

Joe laughed before saying, "I reckon you found out pretty soon that you were wrong when you thought you had nothing else to lose."

"Yup. When the colonel finally stopped yelling, he told Lieutenant Williams to take me to the stockade. Then he said I'd be court-martialed for mutiny and hanged. After the lieutenant escorted me outta the command building, he told me I really screwed up, as if I didn't need reminding. But he also said he'd be willing to act as my defending officer for the court martial.

"I was kept in the stockade for two days without hearing a word about the court martial or anything else. I reckon that after the colonel cooled down some, he figured out he'd have an even bigger problem with the troopers if he put me on trial. So, he sent the lieutenant to tell me I was gonna be mustered out without pay."

"Does he have the authority to do that?"

Rock shrugged as he replied, "I don't know. But I didn't want any of the others to get in trouble by making a fuss, so I just took my medicine."

The small man then arrived with their lunch and as he set the tray on the table, he said, "I reckon this is the last time we'll be seein ya, so good luck, Rock."

Rock nodded and said, "Thanks, Jim."

Jim turned and walked away, and Joe and Rock began moving the plates from the tray to the tabletop. Each was filled with an unidentified meat smothered in brown, greasy gravy, a baked potato and boiled onions.

As they began eating, Joe asked, "What are you going to do now?"

"I gotta go back to my quarters and pick up my duffle."

"I meant after you leave the fort. You didn't get your mustering out pay, so you'll need to find a job."

Rock swallowed his first bite of greasy meat that turned out to be salt pork, then said, "I reckon I'll walk to Boise City and start looking for one."

"Don't you have a horse?"

"Only the one the army let me use."

"I really don't need Barney. Do you want him?"

Rock was surprised by Joe's offer but quickly replied, "Sure. He's a nice-looking animal. What's the catch?"

Joe grinned and said, "No catch. But I did have a reason for wanting to talk to you. When the private in the admin building stopped calling you corporal, I figured you were being mustered out. It was also obvious that he respected you, so I wanted to know why the army was letting you go."

Rock was making short work of his lunch as he waited for the deputy to explain why he needed to learn the circumstances of his dismissal from the army.

Joe snuck in a bite of his potato before saying, "I was hoping you weren't being punished for being abusive to your men. It didn't take long for you to dispel that notion."

Rock asked, "So, why did you need to know that I wasn't a mean son of a bitch?"

"Do you know how many lawmen are in Boise County?"

SPRING SURPRISES

"You got three or four up in Idaho City, don't ya?"

"We should have a half dozen, but there's only Sheriff Fulmer and me. The sheriff has been searching for good men to hire, but they're either afraid or unqualified. I was hoping to convince you to join us."

Rock grinned as he said, "I don't need much convincing, Joe. If I knew you were shorthanded up there, I woulda made that long walk to Idaho City."

Joe smiled then said, "Let's finish eating, then you can pick up your duffle before we ride to Idaho City."

Rock nodded before he and Joe viciously attacked the defenseless food on their plates.

Joe wasn't even surprised by the fortunate timing of his arrival at Fort Boise. He simply accepted the chance meeting with Rock as another of the string of almost providential events he'd encountered over the past year. They'd become commonplace ever since the day he needed to help Captain Chalmers. Now he wondered what the next one would be and how it would affect his life.

―――

It wasn't until they rode out of Fort Boise before Rock asked, "How'd you get to be a deputy, Joe?"

Joe smiled as he replied, "I thought the first thing you'd ask me was how much the job paid."

"I figured it was around thirty dollars a month, which is more than twice what I was making as a corporal. But they did feed us and give us a place to sleep."

"The county just raised the salary for deputies to a hundred dollars a month."

Rock quickly looked at Joe and exclaimed, "*A hundred dollars a month?* That's a lot of money!"

"That's because it's dangerous and most of the unmarried men are out looking for gold."

"I reckon so, but that's still a lot of money. That's a lieutenant's pay."

"I thought eighty dollars a month was too much, but I'm not complaining. Even though it'll be the sheriff's decision to hire you, I don't think that'll be a problem. When I arrived in September, he only had one deputy and he quit in October. Then he hired another deputy, and he was killed a month later."

"So, tell me how you got to be a deputy."

Joe nodded as he said "I was scouting for a wagon train and another scout wanted to start prospecting, so…"

SPRING SURPRISES

Joe's brief explanation was just the start of their long conversation. Rock's many questions meant that Joe did most of the talking, but he did learn more of Rock's background. He was fourteen when his family left Ohio in the spring of '53. When he was eighteen, he enlisted, and his unit was sent to man the recently established Fort Boise.

They had the road mostly to themselves as they rode north, and Joe didn't recognize any of the men who passed by on their way to Boise City.

When they reached the creek that crossed the road, they pulled up to let Duke, Barney and Bernie drink.

Rock watched Barney as he dipped his muzzle into the icy water and said, "Joe, I hate to bring this up, but I've don't even have two dollars to my name."

Joe smiled as he said, "That's not a problem, Rock. You can stay with me and Faith 'til you get paid."

"I don't wanna be a nuisance, Joe."

Joe chuckled before saying, "You won't be a nuisance. Faith will be so happy when I tell her that you're going to be a deputy that she'll probably bake you a cake."

"But ain't your place is gonna be pretty crowded when she has your baby."

"Trust me. It won't be crowded. We just made one of the downstairs bedrooms into a nursery and still have four empty bedrooms upstairs."

Rock stared at Joe as he asked, "How'd you manage to buy a house that big?"

"Let's get moving again and I'll tell you about it."

Rock nodded before they walked their horses out of the creek and Joe began telling him the story of the bank robbery. That led to a discussion about the bizarre real estate market in the town.

They were talking about the expected flood of gold seekers and families when Joe spotted his small canyon and knew he'd have to postpone his exploration. But with Rock joining them, he'd should have a little more personal time. Of course, when Kathleen Maureen arrived almost all of their free time would vanish.

It was late afternoon when Idaho City came into view and Rock said, "It's a lot bigger than I expected."

Joe looked at him and asked, "Haven't you seen it before?"

"Nope. Our job was to keep the Injuns quiet, so we patrolled south, east and west. Where's the sheriff's office?"

Joe pointed as he said, "See that big brick building on the right? That's the county courthouse. The jail is a couple of buildings to the north. Most of the saloons line up along the west side of Main Street until you reach the opera house. Most of the big businesses are on the other side of the opera house or the east side of Main Street. Sheriff Fulmer's house in on Second Street and my place is on Third."

Rock was still scanning the street traffic and buildings when they entered Idaho City and soon passed the courthouse.

After pulling up in front of the jail, they dismounted and as they tied off Duke and Barney, Joe said, "Let's surprise my boss."

Rock replied, "I hope he'll be my boss pretty soon, too."

Joe grinned as he opened the door and stepped inside.

Tap looked over the top of *The Idaho City Bugle* and asked, "Did the army take Feldman, Joe?"

Rock followed him into the jail and closed the door before Joe replied, "Yes, sir. But only if I agreed to take Corporal Roche off their hands."

Tap glanced at Rock before asking, "What in tarnation are you talkin' about?"

Joe laughed before saying, "I was just kidding, Tap. After they took Matt Feldman away, I met the corporal. He'd just been mustered out of the army because he'd had a disagreement with his pompous commanding officer. He told me about it, and I thought the colonel was wrong to even punish him. As he didn't have a job, I asked him if he'd be willing to come to Idaho City and join us as a new deputy."

Tap set his paper on the desk, stood then stepped close to Rock and shook his hand as he said, "If Joe thinks you'll be a good lawman, that's good enough for me. I'm Tap Fulmer."

Rock wore a giant smile as he shook Tap's hand and said, "My name's Aubrey Roche, but everybody calls me Rock."

"I'm glad to know ya, Rock. Have a seat and we'll chat for a little while before we close up for the night."

———

The 'little while' lasted for almost an hour, but by the time they left the jail, Tap was convinced that Rock would be a valuable addition to the office.

Tap waved before he turned onto Second Street, and Joe and Rock waved back before they continued riding along Main Street. When they turned right, Joe was still telling Rock how happy Faith would when she met him.

When Joe pointed to his home, Rock said, "That's a mighty impressive house, Joe."

"So, now you know that you won't be a nuisance."

"I'll still be a fly in the ointment 'til I get my own place."

SPRING SURPRISES

Joe snickered as they walked their horses down the graveled drive and pulled up before the small barn.

After stabling Duke, Barney and Bernie, they left the barn and headed to the house. Joe had his saddlebags over his shoulder and Rock wore his heavy duffle on his back when they stepped onto the porch and Joe opened the kitchen door.

Faith had finished cooking supper and was sitting at the kitchen table waiting for Joe when she heard him return. She waddled to the kitchen window and watched as Joe and a stranger dismounted before entering the barn. The other man was riding Barney, so she thought the army might have declined to accept the church thief. Why Joe was bringing him to their home instead of the jail was a surprise. But she trusted Joe's judgement, and knew he had a good reason.

Joe was smiling as he closed the door, set down his saddlebags and said, "Faith, I'd like you to meet Mister Aubrey Roche, who prefers to be called Rock."

Rock had set down his duffle and was taking off his hat when he smiled and said, "Pleased to meet you, ma'am."

After hearing Joe's introduction, Faith was relieved and smiled warmly as she replied, "It's a pleasure to meet you as well, Rock."

Joe hung his hat and was unbuttoning his coat as he said, "In case you haven't noticed, until recently Rock was a corporal in the Union army. I was able to convince him to take the less reputable position as a Boise County Deputy Sheriff. With your permission, he'll be staying with us for a little while until he finds someplace to hang his hat."

Faith looked at Rock and said, "Of course, you can stay with us. We certainly have the room."

Joe said, "Let me help you set the table, and we'll explain everything while we eat."

Faith nodded then smiled at Rock and said, "I'm sure you won't be another Eddie Pascal, Rock."

Rock snickered then said, "No, ma'am. Joe told me about him, and I don't even own a stovepipe hat."

―――

Two hours later, Rock entered his assigned bedroom on the second floor and closed the door. He knew he'd been extremely fortunate to have met Joe and was determined to be a good lawman. He still found it difficult to believe that Joe had just turned seventeen. Faith looked closer to her real age, but she behaved and spoke as if she was much older. Despite Joe telling him how pretty Faith was, Rock was still impressed when he met her, even in her late stage of pregnancy.

After just a few minutes with them, Rock knew that they were a perfect match. Joe said there were more women in Idaho City than in most Western towns and hoped he would find his own Faith was among them.

SPRING SURPRISES

Joe finished adding wood to the heat stoves and the fireplaces before entering their bedroom. Faith was already beneath the layers of blankets and their heavy quilt as he began to disrobe.

She softly said, "I like Rock and think he's going to be a good deputy, too. I imagine Tap was dancing around the jail when you told him that Rock was going to be a deputy."

Joe pulled off his left sock and replied, "He may not have waltzed around the office, but it was close. Rock wasn't even given his mustering out pay, so is it alright if I give him some money to help him get by?"

"You didn't have to ask me, Joe."

"Of course, I did. A lot of husbands treat their wives like servants, but I'm not one of them. You're an equal partner in our marriage, and I value your opinion."

Faith smiled as she asked, "Even when it comes to your job, Deputy Beck?"

Joe stood and slipped off his britches before replying, "I value your opinions, Mrs. Beck. That doesn't mean I always have to accept them."

Faith laughed before Joe slipped beneath the covers, and as he pulled her close, she asked, "How is Joseph doing?"

"Doc Wallace said there were no early indications of infection. And it was a good sign that Joseph's biggest complaint was that he's always hungry."

Faith smiled as she said, "I can empathize with him. Kathleen Maureen is always demanding more food."

Joe's right hand was resting on Faith's bulging bump when he felt a sharp kick.

He grinned and said, "She apparently disagrees and insists that you're the one who demands the extra food. At least after she's born, she'll have all the nourishment she needs."

"I know that you're pleased with my burgeoning bosoms, but I didn't expect them to get this large so quickly. Do you think it's normal?"

"I think it's perfectly normal. It's just different for each woman for a number of reasons. Did you ask Doctor Taylor?"

"No. And I didn't ask Mary, either. I guess it doesn't matter."

"What matters to me is that shortly after spring arrives, my perfect wife will feeding our perfect daughter."

Faith kissed him then said, "I could be feeding our perfect son, Papa Joe."

Joe wrapped her in his arms before saying, "Maybe. Now close your blue eyes and get some sleep."

SPRING SURPRISES

Faith sighed, closed her eyes and hoped that Kathleen Maureen or Sam Grant decided to rest for the night.

CHAPTER 4

Early the next morning, Joe and Rock rode to the jail rather than walk. Joe figured that after Rock was sworn in, either he or Tap would give him a tour of the town on horseback. It would be a lawman's inspection which would include descriptions of each of the shops and businesses as well as their owners. Rock also needed to know which saloons were the biggest source of trouble.

Joe was usually the first to arrive each day, so he wasn't surprised to find the office empty when he and Rock entered the jail. After they removed their outerwear, Joe sat behind the desk and Rock made use of one of the straight-backed chairs.

Rock slid the Colt Navy from his holster and said, "When you gave it to me, I was kinda surprised when you said it belonged to Faith."

Joe grinned as he said, "Tap's Henry used to be hers before I gave it to him. She was a pretty good shot with both of them, too."

"I wouldn't mind having a Henry, but they're hard to find."

"You can't have mine, but I'd be willing to part with my Spencer."

"I'd sure appreciate it, Joe. We were issued Spencers last October, but they weren't gonna let me keep mine."

"You should be grateful the colonel didn't make you take off your army britches."

Rock snickered before saying, "That's just 'cause he didn't think about it."

Joe pulled the book of Idaho Territorial Laws and began explaining some of the stranger ones to Rock as they waited for Sheriff Fulmer. Some of them were so bizarre, Rock thought Joe was pulling his leg. Rock asked if the blanket prohibition of spitting in public on Sundays applied to wet sneezes.

Thirty-five minutes later, Joe returned the book to the shelf and said, "The boss must have had a busy saloon stroll last night to be this late."

"You woulda heard if he'd been shot, wouldn't ya?"

"If he'd been hurt, someone would have been pounding on my door within minutes."

"Is it always this quiet in the morning?"

"It's not unusual on Saturday or Sunday mornings because the rowdy crowd is either sleeping or suffering. Things will pick up before noon, though."

Rock nodded before he turned his eyes to the front door.

Joe wasn't looking at the door. He was studying Rock and debating with himself. Even after receiving Faith's blessing, Joe was still uncomfortable about offering Rock some money to get by. But it wasn't about the money, he was just concerned Rock might be offended.

He was still undecided when Sheriff Fulmer opened the door and stepped inside.

Tap closed the door and as he removed his hat, he grinned and said, "Sorry I'm late, boys. I was busy with the county bosses."

As the sheriff removed his coat, Joe asked, "You're authorized to hire as many as four more deputies, so what did they want?"

"It wasn't what they wanted. I wanted somethin' from them."

Joe didn't ask what it was but just watched as Tap walked to the desk, opened a drawer and took one of the six untarnished deputy badges.

Without a hint of ceremony, he handed it to Rock and said, "Consider yourself sworn in, Deputy Aubrey Roche."

Rock glanced at Joe, then smiled and pinned on the badge before saying, "That was quick."

Sheriff Fulmer then said, "Now that you're officially a deputy, I need to pay you your salary for the month of March."

SPRING SURPRISES

He reached into his pocket and pulled out a wad of bills and handed it to a stunned Deputy Roche.

Rock stared at the money as he said, "But…it's…I only…"

Joe laughed then said, "Just put it in your pocket and say, 'thank you, boss.' You've already earned it by just puttin' on the badge."

Rock grinned and said, "Thank you, boss."

Tap slapped Rock on his left shoulder before saying, "You're welcome. Now let's ride around the town you'll help to safe. Joe, you can take the desk while I give Rock the tour."

Joe scanned the room for invisible deputies then smiled and said, "Yes, sir," before Tap and Rock walked to the peg wall to retrieve their coats and hats.

After they left, Joe smiled and said, "So much for being worried about offending Rock."

―――

While they were gone, Joe shifted from lawmaker to housekeeper. His first job was to empty the heat stove. After scooping the black dust into the ash bucket, he carried it out the back door and scattered it into the wind. Joe returned the bucket to the closet, took out the broom, headed back to the front of the jail and began sweeping.

He worked his past the four cells, swept out Tap's private office and finished in the small back room. He opened the back door then reunited the large pile of dirt with the rest of Idaho Territory. After the floor was reasonably clean, Joe dusted the furniture and made the small bed in the back room and the cots in each of the cells.

Satisfied that the jail was as clean as it would ever be, Joe decided to service the two shotguns. It took him nearly an hour to meticulously clean and oil the scatterguns, but when he returned them to the rack they looked as if they were straight out of the factory.

Joe returned to the desk and wondered where his fellow lawmen were. They'd been gone more than two hours, and even though Idaho City was growing quickly, he thought they'd be back by now. He figured that Tap must have stopped to introduce Rock to his family and check on Joseph. Whatever the reason for the extended tour, Joe was getting so bored that he began to wish someone would commit a crime. Something like the O'Connor brothers' sweet cake heist.

Joe opened the large bottom right-hand drawer and pulled out the incident logbook. The thick ledger's first entry was September 3, 1863, yet there were only eight blank pages remaining before they started a new one. As he began reviewing the events, he smiled when he identified Eddie Pascal's handwriting. He may have been a poor excuse for a lawman, but his penmanship was perfect.

SPRING SURPRISES

As he flipped the pages, Joe recalled most of the serious situations. He was actually surprised when he realized that most of the entries were his, even before Eddie Pascal quit.

Joe thought it was close to noon when he returned the logbook to the drawer, so he looked through the window to check the shadows. He was thinking about heading home for lunch when he saw Tap and Rock pull up and dismount.

As they entered, Joe was about to ask if they rode to Centreville to find Eddie Pascal when Tap said, "Sorry we took so long, Joe. Anything happen while we were gone?"

"No, sir. I was getting pretty bored. I cleaned the jail and just about overhauled the shotguns."

Sheriff Fulmer said, "I noticed the place looks a lot better. And now you and Rock will have clean scatterguns on tonight's saloon stroll. One of the reasons we took so long is that I took Rock to meet Mary and my young'uns."

Joe said, "That's what I thought. How's Joseph doing?"

Tap snickered and replied, "He's still whinin' about bein' hungry, but the doc said that's a good sign."

Rock then said, "But the other reason we took so long is that I got a room at Fletcher's Boarding House. When Tap told Henry Fletcher I was a deputy, he was really happy that I'd be staying there and is only going to charge me ten dollars a month."

Joe smiled as he said, "That's a good deal, Rock."

Sheriff Fulmer said, "You can head home for lunch, Joe. Why don't you take Rock with ya so he can move out?"

Joe nodded, said, "Yes, sir," before he stood and stepped away from the desk.

———

Five minutes later, they dismounted then tied off Duke and Barney before stepping onto Joe's back porch and entering the kitchen.

As Rock closed the door, Joe noticed that Faith wasn't alone and realized he'd forgotten to tell Rock about Sarah.

Faith remedied his oversight when she smiled and said, "Rock, I don't believe you've met my friend, Sarah Walker."

Then she turned to Sarah and said, "Sarah, this is our new deputy I told you about, Aubrey Roche, but he prefers to be called Rock."

As Joe removed his hat, Rock smiled and said, "It's a pleasure to meet you, Miss Walker."

Sarah blushed just enough to be noticeable as she smiled back and replied, "I'm happy to meet you as well, Rock. Please call me Sarah."

Rock's smile expanded as he said, "Thank you, Sarah."

SPRING SURPRISES

Sarah said, "Faith told me about how you'd been forced to leave the army, Rock. I think it was horribly unfair and your colonel should have been the one to be sent away."

"I shoulda kept my temper, Sarah. Of course, if I just said I was sorry then Joe…"

Joe interrupted Rock by saying, "Rock, you can take off your hat and coat now and talk to Sarah while we have lunch."

Rock sheepishly replied, "I reckon so," then pulled off his hat and hung it next to Joe's.

Rock was taking off his coat when Joe kissed Faith then said, "After lunch, Rock will be moving to his room at Fletcher's Boarding House."

Faith said, "That was fast. But let's get you both fed before Rock packs his things."

Joe nodded then said, "I'll be right back," then walked to the hallway and turned into his office

Less than a minute later, he returned carrying his Spencer and his remaining supply of the .56 caliber cartridges.

He handed the carbine to Rock and said, "I'll get you a scabbard from the barn before we leave."

Rock examined the weapon and said, "This is in better shape than any of the ones we had at Fort Boise, Joe. It looks like it ain't even been fired."

"It hasn't been fired as much as the ones you used at the fort, but the rounds that traveled down that barrel were aimed at Union cavalrymen."

Faith forced a postponement of what she suspected would be a long conversation by saying, "You can tell Rock about the gunrunners when you return to the jail, Deputy Beck."

Joe grinned, said, "Yes, ma'am," then carried the boxes of cartridges to the far wall and set them on the floor beneath Rock's coat.

Rock leaned the Spencer against the wall before he and Joe helped Faith and Sarah set the table.

After they took their seats, Joe glanced at Faith. When she nodded, he bowed his head and said grace.

As they began eating, Sarah said, "When Faith told me that you were a corporal, I thought you'd be much older, Rock. But you don't look much older than Joe."

Rock smiled as he replied, "I'm six years older than Joe, Sarah. I was kinda surprised when he told me he was just seventeen."

Sarah said, "So was I when I first met him. But if you hadn't told me your age, I would have guessed you to be no older than twenty."

Rock was becoming pleasantly uncomfortable as he replied, "Thank you for the compliment, Sarah."

Sarah smiled as she said, "I have the same problem as Joe does. Most people think I'm older than I really am. Do you want to guess my age?"

Rock glanced at Joe for help but didn't get a hint from his poker-faced fellow deputy.

When Rock didn't answer, Sarah grinned and said, "I'll be seventeen in May."

Rock wasn't sure how he should respond, so he just smiled and said, "I was eighteen when I enlisted."

Sarah softly said, "You must be a very brave man to be made a corporal so quickly."

Rock flushed and sought refuge in his ham sandwich as Sarah gazed at him with her big brown eyes.

Joe had a mouthful of sandwich as he looked at Faith and found her blue eyes focused on Sarah. He understood why, too. Sarah was uncharacteristically flirting with Rock. When he first met Sarah, her full figure reminded him of Marigold. Now it was as if she had also inherited Marigold's character.

When Joe looked at Rock and noticed his uneasiness, the discomfort he'd always felt when Sarah was nearby vanished. Whatever the reason for Rock's reaction, Joe decided to ease his condition by saying, "I was going to have our barn extended about twelve feet, but now I think I'll make it twenty-four feet."

Faith asked, "Why do you want that much extra space? The foals won't need their own stalls for a year or so."

"It's not for the foals, sweetheart. I think it would be a good idea if we bought a buggy or a buckboard."

As Joe took a bite of his sandwich, Faith said, "That is a good idea. It'll make it easier for me to get around when I have to bring Kathleen Maureen with me."

Sarah giggled before saying, "You could be driving the buggy with Sam Grant instead, Faith."

Faith laid her left hand onto her swollen abdomen as she replied, "I don't want to ruin Joe's perfect prognostication percentage by having a boy, Sarah."

Joe chuckled but didn't comment. He knew his record was far from perfect, but hoped he was right about Kathleen Maureen. He didn't know why he wanted their firstborn to be a girl. Maybe it was because he had older brothers who weren't nearly as nice as his little sister. Whatever the reason, he wasn't going to be disappointed if Sam Grant arrived in April, as long as Faith was happily caring for him in May.

———

SPRING SURPRISES

Ten minutes later, Rock left the kitchen and went upstairs to pack his duffle while Joe helped Faith and Sarah clear the table.

As she set her plate into the sink, Sarah said, "I think you're very lucky to have Rock as a deputy, Joe."

Joe nodded as he replied, "I know, and Tap does too. I wish we had at least two more, though."

Faith said, "So, do I."

Sarah looked at the hallway entrance before saying, "I don't think you'll find another man as good as Rock."

Faith didn't reply but just looked at Joe and raised her eyebrows.

Joe winked, then looked at Sarah and said, "You're probably right."

Faith asked, "If he was coming back, shouldn't Eddie Pascal be here by now?"

"The road should be open by now, so I'm pretty sure we've seen the last of Eddie in Idaho City. I might bump into him the next time I visit Centreville, though."

"Maybe they decided to have a town marshal and gave Eddie the job."

Joe snickered before replying, "Placerville is bigger and they're talking about it, but even if Centreville decided to have a town marshal, I doubt if they'd give it to Eddie. Even if he wasn't wearing his stovepipe hat."

Faith laughed then said, "It still would great if those towns hired marshals."

Joe heard Rock's heavy footsteps descending the stairs as he said, "It might make things worse if they hired the wrong kind of marshal. Rock is already finished packing, so we'll be on our way."

Joe gave Faith a quick kiss before he walked to the far wall and took his coat from its peg. He was slipping it on when Rock entered the kitchen lugging his duffle.

Rock set the heavy canvas bag onto the floor then smiled and said, "It was nice talking to you, Sarah."

Sarah gave him a big smile and replied, "I enjoyed meeting you too, Rock."

Joe was surprised by Rock's swift recovery and noticed Sarah's optimistic reaction. He hoped that Rock was just being polite but already wondered if he should tell Rock about Jimmy Pritchard when they returned to the jail.

As Rock donned his coat, Joe decided to wait until after he had asked Faith for her opinion. He was certain that Sarah's shift in behavior would be the leading topic of their next private conversation.

Joe picked up the boxes of cartridges and Rock grabbed his Spencer before they left the kitchen.

Joe dismounted in front of the jail after leaving Rock at Fletcher's Boarding House to move into his room. He tied off Duke then entered the jail only to be surprised when he found it empty.

He hung his hat and shouted, "Tap, are you in your office?"

When the jail remained silent, Joe walked to the desk expecting to find a note but found nothing to let him know where Tap was. He was growing concerned and was about to leave the jail when he heard the back door open. He turned just as Sheriff Fulmer entered and closed the door.

When Tap spotted Joe, he grinned and said, "I had to make a quick run to the privy."

"Do you have stomach troubles?"

"I musta ate too much last night, but I'll be okay."

Joe nodded then as he pulled off his coat, he asked, "You're still going home for lunch, aren't you?"

"I'll head home, but I ain't sure I'm gonna eat anything."

"Why don't you just stay at home, boss? You have two deputies now. Rock will be back after he moves his things into his room at the boarding house."

"It's been a long time since I had two real deputies, so I reckon you can get along without me for the rest of the afternoon."

"We'll manage, Tap."

As Joe stepped to the desk, the sheriff popped him on his right shoulder before he walked to the peg wall and took down his coat. Joe noticed that Tap was moving more slowly than usual and hoped it was a temporary condition.

Joe's memories of losing his entire family because of tainted meat were still vivid. Ever since that tragic experience, Joe had been very particular about the food that he and Faith consumed. He knew that few people were as careful as he was but hoped that Tap was one of them.

Sheriff Fulmer had been gone for just five minutes when Big Bob Glass entered the office. While Joe was at least two inches taller than the blacksmith, Big Bob probably outweighed Joe by forty pounds and none of it was fat, either. His arms alone made up around ten pounds of the difference.

Joe asked, "What can I do for you, Bob?"

"It ain't much, Joe. But somebody's sneakin' in at night and stealin' old horseshoes. I didn't notice it until the barrel was only half full. I had one of my boys watch the shop every night for a week or so and I didn't lose any. So, I figgered they had enough of 'em, so I didn't have anybody watchin' last night. But this mornin', another batch was missin'."

"Did you try moving all the old shoes into a crate with a lid?"

"I did that the first time I found some missin', but the thief found 'em right off."

Joe said, "I can't imagine why anyone would steal used horseshoes unless Mister Brown was running low."

"That's what I figgered, but when I asked Charlie about it, he told me he was missin' some, too. Maybe a new blacksmith opened up a shop in Centreville and is ridin' in at night."

"That's a long ride to steal old horseshoes, Bob. How often does it happen?"

"Between me and Charlie, I reckon it's once or twice a week."

Joe nodded as he said, "I'll tell the sheriff about it, and we'll check on both smithies when we do our nightly walk past the saloons."

"I know it ain't important like a bank robbery, but it really sticks in my craw."

"It's still a crime, and all crimes are important to me, Bob. I just need to figure out his motive, then I'm sure we'll find your horseshoe thief."

Big Bob grinned and said, "Thanks for listenin', Joe. I've gotta get back to work and I hope you catch him soon," then the muscular blacksmith turned and left the jail.

The door hadn't even closed before Joe began trying to figure out why someone other than a blacksmith would steal worn-out horseshoes. As Bob said, it wasn't a serious crime, but its oddity intrigued Joe. And it was a puzzle he was determined to solve.

Iron needed to be heated to extremely high temperatures before it could be reworked, so Joe quickly discarded the idea that the horseshoes would be melted down. If they couldn't be reused as horseshoes or transformed into something else, their only value was their weight. But even that didn't make much sense. The total weight of the stolen horseshoes was probably less than two hundred pounds. A large chunk of granite could weigh that much.

After eliminating any motive for anyone else to steal used horseshoes, Joe returned to his first suspect, the town's other blacksmith, Charlie Brown.

Big Bob was Idaho City's first blacksmith, and his shop was much larger than Charlie's. Bob had another blacksmith working for him and four apprentices, including his two sons.

Charlie only had one apprentice, his thirteen-year-old son, Linus. Five of the six liveries in Idaho City used Big Bob's shop, so he had the used horseshoe market cornered.

Because Charlie has a much smaller operation, he should have been the first to notice the missing horseshoes. Then he would have visited Big Bob and reported the crime.

The timing was another indicator that Mister Brown was Big Bob's horseshoe thief. The scrap shoe stealer knew where Bob kept them even after they were hidden. He knew about the night watch, too.

Once Joe had his suspect, he needed to find proof and a reasonable solution. Joe didn't want to search Mister Brown's smithy and brand him as a possible thief if he was innocent. It might ruin his business, and competition was always good for customers. It was just a few seconds later when he realized the most obvious method to quietly end the horseshoe thievery.

Joe was adding a few touches to his plan when Rock returned and asked, "Anything happen while we were gone?"

"Tap's stomach his giving him trouble, so he won't be back this afternoon. Then Big Bob Glass just stopped by to report a theft."

Rock was hanging his coat as he asked, "What was stolen?"

"He's being robbed of used horseshoes."

Rock stepped to the desk, took a seat and asked, "Why would anybody steal used horseshoes? I figure the only one who'd want 'em would be a blacksmith."

"That's true. We only have two. Big Bob Glass and Charlie Brown. Big Bob visited Charlie, and Charlie told him he was missing some as well."

"Big Bob owns that really big shop that Tap showed me yesterday, doesn't he?"

"Yup. Charlie Brown's smithy is a lot smaller and even though Charlie told Big Bob that someone was stealing his used horseshoes as well, I still think he's the thief."

"I figure there's gotta be more'n a thousand horses and mules in town, so why would he need 'em that bad?"

"I'm not sure of the reason, but I think I can put an end to the night thefts as quietly as possible."

"How are you gonna do it?"

"I told Bob we'd swing by after our nightly whiskey walks and see if anybody's prowling around their smithies. So, I'll head down to Charlie's shop to let him know that we'll be watching his place, too."

Rock snickered then said, "I reckon that'll put an end to it."

"I'll be able to see his reaction and maybe do a casual search while I'm there, too."

"Do you want me to come along?"

Joe thought about it for a few seconds before replying, "Sure. I can introduce you to Charlie before I tell him about Big Bob's visit."

"When do you wanna head over there?"

Joe stood then said, "Let's pay Charlie a visit right now. It's a Saturday and a payday for a lot of men, so things will start getting hectic pretty soon."

Rock grinned as he said, "This oughta be interesting."

It was mid-afternoon as they rode down Main Street, yet there was already more noise coming from the saloons than on most weekday nights. Joe knew they'd be lucky with only four saloon visits on tonight's stroll and hoped Rock's first whiskey walk wasn't too violent.

They turned onto B Street and soon pulled up before Brown and Son, Blacksmiths. They dismounted, tied off Duke and Barney then left the cool Idaho air and entered the oven-like shop.

Charlie was watching his son Linus hammer a glowing iron rod, and neither of them looked at Joe and Rock until Linus stuck the red-hot piece of metal into a barrel of water. After the cold water burst into a bubbling, steaming cauldron Charlie nodded then turned and approached Joe and Rock.

Joe could sense Charlie's nervousness before he stopped and asked, "What can I do for ya, Joe?"

"First, I wanted you to meet our new deputy. His name is Aubrey Roche, but he prefers to be called Rock."

Charlie shook Rock's hand and said, "It's about time Tap hired more deputies."

Rock said, "Hopefully, we'll add a couple pretty soon."

Joe then said, "The other reason we stopped by is that Bob Glass just reported that somebody has been stealing used horseshoes. And he said that you had the same problem. How many did you have stolen?

"Not a lot."

"Do you have any idea who would bother taking worn horseshoes?"

Charlie shook his head and simply replied, "Nope."

"I couldn't figure out why anyone would steal them either. But I told Bob that we'd check on both of your shops after we do our nightly visits to the saloons. We'll do random checks when we get called out late at night, too."

SPRING SURPRISES

Charlie glanced at Rock before he said, "You don't hafta waste your time, Joe. They're just worn-out horseshoes. I can't figger out why Bob reported it in the first place."

"He did seem a bit embarrassed when he reported the theft. I was a surprised that you didn't tell us about it before Mister Glass did."

Charlie was growing more nervous as he said, "It ain't...I'm okay."

"It's still a crime, Mister Brown. If we let the small ones go, the criminals will think we don't care and commit bigger crimes. What if the horseshoe thief shows up tonight and takes your anvil?"

"I couldn't afford to lose my anvil or any of my tools, not now. I'm almost finished makin' six sets of barred windows for the Landsman Bank."

Joe smiled and said, "I hope the rich Mister Brown pays you well for the job. You do excellent work."

"Thanks, Joe."

"We'll be heading back to the jail, Mister Brown. If you find anything else missing, let us know."

Charlie just nodded before Joe and Rock turned and left the smithy.

As they rode back to the jail, Rock asked, "Do you still think he was stealing the other blacksmith's horseshoes?"

"I'm pretty sure. Charlie was nervous as soon as he spotted us and only got worse after I told him that Big Bob had reported the theft. But I think I know why he did it, too. He was probably low on scrap iron when he was asked to make all those cages for the bank's tellers. He must have figured that Big Bob wouldn't miss the horseshoes if he didn't take them all at once."

"How could he figure out when to take 'em and where they were after he moved 'em?"

"My best guess is that his son is a pal of one of Big Bob's boys. Bob's kid probably thought it was funny and told Linus about it. But it doesn't matter. I think we've seen our first and last of case of horseshoe rustling."

Rock snickered then asked, "Are we still gonna swing by their shops after we visit the saloons?"

"We'll visit them tonight then it'll be up to Tap if we keep it up."

"I hope he's feeling better."

As they pulled up before the jail, Joe said, "So, do I. If he's not, then Mary is going to need help. She already has her hands full nursing Joseph while doing her other chores."

SPRING SURPRISES

Shortly after Joe took his seat behind the desk, Rock leaned against the nearby wall then folded his arms and asked, "When will we be starting the saloon stroll?"

"It's usually an hour or two after sunset, but we vary the time to ensure they don't just behave themselves when they expect us to show up. I usually go home, have supper then when I think it's a good time to leave, I come back here to pick up a shotgun. Tonight, I'll meet you here around seven o'clock."

"I was just asking because they serve supper at the boarding house at six o'clock."

"There's no rush, just don't eat too fast and get a belly ache like our boss."

Rock snickered then after a short pause, he quietly said, "Sarah sure is a nice gal. And she's really pretty, too."

Even though it was impossible to imagine, Joe was beginning to believe that Rock hadn't noticed Sarah's interest. But Rock's out of the blue comment destroyed that unlikely notion.

Joe replied, "She is very pretty, and she's Faith's good friend, too."

Rock nodded as he stared at the opposite wall as if he was studying the lone wanted poster.

Neither of them said a word for almost a minute before Rock broke the silence by saying, "I'm really surprised she ain't married yet. Is it 'cause her folks don't want her to leave?"

"No, it's not her parents. She's been visiting Jimmy Pritchard, the butcher's son, for around two years."

Rock looked at Joe and snapped, *"Two years? Why hasn't he already married her?"*

Joe sighed then answered, "I'm sure he wants to, but he hasn't been able to summon the nerve to propose. Jimmy is a good man, but he's shy and stutters. That's why I was surprised when he showed up a few days ago and asked if he could be a deputy. I think he only asked because he thought that if he became a lawman, it would give him confidence. He wanted to prove to himself that he was good enough for Sarah.

"Tap talked him out of it because he knew Jimmy wouldn't last a week. When I saw his disappointment, I felt bad for him and thought if I befriended him, he'd think better of himself. He perked up after I asked him to stop by the house sometimes, but I haven't seen him since that one meeting."

Rock left the wall and sat down before saying, "I'm glad you told me about Jimmy Pritchard, Joe. I feel like a fool for thinking that Sarah wasn't spoken for."

SPRING SURPRISES

"You're not a fool, Rock. Any man with eyes to see Sarah and ears to hear that she wasn't married would ask that same question."

"I reckon so. Sarah must be really smitten to wait so long."

"I couldn't tell you how she feels about Jimmy. The only woman I can understand is Faith. But I wonder if there might be another reason for Sarah's patience. Her father owns the biggest dry goods store in Idaho City and Jimmy's father is a butcher who also owns a greengrocery. Maybe their fathers are encouraging the match."

"I reckon that might be so, but Sarah seems too independent-minded to be told who she's gotta marry."

Joe replied, "Well…" then stopped when the door opened, and two incredibly filthy men entered the jail.

Both lawmen stood as Joe loudly said, "Stay right there and tell me what you want."

The two unkempt men didn't even take off their grubby hats as the shorter one said, "We was workin' our claim when a couple of claim jumpers showed up and started shootin' at us. We didn't have our pistols, so we just skedaddled."

"What are your names?"

"I'm Pappy Hillary, and he's Lou Toomey."

Joe was examining the two men as he asked, "What kind of guns did they use?"

Pappy glanced at his partner before saying, "One had a Spencer, and the other feller was usin' a pistol."

Joe then asked, "Where is your claim?"

"Northeast of here about six miles or so. But we ain't goin' back 'til you get rid of them bastards."

Joe nodded as he said, "We'll get our guns then head out there in a few minutes."

Pappy nudged his filthy friend before they turned and left the jail.

After the door closed, Rock walked to the peg wall and grabbed his coat before asking, "How are we gonna handle this, Joe?"

Joe was looking out the window as he said, "I think their story was even dirtier than they were, Rock. Prospectors are always worried about claim jumpers, so I find it hard to believe that those two could be caught by surprise in the middle of the day. Prospectors usually keep a gun handy, too. But the biggest reason I have for doubting their story is because of their boots."

Rock looked at Joe as he asked, "Their boots?"

SPRING SURPRISES

"Prospecting is hard on boots. And even though they looked as if they hadn't washed or changed clothes since '63, their boots were in pretty good shape. And they were riding boots, not heavy work boots. Their clothes weren't torn or patched, either. They were just covered in mud.

"So, I don't believe they're prospectors at all. I think they want us to leave town for some reason, so let's oblige them. We'll ride north until we round the curve then cut into the trees. Then we'll return to find out why they wanted to get rid of us."

As Joe pulled on his coat, Rock said, "They coulda been telling the truth, Joe."

"Maybe they were. But we won't be wasting too much time if I'm wrong. If there are claim jumpers, they won't be going anywhere for a while."

As they tugged on their hats, Rock asked, "So, if they aren't prospectors, then what do you think they're up to?"

"I imagine they're planning to rob one of the banks before they close for the day. The other question I have is if they have more partners."

As they headed to the door, Rock said, "I hope you're wrong."

———

As they rode down Main Street, Joe wasn't surprised that he couldn't find the two prospectors. When he'd looked through the window after they left the jail, the two men just walked away. They'd raced into town just minutes earlier, so there should have been two exhausted animals tied at the hitchrail. But there was just empty space beside Duke and Barney, which was even more evidence that they were using a ruse to empty the town of lawmen.

When they passed by each of the town's three banks, Joe noted the horses waiting in front or tied to hitchrails of nearby the buildings and marked the ones he'd never seen before. There were two tied in front of The Idaho City Bank that particularly attracted his attention. They were both fairly young geldings, and one was lashed to a heavily loaded pack mule.

They were approaching the northern edge of Idaho City when Rock said, "I didn't see 'em anywhere, Joe."

"I didn't think we would. I watched them walk away and noticed they didn't have their horses tied out front as they should have. I imagine they turned into to the alley north of the jail then waited in the shadows to watch us ride past."

Rock shook his head and said, "I shoulda noticed that."

"You've only been a lawman for a day, Rock. You'll probably pick it up faster than I did."

Rock snickered then asked, "Did I miss anything else?"

"Nothing you'd be able to notice because you haven't been in town very long. But when we passed The Idaho City Bank, I spotted two horses that I hadn't seen before, and one was trailing a pack mule. I'm pretty sure they were our phony prospectors' animals."

Rock resisted the temptation to look behind them as they approached the bend in the road. Instead, he looked at Joe and suspected that it hadn't taken him very long at all to learn how to be a good lawman.

They entered the curve then less than a minute later, turned east into the tall pines. After making another right turn, they began ducking branches as they wound their way back to Idaho City.

———

After Pappy and Lou saw Joe and Rock ride past, they turned and headed deeper into the alley before turning onto the side street.

As they walked behind the businesses, Pappy said, "By the time we walk into that bank, they'll be too far away to hear any gunfire."

Lou replied, "This is workin' out even better'n we figgered, Pappy."

"Yup. That sheriff and deputy will likely spend an hour out there lookin' for our claim. By the time they get back, they won't know where to look for us."

Lou snickered as he slid his fingertips over his Remington's grip. When they arrived in Boise City two days ago, they were amazed when they learned there were only two lawmen in Idaho City protecting all that money and gold. Pappy came up with the plan on the ride from Boise City, and now there was no one to stop them from taking all the cash and gold they could carry before they rode out of town.

———

As Lou and Pappy anxiously waited, Joe and Rock left the trees and pulled up less than a thousand yards from the town.

Rock asked, "How do you wanna handle this, Joe?"

Joe was staring down Main Street as he replied, "The bank will be closing in the next few minutes and their horses are still out front, so let's go meet them before they try to make a withdrawal."

Rock nodded before he and Joe began walking their horses into town. Joe unbuttoned his coat to give him faster access to his Colt if necessary.

After Rock did the same, he asked, "Do you think they'll try to shoot it out?"

"The taller guy, Lou might think about it, but it's more likely that they won't take the risk. They could have just walked into the jail and gunned us down. But they came up with that whole dirty prospector scheme just to get us out of the way."

"So, we're just gonna talk to 'em?"

"I hope so. It's better than getting into a shootout on Main Street with a lot of townsfolk nearby. We'll be out of pistol range when they see us, so don't react if one of them reaches for his pistol. Only pull your Colt if they start to draw when we're close."

"Okay, Joe. But I gotta admit that this job is a lot different than my last one. We usually only talked after the shooting was over."

Joe grinned as they entered town but focused on the two alleys across the street from The Idaho City Bank. He still studied the street traffic and the pedestrians on the boardwalks in case bullets started flying.

Joe had to consider the condition of the street, too. It was almost dry, but there were lines of deep ruts which acted almost as train tracks for passing wheeled traffic. The deep, foot-wide gouges made it hazardous for crossing pedestrians, and also for riders' horses. So, Joe and Rock would have to use a slow and careful approach.

They were around fifty yards from the bank when the two mud-coated men stepped into the late afternoon sun. What alarmed Joe was that they now wore their gunbelts outside their jackets but didn't have time to tell Rock.

The pseudo-prospectors carefully stepped across the road as they focused on the street to avoid the ruts and piles of horse dung.

Joe wasn't about to let them reach the bank, so he shouted, "Hey! I need to ask you something!"

Pappy and Lou quickly turned and were startled when they saw Joe and Rock just a hundred feet away. Pappy immediately recovered and started to bring his right hand up to wave, but Lou had a very different reaction. Because the lawmen had their pistols under their coats, Lou was confident he'd could kill them both. So, his right hand dropped to his Remington and as his fingers wrapped around the grip, his right thumb flipped off the hammer loop.

Joe had been in his enhanced state before they left the pines, so when he finished shouting, he'd been able to see the fierce look in Lou's eyes. So, before Lou even began to reach for his pistol, Joe threw open his coat and drew his Colt from its holster.

Lou couldn't believe the deputy was able to draw his pistol so quickly and the shock made him rush his shot. He yanked his trigger and the Remington recoiled after releasing its .44 caliber slug. The ball of lead passed over Joe's head by three feet before it arced into the sky just before Joe pulled his trigger.

Joe's .45 caliber round followed a downward path before it ripped into the center of Lou's gut just below his diaphragm. The bullet just nicked the abdominal aorta as it passed before it left Lou's body and buried itself into Main Street.

As blood flooded his abdominal cavity, Lou dropped his Remington then looked down at his filthy coat and grabbed his stomach with both hands.

Rock was throwing back his coat to reach for his pistol when Lou Toomey collapsed, and Joe cocked his hammer and shifted his sights to Pappy.

Pappy had been stunned when Lou chose to shoot the lawmen. But he knew if he let his fingers go anywhere near his Colt, the deputy would kill him. So, he threw up his hands then took one more step to face the deputy. When he did, Pappy's left boot heel caught the edge of one of the deep ruts. He was still staring at Joe's muzzle as he started to fall, so by the time he saw the large pile of fresh horse dung, it was too late. He did manage to turn his face away, but still planted his left ear into the warm manure.

From the time Lou decided to reach for his pistol until Pappy fell had taken less than four seconds.

Rock was cocking his pistol when Joe shouted, "Hold your fire, Rock! But if he even twitches, shoot him!"

"Okay, Joe. After you start walking, I'll follow and bring Duke with me."

Rock held his sights on Pappy as he watched Joe holster his smoking Colt. Even after hearing some of Joe's amazing exploits, he was still awed by what he'd just witnessed. He couldn't believe that anyone could make a killing pistol shot at this range, much less to do it so quickly.

Crowds were beginning to gather as Joe dismounted and walked to Lou's body. He snatched his Remington from the ground, dropped it into his coat pocket then stepped to where Pappy lay motionless with his left ear still buried in manure.

Joe stopped near his feet and said, "Alright, mister. You can stand up now then wipe that mess off with your shirt sleeve."

Pappy slowly rose from the ground, then as began to remove most of the smelly coating with his right shirtsleeve, Joe asked, "Why did your partner pull his pistol? We were just going to ask you if those claim jumpers had horses."

Pappy was astonished that the deputy still believed the story. Just a few seconds ago, he thought he was about to die. Now, if he played his cards right, he thought he might be able to ride out of town before the lawmen realized they'd been tricked.

He continued to wipe the stinking mess from the side of his head as he said, "All I can figger is that Lou musta mistook you for them claim jumpers."

"Alright. Where are your horses?"

Pappy pointed to the two geldings and the pack mule in front of the bank and said, "They're right over there."

"I'll help you load your partner onto his saddle then I'll lead you to the mortician."

Pappy nodded then said, "I appreciate it, Deputy. I'm real sorry for causin' all this trouble."

Joe nodded then said, "Go get your horses while I talk to my boss."

As Pappy carefully stepped over the ruts to retrieve his horses and pack mule, Joe took Duke's reins and said, "I told him that to keep him from even thinking of trying to shoot his way out."

"Are you gonna let him go?"

"I don't think he's going to admit he was planning to rob the bank. And trying to prove his phony claim jumping story would be a waste of our time. But I'll have a chat with him on the way to the mortuary."

Rock glanced at Pappy before saying, "I can't believe you were able to get your Colt ready so fast and be so accurate at that range."

Joe shrugged then said, "After we get Lou's body hung over his saddle, go tell Tap what happened."

"Okay."

A few minutes later, Joe and Pappy rode down Main Street past lines of onlookers on both boardwalks. They turned onto A Street and pulled up before Moran's Mortuary.

After Lou's corpse had been moved to the mortician's table, Joe had Pappy pay the fee before they left the mortuary.

They had just mounted their horses when Joe said, "Before you and your dead friend even left the jail, I knew you were lying about those claim jumpers. You overdid it with the mud you spread on your clothes, but you should have been wearing work boots."

Pappy was startled and snapped, "*Then why did you ride off?*"

"I couldn't toss you in a cell just because I didn't believe you. If we just stayed put, you'd probably hang around until you could come up with another plan to rob one of the banks. We needed to catch you as you approached the bank."

"You can't prove we were gonna do any such thing!"

Joe's green eyes bore into Pappy's as he said, "You're right. I can't prove it. But I'm still going to escort you out of town. And if I ever see you anywhere in Boise County again, I'll shoot you on sight."

Pappy felt a chill run down his spine and the hair on the back of his neck came to attention before he quietly said, "I ain't ever comin' back here."

"Then let's get moving."

———

Joe escorted Pappy until he reached the shallow canyon he had yet to explore then pulled up and watched him ride away. He continued monitoring him until he rounded a curve then wheeled Duke around and headed back to Idaho City.

———

As he stood in the foyer of Fulmer home, Rock quickly said, "It was almost like he knew what they were thinking and what was gonna happen before it did."

Tap shook his head as he said, "I've seen him do that kinda thing a lotta times and it still spooks me a bit. It's almost like he's not human, but I know that ain't true. I reckon he's the best man I'll ever meet."

Rock nodded then said, "I'm glad you're feeling better, boss."

"And I'll have another day of rest to get everything settled."

"I'll go back to the jail to wait for Joe."

"Okay, Rock. I'll see ya Monday mornin' unless you're a Catholic. Then I'll see you at Mass tomorrow."

Rock smiled as he stood and said, "Sorry, Tap. I'm a Methodist in good standing."

Tap snickered before Rock waved and left the house.

After he'd gone, Mary said, "I know that Joe's a remarkable young man, but he should be more careful with their firstborn about to arrive."

"He promised Faith he'd always be careful, sweetheart. And he always keeps his promises."

The sun was setting when Joe locked the jail door. Most of the remaining office time had been spent telling Rock what he'd said to Pappy. While he hadn't had enough time to write his report, he had made an entry in the incident log book.

As he turned onto #15 Third Street's gravel drive, Joe looked at the small barn and pictured it with the new extension. He'd need to buy the buggy before Kathleen Maureen arrived, too.

After unsaddling Duke and brushing his midnight black coat, Joe left the barn, closed the wide door then headed to the kitchen. He looked through the two back windows but didn't see Faith. He hoped that Sarah wasn't with her because he wanted to talk about the effect she'd had on Rock.

When he entered the warm kitchen, he was relieved to find Faith sitting at the table by herself.

As Joe took off his hat, Faith asked, "Was that gunfire I heard a couple of hours ago?"

Joe hung his hat and was unbuttoning his coat as he replied, "Yes, ma'am. I had to shoot a man on Main Street. I'll tell you about it shortly. How are you feeling?"

"I'm all right. But I was worried for a while after I heard those gunshots. I only relaxed when nobody arrived with a sad face to tell me you'd been hurt."

Joe draped his coat over a hook, then unstrapped his gunbelt and looped the buckle over another hook before he walked to the table. He leaned over, shared a long kiss with his wife then sat down.

"I promised you that I'd always be careful, my love, and that is one promise I will never break. Especially now that we'll soon be welcoming Kathleen Maureen into the world."

Faith smiled as she said, "And then you can be careful when you're changing diapers."

Joe chuckled then stood before saying, "We'll have the diaper-changing debate after she arrives. But I'll tell you about the shooting incident while I put our supper on the table."

"Thank you, Deputy Beck."

As Joe stepped to the cookstove, he said, "Rock and I were talking when these two filthy men entered the jail. I had just cleaned the place, so I told them to stay put and asked…"

Joe talked for almost ten minutes as he filled their plates and glasses then moved them to the kitchen table. When he sat down, he said grace then took a long drink of ice-cold water.

With the lawman part of their conversation over, Faith said, "I was surprised with Sarah's behavior when you and Rock were here at lunchtime. She was obviously flirting which seemed out of character. I assume that you noticed it as well."

"I certainly did. I was going to ask you about it as soon as we could have a private conversation. What did she say after we were gone?"

"She behaved like a giddy schoolgirl. She gushed about how handsome he was and asked me all sorts of personal questions about him. What did Rock say when you returned to the jail?"

Joe swallowed his mouthful of stewed chicken before replying, "We had to leave right away to resolve a case of stolen used horseshoes. But after we returned, Rock seemed to drift off and almost whispered how pretty she was. Then he asked me why she wasn't married, and I told him about Jimmy Pritchard and why he hadn't proposed. I even mentioned that Jimmy asked to be a deputy and that I asked him to visit the house to help build his confidence."

"What did he say after you told him?"

"He said he felt like a fool for not even asking if Sarah had a beau. I'm pretty sure he's smitten, but he won't do anything about it."

"Sarah believes that even after all this time, Jimmy is still afraid of her. I have a feeling that she is already planning to switch beaus."

Joe took a drink of water before saying, "After Rock expressed his disbelief that Sarah wasn't married yet, I realized that it was a good question. She's a handsome young woman with a good figure and has a father who owns a successful business. Even plain girls from poor families are usually married before they reached Sarah's age."

Faith laughed then said, "Or she'd be put on display near a wagon train with a sign hanging from her neck."

Joe smiled as he said, "You were never even close to being plain, Faith Hope Charity Virtue Goodchild Beck. But I was wondering if their fathers had something to do with the match.

Did Sarah ever say anything that sounded as if that was the case?"

Faith thought about it as she chewed and after she swallowed, she replied, "I don't believe she was ordered to accept Jimmy as a suitor. But she did say her parents were very enthusiastic when he asked if he could formally visit her."

"I'll feel really bad for Jimmy if Sarah ends their courtship, and I can't imagine how Mister Pritchard will react if she does. I know it's not our business, but I feel somewhat responsible."

"You aren't accountable for whatever they choose to do, Joe. You're responsible for keeping the people in Boise County safe and you do it better than anyone else."

Joe smiled as he said, "I'm also responsible for making your belly balloon like a watermelon."

Faith laughed then said, "And had a wonderful time doing it, too."

Joe took Faith's hand and quietly said, "I love you, Faith."

Faith whispered, "I love you too, Joe."

After twelve silent seconds, Joe said, "Let's finish supper then I'll clean up before I leave to join Rock on his first saloon stroll."

"Which also happens to be on the last Saturday night of the month."

SPRING SURPRISES

Joe nodded before biting a buttered biscuit in half.

———

A little more than two hours later, Joe and Rock returned to the jail. The saloon stroll had been amazingly uneventful. They'd only had to enter two drinking establishments and hadn't needed to intervene in either of the loud arguments. They would have finished twenty minutes earlier if they hadn't had to swing past the two blacksmith shops.

Rock hadn't said a word about Sarah during the long stroll, but that changed when Joe was returning his shotgun to the gunrack.

Rock asked, "How often does Sarah visit Faith, Joe?"

"She's spending more time at the house now that Faith needs her help."

"Oh. I was just wondering."

Joe just nodded before they walked to the door and left the jail.

———

When Joe stepped into the kitchen, there was enough moonlight coming through the window to make lighting a lamp unnecessary. He added wood to the heat stoves and fireplaces before silently sneaking into their bedroom to avoid waking Faith.

He undressed as quietly as possible before slipping beneath the covers and laying his head on the pillow. It was times like this that he wished he didn't have a job that kept him away from Faith for so long each day. But he was intensely grateful to be able to return to her almost every night. He knew he was much more fortunate than the millions of men who hadn't seen their families for years, and the many thousands who would never return home.

CHAPTER 5

Joe handed Faith her cup of steaming coffee before he sat down beside her.

She smiled as she said, "You are spoiling me, sir."

Joe snatched a strip of bacon from his plate then replied, "Sunday is the only day I have the opportunity to spoil you, ma'am."

"Maybe if Tap hired more deputies, you could spoil me more often. But I suppose I should be satisfied with just one day each week."

Joe devoured the entire strip before he said, "Maybe more good candidates will apply now that Rock's here. But until that happens, I'm just grateful for the twenty-four-hour armistice."

"Do you have any plans for this afternoon?"

Joe sipped his coffee then answered, "When I escorted that wannabe bank robber out of town, I thought about exploring the shallow canyon but didn't have the time. Maybe I'll head down there after lunch."

"Are you going to finally going to try your luck at feather fishing?"

Joe grinned as he replied, "No, ma'am. I don't think the stream is deep enough. I'm just curious to discover what's behind those trees."

"Sarah said she would stop by after lunch. So, while you're exploring, we'll be able to have an interesting chat. I'm sure her first question will be, 'Is Rock going to visit this afternoon?'"

"Just before we left the jail last night, Rock asked me if Sarah visited you often. So, even if I'm not here, don't be surprised if he stops by."

"I won't be surprised, but Sarah will be ecstatic if he does."

"Despite my concerns about Jimmy Pritchard, I'm somewhat glad that Rock's attracted her attention."

Faith's eyebrows arched as she quickly chewed her mouthful of scrambled eggs.

Five seconds later, she gulped and asked, "Why would that please you?"

"I never told you before because Sarah's your friend. But for some reason, she always made me uncomfortable. The good news is that my irrational feeling disappeared when she met Rock."

Faith's blue eyes widened as she asked, "Did she flirt with you as she did with Rock, and you just didn't tell me?"

"No, no. Not at all. That's why I couldn't figure out why I was uncomfortable."

Faith sighed before quietly saying, "Maybe it's because I'm not very…" then after a short pause, she said, "Never mind."

Joe leaned over and kissed her, then said, "I imagine every husband who ever lived has told his wife at least once that he's never even looked at another woman. I won't go that far, but I will tell you that no other woman could ever take your place."

Faith sniffed then smiled and whispered, "I'm getting silly again, aren't I?"

"No, my love. You're getting ready to have our baby."

Faith laughed, then kissed Joe before finishing her breakfast.

―――

After cleaning up, Joe and Faith walked to the parlor and sat on the couch. Joe opened their Bible and read from Paul's Letter to the Corinthians.

They had attended Mass at St. Joseph's with the Fulmers until Faith's condition became noticeable. Father Burns didn't object to her presence, but it was obvious that some members of the congregation weren't pleased with her growing bump. So, each Sunday morning after breakfast, Joe would read some passages from their Bible then they'd discuss their significance. Father Burns would arrive after Mass to administer the sacrament of Holy Communion.

After their private service ended, Joe turned to the last pages of the Good Book and showed it to Faith.

She smiled and said, "After spring arrives, I'll be entering our baby's name."

Joe closed the Bible, set it on the side table and put his arm across Faith's shoulders before he said, "I'm still amazed how quickly you learned to read and write. Your penmanship is much better than mine, too. How current are you on your journals?"

"I only need to add the last two days' of Joe Beck stories. I still have another twenty pages in this book, but maybe you'll buy me a couple of new ledgers before Kathleen Maureen arrives."

"I think we can afford the outrageous cost, Mrs. Beck."

Faith nodded then closed her eyes and rested her head on Joe's shoulder. She'd been overjoyed when she learned she was pregnant but now wished for April to arrive quickly and she wouldn't be so big. Even before he told her, she knew Joe would never touch another woman but was still jealous when Sarah looked at him. So, when Sarah flirted with Rock, she'd felt a much greater sense of relief than Joe had.

But while her spate of jealousy was gone, Faith knew her other secret concerns wouldn't be as easily dismissed. Her old worries about dying during childbirth had resurfaced, and she prayed that she could keep them hidden from Joe.

―――

Sarah had just arrived before Joe kissed Faith and left the house. As he trotted down the back porch steps, he stopped when he noticed a knot in the second stair tread that hadn't been there before. He soon realized that it wasn't a knot at all. It was the back end of a .44 caliber slug of lead. He slid his index finger across the hole before he whistled then headed to the barn. He'd discovered where the shot Lou fired from his Remington had found its home and would tell Tap and Rock about it tomorrow.

―――

Forty minutes later, Joe turned Duke into the small canyon and rode alongside the churning waters of the clear stream. As he rode among the tall pines, he realized he'd underestimated the depth of the stream. It was certainly deep enough for trout and even salmon, but he didn't believe it was nearly long enough.

He wasn't looking for fish of any sort as Duke carried him deeper into the canyon. He guessed he was a little more than eight hundred yards from the road when the trees gave way to a large clearing, and he quickly pulled Duke to a stop. He wasn't planning on doing any hunting, but when he saw the small herd of white-tailed deer, he wasn't about to miss the opportunity to get some fresh meat.

He slid his Sharps from its scabbard and cocked the hammer. He was about two hundred yards out and with the wind coming down from the mountain and blowing in his face, he knew he could get closer. But he felt as if he'd be cheating if he did, so he brought the carbine level and set the sights on a large doe. He was about to fire when he changed his mind. It wasn't because he felt any sympathy for the animal. He just didn't have the time to properly dress the carcass.

Joe released the carbine's hammer then slid the Sharps back into its scabbard before starting Duke across the clearing. The large buck suddenly noticed him, and the herd scattered into the trees that ran alongside the clearing.

After watching their frantic escape, Joe let his eyes follow the stream. As he'd expected, it began at the base of the mountain just beyond the clearing. He dismounted then walked along the stream leaving Duke to graze on whatever greenery he could find.

He smiled as he imagined the prospectors who'd visited the stream searching for gold only to find disappointment. As he wasn't looking for any of the yellow metal, Joe was far from disappointed. The stream might not be suitable for feather fishing, but the canyon was a natural masterpiece.

Before Joe reached the end of the clearing, he saw a small pool that had been created by the water rushing down the side of the mountain. He stopped at the pool's edge and let his eyes climb the mountainside to trace the water as it raced across the rocks. While there wasn't a good-sized waterfall, there were small cascades every few yards that he found mesmerizing. The largest of the miniature falls was the one just above the pool. It was about ten feet wide and four feet high and had its own tiny rainbow.

On a ledge about a couple of hundred feet overhead Joe spotted an enormous nest. He stared at it for almost two minutes before one of its residents leapt into the air and spread its wings. A few seconds later, another golden eagle flew from the nest to join its mate.

Joe smiled as he saluted the avian king and queen and said, "Good hunting, Your Majesties."

The sight of the magnificent birds of prey only added to Joe's desire to own the small valley. As he slowly walked back to Duke, Joe scanned every detail of the canyon.

A few minutes later, as he passed through the trees, Joe began to estimate how much it would cost to buy the canyon. The entire canyon wasn't even a full section, but because it didn't have any gold, it was probably much less expensive than the land north of Idaho City. If it wasn't too much, he'd ask Faith what she thought about buying it. If she'd been able to join him, Joe knew she'd want it, even if it drained their bank account. That was because the canyon was a smaller version the one that he and Faith had visited at the bottom of Cheyenne Pass, only without the mad cougar.

After unsaddling Duke, Joe left the barn and after reaching the porch, he glanced at the .44 caliber knot in the porch step and wondered if Faith would want it repaired.

When he entered the kitchen, he wasn't surprised that Sarah was still visiting Faith but was relieved that Rock wasn't with them.

As he removed his hat, Faith asked, "Did you find any fish in the stream, Deputy Angler?"

Joe laughed as he hung his coat then replied, "No, ma'am. But I did see a herd of white-tail deer in a clearing near the back of the canyon. It's a beautiful but smaller version of the one where we met the rabid mountain lion."

As he sat at the table, Sarah said, "Faith told me how you and Rock stopped two men from robbing the bank yesterday. She said that one of them took a shot at you before you shot him. Did Rock stop the second one from shooting you, Joe?"

Joe obfuscated his reply by saying, "He was ready to shoot him if he so much as twitched."

Sarah beamed before she asked, "Why did you let that man go after his friend tried to shoot you?"

"His partner shot at me, but he didn't even reach for his pistol. Even though they were going to rob the bank, we can't arrest a man for having bad intentions. If that was true, our jail would have to be the size of the opera house."

Faith smiled and asked, "How much snow was left in the canyon?"

"Not as much as I expected. The deep drifts were along both sides and at the base of the mountain. There was a clear area where the stream slid down the mountainside and formed a small pool."

Faith asked, "You didn't take a swim, did you?"

Joe replied, "I was thinking about it but was dissuaded when I saw that monster-sized snapping turtle rise from its depths."

Faith laughed as Sarah exclaimed, "*There was a giant snapping turtle in the pool?*"

Joe grinned as he said, "No, ma'am. I was just reminding Faith of the last time we came face-to-face with one."

Sarah said, "Oh. Well, now that you're back, I'll be going home to help my mother with the Sunday dinner."

As Sarah rose from her seat, Joe stood and walked to the brass hooks and took down her coat. He held it out and after she slid her arms through the sleeves, she buttoned the coat then took her bonnet from its hook and pulled it on.

She was tying the cloth strips when she smiled at Faith and said, "I'll see you tomorrow," then turned and stepped to the door.

Joe watched Sarah until she reached the ground before closing the door and asking, "So, was your chat as interesting as you'd expected?"

As Joe started back to the table, Faith stood and replied, "It was for a few minutes then it became quite boring. Can we sit on the couch while I tell you about it?"

Joe nodded, said, "Yes, ma'am," then took her arm.

When they were comfortably seated on their soft couch, Faith said, "You were still in the barn when she asked me if Rock had talked to you about her. When I said that he had, she was so excited that she almost started bouncing as she begged for details. You can imagine how she reacted when I told her that Rock thought she was nice and very pretty, too."

"I'm sure she was ecstatic when you told her. But I assume she wasn't pleased to hear that I informed Rock about Jimmy Pritchard."

"She was so happy that I didn't have the heart to tell her. For the rest of her visit, it was difficult for me to bring up a topic that didn't involve Rock. I was beginning to wish I'd told her that Rock never even asked about her."

"You can't tell a lie, Mrs. Beck."

Faith smiled and said, "Speaking of lies, I noticed that you fibbed when you told Sarah that Rock stopped the other man from shooting you."

"I didn't fib, ma'am. I simply obfuscated my answer by changing the timing a bit. If you recall my exact wording, I said that Rock was going to shoot him if he so much as twitched. That was exactly what he was going to do after Pappy planted his head in that pile of horse manure."

Faith laughed then leaned her head onto Joe's shoulder before saying, "I stand corrected."

"Speaking of that shootout. The one who did try to shoot me missed wildly. And believe it or not, I discovered where his bullet landed."

Faith quickly turned to look at him then sharply asked, "How on earth did you find it? And how do you know it's the same bullet?"

"Because, my love, until yesterday, there wasn't a .44 caliber slug of lead buried into one of our back porch steps."

Faith exclaimed, "*It hit our house?*"

Joe grinned as he said, "Better our house than your husband, don't you agree?"

Faith rested her head back onto Joe's shoulder before she sighed and said, "Of course, I do. I guess it had to land somewhere."

"Do you want me to pry it out of there and repair the hole?"

"Only if you think it's necessary, but I think you should leave it. It'll be a unique addition to our home."

Joe then said, "When I was watching the water cascade down the mountainside to form the pool, I spotted a large nest high on a ridge. A minute or so later, a pair of golden eagles took to the sky. It was an impressive sight."

Faith smiled and asked, "Did you want to buy some land in the canyon?"

Joe smiled as he replied, "I was going to ask you, but only after I found out how much it would cost. I'll do that sometime this week and then we'll talk about it."

As Faith nodded, Joe slid his arm over her shoulders and pulled her close.

For more than an hour, they talked about a variety of subjects, including the canyon, the Sarah, Rock and Jimmy Pritchard situation, Kathleen Maureen, and even the weather.

SPRING SURPRISES

They knew the reasonably warm respite would soon end and winter might return with a vengeance. The pleasant days of spring would arrive in the mountains just before Kathleen Maureen entered the world.

―――

The winter weather returned while Joe and Faith were sleeping, but it wasn't as vengeful as they'd expected. When Joe left the house Monday morning, there was a dusting of fresh snow on the ground, but the wind wasn't howling, and the air temperature was still a few degrees above zero.

When Joe entered the jail, Rock closed the heat stove door then turned and asked, "How deep do you reckon it's gonna get, Joe?"

Joe hung his hat and began unbuttoning his coat as he replied, "I can't give you an accurate answer because I didn't bring my copy of The Old Farmer's Almanac with me. But I'd guess it's not going to be more than a few inches."

Rock snickered as he sat behind the desk then said, "At least it's not a blizzard. But those streets are gonna be a real mess when it melts."

Joe sat down on one of the straight-backed chairs before he said, "That might not be for a while. It should keep things quieter for us, too. What did you do with your day off, Rock?"

"I went to services then spent the rest of the day exploring the town. I was thinking of riding to Centreville but didn't want to get buried in an avalanche."

Joe grinned as he said, "I did a little exploring myself. I finally got to visit that small canyon about a mile south of town."

"Did you find any gold nuggets while you were looking around?"

"The prospectors discovered there wasn't any gold south of town, and I'm glad they didn't find a speck of it. It's just a beautiful, secluded small valley. And if it's not too expensive, Faith and I are planning to buy it."

"You're thinking of buying it? Are you gonna build a house and live down there?"

"Not a house. I might build a small cabin, but we're not about to move out of our home. Especially with Kathleen Maureen about to arrive."

Rock said, "If you buy it, then I'll be glad to help you build the cabin."

Joe was about to thank Rock for his offer when Sheriff Fulmer entered the jail and stomped the snow off his boots.

After closing the door, Joe asked, "Is your stomach behaving itself, Tap?"

"Yup. And Joey is eatin' everything is sight, too."

Rock said, "That's good to hear."

Tap said, "That was some mighty fine work you boys did on Saturday, Joe. I was kinda surprised you let that other feller go, though."

Joe shrugged and replied, "All we had on him was lying about the claim jumpers, boss. With as many cases as Judge Oliver has on his calendar, I didn't think Mister Blanton would even charge him. But before I sent him on his way back to Boise City, I told him that if I saw him again, I'd shoot him on sight. So, I don't think we'll see him again."

"I reckon you're right about Blanton. And after that feller saw you shoot his pal, you're probably the last man he ever wants to see."

As Tap walked to the heat stove to warm his hands, Joe asked, "Do you know what the most bizarre thing about that shootout was?"

Both of his fellow lawmen looked at Joe before he said, "The bullet that Lou fired at me found a home in one of my back porch steps."

Rock sharply asked, "Is it still there?"

"Yup. I asked Faith if she wanted me to fix it, but she thought it would be an interesting conversation piece."

Tap said, "I've gotta take a look at it the next time I pay a visit."

Rock nodded then said, "Joe's thinking of buying a small canyon south of town."

Tap looked at Joe and asked, "You finally rode down there and looked around?"

"Yes, sir. I know The Landsman Bank handles the sale of mining claims, but do they deal with regular property as well?"

Tap replied, "I reckon so, but I ain't sure that the canyon's been surveyed."

"I guess I'll have to visit the bank to find out."

The conversation moved back to Saturday's bank robbery as the light snow continued to fall. After almost an hour of discussion, Joe was a bit surprised that Rock had yet to mention Sarah, and he wasn't about to broach the subject.

When Joe left jail about ten o'clock, the snow had stopped falling, but the sun was still hidden behind the gray clouds. The wind had picked up a bit making it feel colder than it was when he walked to work.

He soon entered The Landsman's Bank and headed to Les Pratt's desk.

SPRING SURPRISES

Les was writing in a ledger but set his pen down when Joe stopped and asked, "Mister Pratt, do you handle land sales that aren't marked for prospecting?"

"I do. But other than the sections that have been split into small parcels for prospecting, we only sell the land that's already been surveyed. And all of that property is within Idaho City's town limits. Are you thinking of buying the empty lot east of your house?"

"No, sir. I was asking about a small canyon that's about a mile south of town, so I doubt if it's been surveyed."

Les opened his large bottom drawer, said, "Let me take a look at the map to be sure, Joe," then walked his fingers along the row of folders until he pulled one onto his desktop.

As the land agent unfolded the large map, Joe knew the canyon was well beyond the town's boundaries and wondered if he could buy the property if he paid to have it surveyed.

Les spread it out on the desktop then seconds later, he jabbed at the map and said, "Well, Joe. It looks like you're in luck. That canyon was surveyed and sectioned off for prospectors before they figured out there wasn't any gold south of town."

Joe quickly asked, "How much would it cost me?"

Les studied the map for less than a minute before he looked at Joe and replied, "The canyon has an area of five hundred and sixty-four acres, so at forty cents an acre, it will set you back two hundred and twenty-five dollars and sixty cents."

Joe grinned as he asked, "Can we do the paperwork, Mister Platt?'

Les said, "It won't take long, Joe. Are you going to build a new place in the canyon and sell your house?"

"No, sir. I might build a cabin, though."

Les smiled as he opened his top drawer and pulled out a sales contract. As he began copying the survey figures to the contract, Joe wondered if he'd been given a discounted price for the property. He'd expected to pay at least a dollar an acre but thought it was more likely that the land simply had no market value. It had no gold, it wasn't good farmland, and there was a lot of forested land closer to Idaho City. Whatever the reason, Joe wasn't about to complain.

———

Forty minutes later, Joe strode quickly down Third Street without even noticing the cold. After registering the land with the county, he was anxious to tell Faith that they now owned the canyon.

He climbed the steps to the front porch, opened the door and entered the foyer.

SPRING SURPRISES

As he hung his hat on the coat rack, he heard Faith say, "You've returned early, sir. I hope you're not expecting me to have your lunch waiting on the table."

Joe pulled off his coat and replied, "I just couldn't bear being away from you for another minute, my perfect wife."

Faith was laughing as Joe entered the parlor, waved to Sarah before taking a seat and saying, "I just took a large bite out of our bank account, Mrs. Beck."

Faith excitedly asked, "You bought the canyon?"

Joe smiled as he replied, "Yes, ma'am. We were fortunate that it had been surveyed before they discovered there wasn't any gold to be found south of town. It didn't cost as much as I thought it would, either. We only paid two hundred and twenty-five dollars and sixty cents for the whole canyon."

Sarah said, "That's still a lot of money, Joe. Why did you spend so much for land that doesn't have any gold?"

"It's hard to explain why I was drawn to the canyon, but Faith understands."

Faith was all smiles as she said, "I can't wait to see what's behind the trees, Joe."

"I'll give you a tour after I buy a buggy. I think there's enough space alongside the stream to drive to the clearing."

Faith said, "I'll get you something for lunch," then started to rise.

Joe quickly popped to his feet and said, "I'm capable of fixing my own lunch, Mrs. Beck."

He had another incentive to make his own lunch besides his consideration for Faith. He knew if he stayed much longer, Sarah would begin peppering him with Rock's virtues.

He stepped across the parlor, kissed Faith, then smiled to Sarah before heading to the hallway.

He was about to enter the hall when Faith said, "Don't limit your lunch to a couple of sour pickles, Mister Beck."

Joe laughed then replied, "I'm not making any promises, ma'am."

As he walked to the kitchen, Joe briefly considered an all-pickle meal, but after Taps recent digestive difficulties, he quickly decided not to test his stomach's resilience.

―――

When Joe returned to the jail, Rock had to rush off to meet the boarding house's meal schedule. Once Rock left the jail, Joe took his notebook from his shirt pocket. He opened it to the next blank page and began to list the things he'd need to do before Kathleen Maureen arrived.

SPRING SURPRISES

The nursery was almost done but he still needed to buy a cradle, so that was at the top of the list. He wrote down the ledgers before moving on to the bigger items. He added the barn extension, the buggy and another horse. He wasn't about to put Duke in harness and with the mares all heavy with foals, that left only Bernie. He smiled when he pictured Bernie pulling the buggy. He didn't think his donkey friend would appreciate being hitched to a buggy even though pulling the tent-cart across the Plains was much more difficult.

He had the pencil poised over the notebook when his mind formed the mental image of the first time that he'd strapped Bernie into his makeshift harness. *Had it really been less than a year ago?* So much had happened in the past twelve months that he found it hard to believe. The tip of Joe's pencil still hadn't moved when Sheriff Fulmer returned.

Joe quickly closed his notebook and slid it back into his pocket as Tap asked, "Did you buy the canyon, Joe?"

As the sheriff stripped off his outerwear, Joe replied, "Yup. It wasn't too costly, either. It only cost me a little more than two months' pay."

Tap took a seat and asked, "Now that you're a big landowner, what are you gonna do with it?"

Joe grinned as he replied, "I might build a small cabin out near the clearing."

"As long as you don't think about handin' in your badge to start raisin' cattle."

Joe snickered before saying, "That's not going to happen, Tap. When I was a boy, I wasn't even fond of the milk cows we had on our family farm."

"I find it hard to picture you as a boy, Joe."

"I just turned seventeen, so it wasn't that long ago, Tap. Although, to be honest, it seems much longer."

"I can't remember much about growin' up myself, especially the bad times. But I do recall some of the good days. So, I reckon in a few years, your bad memories will fade away, too."

Joe smiled as he said, "I wish that was true, but I think this brain of mine has too much storage space to let that happen. I can still recall almost every important event of my life. I can still see my father's smiling face when he gave me a gift for my fourth birthday. It was a toy pistol that he'd carved himself."

Tap shook his head before saying, "You're really scary sometimes, Joe."

"I know. I'd probably be branded as a warlock and burned at the stake a few centuries ago."

Tap chuckled before saying, "At least now all you gotta worry about is gettin' shot."

"That reminds me, do you mind if I keep Lou's Remington?"

"I figgered you'd want the pistol that sent that bullet into your porch step."

"There is that I suppose, but it's really because I like it better than my Colt."

Joe's comment triggered a long conversation about firearms that was still ongoing when Rock returned from lunch. Less than a minute later, he inserted himself into the discussion.

After almost an hour of gunpowder-related talk, Joe looked at his fellow deputy and said, "When Faith and I were deciding on a boy's name just in case I'm wrong about Kathleen Maureen, one of the things that I thought about was how it sounded. I wanted a name that flowed. That's why we decided to address Kathleen Maureen as Katie. Katie Beck is easier on the tongue than Kate Beck or Kathleen Beck. Sam Beck works the same way and sounds like one word."

Rock looked at Joe and asked, "Where are you going with all this, Joe Beck?"

"Your name is Aubrey Roche, and we all call you Rock. But it doesn't flow, does it? Rock Roche is awkward. Even Aubrey Roche is smoother. But I was thinking that Rocky might work better than just Rock. What do you think?"

Tap snickered then said, "I think Joe's got somethin' there, Rocky. It does sound better when you gotta tell some troublemaker you're Deputy Sheriff Rock Roche."

Rock was about to decline Joe's suggestion when Joe said, "Besides, Rock Roche sounds a lot like cockroach. I'm surprised nobody ever tried to make light of the similarity before. But I reckon it won't be very long before some drunk uses it when you try to break up a fight."

Rock was even more surprised than Joe. He'd been called Rock since he was a boy, yet not a single person had mentioned the phonetic resemblance of Rock Roche to cockroach.

After that startling realization, Rock said, "You're right, Joe. I don't wanna be associated with those crawling bugs, so from now on, I'll be Rocky. Like you said, it flows better, too."

Tap nodded as he said, "Now when you can face down some hoodlum, you can tell him you're Deputy Sheriff Rocky Roche."

The renamed deputy grinned before saying, "Rocky Roche. I like the sound of that."

Joe was pleased that Aubrey Roche genuinely appreciated his suggestion but was even more pleased that Rocky Roche hadn't spoken Sarah's name once all day. He didn't think Rocky had lost interest but believed he was just keeping his feelings to himself after learning about Jimmy Pritchard.

Joe then wondered why Jimmy hadn't visited the house yet. Granted, he worked with his father each weekday and Saturday, but he had his evenings and Sundays free. He must have known that Sarah was with Faith yesterday, which should have been an added incentive for him to pay a visit. Maybe it was time to pick up some fresh meat at the Pritchard's butcher shop.

The late winter sun broke through the clouds just as Joe turned onto Third Street. Even though he knew that it had almost no effect on the temperature, it still felt warmer.

A couple of minutes later, he entered the foyer and hung his hat, coat and finally his gunbelt on the coat rack. When he stepped into the parlor, Joe found that Faith had a woman visitor not named Sarah.

Joe smiled as he said, "Hello, Sister."

Faith said, "Joe, this is Sister Mary Catherine. She's a nurse as well as a teacher and has offered to be my midwife. I'd rather have Sister Mary Catherine with me than Mrs. Taylor. Is that alright?"

"Of course, it is. I'm very pleased to meet you, Sister."

Sister Mary Catherine smiled as she said, "I'm happy to finally meet you as well, Mister Beck. You've been in all our prayers since you returned Father Burns' chalice. It was Father Burns who suggested I offer my services as a midwife."

"I'll thank Father Pat when I see him. And please call me Joe, Sister."

The nun nodded then stood and said, "I must return to the convent before vespers, but I will see you again tomorrow, Faith."

Joe and Faith both rose before Sister Mary Catherine pulled her heavy shawl over her shoulders then walked to the foyer and left the house.

After the door closed, Faith said, "I was surprised when Sister Mary Catherine arrived, but Sarah seemed almost terrified. Sarah left before Sister Mary Catherine even explained why she had come to the house."

Joe kissed Faith before saying, "You can tell me all about it over supper."

Faith smiled as she hooked her arm through his before they entered the hallway.

―――

As they ate, Faith related the early afternoon conversation with Sarah which had abruptly ended with Sister Mary Catherine's unexpected arrival. While the chat hadn't been very interesting, Faith suspected Sarah was preparing to tell Jimmy Pritchard she was no longer interested.

Joe said, "I wonder if Jimmy already knows she's changed her mind. He's probably been worried about it ever since he started visiting her."

"I wouldn't be surprised. So, how was your afternoon, Deputy?"

"It was quieter than normal. But I did convince Rock to start calling himself Rocky."

Faith laughed then asked, "Why did you even think of asking him to do that?"

Joe grinned and began listing the reasons he'd given to Aubrey Roche. He didn't reveal the Rock Roche-cockroach similarity until it could serve as a punch line. When he finally told her, he was rewarded by Faith's jubilant reaction. When she began laughing, he focused on her sparkling blue eyes as tears rolled down her cheeks.

Faith was dabbing her eyes with her napkin as Joe said, "So, now he's Rocky Roche. Are you going to help Sister Mary Catherine come up with a less cumbersome form of address?"

Faith shook her head before replying, "No, sir. Sister is far from cumbersome, and don't even think of calling her Sis."

Joe chuckled before saying, "I'll behave myself, ma'am. After all, Sister will be helping to bring our Katie into the world."

Faith nodded and smiled before she took a bite of the thick beef stew. While she'd been genuinely surprised when Sister Mary Catherine arrived, Faith immediately understood why she'd come, even if the nun didn't know the reason. It was because she'd told Father Burns of her resurgent dread of dying during childbirth. He probably sent Sister Mary Catherine hoping she would help calm Faith's fears.

While Faith wasn't certain the good sister could put an end to her worries, she hoped she'd be able to keep them at bay until she entered labor. Even though Joe had already pushed her irrational fears aside months earlier, she was still determined to keep him from learning of their return. Her perfect husband had enough to worry about, especially with the warmer weather about to arrive.

That night, as Joe held his sleeping wife close and listened to her soft breathing, he wished March would pass quickly for her. He suspected that her old childbirth demons had resurfaced, but he wasn't about to ask her. If he was wrong, he might be the one to open the vault and release those hidden fears. All he could do was to care for her as well as he could, but he was enormously grateful that Father Burns had sent Sister Mary Catherine to be her midwife. Maybe the holy sister could help Faith with her troubled soul as well.

CHAPTER 6

The rest of the week was mostly uneventful for the men of the Boise County Sheriff's Office. There were a few minor scuffles and the usual vagrants and drunks, but there were no serious crimes that required their immediate attention.

Deputy Roche appreciated being addressed as Rocky and was becoming more comfortable in his new job as a lawman.

Sarah had only visited Faith once since her last visit, but Sister Mary Catherine had stopped by each afternoon when classes ended for the day.

Joe had arranged for M.D. James Construction to build the barn's extension, and they'd begin work on Monday. When he'd gone to Walker's to purchase the ledgers, he didn't see Sarah, but that wasn't a surprise as she usually helped her mother.

When he stopped at Pritchard's on Wednesday, he thought he'd finally have a chance to ask Jimmy why he hadn't visited the house. But Jimmy was in the back room butchering a hog, so he just bought some steaks from Orin Pritchard before leaving.

Friday morning, Joe was behind the desk talking to Rocky about last night's whiskey walk when Sheriff Fulmer entered the jail.

Before he even took off his hat, Tap said, "Now that it's warmin' up some, I figger I'll take Rocky out to Centreville and show him around."

Joe said, "I can take him, boss. I'd like to see what's become of Eddie Pascal, too."

"I know the town better'n you and I wanna find out what he's doin' myself."

"Okay, Sheriff. But I'll expect a full report on Eddie's situation when you return this afternoon."

Tap grinned as he said, "Maybe he'll wanna come back now that we have Rocky to keep him safe."

Rocky snickered then stood and walked to the peg wall to grab his coat and hat. So, just twenty minutes after opening he jail, Joe found himself alone. It was about a two-and-a-half-hour ride to Centreville, so Joe figured they'd return by mid-afternoon. He knew they wouldn't be returning with Eddie but was curious why he hadn't reclaimed his badge. He had seemed pretty enthusiastic with the notion but probably had second thoughts.

Thirty minutes later, Joe was already bored, so he decided to make a full circuit of Idaho City. After putting on his hat and coat, he left the jail, locked the door then turned south along the boardwalk. He greeted the folks as they passed by and soon reached the intersection with D Street. When he stepped onto the cross street, he looked east and saw Jackson's Wagons and Carriages. He thought about buying a buggy but decided to wait until after the barn extension was finished sometime late next week.

Joe's long morning stroll took almost an hour, which included a detour past his house. He didn't want to startle Faith with his unexpected return, so he just took off his hat and waved it overhead three times as he walked past, just in case she was looking out the window.

When he cut across the open field, he looked at St. Joseph's school and wondered which of the classrooms belonged to Sister Mary Catherine. She taught the first- and second-year students and would have Joseph Fulmer as one of her pupils in September. Joe turned right and walked behind the school then past the convent and the church before heading back to Main Street.

Twenty minutes later, as he sat behind the front desk, Joe found boredom creeping up on him again but knew he should appreciate the lack of excitement while it lasted. The road from Boise City would soon be filled with hopeful prospectors and other men looking to earn an honest living. But it was those other men seeking to enrich themselves by more sinister means who would make a quiet week like this one a rarity.

But even as he acknowledged the benefit of boredom, Joe felt as if there was something evil lurking nearby. It was as if the quiet morning was just the lull before a violent afternoon. It may only be a feeling, but Joe wasn't about to completely dismiss it, either.

Without any real reason, Joe slid the Remington from his holster and pulled the hammer back to its half-cocked position. As he rotated the recently oiled cylinder, he verified each of the five loaded chambers. After making sure the empty chamber was behind the firing pin, he released the hammer and returned it to his holster.

Joe hadn't done any target practice with the pistol yet and hoped he didn't need to use it before he checked its accuracy. After all, the only bullet he'd seen leave its muzzle was embedded in one of his back porch steps.

———

As Tap and Rocky rode down the main street of Centreville, Rocky asked, "Are we gonna head over to Placerville now?"

Tap rubbed his left shoulder before replying, "Nope. I reckon we oughta head back after we find out where Eddie is hidin'. Joe can show you around Placerville next week before he gets distracted 'cause of Faith."

Rocky snickered before saying, "I can't imagine Joe getting distracted by anything, boss. Not even being a papa for the first time."

"Maybe he won't get as silly as I was when Mary was havin' Joseph, but Faith means everything to him."

"It's kinda hard not to notice how much he cares about her. I wish I had a woman who made me feel that way about her."

Tap looked at Rocky but didn't ask if he was thinking about Sarah Walker.

They were about to turn onto the road back to Idaho City when they were flagged down.

When they pulled to a stop, Wally Earhart looked up and said, "Howdy, Sheriff. Is this your new deputy you hired to replace Joe Beck after he got buried under Eddie's avalanche?"

Tap quickly replied, "Joe ain't dead. Who told you he was dead?"

"Clark Kingsley. He was Eddie's pal and said Eddie was braggin' about it all over town before he run off."

"Eddie's gone? Where did he go?"

"I ain't got a clue, Sheriff. But I reckon he musta skedaddled 'cause he knew Joe Beck wouldn't be happy when he heard Eddie was tellin' everybody he dumped a mountain of snow on him."

"I guess so. If you do see Eddie around, tell him I recommend he leaves Boise County altogether."

Wally grinned then waved before Tap and Rocky rode away.

———

It was just after the noon hour when Joe left the jail to head home for lunch. As he walked along the boardwalk, he scanned the busy street searching for any signs of potential trouble. Nothing seemed even remotely out of the ordinary, which strangely enough, only reinforced his sense of impending violence.

For the second day in a row, when Joe entered his house, he found Faith with non-Sarah visitors. At least this time, he wasn't surprised. One of them left the couch and trotted across the parlor as he was hanging his hat.

He was unbuttoning his coat as he smiled and said, "I'm glad to see you up and about, Joseph."

Joseph looked up and grinned as he asked, "Wanna see my stitches, Uncle Joe?"

Uncle Joe laughed then replied, "Not in front of the ladies, Joseph. We'll compare our wounds when we're alone. Okay?"

Joe hung his jacket as Joseph said, "Okay."

As they entered the parlor, Joe said, "Good afternoon, Mary. And I'm happy to see you too, Grace."

Joseph plopped onto the couch next to his mother as Joe stepped to Faith.

He gave her a reasonably chaste kiss, then said, "It's been a boring day thus far. I guess Tap told everyone to behave while he and Rocky were visiting Centreville."

Faith smiled as she said "I'm sure that's what happened. And yes, I did see you walk by and wave your hat. Why didn't you come inside?"

"I didn't want to startle you and disturb Kathleen Maureen."

Mary laughed before saying, "I don't think your son or daughter would be annoyed if you walked into your house unexpectedly, Joe. Tap surprised me more than a few times when I was near term with Joseph and Grace."

Grace asked, "What does 'near term' mean, Mama?"

Mary patted Grace on her knee before replying, "I'll tell you when you're ready for school."

Faith said, "I told Joseph that Sister Mary Catherine would be his teacher when he went to school."

Joe grinned and said, "She's much nicer than my first-year teacher. We used to call her Miss Meany but had to be very careful when we did. Her ears were as big as chalk boards, and she could hear us whispering even when she was in the next room."

Joseph and Grace giggled as Joe spread his hands behind his ears and wagged his fingers.

Joe smiled and said, "I'll grab something quick for lunch then head back to jail. Tap and Rocky should return within an hour or so, and I want to look busy when they do."

Faith said, "Well, maybe you'll get lucky, and a large gang of notorious outlaws will ride into town and try to rob all three of the banks before Tap and Rocky return."

Joe chuckled, said, "I can't be that lucky," then walked down the hallway.

―――

Forty-five minutes later, Joe was sitting behind the desk reading an editorial in *The Idaho City Bugle* arguing that Stephen Douglas should have been elected in 1860. The author claimed that he would have allowed the South to keep their slaves and war would have been averted.

Joe couldn't imagine how anyone who was smart enough to write a coherent sentence would believe that if Douglas had defeated Lincoln, the Southern states would have been happy about it. Even though Douglas vaguely supported the institution of slavery, no Southern Democrats would have voted for him anyway. They had two pro-slavery candidates of their own, which almost assured Mister Lincoln of electoral victories in the Northern states.

SPRING SURPRISES

He'd just begun reading the highlights of the last town council meeting when the door flew open, and Mister Chen Ping rushed inside without closing the door behind him.

The small Chinaman's hands were flailing as he shouted, "Come quick! Hurry!" before he turned and hurried out the door.

Joe had popped to his feet as soon as Chen entered, so when the laundryman turned to leave, he was already racing across the floor. He slammed the door behind him and caught up with Mister Chen on the boardwalk.

Joe trotted alongside the Chinaman and loudly asked, "What's wrong?"

"My brother is shot!"

Joe pulled his Colt as he asked, "What kind of gun did he use?"

"A pistol."

Just as Joe was about to ask if the shooter had ridden away, he heard a gunshot coming from Chen's Laundry. He shouted for Mister Chen to stay back then sprinted to the laundry.

Before he reached the front of the laundry, Joe turned down the narrow alley between the laundry and the druggist, then hurried to the back entrance. When he exited the alley, he found the back door open and could hear women wailing but not the shooter. He pulled his Remington just before he entered the hot, humid workplace. When he saw a small huddle of terrified Chinese women, he shushed them before he stepped deeper into the laundry and cocked his pistol's hammer.

He quietly passed the four large washtubs then walked between two lines of drying clothes.

Joe was tiptoeing closer when he heard a woman shout, "Go away!"

As more of the front of the laundry came into view, Joe heard a man yell, "Get outta the way! I don't wanna shoot any Chink women, but I'll do it if you don't move!"

Joe took one more step then spotted the feet of two male victims on the floor with four Chinese women surrounding them. Two of the women were kneeling and bandaging the two men who'd been shot while the other pair was facing the shooter and defiantly protecting them. Joe still couldn't see the shooter, but knew he had to act quickly.

Joe quickly stepped out into the open area and swung his Remington's muzzle toward the door where he expected to find the shooter. His front sight almost immediately reached a tall man standing just to the right of the doorway with his pistol aimed at the women.

SPRING SURPRISES

When the shooter first saw someone step out from behind the line of clothes with his peripheral vision, he mistakenly assumed he was the Chinaman who'd run off. A heartbeat later, his brain corrected his assumption. As soon as he identified the new arrival as a white man with a pistol, he quickly turned his Colt toward the unexpected threat.

In Joe's enhanced state, that short delay seemed like a full minute. His centered his sights on the man's chest and squeezed his trigger. The Remington bucked in his hand, and a small fraction of a second later his .44 caliber bullet found its mark. The slug of lead slammed into the left side of shooter's chest, splintered a rib then drilled through the center of his heart. It shattered another rib before exiting his body, then created a small tent in the back of his coat before bouncing off the door jamb and falling to the floor.

The tall man stumbled backwards until he banged against the counter. As he bent over backwards, his hat fell from his head and landed on the wide counter. He took one awkward step forward then dropped to his knees. His Colt Pocket pistol slipped from his hand and clattered to the floor before he fell face down onto the pine boards.

Joe holstered his pistol as he hurried past the women and when he reached the shooter, he gave him a hard kick in the chest. After verifying the man was no longer a threat, Joe picked up his small pistol, released its hammer and dropped it into his coat pocket. He took a longer look at the shooter without recognizing him before stepping back to the four women and the wounded men.

He dropped onto his heels and loudly said, "Let me see them."

The two women who were protecting them moved away just enough for Joe to look at the injured men. The women had already bandaged both men's wounds, but the location of the blood stains told him that neither gunshot was fatal. One had been shot in the outside of his left upper arm and the other had a long grazing wound on the right side of his head just above his ear.

He looked at the oldest woman and said, "You are all very brave, but they will need a doctor."

The woman shook her head and exclaimed, "No doctor! No doctor!"

Joe wasn't about to waste time arguing, so he stood and walked around the counter to the door. There were two small crowds gathering on the other side of Main Street leaving a gap opposite the open doorway to avoid any errant bullets.

He spotted Mister Chen on the outer edge of the group to his right and shouted, "He's dead, Mister Chen!"

As the laundryman hurried across the street, the two small crowds followed at a slower pace and began to coalesce into a larger group.

SPRING SURPRISES

Just before Mister Chen stepped onto the boardwalk, Joe spotted Tap and Rock about three blocks away and riding quickly towards him. He waved them over then escorted Mister Chen into his business. Three of the women were guiding the two wounded men to the back of the laundry when they entered. The one who'd told him not to bring a doctor remained near the counter and said something to Mister Chen in Chinese. Mister Chen then quickly asked her a short question which she answered. When she finished talking, she smiled at Joe, then hurried away before Joe and Mister Chen turned to look at the dead shooter.

Joe asked, "Do you know him?"

Mister Chen shook his head and said, "No. He just walked in and shot my brother. We have no guns, so I ran to the jail. My wife told me that he shot my son and was angry they were still alive. She and my daughter stood in front of my son and brother to protect them."

"I witnessed their bravery, Mister Chen. Your brother and son didn't suffer mortal wounds, but your wife said not to fetch a doctor."

Mister Chen nodded as he said, "My wife will heal their wounds."

"That's your choice, sir. I'll move the body out of your business. He didn't bleed very much because his heart stopped immediately after being shot."

Mister Chen sighed then looked up at Joe and said, "If you did not act as you did, my son and brother would have died. And I would probably have lost my beloved wife and daughter as well. I am very grateful."

Joe quietly said, "I was just doing my job, Mister Chen."

"That is so. But to thank you for doing it well, you can tell your wife that she will never do laundry again."

Joe smiled as he said, "Thank you, Mister Chen. Your gift will make my wife very happy."

Mister Chen bowed, said, "I must see my son and brother," then quietly walked away.

Joe rolled the dead man onto his back and began searching his pockets for anything that might identify him. His coat's right pocket produced another Colt Pocket pistol, which was a surprise. He slipped it into his left coat pocket and was emptying the shooter's pants pockets when Tap and Rock hurried into the laundry.

They stepped around the counter and Sheriff Fulmer asked, "What happened, Joe?"

"I was in the office and didn't even hear the first shot, so I don't know what triggered the shooting. After Mister Chen burst into the jail and told me, I hurried this way and heard a gunshot. I snuck in the back and heard the shooter shouting that he'd kill the women if they didn't get out of the way.

"When I spotted four women surrounding two men lying on the floor, two were already bandaging the wounded men. Mrs. Chen and her daughter were standing in front of Mister Chen's brother and son to protect them from the shooter. I didn't see him until I stepped out from behind those hanging clothes. Then I shot him before he could get me in his sights."

Rocky was looking at the body as he exclaimed, "Damn, Joe! You hit him right in the heart!"

Joe replied, "He was just eight feet away, Rocky. Anyway, he was using a Colt Pocket pistol, which is probably why both men are still alive."

Joe pulled out the one with two chambers and handed it to Tap as he said, "And I found a second one in his coat pocket," then took it from his other coat pocket and gave it to Rocky.

Tap examined the small Colt and said, "It sounds as if he was ready to unload both of them."

The sheriff looked at the shooter and asked, "I never saw him before, but did Mister Chen recognize him?"

Joe shook his head as he replied, "No, sir. He must have arrived in town in the last day or two. I don't know what set him off, but it sounded like he just hated Chinamen. If he didn't have a qualm about shooting women, it would have been a lot worse."

Tap said, "Finish checkin' his pockets while we fetch Mister Moran to come and pick up the body."

Joe nodded then resumed his search before Tap and Rocky left the laundry. He found thirty-seven cents in his britches, but nothing to identify him. He opened his coat and discovered a wallet in its inside pocket. It held seven dollars in currency but nothing more.

Joe stood and was about to leave the laundry to find the man's horse when he spotted the shooter's hat sitting on the counter as if it was on a store shelf. He picked it up, and when he looked inside, he found the initials D.E.W. scrawled inside. It wasn't much, but maybe he'd learn D.E.W.'s name when he searched the man's saddlebags.

He kept D.E.W.'s hat as he stepped onto the boardwalk then approached the only horse tied to the hitchrail. He was a handsome black gelding linked to a dark brown pack mule. They were such a noticeable pair that Joe was certain he'd never seen them before. That meant the shooter must have just ridden into town, maybe while he was reading *The Idaho City Bugle*.

The crowds of spectators were dispersing as he untied the gelding's reins and led him away from the laundry. He soon reached the jail, then tied off the gelding before removing the shooter's saddlebags. He'd search the panniers on the pack mule after Tap and Rocky returned.

After entering the jail, Joe walked to the desk and set the hat and saddlebags onto the desktop. The left saddlebag contained nothing noteworthy. But even though the right one didn't provide the shooter's name, it proved to be much more informative.

He found a folded copy of *The Oregon Voice* that had its entire front page dedicated to one story. The headline read YELLOW WAVE FLOODS MINES. The article was filled with hateful rhetoric about the mine owners' decision to hire Chinese laborers. It didn't demand violent reprisals against the Chinese, but it was obvious that the author hoped it would inspire the displaced white miners into action.

Joe suspected that D.E.W. had been one of the displaced miners and decided to mine for gold in Idaho City. When he saw Chen's Laundry, he probably believed the Chinese had already started taking over the gold fields. Why he decided to just walk into the laundry and start shooting would probably remain a mystery.

He was folding the newspaper when Tap and Rocky entered the jail and Tap asked, "Find anything?"

"So far, all I know is that his initials were D.E.W., and he probably hated Chinese. I've never seen his horse and pack mule before, so he probably just rode into town."

As Tap and Rock took off their hats and coats, Sheriff Fulmer said, "I reckon it doesn't matter what his name is. Do you wanna take his horse and mule down to Frank Smith until we figger out what to do with 'em?"

Joe replied, "If it's alright with you, boss, I'll drop off his mule and check the packs, but I'd like to keep the gelding."

Tap said, "That's alright with me, but I figgered you already had too many horses."

"I need a horse for the buggy I plan to buy. I can't use the mares for a while, and I'm not about to put Duke in harness."

Tap nodded then said, "To be fair, I'll keep one of his Colt Pockets and Rocky can have the other one. I figgered you had enough firepower already."

Joe smiled as he stood and said, "I'll never have too much firepower."

Rocky was grinning as he took D.E.W.'s unfired pistol from his coat pocket and asked, "Did you find any .31 caliber ammunition in his saddlebags?"

As Joe walked by, he replied, "There's an ammunition pouch in the left one."

———

After leaving the jail, Joe rode the black gelding to Frank Smith's livery with the pack mule trailing. While the gelding was no match for Duke, he was a good-looking horse.

SPRING SURPRISES

He pulled up outside the livery, dismounting then tied the gelding's reins to the hitchrail. He detached the pack mule from the gelding and was about to take him into the big barn when Frank Smith stepped outside.

He grinned as he asked, "What you got there, Joe?"

"These belonged to a stranger who walked into Chen's Laundry and began shooting. He's being taken to the mortuary, so he won't be needing them anymore. I'll need to have the mule boarded after I inspect what's inside his packs."

"Are you keepin' the gelding?"

"Yup. I'm going to buy a buggy and put him in harness."

"If you need a buggy, I think John Post is plannin' on sellin' his now that he bought that fancy carriage."

"Thanks for letting me know. I'll talk to him later, so let's get the mule inside and see if there's anything interesting in those packs."

Twenty minutes later, Joe rode the gelding back to the jail. The only interesting item he'd found in the packs was a small cask of gunpowder.

While he was rummaging through the panniers, Frank inspected the gelding. He was around eight years old and aside from needing new shoes, the horse was in excellent condition.

Joe was deciding on a name for the gelding when he entered the jail. He smiled when he saw two petite Chinese women standing before the desk looking at him.

Tap grinned and said, "Mrs. Chen and her daughter wanted to thank you for stoppin' the shooter."

Joe removed his hat, smiled at Mrs. Chen and said, "You were both very brave, ma'am. I just pulled my trigger."

Mrs. Chen smiled as she replied, "We would be with our ancestors if you did not come. We are very grateful."

Joe nodded then asked, "Are your son and brother-in-law doing well?"

"Yes, thank you. My daughter and I will now return to care for them."

Joe was about to turn around to open the door for them when Rocky hurried past him, opened the door and smiled at the ladies as they left the jail.

After Rocky closed the door, Tap lifted a large basket onto the desk and said, "They brought you this for your laundry, too."

Joe was somewhat embarrassed as he walked to the desk and moved it to the floor before sitting down.

When Rocky took a seat, Tap said, "Just before we left Centreville, some feller told us that Eddie Pascal left town. He was tellin' everybody that he buried you under the avalanche, so I reckon he didn't want to be around when you rode into town. I just can't figger out why he'd be that stupid."

Joe's eyebrows rose slightly as he said, "I can imagine how that might have happened. When he got back to town, that pal of his who reported the fake shooting probably asked him if he went through with it. Eddie didn't want to admit he'd failed, so he told a long, embellished fairy tale about his successful assassination. He knew we wouldn't be visiting Centreville for a few days, but as soon as the warm weather began melting the snow, he left town."

"I reckon he won't be showing his face in Boise County again."

"Probably not."

Rocky said, "I bet Faith is gonna be really happy now that she doesn't have to do laundry anymore."

Tap grinned as he said, "Joe's been washin' their clothes for the last month, but I figger Faith will be glad to have the Chens take over 'cause they'll get 'em clean."

Rocky snickered before saying, "I reckon that I've got to take my dirty clothes over there tomorrow."

Joe smiled as he stared down at the large basket and noticed the Chinese figures written along the edge. He had no idea what they meant but assumed they would translate into Joe Beck. Faith would definitely be pleased when he told her, but he was even happier to put his days of doing the laundry behind him.

―――

The sun was touching the western mountains when Joe left the jail carrying the empty basket. He didn't bother mounting the gelding but just untied his reins and began leading him down Main Street.

The saloons were already noisy as he passed by, and he hoped Rocky didn't have a bad night. His first two whiskey walks were pretty tame, but Joe believed this one would probably require at least four visits into the drinking establishments. As he led the gelding onto Third Street, Joe could even name which ones would demand Rocky's attention.

When he turned onto his graveled drive, Joe glanced at the gelding and said, "I'll let Faith give you a name, sir. It'll be interesting to hear her choice, too."

He was smiling as he led the gelding into his new home.

Joe set the basket on the wide tack shelf before he began unsaddling the gelding. After he was stripped, he had to squeeze him in with Bernie.

He patted the donkey on his flank and said, "By this time next week, you'll have a bigger stall all to yourself, Bernie."

Joe snatched the basket from the crowded shelf and took a minute to examine the mares with their swollen bellies. Joe figured that Bessie would be the first to foal her mule but hoped that Betty, Nellie and especially Duchess all foaled baby horses.

He closed the barn door then quickly crossed the open ground to the back porch. He took a short glance at the bullet knot before stepping onto the porch and entering the kitchen.

Faith was smiling as he closed the door and said, "I imagine there's a story behind that basket."

Joe set it on the floor and as he hung his hat on a brass hook, he replied, "Yes, ma'am. The basket is an unexpected reward for just doing my job this afternoon."

Sister Mary Catherine asked, "Someone gave you a basket for helping them? Can you accept honoraria for doing what the county pays you to do?"

Joe hung his coat and was unbuckling his gunbelt when he answered, "There's no law against it, but I've always declined those I've been offered. I only accepted this one because it's a really a gift for Faith."

Faith asked, "What did you do that prompted someone to give me a basket, Joe?"

Joe walked to the cookstove, lifted the lid from a pot and took a deep sniff before returning the lid and saying, "I was sitting at the desk reading the paper when Mister Chen, the laundryman, rushed through the door…"

He continued telling the story as he filled a cup with hot coffee and took a seat at the table. Neither Faith nor Sister Mary Catherine interrupted him with a question until he told them what the shooter had shouted just before Joe shot him.

Then Faith exclaimed, "*He was just trying to kill them for being Chinese?*"

Joe nodded and replied, "Yes, ma'am. And if he hadn't been a bit squeamish about shooting women, I would have been too late to stop him from finishing what he started."

When Joe finished, Faith looked at the basket and said, "I'm proud of you for stopping the hate-filled crazy man, Joe. When you take our first basket of dirty clothes to the laundry, please tell Mr. and Mrs. Chen how grateful I am for their gift."

"I'll let them know. Oh, and the shooter's black gelding is in our barn. I plan to use him as our buggy horse, but I'll give you the honor of naming him."

Sister Mary Catherine stood then said, "I wish I could stay longer, but I must hurry back to the convent. After vespers, I'll regale my sisters and Father Burns with your recent heroics, Joe."

"It was hardly heroic, Sister."

The nun smiled, said, "That is your perception, not mine, Joe," then took her shawl from the back of her chair and quickly left the house before Joe could comment.

While they set the table for their supper, Joe told Faith what he hoped would be the last chapter of the Eddie Pascal story.

After saying grace, Joe asked, "No Sarah today?"

"No. She hasn't visited since she met Sister Mary Catherine. I know the sister makes her uncomfortable for some reason, but she still could come by during school hours."

"Maybe it's because of Sister M.C.'s black habit. Most of the time we see people dressed all in black, someone died."

Faith laughed then said, "Sister M.C., Joe? Really?"

Joe finished chewing a chunk of stewed beef, swallowed and replied, "It's three fewer syllables, ma'am."

"Just don't use it in front of the sister."

"You underestimate Sister M.C., Faith. She has a wicked sense of humor under those layers of black cloth. I wouldn't be surprised if she laughed if I did use the shortened appellation. Then she'd call me Deputy J.B., even though it's still only two syllables."

Faith smiled and shook her head before asking, "How about Porch?"

Joe was about to assault a buttered biscuit when he asked, "What do you want me to do about our porch? I thought you didn't want me to remove the bullet."

"I meant as a name for the gelding. That way, when anyone asks why you named him Porch, you could tell them how the bullet became stuck in our porch step."

Joe chuckled before saying, "Then Porch it is, Mrs. Beck."

After the gelding had been named, Joe said he'd visit Mister Post about his excess buggy before they started discussing the strange situation with their friends. Joe was more curious about Jimmy's failure to visit, while Faith was more interested in Sarah's intentions. Faith postulated that Sarah was avoiding her company because she'd told Jimmy and her parents that he was no longer her beau. While Joe admitted to that possibility, he reminded her that she's already noted that they had no role in the situation.

―――――

Rocky left the jail with his shotgun leaned over his right shoulder then turned left to walk to the end of Main Street. The cacophony of sounds coming from the saloons on the other side of the street were louder than they'd been on his earlier whiskey walks. But Tap had explained they would continue to add volume and violence as the weather warmed. While it wasn't close to summer-like conditions, it wasn't nearly as cold as it had been just a week earlier.

After he crossed to the other side of the street, he approached Conner's Irish Pub at the end of the row of saloons. Because it attracted most of the men with Irish roots, it tended to be one of the more active saloons. As he approached the entrance, Rocky heard a heated argument about whose horse was the fastest but didn't enter the establishment. Joe had told him that as much as the regular patrons loved their whiskey, Irish or otherwise, they also preferred to settle their many arguments with fists and not pistols.

Rocky walked past four more saloons before hearing a much louder shouting match coming from The Lady's Garter. He opened the outer doors before pushing through the swinging doors and stepping into the smoky, crowded saloon. It wasn't difficult to locate the source of the volatile quarrel and headed toward the four men standing around a poker table.

Rocky left a wave of silence in his wake as he approached the still-screaming poker players. It was soon obvious that it was the very common issue of the game's big loser accusing the big winner of cheating. In this case, it was pretty clear that the accusation was valid.

The big loser pointed at the big winner's hand laying on the table as he shouted, "Ain't no deck of cards got five kings, mister!"

The big winner yelled back, "I only got three of 'em, and your pal got the other two! He's the cheater!"

They glared at each other, but neither man made a move for his pistol when Rocky loudly said, "Calm down, boys! Why don't you all just take back what you got in the pot and play another hand? Just check to make sure the deck has fifty-two different cards before you deal."

The big loser grumbled, "I'll check 'em real good."

The four men slowly lowered themselves back to their chairs and began taking their money from the pot. As the loser gathered the cards, Rocky turned and left the saloon.

After he resumed his saloon stroll, Rocky was pleased with how he'd handled the problem. He imagined it was what Joe would have done in the situation.

Rocky was passing Foley's Beer Hall when he snickered and said, "You're trying to mimic a man six years younger than you are, you moron. You were an NCO in the Union army, for God's sake!"

He only needed to enter three more saloons before returning to the jail to drop off the shotgun, and each of them only required a brief appearance. Even though he'd had a relatively quiet night, by the time Rocky returned to his room at Fletcher's Boarding House, he was finally beginning to feel like a real lawman.

SPRING SURPRISES

Joe and Faith had gone to bed an hour earlier but not to enjoy an extended night's sleep. Joe held his wife close and asked, "You'll let me know when this becomes uncomfortable, won't you?"

Faith smiled, then kissed him before replying, "Maybe. That might not be until I go into labor, though."

Joe placed his right palm of her damp bulging middle and said, "I think Kathleen Maureen's unhappy for disturbing her."

Faith said, "I can't think of a better reason for disturbing her, Joe. Even if we don't upset her, she's kicking even more now. I can't imagine how much she'll be protesting over the next weeks."

"Does Sister M.C. think our daughter is too busy?"

"No, she's very pleased with both of us. And on his last visit, Doctor Taylor told me that everything was going well. He'll be checking us again on Monday afternoon, too."

Joe nodded but the increased frequency of Doctor Taylor's visits made him wonder if the physician was concerned. He quickly dismissed the idea as nothing more than a side effect of having a lawman's necessarily suspicious mind.

Faith was sure that neither Doctor Taylor nor Sister Mary Catherine had any concerns about her or Kathleen Maureen.

But their assurances did nothing to diminish her fears about what would happen on the day she went into labor. She desperately wanted to be able hold her baby in her arms and give her the love only a mother could provide. But that intense need only added to her growing sense of a terrible fate that awaited her.

Faith felt herself slipping into despair when Joe said, "I wonder if our friends from the wagon train are all neighbors in Oregon."

Faith asked, "What made you think of them all of a sudden?"

"When I felt Katie's kick, I realized Marigold might have had her baby already. I find it hard to picture Marigold as a mother."

"I can't either. But I don't have that problem with Becky. I can still remember her ecstatic face as she rocked her imaginary baby."

Joe kissed her on her forehead before saying, "And seeing the love Becky had for a baby she believed she would never hold was what expelled your fear of childbirth. Soon, Becky will be even happier when she holds her human baby in her arms. And next month, when you gaze down at Kathleen Maureen's small, perfect face, you'll have the same overwhelming sense of joy.

SPRING SURPRISES

"I love you with all my heart, Faith. But I know that no man can ever fully understand the pure, absolute love only a mother can have for her baby. I should be jealous, but I'm just enormously happy for you."

Faith looked at Joe's green eyes in the moonlight and wondered if he knew her fears had returned, but now it no longer mattered. Just as her worries had disappeared after that soul-changing day with Becky, that memory alone now pushed them back into their locked vault. And if they tried to make another appearance, Faith hoped she now had a weapon to keep them at bay.

She kissed Joe softly before whispering, "I love you, Joe. And thank you for being you."

Joe quietly replied, "I'm the luckiest man God ever put on this planet, Faith. Now close your blue eyes and have a night filled with pleasant dreams."

Faith sighed, then closed her eyes as Joe tugged their blankets over her shoulders.

CHAPTER 7

Saturday morning, Joe was the first one to enter the jail, which was usually how each day began. Tap usually helped Mary with the children, and Rocky abided by the boarding house's breakfast schedule.

He started a fire in the heating stove before taking off his coat and taking a seat behind the desk. Joe opened the logbook to see if Rocky had any problems on last night's saloon stroll and was a bit surprised to find no new entries. He hoped it was as quiet for him on tonight's walk.

The jail was beginning to warm when Sheriff Fulmer entered and as he hung his hat, he said, "When I told Mary about the shootin', she was glad you stopped the shooter. But she was kinda jealous when I told her about the laundry basket."

Joe grinned as he replied, "You should get her a basket, Tap. It's only six dollars per month, and that's a little more than a quarter of our recent increase in pay. I was going to do it myself before the shooting because I wasn't looking forward to washing dirty diapers."

Tap snickered then took a seat before asking, "Anything in the log book?"

SPRING SURPRISES

"No, sir. I was a bit surprised, too."

"That's kinda scary, Joe. It's like they're all buildin' up for one really bad one. Maybe two of us should start makin' the walks."

Joe said, "You're the boss, Tap."

The boss replied, "I'll think about it," then asked, "Did you hear about the telegraph comin' in a couple of weeks?"

"Nope. Idaho City should have had a telegraph office before it had its second saloon. But I imagine the army is using almost every inch of Western Union's wire and most of their telegraph sets."

"You're right about that, but I'm just happy we're finally gonna get one."

Rocky interrupted further telegraph talk when he loudly entered the office. As he began stripping off his coat, he started to tell them about the poker game incident. Before he moved on to the minor problems he'd handled, Joe abdicated his front desk throne to Rocky.

Joe just leaned against the wall and listened until Rocky finished before he said, "Now that I have a buggy horse, I'm going to head down to the feed and grain to talk to Mister Post about his excess buggy."

Tap grinned as he said, "I reckon we can keep the town peaceful 'til you get back, Deputy."

Joe smiled then stepped to the peg wall and took down his coat.

Joe didn't bother haggling with John Post over the price for his buggy. So, just fifteen minutes after leaving the jail, Joe was the proud owner of a used buggy. Mister Post agreed to keep it in his large warehouse until Joe's barn extension was finished next week.

On his way back to the jail, Joe looked forward to driving the buggy to their canyon with Faith riding beside him. Tomorrow afternoon, he'd return to the canyon to make sure the path was wide enough for the buggy to reach the clearing.

When Joe went home for lunch, he told Faith about the buggy and his planned visit to their private canyon tomorrow. As they shared their noon meal, they chatted about the future buggy ride into the hidden valley. Faith was bubbling in anticipation of seeing the hidden clearing and the small, snapping-turtle-free pool on the following Sunday.

SPRING SURPRISES

The rest of the day was as uneventful as the morning had been. So, as Tap locked the door, and the three lawmen left the jail, each of them felt as if all hell was about to break loose. But no one mentioned it as if it would light the fuse to the powder keg.

Just over two hours later, with the half-moon overhead, Joe was crossing Main Street before it became the road to Boise City. On his walk to the south end of town, he'd heard the expected sounds of boisterous revelry coming from the saloons. As loud as it was tonight, he knew both the noise and trouble would increase along with the rise in temperature. When Joe reached the western boardwalk, he turned and began the night's saloon stroll.

He had to enter The June Bug Saloon when he heard a loud crash that turned out to be the death of a thrown chair. When he stepped onto the barroom floor, the clientele became as silent as an empty barn. Joe just turned and left. As he resumed his stroll, he heard the barroom noise rising to match its earlier volume.

After leaving the June Bug, Joe needed to show his face in three more drinking establishments before he even reached the halfway point.

Joe soon approached the front entrance to one of the larger and more disreputable saloons, Pete Parker's Palace. The intense volume of the racket going on inside the place was causing the windows to vibrate, but he wasn't able to detect any sounds of violence which would require his attention. He was just ten feet past the entrance when the sharp crack of a gunshot echoed from the saloon. Joe pulled the shotgun into his hands before he whipped around and raced to the doors.

When he burst through the inner doors, he saw the back of a man standing with a smoking pistol in his hand looking down at his unmoving victim.

He cocked the shotgun's hammers before stepping closer and shouting, "Drop the gun, mister!"

The man didn't let the pistol fall from his fingers but continued to stare at the body lying on the floor just eight feet from where he stood.

With the two shotgun barrels leveled at the man's back, Rocky slowly approached the shooter then stopped when he was six feet away.

"Mister, I told you to drop the pistol. I've got a cocked shotgun aimed at your back."

The Colt remained in his grip and without turning, the man quietly said, "I…I did…did…didn't w-w-w-want to shoot him."

Joe was stunned when he realized that Jimmy Pritchard was the shooter. He released the shotgun's twin hammers, then lowered the scattergun before he stepped closer and pulled the pistol from Jimmy's hand.

He dropped the revolver into his coat pocket before he looked at the closest onlooker and asked, "What happened?"

Willy Norton pointed at the dead man and said, "Rich Smith was makin' fun of Jimmy's stutterin' and callin' him all sorts of names. I figgered that Jimmy would just leave like he always did, but then Rich said if Jimmy was a real man, he woulda bedded Sarah Walker right off. Jimmy got really mad and started yellin' at him, but he was still stutterin'.

"Then Rich said he was gonna…well, he kinda said he was gonna visit Sarah himself and started laughin'. Jimmy said he was gonna shoot Rich and started to reach for his pistol. But he forgot about his hammer loop, so by the time Jimmy pulled it out of his holster, Rich already had his Colt cocked and pointed at his face."

Joe shifted his eyes back to Jimmy as Willy said, "Jimmy was shakin' real bad when he tried to cock his hammer, but Rich didn't pull his trigger. We reckon that he wanted to be able to say it was a fair fight. Anyway, Jimmy got his hammer all the way into firing position but closed his eyes just before Rich pulled his trigger. We figgered Jimmy's brains were gonna be splattered all over the saloon but all we heard was the pop from Rich's percussion cap goin' off.

"Rich musta been more surprised than we were and was pullin' his hammer back for a second shot when Jimmy opened his eyes and pulled his trigger."

Joe nodded, said, "Thanks, Mister Norton," then stepped past Jimmy and picked up Rich Smith's Colt and released the hammer before dropping it into his left coat pocket.

He looked at the bartender and said, "Have somebody take the body down to Moran's Mortuary," then turned back to face Jimmy.

Jimmy was staring at him with blank eyes when Joe took his elbow and said, "Let's get you out of here, Jimmy."

Jimmy didn't reply but simply turned around and walked with Joe out of the saloon.

Once they reached the cold night air, they turned left on the boardwalk and walked past the next saloon before Jimmy quietly asked, "Am I gonna hang for killing him?"

"No, Jimmy. You didn't do anything wrong. You shot him in self-defense and you're lucky to be alive. But why did you even go to Pete Parker's place? There are other saloons that are more peaceful."

They walked past The Watering Hole before Jimmy replied, "I…I w-wanted to…my f-f-father said not to g-g-go there."

Joe ignored the shouting coming from The Rich Racoon as he sharply said, "I think you're a better man than your father, Jimmy, and you don't have to prove a damned thing to him."

SPRING SURPRISES

Jimmy looked at Joe but didn't say anything as they continued past Gentleman Jack's Gambling Parlor. They passed three more drinking, gambling and bawdy houses before they crossed the Main Street's intersection with B Street.

Joe finally asked, "Will you be all right now, Jim?"

Jimmy nodded then asked, "Why did you call me Jim?"

"Because I figure your folks called you Jimmy since you were in diapers. But I've only known you as a man, so I think of you as a Jim."

Jimmy smiled as he said, "Okay."

Joe popped Jim on his shoulder before saying, "I don't know why you still haven't paid me a visit, but I do need you to stop by the jail on Monday to make a statement. Okay?"

"Okay. I'll be there, but now I've gotta go home and tell my folks what happened."

Joe nodded and said, "Don't be ashamed of what happened, Jim. Tell them as if you were reciting a speech, and I'll see you Monday morning."

Jimmy managed a weak smile before waving and hurrying away.

Joe stopped and watched as Jimmy disappeared into the shadows and hoped he was able to stand up to his father.

Maybe his father would even be proud of him, but Joe hoped that Orin didn't praise Jimmy for killing a man.

When he resumed his whiskey walk, Joe noticed that Jimmy hadn't stuttered when he said he had to tell his parents about the shooting. It might have been because Jimmy had been distracted but Joe hoped the rechristened Jim was finally beginning to have a measure of confidence in himself.

―――

Twenty minutes later, Joe turned down 2nd Street and soon stepped onto the Fulmers front porch. He knocked on the door and just seconds later, Tap swung it open.

The sheriff said, "Come on in and tell me what happened, Joe."

Joe stepped into the foyer and after Tap closed the door, Joe removed his hat and said, "There was a fatal shooting in Pete Parker's Palace. Rich Smith was the instigator, but he's dead and I had them take his body to Moran's. The shooter was Jimmy Pritchard."

Tap's eyebrows shot up as he exclaimed, "*Jimmy Pritchard killed him?*"

Joe nodded as he replied, "It's a long story, but basically Rich taunted Jimmy probably to get him mad enough to go for his pistol. I didn't even know he had one. Anyway, when Jimmy finally reached his boiling point and drew his pistol,

Rich already had his cocked and aimed at Jimmy's face. He had a misfire and was cocking his hammer for a second shot when Jimmy fired. I'm not even sure Jimmy knew where his muzzle was pointing.

"I checked both of their pistols which corroborated what I was told by Willy Norton. Both of their pistols are on the desk and Jimmy will come by Monday morning to make his statement."

"Rich Smith always was a troublemaker. Is Jimmy gonna be all right?"

"I think so. He's probably already told his folks what happened."

"Okay. I reckon we'll find out how he's doin' when he shows up."

Joe nodded then pulled on his hat, crossed the foyer and left the house. As he walked through the empty lot east of the school, Joe looked for the welcoming light coming from his home's kitchen windows. Despite the shooting, the night's walk hadn't been as dangerous as he'd expected, but he was still anxious to return to Faith.

When he entered the kitchen, he heard Faith's voice echo from the hallway as she loudly said, "I'm in the parlor, Joe."

Joe quickly hung his hat before replying, "I'll be there shortly, ma'am."

He soon entered the warm parlor and sat beside his wife on the couch. Before Faith could ask about his night, Joe began telling her about the shooting. Faith had almost an identical reaction to Tap's when he revealed the name of the shooter. He spent more than five minutes explaining the incident then another fifteen answering her questions.

After Joe had replied to her last query, he said, "You look tired, sweetheart. So, it's off to bed where you can get some much-needed sleep."

Faith sighed before she said, "Alright. I am a bit weary."

———

Faith drifted into a deep sleep less than a minute after her blonde head touched her soft pillow. But Joe stayed awake for almost another hour as he thought about tomorrow's ride to the canyon and Jimmy Pritchard's visit Monday morning. He was curious if stuttering Jimmy or confident Jim would walk through the door.

———

Early Sunday afternoon, Joe turned Duke onto the bank of his canyon's stream. He walked his stallion a few feet away from the rushing water to make sure there was enough space for the buggy. It was close in two spots, but when Joe pulled up at the edge of the clearing, he was sure the buggy wouldn't have any difficulty.

SPRING SURPRISES

He sat in his saddle and counted the deer in the small herd before he raised his eyes to watch the pair of eagles already soaring high above the clearing. He suspected that a few of the does would have fawns in the next month or so and wondered if the giant golden eagles would snatch one of the newborns to feed their chicks.

He didn't pull his Sharps or his Henry before starting Duke across the clearing. Just seconds later, the deer scattered, and Joe watched them until they disappeared into the line of trees along the southern edge of the clearing.

He smiled and said, "I won't be doing any hunting for a while, so your biggest worry is those two big birds a few hundred feet over your heads. Of course, you might run afoul of a wolf or bear in the woods if you're not careful."

After he'd issued his warning, Joe kept Duke at a walk as he headed toward the pool. When he was close to the bank, he dismounted and led Duke to the water's edge.

Duke dipped his muzzle into the pond before Joe sat on his heels and dipped his cupped hands into the frigid water. After satisfying his thirst, Joe was drying his hands on his britches when he saw something reflecting sunlight close to the bank just below the water's surface. It knew it wasn't gold, but his curiosity made him plunge his recently dried hand back into the water and snatch the rock from the bottom.

He opened his fingers and looked at the dark red, almost purple rock but wasn't sure what it was. He examined it for almost a minute and was about to toss it back into the pond but thought Faith might like to see it. So, he dropped it into his coat pocket before he stood and dried his hand again. He was about to mount Duke when he decided to look around and see if he could find another example of the unusual stone.

Joe searched the pool and the nearby stream for almost twenty minutes before he found a second one. It was much larger than the first, but he still had no idea what it was. He had plenty of time, so he continued prospecting for more shiny rocks.

He found four smaller ones when he decided to end his exploration. Before he returned to Duke, he took all six of the stones from his coat pocket and held them out in the afternoon sun. The sunlight seemed to bring the stones to life and the effect from the largest of them was almost hypnotic. After a few seconds, he pried his eyes from the stones, slipped them back into his pocket then trotted back to Duke.

———

Forty-five minutes later, Joe left their small barn that would start growing tomorrow and trotted to the house. He may not know what kinds of stones he had in his pocket but was still anxious to show them to Faith.

SPRING SURPRISES

When he entered the kitchen, he wasn't surprised to find Faith sitting at the table waiting for him. He hung his hat but left his coat on as he walked across the kitchen floor.

After Joe gave her a warm kiss, Faith smiled and asked, "So, will you be able to drive our new buggy to the clearing next Sunday, Mister Beck?"

Joe sat down and replied, "Yes, ma'am. And you'll be pleased to know that while I may not have seen a snapping turtle in the pool, but I did find some unusual stones. I have six of them in my coat pocket."

"What do they look like?"

Joe reached into his coat pocket and handed Faith one of the smaller stones.

She held it between her thumb and index finger and began tilting it in the late afternoon sunlight that streamed through the window.

She was still examining the rock as she asked, "Do you have any idea what it is?"

"No, ma'am."

"It's a dark red, so do you think it could be a ruby?"

"I don't think so. But that's one of the smaller ones. Here's the biggest one I found."

When Joe handed her the much larger stone, Faith set the small one onto the table then stared at the egg-sized rock in the sunlight.

After gazing at the play of the sun's rays on its surface for almost a minute, she quietly said, "This is amazing, Joe. It's not only large but it's also a deeper shade of violet than the small one. More than that, it has an almost hypnotic effect when you turn it in the sunlight. On the clear part, it has three crossing lines that look like a star. I wonder what it would look like if it was polished."

"I was impressed with it myself and was thinking of taking it to Mister Faircloth to have it polished. He could tell us what it is, too."

Faith gave both stones back to Joe as she said, "I think that's a wonderful idea."

Joe slid them into his pocket before he stood and took off his coat then hung it on a brass wall hook.

After hanging his gunbelt, he returned to his seat and asked, "You haven't had any visitors after Father Burns left?"

"No. I was surprised, too. After Jimmy's shooting last night, I expected Sarah would have rushed over to ask you what happened."

"That's what I thought, too. She must have heard about it by now. Jimmy and Sarah both go to the Methodist church, so maybe he told her after services."

"That could be the reason. But isn't Rocky a Methodist, too? Even if he didn't attend services, I'm sure he's heard about it."

"I guess…"

Joe stopped talking when they heard loud knocking on the front door, then he said, "That doesn't sound like Sarah's knock. I'll go let Rocky in."

He stood and trotted down the hallway and soon entered the foyer and opened the door.

Rocky exclaimed, "I just heard that Jimmy Pritchard shot some feller last night. What happened, Joe?"

"Obviously, you slept most of the morning. Come on in and I'll tell you about it."

Rocky entered the foyer and replied, "I didn't oversleep, Joe. I rode outta town to try my new Colt Pocket pistol."

Joe closed the door and waited until Rocky hung his hat and coat on the coat rack before he escorted Rocky down the hallway to the kitchen. They joined Faith at the table and Joe began his explanation.

After Joe finished telling him the story, Rocky asked, "What did Tap say when you told him?"

"He agreed with me that it's a clear-cut case of self-defense. I got all the facts from a bystander. Jim didn't say anything about the shooting, but he's coming to the office tomorrow morning to make a statement."

"I reckon Sarah musta stopped by already to ask about it."

"No, she didn't. Faith and I were just talking about it. They both attend the Methodist church, so she probably talked to him after services this morning."

"I reckon I picked a bad day to miss church. Do you think Jimmy Pritchard even went to church after killing that loud-mouthed bastard?"

"I have no idea. I guess it depends on what happened when he got home. He seemed more concerned about what his father would say than he did about shooting Rich Smith. And he was really shaken after he saw Smith lying on the floor."

Rocky stared at the tabletop as he quietly said, "I wonder what Sarah will think of him now."

Joe looked at Faith who just shrugged before he asked, "So, how accurate was that baby Colt?"

Rocky raised his eye to Joe, grinned and said, "It's pretty accurate up to about thirty feet, but that .31 caliber bullet sure does stray after that. I reckon that D.E.W. character musta been rushed when he tried to shoot Mister Chen's brother and son."

SPRING SURPRISES

"He was probably shaking with hate, too."

Rocky then asked, "Do you know Mr. Chen's daughter's name? The one who came to the jail to leave the basket?"

Joe replied, "I believe her name is Chen Ai."

Rocky tilted his head slightly before asking, "It ain't Ai Chen?"

"Nope. Chinese folk put the family name first, so it's Chen Ai. Mister Chen is Chen Ping and Mrs. Chen is Chen Ju. I hope you don't want me to give you all of their names."

"No, that's okay. I'm kinda surprised that you know 'em."

"Ever since I arrived, the first time I visited a business or a home, I made a point of asking each person's name. I didn't want anyone to think of me as a stranger. I haven't met everyone, of course. There are the prospectors and most of the folks in Centreville and Placerville, too."

"Maybe I oughta start introducing myself."

Faith smiled and said, "You can start when your drop off your dirty laundry tomorrow."

Rocky blushed just enough for Joe to notice before he stood and said, "Well, I gotta get back to the boarding house. They have a big dinner on Sundays."

Joe said, "See you in the morning, Rocky."

Rocky waved and headed down the hall.

After they heard the front door close, Faith said, "I think Rocky is just lonely."

Joe smiled and said, "He's also a man who's been living with a bunch of men in blue suits for six years, Faith. He needs the company of a woman, but I hope he finds a good one. It's too bad that I've already stolen the best woman."

Faith laughed before saying, "A woman who now has a belly the size of giant pumpkin."

Joe leaned over and kissed her then said, "But not for much longer, my love."

———

They had no more visitors by the time they blew out the last lamp and retired for the night. Faith had added the Jimmy Pritchard incident into the journal and included a few personal observations about Sarah.

While Faith was writing in her journal, Joe opened his notebook and added the visit to Mister Faircloth. Tomorrow they'd start building the barn addition and by Friday, he'd be able to pick up the buggy. But the most interesting event on Monday morning would happen in the jail. Joe hoped it would be Jim Pritchard who showed up and not stuttering, shy Jimmy.

CHAPTER 8

Joe arrived at the office even earlier than usual. He needed to write his report of the shooting and add two entries to the logbook.

He was almost finished with his report when Sheriff Fulmer entered the office, so he didn't stop writing.

After Tap took a seat, he waited until Joe set down his pen before he asked, "Did you hear anything more about that shooting, Joe?"

Joe shook his head as he replied, "Rocky stopped by yesterday afternoon to ask about it, but no one else paid me a visit."

"I talked to a few folks after Mass yesterday and they were all shocked when they heard that Jimmy Pritchard killed a man, especially in a rathole like Pete Parker's saloon. He just ain't the kinda feller who uses that place."

"You can imagine my reaction when I realized who had pulled the trigger. I hope he'll be all right when he shows up to write his statement. After he leaves, I'll take his statement and my report to Mister Blanton. You don't see any chance that Jim will be charged, do you?"

"Nope, but I ain't a lawyer. And I'm damned happy about it, too."

Joe snickered then said, "So, am I. We have plenty of lawyers in town, but you're the only sheriff. I know none of those attorneys could do your job, and doubt if any could do as well as Eddie Pascal did as a deputy."

Tap grinned and said, "You ain't bein' very fair, Joe. I reckon there are a couple of those shysters who could do a good job pretendin' to be President Lincoln."

Joe laughed and was about to continue the Eddie Pascal tribute when Rocky made his appearance.

―――

A few minutes later, the three lawmen were reviewing the weekend's events. The discussion lasted for more than thirty minutes before Rocky shifted topics when he asked Tap if he'd tried his Colt Pocket pistol.

Joe didn't listen to them discuss their five-shot revolvers as he stared at the door and wondered when Jim or Jimmy would arrive to write his statement. He'd expected him to show up early just to get it done. Now Joe began to suspect that Jimmy's father might be the reason for the delay.

Joe was still focused on the door when a shadow passed by the window just before the door swung open.

SPRING SURPRISES

Jim Pritchard closed the door, took off his hat and said, "Good morning, Joe. I'm here to write my statement."

Joe noticed that Jim hadn't stuttered before he stood and asked, "Sheriff, do you mind if Jim uses your office?"

Tap replied, "Go ahead. Me and Rocky will find somethin' to keep us busy."

Joe smiled then stepped away from the desk and waved for Jim to follow before he led him down the hallway to the sheriff's private office.

Once they entered the small room, Joe closed the door and said, "Have a seat behind the desk, Jim. I'll get you some paper and a pencil."

"Okay."

Jim set his hat on the desk and took off his coat which he laid across the back of the chair before sitting down.

Joe set four sheets of blank paper and a reasonably sharp pencil in front of him, and Jim began writing his statement. Joe studied Jim as he relived last night's experience in written words. He watched his expression and his hand as he wrote and didn't see a hint of nervousness. Each letter was smoothly formed, and the sentences were coherent and concise.

What impressed Joe even more than Jim's penmanship was the content of his statement. Joe noticed that Jim included each of Rich Smith's insults and what was almost astounding, he didn't gloss over his fear of stuttering when he tried to respond, or his abject terror as he stared down the barrel of Rich's Colt.

When Jim finished writing, he set down the pencil then looked at Joe and asked, "Do you want to read it to make sure it's good enough?"

Joe picked up the three sheets and said, "I already read it, Jim. It's better than the report I wrote about the incident. How are you doing?"

Jim exhaled before replying, "I'm a lot better."

"What did your father say when you told him?"

"He was really mad when he found out I went to Pete Parker's, but not so much when I told him about the shooting. Sunday morning, he and my mother acted as if nothing had happened at all."

"Did you tell Sarah?"

Jim nodded as he answered, "After we left the church. After I told her about it, she said she was proud of me for defending her honor. I was surprised, but when she told me that, it made me feel a lot better."

Joe smiled as he asked, "So, how much longer are you going to wait before you propose, Jim?"

SPRING SURPRISES

Jim grinned before he said, "I already did. I asked her last night and she said yes. She seemed really happy, too."

Joe stood and offered his hand, as he said, "Congratulations, Jim."

As Jim exuberantly shook Joe's hand, he said, "Thanks. We're getting married on the twenty-first of March, the first full day of spring."

"That's a good way to start a new season."

Jim's broad smile faded before he asked, "Do you still think I won't be in trouble for shooting Rich Smith?"

"I'm going to visit the county prosecutor in a few minutes. But I'd be shocked if he even thought about charging you with a crime."

"Will you come to the shop and let me know what he said?"

"I'll do that. And Jim, I noticed that you're haven't stuttered since you arrived. Is that permanent?"

"I hope so."

"If you feel a stutter coming on, just remember that you're marrying Sarah in two weeks."

Jim laughed as he stood and followed Joe out of the sheriff's office.

After Jim left the jail, Joe said, "I'll go see Mister Blanton then head over to Pritchard's to tell Jim about our prosecutor's decision."

Tap nodded as he said, "Jimmy seemed kinda different and he didn't stutter, either."

Joe was putting on his coat as he said, "He didn't stutter once when I was talking to him, either. Maybe that's because he's marrying Sarah Walker on the twenty-first of the month."

Tap exclaimed, *"They're gettin' married after all this time?"*

Joe just winked, pulled on his hat and left the office.

———

His visit with the county prosecutor took longer than he'd anticipated but not because Mister Blanton was debating whether or not to charge Jim with a crime. After reading Joe's report and Jim's statement, he asked for every detail in the shooting. Then, just as Joe thought he would be able to leave, Mister Blanton asked for more information about the shootout in Mister Chen's laundry.

When Joe finally left the county courthouse, the sun only needed another hour of travel before it reached its zenith. As he headed for Pritchard's, he reached into his coat's right pocket and felt the six red stones. If it was as pretty as he expected it to be after Mister Faircloth polished the biggest one, he'd have the jeweler make it into a necklace for Faith.

He knew it wouldn't matter to her if it wasn't a valuable gemstone. It would be important to her because it had come from the pool in their canyon.

Before he reached Pritchard's Butcher Shop and Greengrocery, Joe prepared for a potentially hostile reception from the older Mister Pritchard. When he entered the large store, Joe saw the proprietor behind the counter talking to Mrs. Olsen. He soon spotted Joe, but his expression didn't change.

As Joe approached the counter, Orin looked past Mrs. Olsen and simply said, "Jimmy's waiting for you in the back room, Deputy."

Joe nodded, said, "Thank you, Mister Pritchard," then headed to the back room where they butchered the meat.

He pushed the curtain aside just as Jimmy slammed a cleaver through a joint of mutton.

Jimmy set the heavy cleaver down and asked, "What did he say, Joe?"

Joe put on his serious face as he stepped closer and said, "He wants to charge…never mind," then smiled before saying, "I was going to make a really bad joke. Mister Blanton agreed it was clearly a case of self-defense, so you have nothing to worry about."

Jim grinned then asked, "What was the bad joke you were planning to use?"

"I was going to tell you that he wanted me to arrest you for murder, but it was probably the stupidest idea that ever popped into my head. I'm just glad another part of my brain kept me from finishing the sentence."

"It woulda been pretty bad, Joe. What did my father say before you came back here?"

"All he said was that you were waiting for me in the back room."

Jim nodded then said, "Even my mother noticed he seemed, um, nicer today."

Joe didn't think Orin's greeting came close to being 'nice' but didn't comment.

Joe was about to leave when Jim said, "Sarah is probably at your house right now. She wanted to apologize for not asking Faith to be her witness."

Joe smiled and replied, "I don't think Sarah needed to apologize. I'm sure Faith understands. It would be a bit embarrassing if she started having contractions in the middle of the ceremony."

"I thought she wasn't going to have the baby until April."

"Doctor Taylor said that Kathleen Maureen might arrive a little early because she's already a big girl."

SPRING SURPRISES

"Oh. And I was going to ask you to be my witness, but Sarah asked me if her brother Tom could stand beside me. Is that alright?"

"Sure. I can't predict what I'll be doing in the next few hours, so I might be in Placerville on your wedding day."

Jim wiped his right hand on his apron before he offered it to Joe and said, "Thanks for being my friend, Joe. You've helped me more than you can imagine."

Joe shook his hand and said, "You're a good man, Jim. But you're still too smart to be a lawman in Boise County."

Jim chuckled before Joe gave him a quick salute and left the back room. Orin was waiting on Mrs. Leviton, so Joe didn't have to acknowledge him as he passed by the counter.

After stepping back into the late morning sunshine, Joe took a few seconds to scan the street before he turned left and headed to Faircloth's Fine Jewelry.

Joe was the only customer when he entered the small shop, so George Faircloth smiled and said, "Good morning, Joe. What can I do for you?"

Joe reached into his right pocket and pulled out the second largest stone.

As he handed it to Mister Faircloth, Joe said, "I don't know what kind of stone this is, but I'm sure you'll be able to tell me."

George held the stone in the palm of his hand for just a few seconds before he said, "This is a very large garnet. While garnets are found in many places in the territory, this one is much more valuable than most. In addition to the large size, it's also a star garnet, which are more beautiful and rarer than red garnets.

"I'd estimate that after cutting, it would yield a stone weighing more than three hundred carats. I won't ask you where you discovered this magnificent example, but would you like to know its worth in its final form?"

"It doesn't matter to me, Mister Faircloth. I was just impressed with how it reflected the sunlight. I was going to ask if you'd be able to polish it, then mount it in a necklace for my wife."

"I can do certainly do that if you'd like. But this is rather a large stone for a necklace. Did you find any smaller stones?"

"I found four smaller ones and one much larger."

George's eyes popped wide as he sharply asked, "*You have a bigger one? Is it a star garnet as well?*"

Joe nodded then took the remaining five stones from his coat and laid them onto the counter.

Mister Faircloth reverently picked up the egg-sized garnet, held it into the light and gazed at the gemstone as if he had just witnessed the appearance of an angel.

He continued to stare at the stone for almost a minute before he looked at Joe and whispered, "This is by far the largest six-star garnet I've ever seen. Words cannot describe the effect it has on me."

Joe smiled as he said, "If you thought the other one was too large for a necklace, I'm sure this one is too big to be mounted on a broach."

George looked at Joe and said, "This should never be mounted in any form of jewelry. I'll have to weigh it later, but I'm sure this stone weighs almost six ounces in its uncut form. After it's cut and polished, it should be more than six hundred carats."

"Would you cut and polish all six of them, Mister Faircloth? When they're finished, I'll pick the nicest of the small ones for Faith's necklace."

George smiled as he replied, "I'd be honored. Do you mind leaving them with me, Joe? I can give you a receipt."

"I don't need a receipt. I trust you, Mister Faircloth."

The jeweler shook Joe's hand and said, "Please call me George."

Joe nodded then said, "I've got to get back to work before Tap figures out that he can get along without me."

George laughed before Joe waved and left the shop. As he headed back to the jail, Joe wondered just how much the large stone was worth. He hadn't even given it a thought before he watched Mister Faircloth's face light up when he saw it. But whatever their value, Joe believed Faith would be pleased just seeing the polished stones.

Joe returned to the jail just before Rocky hurried away to reach the boarding house before they began serving lunch.

When he took a seat in front of the desk, Tap asked, "What did Jimmy say when you told him that he wasn't gonna be charged?"

"He was pretty excited. Then he told me that Sarah had gone to my house to break the news to Faith that she'd selected another woman to be her witness."

Tap snickered before saying, "I don't reckon Faith's gonna be too upset about it. I can't see her standin' on her feet for an hour."

"Then Jim said he was going to ask me to be his witness, but Sarah wanted her brother Tom instead."

"I don't suppose he told Sarah it was his choice who was gonna be his witness, did he?"

"Nope. He may not stutter anymore, but I think Sarah will rule the roost after they're married."

"Sounds like it. I reckon Rocky missed a bullet and didn't even know it."

"I think so, too. At least when that bullet landed, it didn't wind up in my porch step. How did Rocky react after hearing the news that Sarah and Jim are getting married after all?"

"Not as bad as I expected. But maybe because he was so impressed with Chen's daughter. Don't go tellin' me that you didn't notice it, Joe."

"I noticed. I told Faith that I think Rocky really needs a good woman after spending six years in the army."

"I reckon so. I wonder how Mister Chen would feel about lettin' a white man marry his daughter?"

"How would some of the townsfolk feel about it? You were already married to Mary when you got here. But I imagine there are still some people in town who don't like her, Joseph, Grace or even you because she's Nez Perce."

Tap nodded and said, "There are more'n a few of 'em, and that's one of the reasons we were really happy when Father Burns had the school built. The nuns won't let any of the boys give Joseph any trouble when he starts goin' to school. It'd be different if he went to the regular school."

Joe smiled and said, "Sister Mary Catherine may be a kind and pretty lady, but I wouldn't want to cross her in the classroom."

"Well, I reckon I'll be headin' home for lunch now that you've ended your wanderin'."

"I'll resume my wandering when Rocky returns, Sheriff."

Tap chuckled then stood and less than a minute later, Joe found himself on his own. He sat behind the desk and opened his notebook. He'd done most of the items on his list, and after telling Jim why it wasn't a good idea to have Faith act as Sarah's witness, he figured he should buy the cradle in the next day or two.

While he didn't care that much about the value of the star garnets, he suspected that there were more of them in the pool and stream. From Mister Faircloth's reaction, he doubted if any of them were nearly the size of the biggest one. But still, they might provide a source of income for Faith and their children in the event that his long string of good luck finally ended.

For a few minutes, Joe reviewed each of the times he'd narrowly avoided death, starting when the rest of his family had perished from bad meat. When he reached ten, he stopped counting as it was becoming morbid.

Joe shook his head then stood and walked to the front window. He watched the road traffic and the folks walking along the boardwalks just as a distraction. As he identified each of the citizens, he said his or her name. Joe studied the folks going about their lives for fifteen minutes before he returned to the desk.

When Rocky returned from his scheduled lunch, he snatched off his hat and said, "I reckon Jimmy Pritchard was happy when you told him he wasn't gonna be charged."

Joe stood and met Rocky at the peg wall and as he took his coat and Rocky hung his, Joe said, "He was definitely relieved. I was going to pull his leg and tell him he was being charged with murder, but my brain figured it was a bad idea in mid-sentence."

Rocky snickered, and as he headed to the desk, he said, "If you pulled a joke like that on me, I woulda punched you in the nose."

Joe pulled on his hat and said, "And I would have deserved it, too."

After he left the jail, Joe turned right and hurried along Main Street's boardwalk. He was anxious to see Faith and hoped that Sarah wasn't still visiting.

He trotted down 2nd Street and after passing the school, he turned left into the open field. He immediately spotted the construction crew working on his barn extension and was surprised to see how much progress they'd already made. He knew it was a simple job but was still impressed. He suspected it would be done by Wednesday. Then he'd fetch the buggy and take Faith for a short test drive.

He waved to the workmen as he strode by and soon hopped onto the lead-filled porch step. Despite its value as a conversation piece, Joe knew he'd have to repair the damage before the wood became dangerously weakened.

Joe was almost nervous when he opened the kitchen door and stepped inside. When he didn't find Faith in the room, he assumed she was in the parlor talking to Sarah. Joe started down the hallway but didn't hear any voices coming from the parlor. As he stepped down the hall, he glanced into their bedroom and came to an immediate stop.

Joe smiled as he tiptoed into the room then picked up one of the two straight-backed chairs and softly set it beside the head of the bed. He kept his eyes focused on Faith before sitting down.

Faith looked so peaceful that Joe almost decided to postpone the surprise until the evening but quickly realized they might have company.

So, he leaned close and kissed her softly before quietly asking, "Would you care to join me for lunch, Mrs. Beck?"

Faith's eyes grudgingly opened before she blinked twice then smiled and said, "After Sarah left, I thought I'd just put my feet up for a little while. I didn't mean to fall asleep."

"You need your rest, sweetheart. But I imagine you're pretty hungry by now, too. So, I'll go fix lunch and let you know when it's ready. Okay?"

"I need to get out of bed, so I'll come with you."

Joe stood and as he helped Faith to her feet, he said, "But I'll still make lunch."

Faith smiled before they left the bedroom and walked to the kitchen.

After filling two plates with last night's leftovers, Joe set them on the table then pumped two large glasses full of icy cold water before joining Faith.

When they began eating, Joe said, "Jim Pritchard told me that Sarah came to apologize for not asking you to be her witness. Then he somewhat apologized to me for having Sarah's brother Tom act as his witness at her request."

"Sarah didn't really apologize. She simply explained that women in my advanced condition should be kept from public view."

Joe smiled as he said, "I seem to recall women in your advanced state walking alongside their wagons as they rolled across the Great Plains. I guess that's not what Sarah considers public."

Faith laughed then took a bite of cold chicken as Joe said, "Oh, and I dropped off those stones with Mister Faircloth. He quickly identified them as star garnets. When I gave him the big one, I thought he was about to start weeping. He said it was a six-star garnet and he'd never seen one that large before."

Faith swallowed before asking, "Did he say how much they're worth after they're polished?"

"I didn't ask. But he said that the large one would be more than six hundred carats when it was cut and polished and even the next largest would be more than three hundred. But neither of the big ones can be used for jewelry, so I was going to have him make you a necklace from the nicest small stone. Is that alright?"

Faith smiled as she replied, "I don't want some giant rock hanging around my neck, anyway. But wearing a necklace with a garnet you found in our canyon will make it special."

Joe smiled back then began devouring his lunch.

He was making good headway when Faith rolled her eyes and said, "All this talk about the garnets made me forget that you received a letter from Captain Chalmers this morning."

Joe quickly asked, "From Captain Chalmers and not his wife?"

"I'm pretty sure that I didn't misread the return address. It's in the parlor on the side table."

SPRING SURPRISES

Joe hopped to his feet and jogged down the hallway. After entering the parlor, he snatched the envelope from the table, glanced at the return address then hurried back to the kitchen.

He barely sat down before he grabbed a butter knife and sliced open the envelope. He pulled out the two folded sheets and began reading.

My Dear Friend Joe,

I can only imagine your surprise when you receive this letter.

Three weeks ago, I gave my parole and was exchanged for two rebel officers. I just returned last week and am doing well. The second thing I did after I came home was to read the warm letters you and Faith wrote to Alice during my absence. (You can imagine what took precedence.)

After talking to Alice about your letters, I immediately penned this missive to let you know how important you and Faith have become to us.

First you saved my life at Lone Jack and then your letters gave my beloved Alice hope when she needed it so badly. After my capture, she became despondent and began to believe I would never return. Despite many visits by our minister and parents to comfort her, she still despaired. But reading how you and Faith had persevered through much more difficult hardships than I might face while being held as a prisoner restored her faith.

She told me how she would reread those letters each time she felt her hope begin to wane. They sustained her through the months I was held captive and we'll treasure them as a family heirloom.

While I have pledged not to take up arms against the Confederacy, I will be traveling to Washington City where I will join the Army of the Potomac to serve on General Meade's staff. But I may be assigned to General Grant's staff as he was just summoned to take control of all of the Union armies. That news was almost universally hurrahed by the boys in blue. They know he won't quit the field until the final battle is won. I have another two weeks on my furlough before leaving St. Louis and hope I have the pleasure of receiving your reply before I go.

I'm sure that you and Faith are anxiously awaiting Kathleen Maureen's arrival, and after she enters the world, be sure to let us know.

I hope that peace will soon settle upon our nation and then one day we will meet again. Yet even if that blessed event never occurs, we will always cherish you as our dearest friends.

Your brother always,

Mil

P.S. God willing, we hope to have our child before Christmas. With your permission we will christen our baby Faith or Joe. God bless you both and thank you for all you've done for us.

Your sister always,

Alice

   Joe sighed then handed the letter to Faith before he resumed eating at a much slower pace.

When Faith gave him back the letter, she said, "I never realized that our letters mattered so much. I just wrote about our journey and how happy we were when we found our home."

Joe returned the letter to the envelope before saying, "I was surprised as well. But I'm glad that Captain Chalmers is safe. I don't believe Alice will worry now that he'll be on the general's staff."

"She'll still worry, only not as much."

"Do you still worry about me, Mrs. Beck?"

Faith looked into his green eyes as she simply replied, "No."

Joe didn't doubt her answer as he'd seen the truth in her deep blue eyes.

After they finished eating, Joe washed their dishes, then before he left, he gave the letter to Faith to store with the Chalmers' earlier correspondence. He and Faith would write a long reply after supper, and he'd post it tomorrow after he dropped off the full laundry basket.

―――

The three lawmen were reunited twenty minutes later, and Rocky was talking about visiting Placerville when the town's mayor arrived. Mayor Quint Williams was almost six inches shorter than Joe yet outweighed him by at least twenty pounds. He was also the owner and president of The Idaho City Bank.

Sheriff Fulmer stood and asked, "What can we do for you, Mayor?"

"I stopped by to make sure you knew that later this week, the Western Union Company will start building their new telegraph office close to my bank. They hope to have it working by the end of next week."

Tap said, "Yes, sir. We knew it was comin', so is there anything else we can do for ya?"

The mayor looked at Joe and said, "I never did thank you for stopping those two men from robbing my bank, Deputy Beck. I only learned of their intention the day after the shooting."

Joe said, "Rocky and I were just doing our job, Mister Williams."

Quint quickly turned his eyes toward Rocky and said, "Of course, I'm grateful to both of you for preventing the robbery."

Rocky nodded as he replied, "Like Joe said, Mister Williams, we were just doing what the county pays us to do."

"It's money well spent, gentlemen. Before I leave, let me commend each of you for doing such a marvelous job protecting the city and its businesses."

Tap grinned and said, "Thank you, Mayor," then waited until the rotund official left the jail before asking, "Do you feel more like gentlemen now, Deputies?"

Joe and Rocky laughed before Rocky said, "I reckon I gotta add another hundred pounds before I'm a real gentleman."

Rocky's reply inspired more laughter which included the sheriff.

SPRING SURPRISES

When they calmed down, Joe asked, "Did you feel that there was another reason for the mayor's visit? He seemed a bit nervous when he first stepped into the jail."

Tap glanced at Rocky who shrugged before replying, "I didn't notice it, but I was kinda surprised he told us about the telegraph office. He's not our boss, so I reckon it doesn't matter."

Rocky grinned and said, "Unless he's planning to make a town marshal and let him hire a few deputies."

Joe said, "He'd need the town council's approval. And if he even mentioned it during their last meeting, the rumor would have roared through town like wildfire."

Sheriff Fulmer was looking at the closed door as he said, "They're havin' a meetin' tonight. So, maybe he figgered he'd talk to 'em first."

Rocky said, "If he does, then I reckon we'll see him again really early tomorrow morning before we hear about it."

Tap nodded before saying, "It could be a lotta help if they could find some good men to take those jobs, but that ain't likely."

Joe said, "I wouldn't give it another thought. I was probably wrong about his discomfort."

Joe then told them about Captain Chalmers' letter and his belief that President Lincoln would soon place General Grant in command of all of the Union armies. That ignited a long discussion about the war back east that had begun to tilt in the Union's favor.

But as they talked about the battles being waged Joe thought about Mister William's visit. Maybe his slight anxiety had nothing to do with his official duties as mayor. He may have been nervous because he was the owner of The Idaho City Bank. If he had an embezzling employee, he'd have good reason to worry about reporting the crime. Once it came to light, he would certainly lose a good number of his customers to the two competing banks. But if that was the reason for his visit, then it would remain his problem until he reported it.

They had three more visitors that afternoon, and each of their minor complaints were quickly remedied. The last one came from Ira Little who claimed the firewood Abner Jones delivered wasn't seasoned properly. By the time Joe resolved the issue, it was close to sunset, so he didn't bother returning to the jail.

The workers had already gone home for the day when he turned onto his gravel drive and saw the growing barn. The extension already had a roof and two exterior walls. As he stepped closer to the house, Joe thought the barn might be ready for the buggy before noon on Wednesday. And that included a new coat of paint for the entire barn.

Faith was standing at the cookstove when Joe entered, took off his hat and waved it three times overhead before hanging it on a brass hook as Faith laughed.

As Joe unbuttoned his coat, Faith asked, "Does that mean you had a quiet afternoon, Deputy?"

"Yes, ma'am. Did you have any visitors this afternoon?"

"Sister Mary Catherine stopped by a little while ago."

Joe wrapped his arms around his wife, then kissed her before he asked, "Did she tell you anything interesting?"

"She believed I was further along than we thought. I told her that it wasn't possible, but she said I shouldn't be surprised if I went into labor before April arrived."

Joe looked down into her blue eyes and asked, "Doctor Taylor doesn't agree, does he?"

"Not in so many words. But he did say that Kathleen Maureen was going to be a big girl and seemed anxious to leave the comfort of my womb."

Joe kissed her again before releasing her and saying, "I guess we'll just have to be prepared if she surprises us with an early arrival. For my part, I'll have to move buying the cradle to the top of my list."

Faith smiled as Joe stepped beside her to help her with their supper.

———

After dinner, they spent almost an hour writing their letters to the Chalmers before heading to the parlor. Joe added four seasoned logs to the fire before he joined Faith on the couch.

Joe had Faith tucked under his arm when he asked, "Did Sarah seem excited when she talked to you about her wedding this morning?"

"She seemed happy but wasn't gushing. Why did you ask?"

"I was just curious."

"Now that you mentioned it, I find it interesting, too."

"Speaking of interesting, the mayor stopped by this afternoon. He told us about the telegraph coming, then…"

Joe added his speculation about the real reason for the mayor's visit which inspired a long discussion about their own bank account in The Landsman Bank.

Forty minutes later, when Faith tried to stifle a yawn, Joe slid his arm from her shoulders, stood and helped her to he feet. She didn't protest as they walked to their bedroom and prepared for bed.

Faith was already sleeping when Joe slid beneath the covers and kissed her softly on her forehead.

SPRING SURPRISES

CHAPTER 9

Over the next two days, there were no significant events in Idaho City or the rest of Boise County.

Tuesday morning, Joe dropped off the laundry basket, posted the letter to the Chalmers and remembered to buy a cradle which met Faith's approval. On Wednesday afternoon, after giving Faith a ride in their buggy, Joe was able to store it in their expanded barn. While Bernie didn't express any gratitude for his private stall, Porch seemed quite pleased with the larger accommodations.

Thursday morning followed the same, routine pattern, but everything changed early that afternoon.

Rocky had just returned from lunch and taken his seat when the door opened, and one of the earliest and least successful prospectors, Jasper Eason rushed into the jail.

Before any of the lawmen could ask him what he needed, Jasper quickly said, "Some crazy feller just shot Hawk, Sheriff!"

Joe and Rock started walking to the peg wall as Sheriff Fulmer asked, "Tell me what happened, Jasper."

"I was pannin' on my claim by Elder's Run when I heard a gunshot comin' from Hawk's claim. I figgered he was huntin', 'til I heard another shot from a pistol. I climbed up on the ridge betwixt our claims and saw this real big feller pickin' up Hawk's pistol. I was real mad, so I yelled at him. That was kinda stupid 'cause he just turned Hawk's pistol at me and fired. He missed, so I ran down the ridge and rode Alma back here real fast."

Joe asked, "Was he alone, Mister Eason?"

Jasper looked at Joe as he replied, "I only saw that one feller, but I wasn't gonna wait to look around. So, I reckon he coulda had a pal in the trees."

As Joe and Rocky donned their coats, Tap said, "Look out for another shooter, boys."

Joe replied, "I'd be relieved if there was only one more, boss."

Jasper asked, "Do you want me to come along, Joe?"

Joe shook his head and said, "No, sir. I know Elder's Run and have a good idea where to find the shooter."

Jasper growled, "I hope you shoot that no-good bastard."

Joe nodded then waved to Sheriff Fulmer before he and Rocky left the jail. Once on the boardwalk, Rocky turned left to retrieve Barney from Smith's Livery and Joe headed in the opposite direction.

———

Fifteen minutes later, the two deputies were riding north on Main Street when Rocky asked, "Where are we going?"

"Elder's Run is about three miles north, but the prospectors' claims are closer to the eastern mountains. So, we'll turn east before we reach the creek and work our way toward the trees that cover the foothills."

"I'm gonna depend on your eagle eyes to find the shooter before he spots us, Joe."

"That's why I don't want to follow Elder's Run to Jasper's claim. If the shooter is still there, he's probably waiting in ambush after he watched Jasper ride off. When we get about a half a mile from the tree line, we'll dismount, so we're less likely to be spotted."

"I'm really grateful for the Spencer, Joe. Are you okay with you okay with your Sharps? It's only got one shot."

"I like the Sharps better and if I need more than one, I'll use my Henry."

"You're gonna bring 'em both after we're on foot?"

"Yes, sir. Better to have too much firepower than not enough."

Rocky grinned as he said, "You got that right."

Joe nodded then began to create a mental image of the terrain surrounding Elder's Run. He'd only seen the area once before and that was four months ago. But he was still able to get a good idea of what lay ahead as Duke carried him out of Idaho City. His biggest concern wasn't the possibility of another shooter in the trees. It was the ridge that separated Jasper's and Hawk's claims because it was an ideal site for an ambush. So, before they made their approach, he and Rocky would have to split up to cover both sides of the ridge.

He looked at Rocky and said, "When we find that ridge Jasper told us about, we'll stop, and I'll cross over to the other side. After about a minute or so, we'll head to the trees. The good news is that the sun will be at our backs, so the shooter will have a hard time seeing us."

"Or the shooters. But if I see somebody with a rifle, do you want me to aim my Spencer at him then yell at him to drop it?"

"Absolutely. But if I spot a shooter, I won't warn him until he notices me, in case there's one on your side, too."

They added a few final touches to their planned approach before Joe spotted the spine of rocky ground which would soon swell to become the higher ridge. He pointed it out to Rocky before they turned right onto the rugged terrain. The two deputies then followed a circuitous path as they climbed the rise.

The tall pines were almost a mile away and while they could only see the top half of the trees, Joe felt his mind's familiar danger warning.

He waved to Rocky and pulled up. He waited until Rocky nodded before pulling his Henry, then dismounting and sliding his Sharps from its scabbard.

Rocky stepped down, pulled his Spencer into his hands and asked, "Did you see something, Joe?"

Joe shook his head and replied, "No. I just had a sense of danger. I've learned from experience not to ignore it. So, let's tie off our horses and I'll climb over the ridge."

Rocky stared at the distant trees as he asked, "Your head warns you about danger?"

"It sounds strange, but it's why I'm still here."

After tying off their mounts, Rocky watched as Joe climbed the twelve-foot-high ridge and then disappeared from sight. He still couldn't see anyone moving but began to count to a hundred which he thought was close enough to two minutes.

SPRING SURPRISES

Once he was back on level ground, Joe didn't wait two seconds before he began walking. He knew his enhanced vision would give him a much better chance of spotting the shooter and didn't want Rocky to be ambushed.

Joe made good use of all of his expanded senses as he drew closer to Jasper's camp. It probably was his third or fourth claim, but even though he'd found just enough dust to keep him fed, Jasper still dreamed of striking it rich.

Joe was smiling when a momentary tiny glint of reflected sunlight caught his eye. It had appeared beside a large boulder near the top of the ridge that Joe estimated to be about six hundred yards ahead. The flash exposed the shooter's location, but Joe didn't focus on the boulder as he continued walking. The sun's rays probably reflected from the shooter's rifle barrel, which meant he was aiming at Jasper's digs. But even if the shooter had spotted him Joe knew he made a poor target at this range. He wanted to get much closer and give Rocky a chance to locate the possible second shooter.

As he continued his approach, Joe wondered what had motivated the shooter to kill Hawk. He doubted if he was a claim jumper. It was probably just to settle a grudge, but whatever his reason, the man was a murderer and must face justice.

―――

On the other side of the ridge, Rocky reached ninety-two before he cocked his Spencer's hammer and began walking.

He was more than a hundred yards behind Joe when he started, and Joe's longer strides added another three or four inches to the gap with each step. As Rocky carefully made his way along the difficult ground, he kept his eyes focused on the ridge which was crowned with boulders and sharp rocky outcrops.

Even though he'd been in several engagements with the Indians, Rocky began to feel an unexpected sense of anxiety. His heart picked up its pace and he felt beads of sweat appear on his brow. He wiped his forehead with his coat sleeve and forced himself to concentrate on the job.

―――

Less than a minute after the first flash, it appeared again only a little lower. This time, Joe was sure the sunlight had reflected off of a gun barrel. But the confirmation didn't affect his approach as he continued moving closer to the probable ambush. He hoped to be within his Henry's effective range before that rifle barrel swung towards him. By then, Rocky should have spotted a second shooter.

Joe was around four hundred yards from the boulder when a small rock suddenly bounced down the ridge's slope. He froze for a few seconds expecting to hear a distant curse, but not even a quick expletive reached his ears. Joe figured that the shooter must not be worried that the rolling stone would give him away. That belief allowed him to pick up his pace when he resumed his stealthy approach.

On the other side of the ridge, Rocky had settled his nerves as he continued his slower walk toward the tree line. He occasionally checked the trees but focused most of his attention on the likely ambush sites along the top of the ridge. In another hundred yards or so, he should be able to see Hawk's body. If he spotted the shooter, Rocky didn't expect to find him on his heels panning for gold.

Rocky had just stepped across a shallow, foot-wide shallow gully when something on the top of the ridge caught his attention. He tried to find it again, but it was too far away for him to be sure of its location. He estimated it was between two and three hundred yards in front of him, so he concentrated on the possible ambush sites in that area.

The slowly rising ridge soon cast a shadow across the ground in front of Joe, so he took advantage of the added natural camouflage as he made his way toward the shooter. He was getting close to Henry range and could clearly see the last six inches of the shooter's rifle barrel. If it hadn't moved a few times, Joe would suspect the shooter was using it as a decoy. He was both surprised and impressed by the man's patience as he must have been lurking behind that boulder for long time. It was as if he was a hunter waiting for his unexpected prey.

Joe walked for another fifty feet before he set his Sharps down and resumed his approach. He moved quickly but carefully as he watched the protruding rifle barrel. He was about eighty yards out when the barrel suddenly disappeared. Joe thought he'd been spotted, so he froze and quickly brought his Henry level.

Rocky was about a hundred and sixty yards further back and still scanning the top of the ridge when something moved in his peripheral vision. He turned his attention toward the trees just in time to see a muzzle flash and a bloom of gunsmoke. For a heartbeat, Rocky was too stunned to move. Then, just as started to dive for cover, the large slug of lead arrived, and he crumpled to the rocky ground in a heap.

When the loud report reached Joe, he forgot about the disappearing rifle and began to climb the ridge.

He'd only taken two steps when he heard someone shout, "I got him, Stan!"

Joe slowed his rate of climb as he heard Stan yell, "Is he dead, Jake?"

Joe worked his Henry's lever as he neared the top of the ridge and heard Jake loudly reply, "If he ain't, I'll finish him with my pistol."

Joe crawled onto the top of the ridge and spotted Jake trotting down from the trees with a rifle in his right hand. He was still almost two hundred yards away from Rocky, so Joe looked to his left and spotted Stan climbing down the ridge with his unfired rifle.

Joe hoped that Rocky had just been wounded but wasn't about to give Jake a chance to use his pistol. But Stan hadn't fired his rifle, so he was the greater threat.

Joe ignored Jake and set his sights on Stan. He had just reached level ground and was less than fifty yards away when Joe squeezed his trigger. When he felt the repeater's kick, he levered in a fresh cartridge then quickly scrambled to his feet.

Stan had been looking at Rocky, so he never knew what hit him when Joe's .44 punched into the right side of his chest. The bullet nicked a rib before it drilled through his right lung's upper lobe then severed his trachea before lodging in his left lung. He fell face first onto a large, sharp rock then bounced before tumbling onto his back.

Jake had been focused on Rocky as well when Joe fired. But instead of reaching for his pistol, he laughed and yelled, "You missed, Stan!" then turned to see his partner's reaction.

When Joe heard him laugh, he was surprised until Jake's shout reached his ears. When Jake turned around, Joe didn't care that he didn't have a weapon ready to fire. He needed to help Rocky.

SPRING SURPRISES

Jake's eyes exploded into white saucers when he realized that Stan hadn't taken the shot. But before another thought entered his mind, Joe's bullet entered his chest. Jake staggered backwards when the .44 shattered his sternum then continued its downward path and blew apart his abdominal aorta before ending its flight by striking his thoracic spine.

Jake's rifle dropped from his hand as he fell over backwards and managed to fall onto a narrow area of flat ground between two large, jagged rocks. He was still alive when Joe began his scuffling descent down the face of the ridge but died before Joe reached level ground.

Joe glanced at Stan and then Jake before he turned and hurried to help Rocky. He was around a hundred feet away when he heard Rocky moan. He was relieved but didn't slow down.

Before he reached Rocky, he could see blood covering the right side of his head and neck. He was still wearing his hat but noticed a bullet hole in the brim close to the crown. He hoped Jack's bullet had only grazed his ear after making that hole.

Joe took a knee next to Rocky, set his Henry down with its barrel on a rock then lifted Rocky's holey hat brim to examine his wound. He soon found a short gash just above and behind his right ear. The wound was just oozing as the blood coagulated, so Joe knew Rocky was out of danger.

He was about to stand to find something to clean the wound when Rocky's eyes opened just a crack before he said, "I screwed up and got shot, Joe. How bad is it?"

"Not too bad. It's almost stopped bleeding already. You need to stay put while I go check on those two bastards and get something to clean your wound. Okay?"

"I can stand up, Joe."

"You'll probably fall down again if you try. And then you'd probably smack your noggin on a rock and have a worse wound on the other side of your head. Stay put, Corporal. I'll be back shortly."

Rocky was about to protest, but knew Joe was right, so he replied, "Okay. But remember I'm still six years older than you."

Joe popped Rocky on his left shoulder before he stood and said, "Yes, sir," then picked up his Henry and hurried back to Jack's body.

He hadn't recognized either shooter but didn't take time to search their bodies for any signs of identification. He trotted past Jake's body then turned towards Hawk's camp. When he reached the crude lean-to, he snatched a recently washed towel hanging from a sagging rope and headed to the nearby stream.

Joe dipped the towel into the icy water then turned back to tend to Rocky's wound. When he spotted his fellow deputy, Joe wasn't surprised to find him sitting up and examining the bullet hole in his hat. He probably tried to stand but when the world began to spin, he thought better of it.

Rocky turned his eyes away from his damaged hat when Joe was a few feet away and asked, "Did you know those bastards?"

Joe sat on his heels next to Rocky and replied, "Nope. I didn't find Hawk's body, either. I'm guessing that after they saw Jasper ride away, they slid it into the trees with their horses. Let's get that wound cleaned up, and I'll get you back to town."

SPRING SURPRISES

As Joe began to gently wipe away the blood, Rocky said, "Get me on Barney and I'll ride back on my own. I'll tell Tap what happened, so he can send some help."

"Only if you aren't so wobbly."

After cleaning off most of the dried blood, Joe wrapped the damp towel around Rocky's head, picked up his Spencer then helped him to his feet. Once he was standing, Joe firmly gripped Rocky's elbow and they began walking to their horses.

They'd gone around fifty yards when Rocky said, "I think I can walk on my own now, Joe."

"Alright. But if you start to tip over, I'm going to grab hold much harder and not let go until you're mounted."

Rocky nodded, said, "Fair enough," then Joe released his grip.

Joe walked closely alongside as Rocky unsteadily made his way down the rocky decline toward their horses. It took them more than ten minutes to reach Duke and Barney, but by then Rocky was moving more steadily. As Rocky untied his gelding's reins, Joe slid his Spencer into its scabbard then watched as Rocky took hold of his saddle horn and set his boot into the stirrup.

Rocky was able to get mounted without assistance, so once he was in his saddle, Joe looked up and said, "Have Jasper come out here to see if he can identify either of them. Tell him the tall one's name was Stan and the short one who shot you was named Jake."

Rocky nodded then asked, "Are they both dead?"

"I'm sure that Stan is no longer with us, but if Jake's still alive, he won't be breathing much longer."

Rocky growled, "Make sure he ain't," then wheeled Barney around and rode away.

Joe watched him for a few seconds to make sure he was steady in the saddle before he untied Duke and mounted. He walked him to the spot where Rocky had fallen and dismounted. He picked up his Henry, returned it to its scabbard then snatched Rocky's hat from the ground and remounted.

Joe stepped down again when he was close to Jake's body. He tied off Duke, approached the carcass and sat on his heels before searching his pockets for information. He found nothing worthwhile, so he picked up the rifle he'd used to shoot Rocky and looked it over. It was a Springfield muzzle loader but offered no clues to its owner's identity. He laid it on Jake's chest before returning to Duke.

After rolling Stan's body onto his back, he laid the unfired Springfield rifle on his chest. Now he had to find Hawk's body.

As he rode toward the trees, his stallion suddenly whickered and turned his eyes slightly to the right, so Joe let Duke follow his nose.

Just before he reached the pines, Joe heard a horse whinny and pulled up. He dismounted and tied Duke to a stout branch before entering the forest. Less than a minute later, he spotted two saddled horses and two mules, but didn't see Hawk's body. One of the mules was being used as a pack animal while the other was bareback, so Joe assumed the pack mule belonged to Stan and Jake and the other one was Hawk's animal. Now he had to find where the killers left Hawk's body.

SPRING SURPRISES

Joe turned left and started on a wide looping path to begin his search. As he passed between the thick tree trunks, he wondered what had motivated Stan and Jake to murder Hawk Owens. While he may never know their reason, their purpose for setting up the ambush was obvious. They hadn't planned on being spotted by Jasper Eason. When he made his escape, they expected him to return with a lawman. They had to cover both sides of the ridge, so Stan was guarding Jasper's campsite and Jake was watching Hawk's.

Joe was still thinking about the ambush when he found Hawk's body. It didn't take long to find the site of the fatal wound. The massive .56 caliber Mini ball had struck him in the back of the neck just above his shoulders. But Joe was looking at the front of his throat where there was a much larger, more grotesque exit wound.

Joe sighed then left the body in place before walking back to the animals. The mules were tied to trail ropes, so he released the horses and led them back to Hawk's body. After securing the horses' reins, he lifted Hawk's stiffening corpse from the ground and managed to drape it over his mule. He loosely tied it down before leading the two horses out of trees.

When he returned to the bright afternoon sunlight, he left Duke in place and led the four animals back to Hawk's camp. When he reached the shabby shelter, Joe tied off the horses then looked southwest for riders before trotting back to Duke.

He was soon riding his stallion back to the campsite when he spotted two riders heading towards him. By the time he dismounted, he had identified Tap and Jasper. Joe tied off Duke and waited for them to arrive.

When they pulled up and stepped down, Tap said, "Rocky told me what happened before he went off to Doc Wallace to get his head fixed up. He said they were both dead, but did you find out anything else about 'em?"

"Not yet, but I haven't had time to go through their gear. All I know is the big one was called Stan and the other one went by Jake. I was hoping Jasper might know who they were."

Jasper said, "When we rode by, I looked at 'em but never saw 'em before."

Joe shrugged and said, "I guess it doesn't matter. But I don't think they were claim jumpers, Jasper. I have a feeling that Stan had a grudge against Hawk he wanted to settle."

Tap said, "I reckon we oughta get those two hung over their saddles and take 'em back to town. We can go through their bags after we drop 'em off at Moran's."

Joe nodded before they began the gruesome task.

Ninety minutes later, Joe and Tap arrived at Moran's Mortuary and left the three cadavers with the mortician. Before they mounted, they spent a few minutes rummaging through the shooters' saddlebags and packs. When they finished their exploration, the two dead men were still just Stan and Jake. After dropping off the four animals at Frank Smith's livery, they headed back to the jail.

Rocky was sitting behind the front desk when they entered the office, and as Joe handed him his wounded hat, Tap asked, "What did the doc tell ya?"

"After he sewed me up, he said I was lucky 'cause if it was another half inch closer, I woulda lost half my head. I didn't bother telling him I would have been a lot luckier if it was a half an inch the other way."

Tap snickered then asked, "Are you still dizzy?"

Rocky hesitated before replying, "Just a little if I move my head too fast. But I'm getting better."

Sheriff Fulmer nodded and looked at Joe.

Before Tap could ask, Joe quickly said, "I'll take the walk tonight, boss."

As the sheriff nodded, Rocky exhaled then said, "I walked right into that ambush, Tap. I wasn't paying any attention to the trees after I thought I saw something move behind the rocks on the ridge."

Sheriff Fulmer grinned as he said, "Live and learn, Rocky. Live and learn."

Joe leaned back lifting the chair's front feet off the floor before he said, "You should keep one of those horses for a spare, Rocky. The brown mare was a pretty handsome lady."

Rocky looked at Tap who said, "You can take your pick tomorrow, Rocky. Why don't you two get outta here? I'll lock up shortly."

Joe dropped his chair onto all four feet before he stood, pulled on his hat and said, "I'm not going to argue, boss," then headed for the door.

He was mounting Duke when Rocky exited the jail and saluted him before Joe waved then turned his stallion and rode north along Main Street.

After Joe unsaddled Duke, he filled his oat bin then took a couple of minutes visiting Bernie, Porch, and the mares before leaving the barn with his Henry.

When he entered the kitchen, Faith's voice echoed from the hallway, "We're in the parlor, Joe."

Joe loudly replied, "I'll be there shortly, sweetheart," then leaned the Henry against the wall.

After hanging his hat, coat and gunbelt he headed down the hallway and found Faith sitting on the couch with Sister M.C. Despite the nun's close proximity, Joe stepped close to his wife and gave her a noticeably unchaste kiss before taking a seat on the nearest chair.

Faith quickly asked, "Did you and Rocky find the shooter?"

Joe nodded as he replied, "We did, but he also had a partner. They were waiting in ambush, and the one we didn't know about wounded Rocky. The bullet just grazed the right side of his head, and he's already back at the office. But I'll be doing the whiskey walk tonight because he's still out of sorts."

Faith sighed then asked, "Did you get hurt?"

"No, ma'am. Neither of them knew I was even there before I started shooting. We left them at Moran's Mortuary along with Hawk Owens."

Sister Mary Catherine exclaimed, "*You killed them without even giving them a warning?*"

Faith turned to look at the nun as Joe replied, "Except for the ones who were already preparing to shoot me, this was the first time I've shot someone without warning, Sister. In this situation, I had no choice. Rocky was down, and the second shooter was on his way to finish him off with his pistol. I had to stop him. but I was in the middle of the two shooters. If I warned them, I'd be caught in a crossfire and Rocky and I would be dead."

Sister Mary Catherine contritely said, "I'm sorry, Joe. I didn't intend for my question to sound accusatory."

"That's alright, Sister. It would be difficult for anyone to understand who wasn't there."

Faith said, "Tell us what happened, Joe."

Joe was convinced he hadn't been wrong in his decision to shoot without warning but still felt ashamed for doing it. So, as Joe told the story, he tried to keep his narration free of even a hint of emotion.

As he spoke, Faith noticed there was something different in his demeanor. She'd listened to him recount each one of his many gunfights, most of them more than once. But now, for the first time, his voice sounded almost apologetic. She knew why and hoped he would talk about it when they were alone.

When Joe finished, Sister M.C. stood, smiled at Faith and said, "I must rejoin my sisters now, but I'll visit you again tomorrow, Faith."

Then she turned to Joe before saying, "You're a good man and didn't do anything wrong, Joe."

Joe stood, said, "Thank you, Sister," then escorted the nun to the foyer and opened the door.

After she'd gone, Joe returned to the parlor and joined Faith on the couch. As soon as he sat down, he slipped his hand behind her neck then pulled her close.

Faith rested her blonde head on his right shoulder and softly asked, "Do you feel guilty for having to shoot those men without a warning?"

Joe hesitated before looking at her and answering, "You know me so well that I should have expected that question. I really believe that I had no other choice, but I do have a sense of shame for what I had to do. It's the only time I've ever pulled my trigger when I couldn't see the other man's eyes."

"Is there anything I can say or do to make your guilt go away?"

"No. I'll just have to live with it and hope it fades away on its own."

After a short pause, Joe said, "I'm only seventeen years old and I've already killed so many men that I'm beginning to lose count. It's as if I'm becoming the Angel of Death."

Faith kissed him on the cheek before saying, "You are nothing of the sort, Deputy Sheriff Joe Beck. If you are an angel at all, you're the Angel of Life. Think of all the good folks' lives you've saved, and not just by stopping bad men. Innocent souls like little Lizzy Dooley and Hanepi Wi."

Joe sighed before saying, "I know. But I often wonder why I seem to find myself in so many of these dangerous situations. It's almost as if I'm a fictional character created by a misguided writer who wants to thrill his readers with one shootout after another."

"Did you want to start farming the clearing in our canyon?"

SPRING SURPRISES

Joe smiled as he replied, "Even if I wanted to go back to farming, which I don't, our canyon would probably be visited by outlaws wanting to steal our star garnets."

"When do you think Mister Faircloth will finish cutting and polishing them?"

"I didn't ask, but I imagine it would take at least a week or so. I'll stop by his shop sometime next week and ask. But now, I'm going to start preparing our supper."

Faith laughed then said, "Really? I don't trust your cooking ability that much, but I'll gratefully accept your assistance."

Joe stood and helped his front-loaded wife to her feet before they walked to the kitchen hand-in-hand.

Thursday's saloon stroll was like most other weeknight walks with four barroom visits without any serious incidents. It took Joe longer than usual as each of his normally short appearances was extended when he was asked about the shootout.

As Joe headed home, he looked up and didn't see any stars on the western half of the night sky. He suspected that Mother Nature was about to remind them that it was still winter.

When Joe left the house the next morning, there was already four inches of heavy, wet snow on the ground and the thick, falling curtain of large flakes limited his vision to less than fifty feet. But there was almost no wind, and the temperatures were barely below freezing, so it was almost a pleasant reminder of the winter season.

He was the first one in the office and after stomping the accumulated snow from his boots, he removed his outerwear then walked to the heat stove to start a fire.

Sheriff Fulmer arrived ten minutes later and after mimicking Joe's arrival sequence, he took a seat in front of the desk and said, "I reckon we'll get more'n a foot of the stuff before we see the sun again, Joe. But that oughta keep things quiet."

Joe nodded then said, "It's a lot better than those blizzards we had earlier, but it'll add a lot of heavy drifts on the mountains."

Tap grinned and said, "At least Eddie Pascal won't be droppin' an avalanche on you again."

"He tried to bury me with one, but he missed, boss. Did Rocky want one of those horses for a spare?"

"I think so. We'll go down to Smith's and look at 'em when he shows up."

On cue, Rocky entered the jail and as he pounded his boots on the floor, Tap stood and said, "Let's go look at those horses, Rocky."

"Okay. I gotta buy a new hat, too."

Joe said, "You should keep your old one as a reminder, Rocky. It's a good conversation piece, too. Just like that .44 in my porch step."

Rocky pulled off his hat, stuck his gloved finger through the big hole and said, "I reckon it would, but I'm still gonna buy a new one."

After the sheriff was ready to confront the cold again, he and Rocky left Joe to mind the store. As soon as the door closed, Joe pulled the logbook from the desk drawer and entered yesterday's event. Less than a minute later, he returned the ledger and took four sheets of blank paper to write his report.

Like all of his written reports, it was concise and accurate. An official report was no place for perceptions or emotion. It took him almost thirty minutes before he set the pen down and returned the blank page to the flat box. Joe leaned back in the chair and stared through the frosty window wondering what was taking Rocky so long. There were only two possible choices: the brown mare or the tan roan gelding. The gelding was much older, so Rocky should have made his selection as soon as he and Tap entered the barn.

He had his answer just two minutes later when Tap and Rocky returned. They'd spent most of the time searching the packs before leaving them with Frank Smith for disposal. The county would collect the sale price of the roan gelding, his tack and the pack mule minus Frank's fees. Those fees including giving the mare a new set of shoes.

The snow began letting up by mid-afternoon and finally stopped giving the sun enough time to make brief appearance.

As Joe waded through the deep snow on his way home, he noticed that despite the weather, the construction of the new Western Union office had continued. He suspected the wires would reach Idaho City early next week and wondered if they'd continue on to Centreville and Placerville.

While the snow hadn't delayed the arrival of the telegraph, it would require a postponement of their buggy ride to the canyon. If Faith wasn't so far along, he'd at least consider making the drive. But he wasn't about to risk Faith and Kathleen Maureen just to give her a tour.

As they shared dinner, Joe told Faith about the delay and was a bit surprised when she smiled and said, "One look outside and I knew we'd have to reschedule it for next Sunday. Even if the snow all melted by tomorrow, the mud would probably be just as deep and a lot messier."

"With any kind of luck, the snow will be gone, and the ground will be dry by next Sunday."

Faith took a large bite of her buttered biscuit as Joe said, "It looks like the telegraph office will be operating within a week or so. It'll be a welcome improvement to the town."

Faith swallowed then smiled and said, "Don't hold your breath waiting for a railroad to show up."

"I don't think we'll ever see a railroad in Idaho City. Once the gold runs out, folks will start leaving. And by the time someone decides to lay tracks across Idaho Territory, there won't be any reason to send a spur here."

Faith's eyebrows rose slightly before she asked, "Do you believe Idaho City will become a ghost town?"

SPRING SURPRISES

"Maybe not a true ghost town because of the timber and other natural resources, but I imagine in ten years or so, there won't be a thousand people living here."

"We won't be leaving, will we?"

"Not unless something makes us decide to pull up roots. But that's a long way off, Faith. And before the population begins to decline, we'll be adding one to the town's census."

Faith smiled as she rubbed her rounded bump and said, "In ten years, maybe we'll add five or six more."

"We have the room, my love."

Faith was about to reach for her cup of coffee when her hidden companion decided to give her a swift kick, almost as a warning that she didn't want to share her room with any siblings.

When she twitched her shoulders, Joe asked, "Katie isn't planning to show up this early, is she?"

"No. She just wanted to remind me that she would be our firstborn and more important than her brothers or sisters."

"But not nearly as important as her mama."

Faith took his hand and avoided the expected reply of 'or her papa' and said, "Or his mama. You could still be wrong, Joe."

"We'll see if I am in a few more days, sweetheart."

"I wish it was only a few more days."

Joe smiled and said, "You have to visit the canyon first."

Faith nodded then resumed cleaning her plate. She was eating more than Joe was now and never seemed to be satisfied, or more accurately, Kathleen Maureen was never satisfied.

CHAPTER 10

The snow slowly began melting Saturday morning, creating an almost impassable mixture of snow, slush and mud. Even horses could barely make their way down Main Street. And those that did turned the surface into an ugly, snowy version of a well-populated prairie dog village.

Joe was still the first one to enter the jail, but even he was delayed after clearing the flagstone path to the privy. After building a fire in the heat stove, he had just settled in behind the desk when Sheriff Fulmer arrived.

Rocky showed up a few minutes later, and soon, the three lawmen were gossiping like a trio of lonely spinsters.

They shared rumors, whispers and real news over the next two hours without interruption before Tap decided to call it a day.

———

When Joe returned home an hour before noon, he found Faith in the parlor with Sister Mary Catherine.

As he sat down, Faith asked, "I'm not complaining, mind you, but why are you home so early?"

"The mess outside is not only delaying our visit to our canyon, but it seems to be preventing any mischief. We were caught up on paperwork, so Tap closed the office."

Sister Mary Catherine said, "I noticed the construction work on your barn is finished. I think they did a very good job overall, but they should have used screws rather than nails on the window bracing."

Joe smiled and said, "I know you're married to a carpenter, Sister, but I didn't think you were one as well."

The nun laughed before saying, "My father was a carpenter as well and as I had no brothers, I helped him in his shop."

Joe asked, "Where did your father have his carpentry shop?"

Sister M.C.'s answer initiated a long discussion about their families. Joe and Faith learned that her family name was Ruiz, and she grew up in Colorado. After she took her vows, she was trained as a nurse before her order sent her to San Francisco. She stayed there for three years before she and the other five nuns were chosen to join Father Burns in Idaho City. What surprised them most was when she told them she was twenty-seven years old. Neither Joe nor Faith would have guessed her to be older than twenty-one.

After the conversation ended, Sister Mary Catherine returned to the convent.

Twenty minutes later, Joe and Faith were sitting at the kitchen table having lunch when Faith said, "I was surprised when Sister Mary Catherine said she was twenty-seven."

Joe replied, "I was more surprised when she told us she worked in her father's carpentry shop. I just can't picture Sister M.C. hammering a nail or sawing a board."

SPRING SURPRISES

Faith smiled as she said, "It is difficult to imagine, but she seems happy with her chosen vocation, just as you are with yours."

"At least she didn't offer to fix our damaged porch step."

"Then you'd better do the repair before she does."

Joe grinned before he took a bite of his leftover stew but mentally added the job to his list of things he'd need to do when spring arrived.

―――

While the spring equinox wouldn't happen for another week, Sunday was blessed with very spring-like weather, and not early spring, either. The temperature was above fifty degrees by mid-morning and the deep snow that seemed as if it would last until June was almost gone by mid-afternoon. There were still drifts in the shadows and on the mountains, but the flat ground that surrounded Idaho City had been turned into a swamp. It made travel extremely difficult, but at least it wasn't populated by mosquitoes, alligators or snapping turtles.

The cycle of warm days and freezing nights continued for the rest of the week, but by Wednesday the sun had converted the mud back into plain old dirt. Business and street traffic returned to normal, and while the townsfolk enjoyed the nice weather, they universally expected winter to give them a dying gasp before submitting to the new season.

Early Wednesday afternoon, the jail had a surprise visitor.

A tall, bearded man with a fierce demeanor entered the office and Tap asked, "What can I do for ya, Elrod?"

Elrod Jefferson closed the door but didn't remove his hat as he replied, "Nothin'. I just wanted to let you know that Mayor Thompson appointed me the new town marshal."

Sheriff Fulmer kept a poker face as he said, "Congratulations."

Elrod then opened his coat to expose the badge on his vest, but Joe suspected he really meant to impress them with the two-gun rig at his waist.

Marshal Jefferson let gravity close his coat before saying, "I got two deputies, so we'll handle any trouble in town, Sheriff."

Tap nodded and said, "See that you do, Elrod."

Elrod didn't smile before he turned and left the jail.

Joe watched through the window as Marshal Jefferson mount and ride away before Tap said, "I reckon we're gonna need two more deputies pretty quick."

Joe said, "I never met him before, but I got the impression he's one of those men who use the badge as a weapon. The kind you don't want to hire, boss."

"You ain't wrong, Joe. Elrod was trouble before he left town more'n a year ago. I knew he headed to Placerville but haven't seen him since. I reckon his deputies are just like him, too."

Rocky asked, "Are we still going to head over there one of these days, Tap? I haven't even seen the town."

"I want to meet his deputies, so maybe I'll give you a tour next week."

Rocky grinned as he said, "Maybe he hired Eddie Pascal."

SPRING SURPRISES

Rocky's suggestion lightened the mood, but Joe suspected the new town marshal would not only fail to keep the peace in Placerville but create even more trouble.

On Thursday, the crew stringing wires for Western Union crew arrived and so did two telegraphers. By Friday morning, there were dozens of citizens lining up to send messages.

When Joe left the jail just before noon, he passed the new telegraph office and The Idaho City Bank before he entered Mister Faircloth's jewelry shop.

Mrs. Faircloth was at the counter and as soon as Joe entered, she turned and loudly said, "George, Joe Beck is here."

Joe stepped to the counter and said, "Good morning, Mrs. Faircloth."

Martha Faircloth smiled as she replied, "Good day to you, Joe. George will be out shortly. He's still working on your smaller star garnets."

Joe was about to ask about the large two stones when Mister Faircloth pushed aside the curtain and stepped out of his workshop.

He wore a giant grin as he shook Joe's hand and said, "I was hoping you'd stop by, Joe. Come into the back room and I'll show you the stones I've already finished."

Joe smiled then stepped around the short counter and followed the jeweler into his workshop.

After Mister Faircloth sat on his tall stool, he slowly slid a blue velvet cloth from his work table exposing the five cut, polished garnets and just watched Joe's reaction.

Despite the dim light, the finished stones still stunned Joe and made him wonder how much more impressive they would be in the sunlight.

He looked at Mister Faircloth and said, "You've taken pretty stones and transformed them into stars, George."

George smiled as he replied, "I'm happy that you're pleased with my work, Joe. I spent more time on the largest one than I did on the other four, but I think it was worth the effort. Don't you?"

Joe nodded then asked, "May I hold it in my hand?"

"Of course, you may. They're still yours, Joe."

Joe took a breath and reverently picked up the largest garnet and held it inches from his dark green eyes. There was enough light in the room to reveal the three lines that formed the six-pointed star against the deep maroon background. He studied the big stone for almost a minute before setting it down and taking the second largest garnet from the table. It was also a six-star garnet, and he wondered if they were as rare as Mister Faircloth had claimed.

After returning it to the tabletop, he selected one of the smaller garnets and found it to be one of the more common four-star variety of garnets as was each of the other three polished stones.

When Joe set the last cut stone back onto the table, he said "I know the small ones aren't very valuable, but they're still just as beautiful."

SPRING SURPRISES

Mister Faircloth nodded as he said, "I agree with you, Joe. But the last one will be prettier than the other small stone when I'm finished. It's a six-star garnet, and I saved it for last because you said you wanted to have one mounted in a necklace for Faith."

Joe grinned and said, "Thank you for remembering."

George looked at Joe and said, "You continue to surprise me, Joe. I'm almost finished, yet you still haven't asked about their value. Before I give you my appraisal, what do you intend to do with the five I've already cut and polished?"

Joe glanced at the polished garnets then replied, "I only had plans for the one you haven't polished. Do you want to sell the others?"

George smiled and said, "I wish I could keep the large one, but I'll be proud to offer them for sale in my shop. Now the small stones are only worth about ten dollars each, but the second largest garnet is valued at three hundred dollars."

The jeweler paused for effect before saying, "The big one will command a price of seven hundred dollars."

Despite Mister Faircloth's earlier weight estimate, Joe was still shaken when he learned the big gemstone's value. He didn't say anything but stared at the large garnet.

George expected Joe's stunned reaction and let it sink in for another fifteen seconds before he said, "If you agree, I'll take a five percent commission on each sale. As part of the bargain, I'll make Faith's necklace at no charge."

Joe blinked then smiled and shook Mister Faircloth's hand as he said, "I think I'm getting the better part of the deal, George."

"And I believe that I'm the winner in our arrangement, Joe. I'll have the necklace done by Monday."

"Thank you, Mister Faircloth."

As Joe prepared to leave, George said, "I won't let anyone know the source of the stones, but if you find any more of them, please don't hesitate to bring them to me."

Joe saluted him, said, "I'll do that, sir," then passed through the curtain, smiled at Mrs. Faircloth as he passed by the counter and soon left the small shop.

As he headed home for lunch, Joe decided to wait until he picked up the necklace on Monday before telling Faith the value of the other stones unless she asked. It wasn't until he turned down his graveled drive that he remembered that Monday was also Jim and Sarah's wedding day. He hadn't talked to Jim since they'd talked in Pritchard's Butcher Shop and Greengrocery, and Sarah hadn't visited Faith after telling her about the wedding. For all he and Faith knew, they could have decided to take a ship and get married in London.

When he entered the kitchen, he smiled when he found Faith sitting at the table munching on one of his sour pickles.

He took off his hat and said, "I thought my pickles were too sour for your taste, Mrs. Beck."

Faith held out the half-eaten ex-cucumber, smiled and said, "I think it was our child who had the sudden urge for one. Did anything exciting happen this morning?"

Joe hung his coat as he replied, "The only interesting news didn't involve the sheriff's office. The Western Union office opened this morning and folks were lining up to send messages."

"I imagine most of them just wanted to see if it really worked."

Joe walked to the breadbox, took out a loaf of bread and set it on the cutting board before he said "You're probably right, ma'am. On my way home, I stopped at Mister Faircloth's jewelry shop."

Faith had just taken a big bite of the pickle, so she just raised her eyebrows as she chewed.

Joe picked up a knife then smiled and said, "He had cut and polished five of the six, including the two largest garnets. I was awed when I saw them, especially the big one."

Faith swallowed and as her eyes watered, she asked, "Did you bring them with you?"

"No. I supposed I should have, but I was too distracted. I'll borrow them this afternoon so I can show you."

"Why do you have to borrow them?"

Joe cringed slightly before he replied, "I suppose I should have asked you before accepting Mister Faircloth's offer to sell them. Do you want to keep them?"

Faith thought about it for a few seconds before answering, "I guess there's nothing we can do with them. Besides, we might find more of them when we visit our canyon on Sunday."

Joe smiled then began cutting the bread when Faith asked, "Did he tell you how much they were worth?"

"Yes, ma'am. He said the small stones are worth about ten dollars each because they're a more common type of garnet. But both of the large ones were rare because of the three reflected lines. He said they're called a six-star garnets, and the second largest one is worth around three hundred dollars, but the biggest one is valued at seven hundred dollars."

Faith's big blue eyes grew even bigger as she stared at her husband and quietly said, "That's over a thousand dollars, Joe."

Joe continued cutting the bread as he replied, "I know. It's a bit scary, isn't it? But Mister Faircloth isn't going to tell anyone how he got them, so we don't have to worry about a hoard of greedy men descending on our canyon."

"I hope he keeps his word."

"I'm sure he will, Now, let's get some bland food into your tummy before that pickle turns your stomach sour."

Faith smiled as she watched Joe make their lunch. While she was surprised and impressed with the value of the garnets, she almost wished Joe hadn't found them. Even if Mister Faircloth kept his promise, she suspected it wouldn't be long before the secret was discovered. Then their canyon could turn into a killing field.

As they ate, they talked about that possibility, and Joe shared Faith's concerns. But they agreed that even if their peaceful canyon was invaded, Joe wouldn't enforce their ownership. It simply wasn't worth shooting anyone over rocks regardless of their value.

After resolving the issue, they discussed Sunday's visit to their canyon before moving onto Jim and Sarah's wedding.

———

SPRING SURPRISES

When Joe entered the jail forty minutes later, he interrupted a conversation Mayor Williams was having with Sheriff Fulmer.

As Joe hung his hat, the mayor said, "I hope you'll keep this confidential, Sheriff."

Tap replied, "I'll do the best I can, Mayor."

The mayor turned and nodded to Joe as he walked by before leaving the jail.

Joe was hanging his coat when the door slammed, so he waited until he took a chair in front of the desk before he asked, "Was it the mayor or the banker who wanted to keep his news confidential?"

"It's the banker's problem. His bookkeeper thought he found a counterfeit five-dollar note around two weeks ago. Quint told him it was just a poorly printed bill but began checkin' his other banknotes. He found another one the day he paid us his visit but decided to hold off 'cause he didn't find any more. Well, he just found two more of 'em and wants us to find out who's makin' em."

"Where does he get his banknotes printed?"

"Some company in San Francisco, and I reckon that's where those counterfeiters are workin'. But we ain't goin' all the way to California to find 'em. But seein' how they're all Bank of Idaho City notes, I figure somebody's got a stash of that funny money somewhere local. We'll just keep our eyes open."

"Is he getting another shipment of currency anytime soon?"

"I didn't get a chance to ask, but he's gonna send 'em a telegram to have 'em change the way they look. That ain't gonna help him much, though."

"Unless there are only a few of them in the county. I can understand why he'd want to keep it quiet, though. If word got out that his banknotes might be counterfeit, a lot of the businesses wouldn't take them. It might be worse than having a really successful embezzler."

Tap snickered and was about to comment when Rocky returned and was soon briefed on the problem.

———

Joe swung by the jewelry shop on the way home and borrowed the largest garnet. The sun was low in the sky when he entered the kitchen, so after taking off his hat, he escorted Faith to the parlor with its southwest-facing windows.

He sat beside her on the couch and took the polished garnet from his coat pocket and handed it to her.

Faith was already awed by the beautiful gemstone before she extended it into the sunbeams.

She gasped before she whispered, "This is even more beautiful than I imagined, Joe. I can't believe this is the same stone you found in our canyon. It's extraordinary."

"Are you going to change your mind about selling it, Faith?"

Faith shook her head as she replied, "No. It's too big to be useful as jewelry, and I wouldn't want to have it just sitting on a shelf gathering dust."

SPRING SURPRISES

Joe studied her face as she gazed at the enormous violet garnet and hoped she'd be as happy with the smaller version she'd soon be wearing. But even as he thought about the necklace, he wondered if he should save another one for Kathleen Maureen. When they visited the canyon on Sunday, maybe he'd find another small six-star garnet to save for their daughter.

Saturday was the last day of winter, but the best the cold season could manage was a freezing drizzle. But by the time Joe harnessed Porch to the buggy Sunday afternoon, the icy crust had already melted leaving just a thin layer of mud.

Twenty minutes after leaving their home, Joe turned the buggy into the canyon and guided Porch alongside the stream.

Faith was anxious to see the clearing and the small pool but was even more pleased to be out of the house.

When they suddenly emerged from the trees, Faith smiled at Joe and said, "It was worth the wait. It's like a world unto itself."

"It is, isn't it? I'm disappointed the herd of white-tailed deer wasn't grazing, but I'll show you the eagles' nest when we're closer. You can already see the water streaming down the mountainside from here. When we're near the pool, you'll see the small waterfalls as the stream cascades over the rocks. The biggest one is already visible above the pool, but it's only about four feet high."

"I think it's perfect."

Joe smiled said, "I think you are too, my love," then leaned over and kissed her as the buggy rocked and rolled across the uneven ground.

Faith patted her bulging coat as she said, "Really, Mister Beck?"

"I never lie, Faith Hope Charity Virtue Goodchild Beck."

Faith laughed as she looked at the pool then followed the streaming water up the side of the mountain until she reached the thick blankets of brilliant white snow.

Joe pulled the buggy to a stop beside the stream about ten feet before the pool before he set the handbrake. Porch dipped his muzzle into the frigid water before Joe hopped out of the buggy then assisted Faith as she stepped to the ground.

The tour began with Joe pointing out the eagles' nest but neither of the two raptors were visible. Not surprisingly, Faith asked him where he'd found the big garnet, so Joe led her to the spot.

Faith studied the myriad stones beneath the clear water and asked, "Do you see any more of them?"

"Nope. That big one was pretty easy to spot, but I needed to get much closer to find the others."

Faith smiled and said, "I won't be getting on my hands and knees to search, if you don't mind. But I can watch while you look for more of them."

"I'll take a few minutes to see if I can find another one but not much longer. We'll have a lot more time during the summer when we can show our canyon to Kathleen Maureen."

SPRING SURPRISES

Faith nodded as Joe dropped to his knees and began exploring. As she watched him, Faith suddenly felt that recently imprisoned sense of doom trying to escape. She didn't know why it had chosen this moment to whisper its return but hoped it was only momentary.

She was still wrestling with the subtle yet troubling thought when Joe exclaimed, "I found one, Faith!"

Joe's excitement shoved her unexpected, brief concerns aside before he stood and showed her the small stone.

He placed in onto the palm of her hand and said, "It's about the same size as the other small ones."

Faith examined it in the bright afternoon sunlight and said, "It's still pretty, though. Are you going to give it to Mister Faircloth even though it's not worth very much?"

"Maybe I'll wait until I find some larger ones. That's assuming I find any of them."

Faith handed the garnet back before she asked, "Do you want to continue searching?"

"Just for a few more minutes, then we'll continue the tour."

"Alright."

As Joe stepped toward the stream, Faith looked up at the eagles' nest but still didn't see the enormous birds. She was still watching when she caught movement out of the corner of her eye and thought the deer had decided to graze in the clearing after all. But when she turned her eyes to the left, she didn't see any deer. Instead, she saw a large black bear loping across the edge of the clearing.

She didn't move a muscle as she loudly said, "Joe, there's a big bear on the other side of the clearing."

Joe quickly hopped to his feet and locked his eyes on the bear as he hurried back to Faith. He knew it probably just left hibernation and would be hungry. Unfortunately, he and Faith were the only prey in the clearing. He had his Henry behind the buggy's seat but still hoped that he wouldn't have to shoot the bear.

He reached Faith and said, "Let's walk to the buggy and after I get my Henry, I want you to get inside, take the reins and start heading toward the road. Okay?"

As they headed to the buggy, she asked, "What about you?"

"I'll be walking behind you. No arguments, Mrs. Beck."

Faith knew he was right, so she remained silent as he slid his Henry from behind the seat then helped her climb into the buggy. She took the reins, released the handbrake then turned Porch to the west and gave the reins a quick snap.

As he stepped quickly behind the buggy, Joe was surprised but grateful that the gelding hadn't reacted to the bear's presence. The bear was about two hundred yards away and had stopped moving but was now staring at him. Joe was beginning to believe the bear had learned to fear humans when it rose on its hind feet and roared.

Faith felt a chill run down her neck when she heard the bear fearsome bellow and was about to pull Porch to a stop when the gelding accelerated. He didn't reach a panicked gallop but was moving too fast for Faith to gain control. When he entered the trees, he felt safe enough slow down, but Faith could no longer see Joe. She pulled back hard on the reins which finally convinced Porch to come to a stop, but she knew she'd never get the gelding to return to the clearing. Faith looked back hoping to see Joe, but her view was blocked by the trees.

Joe was relieved when Porch took Faith out of the clearing and prayed that she was able to avoid an accident. Now all of his attention could be focused on the bear. After its impressive display, the bear had dropped down to all fours and began lumbering towards him. It was still more than a hundred yards away when Joe levered a live cartridge into his Henry's breach. He wasn't about to waste a bullet at this range as it would only anger the bear.

The bear continued its swaying approach for another thirty yards before it slowed and roared. Joe suspected that despite its hunger, the bear was unsettled when its prey didn't run which was the last thing he was going to do. Even with his long legs, the bear would be able to run him down in just a few seconds.

Joe tilted his hat back and glared at the black bear with his bright green eyes before he shouted, "I'm not some defenseless doe, Mister! You may have sharp teeth and long claws, but I can bite you long before you get here!"

The bear didn't roar his reply but stopped walking and simply snarled at Joe.

Joe felt it was becoming a stand-off and didn't want to keep Faith worrying, so he raised his Henry, aimed at the ground just in front of the bear's left paw and squeezed his trigger.

The sharp crack and the .44 slug of lead both arrived at the same time and the combination startled the bear. He hopped back and roared before turning and trotting away.

Joe watched until he disappeared into the trees on the south side of the clearing before he began jogging along the stream.

Faith was actually relieved when she heard the single gunshot. It meant that Joe had probably driven the bear away. He'd need to take a second or third shot if he had to kill the bear with his Henry. She suspected he'd be bringing his Sharps the next time he visited the canyon. She was still focused behind the buggy when Joe appeared.

As soon as Joe saw Faith looking back at him, he slowed to a walk, then took off his hat and waved it three times over his head.

Faith still felt that same rush when he let her know he was safe then waved back just before he reached the buggy.

He climbed inside, handed her his repeater and took the reins before he said, "After I introduced my Henry to our four-footed neighbor, he bid me farewell and returned to the trees to look for more suitable prey."

Joe snapped the reins and as the buggy began rolling again, Faith said, "Porch got a bit excited but calmed down once he thought he was safe. Can I assume the next time you visit our canyon you'll have your Sharps with you?"

"That's a very good assumption, Mrs. Beck. Now let's get home and enjoy a quiet Sunday afternoon and evening."

Faith wrapped her arm around his elbow then said, "This may sound strange, but I almost miss the excitement we experienced almost daily on our long journey."

"I don't have that problem, ma'am. I'm grateful for the quiet days."

Faith smiled and said, "I said almost, sir. But I'm even more pleased to have those quiet days, too."

When Joe turned the buggy onto the road, he noticed two covered wagons about four hundred yards ahead of them. He knew that soon the road would witness a steady stream of wagons and riders and those quiet days would soon be few and far between.

But as they drew closer to the wagons, there was something about one of the horses trailing the rear wagon that tickled his memory. He continued studying the unremarkable brown horse for another twenty seconds when he realized what had brought the animal to his attention. It was its unusual gait and after making the connection, he examined the second horse tied to the back of the wagon which confirmed his identification.

Joe kept his focus on the wagons as he smiled and said, "I think that the bear isn't the only surprise we'll have on this first day of spring."

Faith looked at him and asked, "What kind of surprise?"

Joe pointed at the wagons and said, "See that brown gelding trailing the second wagon? Have you ever seen it before?"

Faith stared at the horse for a few seconds before saying, "No. It looks like a lot of other horses. Why is it a surprise?"

Joe was about to answer her question then changed his mind and replied, "You'll have your answer in a few minutes when we reach Main Street."

They were less than fifty yards behind the wagon, yet Faith still couldn't make the connection. She was preparing to repeat her question more forcefully when a flash of white appeared at the back of the wagon and barked.

It took her a few seconds before she exclaimed, "*Is that Laddie?*"

Joe grinned and replied, "I imagine so. That's Will Boone's horse, so I imagine we'll meet Mary and their boys shortly. And unless I'm mistaken, the other wagon is being driven by Bo Ferguson."

Faith leaned to her right to glimpse the leading wagon, and Joe gave her an assist by angling the buggy to the right edge of the road. Faith didn't recognize Bo's horses, but easily identified the wagon she'd considered a prison until she married Joe.

Laddie stopped barking when five-year-old John left the shadows to see what had excited the collie. When he saw the buggy, he disappeared for a moment then reappeared a few seconds later with his now four-year-old brother Alfred.

It was obvious that neither of the boys had recognized them, so Joe took off his hat and waved it just once before pulling it back on. John and Alfred grinned and waved back, but still didn't seem to know who was in the buggy.

Faith had been smiling since she'd seen Laddie and was surprised by the boys' lack of enthusiasm. She expected to see their delayed excitement when they stopped on Main Street but didn't have to wait that long.

She was still watching the boys and Laddie when Mary leaned out from the driver's seat and looked for the buggy that had interested two of her boys.

SPRING SURPRISES

When she saw Faith's blonde hair, she shouted, "Is that you, Faith?"

Faith nodded and waved as she yelled, "I'm surprised to see you, Mary!"

Faith's reply was still echoing from the nearby rocks when the loud, almost panicked clanging of the lead wagon's bell filled the air.

Joe laughed and said, "I guess that Bo and Nora know we're back here now."

Nora stopped ringing the bell then she hung out from the right side of the driver's seat and waved to Joe and Faith. Joe couldn't see her from his position, so only Faith waved back.

Joe pulled the buggy close to Will's two horses just as they rounded the last curve before Idaho City. By then, Mary had scrambled to the back of the wagon to join John, Alfred and Laddie.

Mary loudly asked, "You weren't in front of us, so where did you come from?"

Joe replied, "We'll explain everything after you stop. And you can tell us why you decided to come to Idaho City."

Mary smiled and said, "It will be an interesting conversation for all of us."

Faith said, "I can assure you that it will be a long one, too."

Mary nodded then slipped back into the wagon. Her boys stayed near the tailgate looking at Joe and Faith as if they were a mirage.

Faith turned to Joe and said, "Neither Will nor Bo seemed to care about searching for gold, so I wonder what brought them here, or if they're going to stay."

"I agree with you about their immunity from gold fever, but I don't have a clue to explain their arrival either. But I'm a bit surprised that Chuck and Marigold didn't join them."

"So, am I. I guess we'll find out in a couple of minutes."

Joe nodded as they approached the beginning of Main Street and hoped that they were planning to stay in town. If so, he knew that if they needed work, Tap would jump at the chance to hire Bo and Will as deputies. With the pending influx of new arrivals and the appointment of Elrod Jefferson as the Placerville town marshal, they'd need all the help they could get. It was just a question of why they decided to come to Idaho City.

Just before Bo reached the first buildings, he pulled the wagon to a stop and set the handbrake. Will didn't need to hear the bell to bring his team to a halt.

Joe drove past Bo's wagon before he tugged on the reins and the buggy stopped rolling. He set the handbrake then bounded out and turned to assist Faith's exit. He kept her hand in his as they walked to the right side of Bo's wagon.

Bo had helped Nora to the ground before Jack and Carl clambered down. Then eight-year-old Anna and seven-year-old Paul left the wagon just as Joe and Faith arrived.

Joe was grinning as he shook Bo's hand and said, "And here I thought I'd seen the last of you, Mister Ferguson. What brings you to our fair city?"

SPRING SURPRISES

Bo's grin matched Joe's as he replied, "I'll wait for Will to tell ya. But how are things goin' for you and Faith?"

"Everything is going really well. As you can see, my beloved wife and I are ready to welcome Kathleen Maureen into the world."

Nora smiled and asked, "When are you due, Faith?"

"Early next month, and it can't come soon enough."

Nora laughed then said, "I understand. Trust me."

Faith nodded just as Will and Mary arrived with Laddie trotting between John and Alfred.

As Mary embraced Faith, she said, "You've filled out nicely, Faith and not just around the middle."

Faith smiled and said, "Where are William and Oscar?"

"They're napping and I didn't want to wake them."

Will and Joe had already shaken hands, so Joe asked, "So, what brings you to Idaho City?"

Bo replied, "Well, me and Will didn't feel like farmin', so we figgered we'd head back to Kansas City and maybe pick up another wagon train."

Joe glanced at Will before saying, "You'd be too late to find one this year, Bo. You'd have to wait until next spring."

Bo exhaled then said, "I reckon you got me there, Joe. The truth is we just ain't cut out for farmin', and I remembered Chuck tellin' us how your sheriff was short of deputies. So, we were kinda hopin' that you still had that problem."

Joe made a sour face before he said, "We just hired a new deputy a couple of weeks ago, Bo."

Bo deflated a bit before Joe laughed and said, "I was just having a bit of fun at your expense, Bo. We did hire a new deputy a couple of weeks ago, but Sheriff Fulmer still has two more slots to fill. I reckon he'll be tickled pink after he meets you and Will."

Bo laughed then slammed Joe on his left shoulder before saying, "I sure missed havin' you around, Joe. So, the first thing we're gonna need is a place to park our wagons."

Joe nodded then said, "Follow me."

Bo said, "Lead the way, Scout," then the Boone family plus Laddie started walking to their wagon and the Fergusons began boarding theirs.

As Joe guided Faith back to their buggy, she asked, "You aren't going to let them sleep in their wagons, are you?"

"Of course not. I wanted you to offer accommodations to Nora and Mary. If I'd asked Bo and Will, they'd probably refuse. Then their wives would remind them who was in charge, and I didn't want to watch it happen."

Faith laughed before Joe helped her board their buggy.

She waited until after he climbed in, released the handbrake and took the reins before she asked, "You know who's in charge in our home, don't you?"

Joe grinned as he replied, "Yes, Your Majesty."

Faith was still smiling when she looked back and said, "They're ready."

SPRING SURPRISES

Joe snapped the reins and Porch began walking along Main Street. He was sure that Tap would be happy to hire Bo and Will, but unlike Rocky, each of them had a family and would need a home. He wasn't sure how much money each of them had but he was sure that Faith wouldn't object if they dipped into their bank account to help. They still had a healthy balance and if Mister Faircloth sells the big garnets, it would almost double.

In the excitement of meeting his old friends, Joe had almost forgotten about the small garnet he had in his coat pocket. He'd leave it with Mister Faircloth when he picked up Faith's necklace, but first, he and Faith needed to welcome the Fergusons and Boones to Idaho City.

Joe didn't turn the buggy down their graveled drive but drove past their house and turned onto the empty lot east of their home.

He kept going until their house's rear porch was thirty yards directly to their right before he pulled up and set the handbrake.

After stepping to the ground, he helped Faith down before they walked to the back of the buggy and stopped to wait for their guests. They watched Bo and Will climb down from their wagons before assisting their wives down. The children all remained inside the wagons as the two couples approached Joe and Faith.

When they arrived, Bo pointed to the big house just a hundred feet away and asked, "Are the folks who live there gonna be unhappy havin' us stayin' here, Joe?"

Joe shook his head as he replied, "No, they won't be very pleased at all. They'll probably raise hell if they see you setting up camp."

"Then why'd you lead us here?"

Joe looked at Faith who smiled and said, "Because that's our home and we're not going to let our friends set up camp when we have so many empty bedrooms."

Will looked at their home and exclaimed, "*That's your house?*"

Faith replied, "It is. And you can be our guests until you find homes of your own."

Nora said, "I can see it's a big house, but there are a dozen of us, Faith."

"There's a lot more open space inside our house than you have in both of your wagons even if they weren't loaded."

Mary was gawking as she asked, "May I ask how much you had to pay for such a magnificent house?"

Joe replied, "We all have a lot to talk about, so let's get everyone settled first."

Faith looked at Joe and said, "While you men take care of the buggy and wagons, I'll take everyone else inside to their rooms."

Joe grinned then saluted and said, "Yes, ma'am," before the three ladies walked to the wagons to retrieve the youngsters.

Bo and Will snickered before they stepped to their teams to begin unharnessing the oxen while Joe led Porch to his barn. He had the gelding in his stall and checked on Duke, the mares and Bernie before Bo and Will had their oxen free of their yokes and leather straps. After leaving Laddie in the barn for a reunion with his equine friends, Joe walked to join his human friends carrying his Henry.

When he was close, Bo asked, "Can we put 'em in your corral, Joe?"

"That's what it's for, Bo. Let's get your team and horses inside then we'll help Will move his big boys."

As they began herding the oxen and his two horses, Bo asked, "How come you're carryin' your Henry? Is it as dangerous as folks said it was?"

"It's not bad at all. I brought it with me when I took Faith to explore our little canyon. I'm glad I did because we disturbed a black bear from his winter nap, so I need to get it cleaned."

"You bought a canyon?"

As the animals entered the corral, Joe replied, "Just recently, but we'll have plenty of time to explain everything."

They settled the oxen and horses into their temporary home but didn't need to help Will as he was already leading his team and two horses in their direction.

Joe was leaning on the top fence rail when Bo asked, "Are you sure your sheriff will want to hire us, Joe?"

"I suppose there's a chance he'll take one look at your ugly face and shoot you instead. But if you'd met the deputy he had before I arrived, you'd know that's not very likely."

Bo looked at Joe before asking, "Have you had any serious trouble since you've been a deputy?"

Joe smiled as he replied, "I had trouble before I was a deputy, Bo. But you know how danger seems to find me wherever I am."

"That's the truth. I was kinda surprised to see how big the town's gettin'."

"And it'll keep growing for at least a couple of more years before the gold starts getting hard to find."

Will drove his team and horses into the corral and Joe closed the gate behind them before they started walking to the back of the house.

―――

Inside the Beck home, Faith had already assigned an upstairs bedroom to Bo and Nora, and Nora chose the adjoining bedroom for the three boys. Eight-year-old Anna was ecstatic when she was given her own room at the end of the hall. Mary and Bo would stay in the nursery with Oscar and William while John and Alfred would bed down in the parlor.

As Faith assigned their sleeping arrangements, Nora and Mary bombarded her with questions about the house and Idaho City. Faith answered some of their queries but deferred most of them until the men returned. She was happy to be reunited with them. but she was already tired and knew it would be a long night.

As the three men walked up the porch steps, Bo looked down and asked, "Is that a bullet in that stair?"

Joe replied, "Yup. I'll explain how it got there tomorrow. I know we have a lot to talk about, but I don't want to keep Faith up too late. I'm sure she's already pretty tired."

SPRING SURPRISES

Will said, "I'm sure she is, and we're kinda run down ourselves."

They crossed the porch and Joe opened the kitchen door and waited until Bo and Will entered before following them inside. They heard the children chattering in the parlor, so after Joe leaned his Henry against the wall, they hung their hats, coats and gunbelts then headed to the hallway.

―――

They only talked for a few minutes before Faith, Mary and Nora along with Anna returned to the kitchen to prepare supper and the boys decided to go upstairs to look at their rooms.

After the boys and the womenfolk were gone, Bo asked, "Can you tell me how much you paid for this place, Joe? I'm only askin' 'cause I'll need to buy a place."

"I'm kind of embarrassed to tell you that we didn't pay anything for the house. When I returned those gold bars, the banker was so grateful that he tore up the mortgage on the house and signed it over to me. But that being said, the mortgage was less than four hundred dollars. The market for houses in Idaho City is really strange. I think you'd be able to find a nice place for less than five hundred dollars."

Bo grinned as he said, "I hope so. We've got seven hundred and forty dollars in our wagon."

Will said, "We've got six hundred and twenty dollars."

Joe said, "Tomorrow, after you meet Sheriff Fulmer, we'll visit Les Pratt at The Landsman Bank and see what he has available."

Will asked, "If the sheriff hires us, how much does the job pay?"

Joe momentarily considered pulling their legs again before he answered, "The county pays deputies a hundred dollars a month."

Bo and Will's jaws dropped, and they just stared at Joe in disbelief for twelve seconds before Bo asked, "Are you jokin' with us again, Joe?"

Joe grinned as he replied, "No, sir. I was thinking of kidding you by telling you it only paid twenty-five dollars a month. I was shocked when the sheriff told me I'd be getting paid eighty dollars a month. In January, the county upped deputies' salaries by twenty dollars because it was hard to find good men willing to take the job."

Will said, "I thought you said it wasn't a dangerous town."

"Most days it's pretty peaceful, but nights tend to be more troublesome, especially with so many saloons. I'm sure you noticed the long line of them when you drove down Main Street, and there are more on the side streets. But we have almost as many lawyers and the new opera house and a theater, too."

Will said, "I was surprised by all those saloons, but Mary kept talking about all the stores and shops."

Bo glanced at the hallway before saying, "I reckon this a good time to tell you about Chuck and Marigold."

Joe was wondering why none of the new arrivals had spoken a word about the other families from the wagon train but seeing Bo's sad expression already suggested the reason.

SPRING SURPRISES

Bo quietly said, "After we reached Oregon, the folks began settling into this nice valley to start buildin' cabins and breakin' the soil for farmin'. There were a few problems but nothin' they didn't expect. But late in November, Marigold lost her baby and kept bleedin'. She died the next day and Chuck got really down for a while. Then he got mad and started drinkin'.

"We tried to help him, but he didn't wanna listen. Anyway, a few days into January, Chuck got himself really boozed up and wandered off. It was really cold and snowin', so nobody even knew where he was. We found his frozen body two days later."

Joe sighed then said, "There was nothing you or anyone else could do, Bo. Chuck was always set in his ways, like when he was infected with gold fever."

"I reckon so, but it still bothered me."

Joe quickly asked, "How are Herm and Becky?"

Bo perked up and smiled before replying, "They're doin' really good. Becky had a baby boy just before we left and was happier than I ever saw her before."

Will then said, "They named him Joseph Herman."

Joe smiled as he said, "I guess that's better than plain old Joe."

With the Chuck and Marigold tragedy behind them, Bo and Will began telling Joe about the other families.

―――

As they prepared the large supper, the ladies' conversation followed a very similar path. They talked about houses and the town for a few minutes before the sad story about Marigold and Chuck surfaced.

After hearing the story, Faith expressed her sadness, but the manner of Marigold's passing was almost devastating. Even after learning of Becky's joyful experience, she couldn't shake the deep impact the news about Marigold had on her.

The conversation continued as they cooked, cut and stirred, and Faith still answered their questions. But she felt almost as if she was an observer and someone else was providing her replies.

―――

When they sat down to eat, they used the dining room for the first time while the older boys ate at the kitchen table. The conversation was pleasant and informative, but even as he said grace, Joe could tell that Faith was troubled and had no doubt about the cause.

After dinner, Mary and Nora insisted that Faith rest while they cleaned up, and Faith simply thanked them before leaving the dining room for their bedroom. Joe wasn't the least bit tired but said goodnight before he followed her down the hallway and into their bedroom.

When he closed the door, Faith weakly smiled at him as she asked, "Are you tired of talking, Joe?"

Joe stepped close, wrapped his arms around her then replied, "No, ma'am. I just wanted to spend some private time with my perfect wife."

Faith rested her head on his shoulder and quietly said, "I keep telling you I'm not even close to being perfect."

"And I keep saying that you're only perfect for me."

Faith sighed then said, "I suppose you're entitled to your opinion, Mister Beck."

Joe kissed her softly before saying, "It feels as if you're about to fall asleep in my arms, Mrs. Beck, so let's get ready for bed."

After Joe released her, Faith smiled then walked to the bed and sat down. Joe sat beside her and began pulling off his boots as Faith took off her shoes.

They could hear their houseguests above their heads and in the other rooms, but neither Joe nor Faith spoke another word before they slipped beneath the covers. After Joe slid his arm under her neck, Faith snuggled close and closed her eyes.

Joe looked at his wife and whispered, "I know that the news about Marigold troubles you, my love. Is there anything I can say or do that would help?"

Faith didn't open her eyes as she quietly replied, "I'll be all right, Joe. I was just shaken when Mary told me."

Joe doubted if she would be able to overcome her demons so easily this time. Earlier, her fears were irrational and distant, but now they were close and personal. He kissed her on her forehead then closed his eyes. As he listened to her quiet breathing, Joe prayed for his beloved wife.

CHAPTER 11

Monday morning at the Beck home was beyond hectic. It was bordering on chaos before the three adult males left the house. As they crossed the empty lot on their way to the jail, Joe pointed out St. Joseph's school, convent and church before they turned onto 2nd Street. After he identified Sheriff Fulmer's house, he told them about the sheriff's family, so they wouldn't be surprised when they met Mary. Despite the frenzied morning, Joe was still the first to arrive at the office.

When Sheriff Fulmer arrived, he found Joe sitting behind the desk chatting with two strangers. The conversation immediately ended, and the two unidentified men turned then stood before the desk.

As he hung his hat, Tap asked, "Do we have a problem already, Joe?"

Joe replied, "Yes, sir. When Faith and I were leaving our canyon yesterday, we trailed these two into town. When I caught up with them, I figured you'd want to have a few words with them, so I told them to show up this morning."

Tap glanced at Bo and Will before he asked, "Why did you think I oughta talk to 'em?"

Joe grinned as he said, "Because we needed a couple of more deputies, Tap. The old codger is Bo Ferguson, the ornery cuss who ruled our wagon train with an iron fist. And the younger, uglier man is Will Boone. He's the ex-sergeant I first met when he was having a lead-filled discussion with some gunrunners."

Tap's eyelids popped wider as he asked, "You're not jokin', are you Joe?"

"No, sir. Faith and I just turned onto the road after our buggy ride to our canyon when I spotted two wagons ahead of us. You can imagine how surprised I was when I identified their wagons. I was hoping that they were planning to stay because I couldn't think of two men who'd be better deputies than Bo and Will."

A big smile grew on the sheriff's face before he shook each of their hands and said, "Joe's talked about you ever since he got here, and I can't tell ya how pleased I am to meet you fellers. Like Joe said, we really need a couple of good deputies and as soon as Rocky gets here, I'll swear you in."

Rocky arrived a few minutes later, and after introductions, Tap swore in Bo and Will as Boise County deputy sheriffs. After the brief ceremony, Sheriff Fulmer took his new hires to the county courthouse to introduce them to Judge Oliver, and Mister Blanton.

SPRING SURPRISES

While they were gone, Joe explained their appearance to Rocky. He was pleased to have them fill their ranks and wasn't even jealous that he was the only one in the office who didn't own a Henry. He felt a special kinship to ex-sergeant Will Boone and expected they'd be sharing war stories by this afternoon.

When they returned, Joe delayed the war storytelling when he took Bo and Will to The Landsman Bank. He introduced them to Mister Brown and explained that they needed to buy houses for their families. The bank president then escorted them to Les Pratt who would handle the transactions.

Joe left them with Mister Pratt and headed back to the jail when, without any particular reason, he began humming Kathleen Mavourneen. As he stepped along the boardwalk, he saw a decorated carriage parked before the Methodist church and realized that he'd forgotten that Jim and Sarah were being married today. He continued to hum as he crossed the street and wondered what else he'd forgotten. Before he reached the other side, Joe recalled the uncut garnet in his coat pocket and Faith's necklace that was probably waiting for him at Faircloth's. He decided to wait until the house was less crowded before visiting the jeweler.

Faith was too busy to allow her renewed concerns to enter her mind. Even though she had Mary and Nora to help with the chores, the house was in a constant state of disruption.

The older children wanted to explore the town and the younger ones seemed to be falling down at every opportunity. When the two mothers weren't busy controlling their offspring, they engaged Faith in conversation. They talked about the town, the families who had remained in Oregon, and what her life had been like since she arrived.

Faith emphasized the positive and downplayed the dangers to make them feel more at home. When she told them about Sister Mary Catherine, it shifted the conversation to her imminent motherhood.

They were sitting at the kitchen table having coffee when Nora asked, "Does Joe still believe you're going to have a girl?"

Faith smiled as she replied, "Yes, he does. There's not a day that passes when he doesn't talk about Kathleen Maureen."

Mary asked, "Have you even chosen a boy's name?"

Faith nodded and answered, "If our baby defies him by having a pointer, then we'll name him Sam. Sam Grant Beck."

Both women laughed before Nora said, "That could get him in trouble if he ever travels south of the Mason-Dixon line."

Mary then added, "Not as much as if he was named Abraham Lincoln Beck."

SPRING SURPRISES

Faith smiled and sipped her coffee, not caring which name their child would bear. She simply hoped to be able to see her baby's face, even if it was just for a few seconds.

———

Joe entered the jail and found Tap sitting behind the desk and asked, "Where's Rocky?"

The sheriff grinned and said, "Otis Litchfield popped in to show us his new Henry. When he said that D.M. had a couple more of 'em, Rocky lit outta here like his tail was on fire."

Joe snickered before taking off his coat then joining Tap at the front desk.

"I left Bo and Will with Les Pratt at the bank. I hope he can give each of them a good deal on house. I'm happy to see them all again, but I'll still be relieved when they find their own homes."

Tap chuckled before saying, "I reckon Faith is prayin' they move out soon, too. After they're settled in, we gotta have a big get-together. Mary's gonna be really happy when I tell her about 'em, too."

"With a crowd that size, we'll probably have to use the dance hall."

Tap started laughing just as Rocky burst into the office brandishing his shiny new Henry and shouted, "I got one!"

Joe grinned as he said, "I can see that. Luckily, we seem to have plenty of ammunition available for target practice. Did D.M. get a shipment of Henry cartridges, or is he running short?"

Rocky didn't even take off his hat or coat before he dropped onto a chair then gazed at his new love as he replied, "He got another full case of cartridges, so he gave me enough to load it."

Joe said, "I hope you don't have one in the firing chamber."

"Nope. D.M. warned me about that. He told me that they're working on a better model that loads faster and safer. But I'm just happy to find this one. Now all of us will have repeaters."

Joe said, "And all of the deputies will have Spencer repeaters as well except for me. Not that I'm complaining, mind you. I'm quite happy with my Sharps. I wished it used cartridges, though. One of these days, I'm going to forget to blow the spilled powder off the back of the breech and give myself an ugly black tattoo on my face."

As Tap and Joe entered a serious firearm conversation, Rocky gently laid his new repeater on the desk then took off his hat and walked to the wall. After he hung his coat, he returned to his chair, retrieved his Henry and joined the discussion.

Joe had just mentioned the Gatling gun when Bo and Will entered the office wearing big smiles.

SPRING SURPRISES

Bo yanked off his hat as he exclaimed, "We got our own houses already! I bought the house at #11 B Street and Will's house is across the street at #14. We're only gonna hafta pay for the leftover mortgages. My place is gonna cost me $385 and Will's is $360."

Tap said, "That sounds like a pretty good deal. Why don't you head to Joe's place and tell your wives the good news?"

Will said, "We gotta get our money to pay the bank, too."

Sheriff Fulmer asked, "So, why are you still here?"

Bo glanced at Will before they turned around and raced out the door. As soon as they disappeared, the three lawmen resumed their Gatling gun discourse.

———

Two hours later, when Joe returned for lunch, it seemed even more chaotic than it had been when the Fergusons and Boones had arrived. Bo and Will were harnessing their teams to the wagons and Mary and Nora were scurrying through the house finding and herding their children.

He found Faith sitting on the couch in the parlor to avoid being stampeded and joined her.

Joe grinned and said, "I guess they're all happy to be moving into their own homes."

Faith smiled as she replied, "You can't imagine how excited they were when Bo and Will told them the news. Mary and Nora went with them to the bank, so I was in charge of their children while they were gone. It wasn't even an hour, but it made me respect all those women who have large families."

"Like your mother?"

Faith nodded as she said, "I guess I was so busy helping that I never really understood how difficult it must have been for her."

Joe kissed her before saying, "I'll do all I can to keep your life from becoming difficult, Mrs. Beck."

Faith smiled and said, "I know you will, but you'll always keep my life interesting too, Mister Beck."

Nora led Anna down the stairs and waved to Joe and Faith as they passed before disappearing into the hall.

Joe looked at his wife and asked, "Have you had lunch yet?"

"No. I was waiting for you."

Joe smiled and said, "Then I'll escort you safely to the kitchen where I'll fix you a big lunch."

Joe stood and took Faith's hand then walked with her to the hallway.

SPRING SURPRISES

He was still preparing their food when Bo entered and said, "We're ready to roll, Joe. We might be late showin' up tomorrow."

Joe replied, "I don't think Tap would mind if you missed a day getting settled."

Bo grinned, said, "Tell him we're grateful," then waved and hurried out of the kitchen.

Faith said, "They'll have to sell their wagons and teams, so I think you'll be lucky to see them on Wednesday."

"They won't have any problems selling their wagons or oxen, but you're probably right about the time they'll need to settle in."

Faith nodded and watched as Joe added a pickle to his plate, but she no longer felt a desire for the sour cylindrical vegetable.

As soon as they began eating, Faith said, "It'll be nice having Nora and Mary around."

"Yes, ma'am. Nora is a nice lady and Mary is completely different from the wicked witch she used to be."

Faith swallowed before saying, "She's married to a much better husband now."

Joe looked into her deep blue eyes as he asked, "Does she still fret about having another baby?"

Faith shook her head and replied, "No. I think she's actually hoping to conceive."

Joe smiled then resumed eating. When Faith didn't mention her own concerns, he was relieved. Maybe she was being honest when she said her sad mood was due to hearing of Marigold's death, and the manner of her death hadn't resurrected Faith's own fears.

―――

The rest of Monday was routine, and even Joe's whiskey walk was more like a cake walk.

Tuesday morning, when Joe told Sheriff Fulmer that his two new deputies would be busy all day, Tap said he'd be surprised if they showed up by Thursday. After Rocky arrived, it was business as usual for the three lawmen.

An hour later, Rocky left for Centreville to deliver two eviction notices, and as soon as he left the jail, Tap said, "I reckon he'll be doin' some practice shootin' with his new Henry on the way."

Joe grinned and said, "He'll probably empty that box of .44s he took with him."

They were talking about Bo and Will when Tom Walker entered the jail and Sheriff Fulmer asked, "What do you need, Tom?"

SPRING SURPRISES

"Somebody broke into our storeroom last night and stole a lotta tins of all kinda food."

Joe stood and said, "I'll check it out, boss," then after pulling on his hat and coat, he followed Tom out the door.

As they walked to his father's store, Tom gave Joe more details about what had been stolen. When he finished, Joe thought it was odd that they'd taken such a wide variety of food tins but hadn't stolen any pricier items.

Before they reached the large store, Joe said, "I'll check in back around storeroom door they used to break in."

Tom nodded and said, "Okay, Joe. My pa already nailed it shut, though."

"That's okay. If I need to ask you anything else, I'll stop by."

Tom waved and headed for the front door while Joe turned down the side alley.

When he stopped by the nailed back door, Joe examined the ground. It was heavily scuffed after Mister Walker had worked to secure the door and just a few feet past the door, the ground was marked with deep ruts from freight wagons. So, he walked past the last of the ruts and soon found two sets of deep footprints which he suspected had been left by the thieves carrying their bags of weighty loot. But what he didn't find was another clue. He didn't find any fresh horse dung behind the storeroom. After crossing the ruts, the footprints just headed north to First Street.

He had first suspected that some down-and-out prospectors had decided to pick up some supplies without bothering to pay for them. But he didn't believe they'd walk all the way into town, so Joe tried to think of who else would need to steal food.

Joe followed the footsteps down the back alley until he lost them among the busy traffic on First Street. He was about to head back to Walker's to let them know there was little chance of finding the thieves when he saw looked west to the end of the street and saw something out of place. Just as the street faded into rough ground, there was an abandoned cabin built by an early settler that was close to collapse. But near the front of the cabin was a buckboard with two saddled horses tied in back.

His enhanced state arrived before Joe turned and began walking at a rapid pace to find an answer to the mystery. He was about a hundred and fifty yards away when he saw two men lugging a large, heavy crate out of the cabin and place it onto the buckboard. Neither of them had spotted Joe before they returned to the cabin, so Joe flipped open his coat and moved his Remington from his holster to his coat's right pocket then picked up his pace.

When Joe was about thirty yards from the buckboard, one of the men backed out of the cabin carrying the front of a large chest, so he slowed to a walk just before his partner emerged gripping the back end of the trunk. The back-ender noticed Joe immediately and said something to his friend who turned and looked at Joe. But rather than stopping to set the chest down, they continued moving to load the trunk onto the buckboard.

Joe stopped just a few feet from the buckboard's horse when they slid the trunk onto the bed and approached him. Joe had seen them around town recently but didn't know their names.

Joe smiled and said, "I was doing my morning rounds and noticed your buckboard. I didn't think anyone lived in that old cabin, so I was curious."

The shorter of the two men said, "We were just usin' it 'til the winter let up. Now that it's over, we'll be movin' on to California. You ain't gonna arrest us for squattin', are ya?"

"Nope. So, what are you going to do when you get to California?"

"We ain't figgered that out yet."

Joe looked at their saddled horses and said, "That's a good-looking mare," then started walking to the back of the buckboard.

He could hear the two men close behind him as he began stroking the tan mare's neck and asked, "What's her name?"

The taller man replied, "I call her Lilly."

Joe detected nervousness in the man's voice as he continued to rub the mare, so when he glanced at the open crate, he wasn't surprised to find it filled with tins of food. He didn't know what was in the trunk but suspected they wouldn't be happy if he asked them to open it.

He smiled as he said, "She's handsome lady. Well, I suppose I'll finish my rounds and head back to the jail. I hope you boys have better luck in California."

Joe saw the relief on their faces before the short man smiled and said, "So, do we."

Joe tipped his hat and started walking away. The two men were at his left as he passed the harnessed gelding and slid his hand into his coat's right pocket and gripped his Remington.

He pulled it free then suddenly turned, cocked his hammer and pointed at the two men as he exclaimed, "Don't move!"

The unidentified men who had been relieved just seconds earlier by the friendly deputy were stunned as they stared at the serious deputy with his drawn pistol.

Joe stepped closer and said, "The owner of Walker's Dry Goods reported that someone had broken into his storeroom and stolen a lot of tinned food. I don't suppose it's a coincidence that you have a crate full of them, do you?"

SPRING SURPRISES

The shorter man quickly replied, "The store was closed, but we were gonna pay for 'em on our way outta town, Deputy."

"You could do your shopping on the way out of town, too. What are your names?"

"I'm Shorty Griswold and he's Ronnie Oglesby."

Joe expected they'd give him false names but knew they hadn't as suspects usually used Smith or Jones.

"So, Mister Griswold, why did you steal those tins of food?"

"I…we were outta cash and figgered on tryin' our luck in Placerville."

Joe's initial examination of their appearance suggested that they were hardly destitute. They may have been somewhat unkempt, but their clothing and boots were fairly new, and they had the buckboard and three horses. He didn't know if they wore gunbelts under their coats but there were rifles in their horses' scabbards, so he assumed they each carried a pistol.

He said, "I want you to unbutton your coats and with your left hand, remove your pistols and drop them to the ground."

Shorty looked up at Ronnie before each of them began popping their coats' buttons. As they pulled their coats open, Joe was surprised to find that they were better armed than he'd expected. Shorty wore a two-gun rig and Ronnie had a

Colt in his holster with a modified sling carrying a smaller pistol.

Shorty quickly said, "I told ya we were gonna pay for the food, Deputy. There ain't no cause for you treatin' us like we were killers."

"Maybe not, but I've learned to be cautious. So, just drop your pistols to the ground then take six steps back."

Shorty grunted before the two men used their left hands to slowly remove and drop their assorted firearms to the ground. Ronnie's Pocket Colt was the last to hit the dirt, then they stepped back about fifteen feet and waited.

Joe kept his eyes on the two men as he picked up the first two Colts and dropped them into his coat pockets. He sidestepped to the buckboard, set them on the driver's seat then returned for the last two. While the two men watched, Joe slid their rifles from their horses' scabbards and set them on the buckboard's bed.

Now that they were disarmed, Joe untied their horses' reins and said, "I want you to mount and then I'll use your buckboard to follow you to the jail."

Shorty snapped, "Why are you doin' all this? There ain't three dollars' worth of tins in that crate!"

Joe began backing to the front of the buckboard as he replied, "Stealing is still a crime, Shorty."

SPRING SURPRISES

As the two men began to mount their horses, Joe quickly holstered his Remington then climbed onto the driver's seat beside the pistols. He released the handbrake, took the reins in his hands then looked back at the two men sitting in their saddles. He was surprised that his prisoners didn't take the opportunity to gallop down First Street. Instead, they started their horses at a walk and headed for Main Street. Joe snapped the reins and followed closely behind them, wondering what was in the trunk.

After they turned onto Main Street, Joe glanced at Walker & Sons Dry Goods but didn't think of stopping to let Mister Walker know he'd found the thieves. Instead, he wondered where Jim Pritchard and Sarah were having their honeymoon.

When they pulled up before the jail, Shorty and Ronnie dismounted and tied off their horses without being asked, which was another surprise for Joe. He figured they must be planning to talk their way out of being jailed without revealing whatever was in the trunk.

After he clambered down from the buckboard, he took one of their Colts from the driver's seat and stepped onto the boardwalk.

They were waiting by the jail's door when Joe said, "Go on in, gentlemen."

Shorty nodded and opened the door and after Ronnie followed him in, Joe stepped into the office and closed the door.

Sheriff Fulmer stood and asked, "Are these the thieves who broke into Walker's?"

Joe replied, "Yes, sir. I'll get them lock them up before I tell you about it."

Shorty pointed at Joe and exclaimed, "Your deputy acted like we were a couple of killers, Sheriff! We only took some tins of food 'cause we were dead broke."

Tap said, "You can tell me your story from behind those bars, mister."

Ronnie was about to add his own protest when he felt a sharp poke in his back from a pistol's muzzle.

After Joe searched Shorty and Ronnie for hidden weapons, Joe locked them in a cell then returned to the desk and set the Colt on its crowded surface.

Joe then said, "I haven't searched their saddlebags yet, so do you want to come along?"

Tap replied, "Let me grab my hat," then walked to the wall snatched his hat from its peg and followed Joe through the doorway.

SPRING SURPRISES

After Tap closed the door, Joe said, "I'm a lot more curious about what's inside that trunk on the buckboard."

The sheriff glanced at the large chest and asked, "Why?"

"They were really nervous when I was looking at the buckboard's bed, and I don't think it was because of the crate of tins."

Tap grinned and said, "Then let's take a peek inside."

The two lawmen left the boardwalk and stepped to the back of the buckboard where Sheriff Fulmer gave Joe the honor of opening the trunk.

Joe lifted the heavy lid and was severely disappointed to find it filled with dirty clothes.

Tap snickered before saying, "I reckon they were just embarrassed for not doin' their laundry."

Joe was stubborn enough to cling to his belief that Shorty and Ronnie didn't want anyone to examine the trunk's contents, so he began tossing the soiled clothing onto the bed.

He had only thrown three shirts and two pairs of britches from the trunk when he found a large canvas bag and pulled it into the bright sunlight.

Tap's eyebrows rose as he said, "That ain't dirty laundry, Joe. What's inside?"

Joe pulled open the drawstrings, stuck his hand into the sack and pulled out a wad of crumpled five-dollar notes issued by The Idaho City Bank.

Sheriff Fulmer quickly said, "I reckon those are the counterfeit bills our mayor is worried about."

Joe returned all but one bill to the bag before examining the banknote. It seemed genuine except for a break in the border on the reverse.

He handed the bill to Tap and said, "You're right that they're the bad bills the mayor found, boss. But I don't think those two in our cell are the ones who printed them. Neither one of them strikes me as being capable of creating counterfeits this good."

Sheriff Fulmer was scanning the five-dollar bill as he replied, "They're really good except for that gap in the border. I ain't run across any counterfeiters before, but I reckon it takes more'n two fellers to do the job. And I gotta agree with ya that they ain't smart enough to make 'em."

Joe grabbed the bag and said, "Let's go ask Shorty and Ronnie how they managed to have all this counterfeit money."

Tap nodded then he and Joe returned to the jail.

Shorty groaned when he saw Joe carrying the bag, and Ronnie cursed under his breath.

SPRING SURPRISES

After taking off their hats, the two lawmen approached the bars and after they stopped, Tap asked, "Where did you boys get this counterfeit cash?"

Shorty sighed before he replied, "We ain't counterfeiters, and that money ain't counterfeit either, Sheriff. We was workin' at J&M Printers in San Francisco when they printed a whole batch of those bills. They didn't notice the mistake 'til they printed more'n a thousand of 'em and I was told to burn 'em. So, me and Ronnie took 'em down to the furnace and burned a bunch of newspapers instead. We figgered we could spend 'em in some hick towns around San Francisco, but nobody would take money from a bank way out here.

"We weren't bein' paid much anyway, so me and Ronnie figgered we'd come out here where we could spend 'em and maybe do some prospectin'."

Joe asked, "Then why did you suddenly decide to leave and steal the tins of food?"

Shorty replied, "We heard the bank found out about the mistake the printers made, so we were gonna move to Placerville 'cause they wouldn't care so much. We just didn't wanna risk spendin' another one of those bad bills in town, so we figgered nobody would care if we grabbed some grub before we left."

Tap looked at Joe, tilted his head and shifted his eyes to the front of the jail. Joe nodded and they walked away from the cell to the door.

When they were out of hearing range, Tap quietly asked, "What do you think, Joe?"

Joe smiled and replied, "I imagine the mayor will be happier than Mister Walker when they hear about the capture. But I think Mister Blanton will have trouble prosecuting them. They stole the badly printed bills in San Francisco, so that's not in our jurisdiction. They weren't technically passing counterfeit notes, either. So, I reckon all he'll be able to charge them with his stealing the tins from Walker's."

Tap nodded as he said, "That's what I was thinkin', too. I'll tell you what I'm gonna do. While you write your report, I'll take the bag of bad money and go talk to Duke Blanton. Then I'll visit our mayor and Cy Walker."

"Okay, boss. If Mister Blanton agrees that it's not worth prosecuting, what will we do with our prisoners?"

"I'll figure somethin' out before I get back."

Joe was writing his report when Rocky entered the jail and saw Shorty and Ronnie in the front cell.

He took off his hat and asked, "What did they do?"

"They stole about a thousand bad five-dollar banknotes from a printer in San Francisco and decided to come here to spend them. But when they heard the bank noticed the problem, they figured to move to Placerville but didn't have any real cash. So, they broke into Walker's and stole some food tins first."

Rocky snickered and said, "That was kinda stupid. Why didn't they just wait 'til they got to Placerville to buy it?"

Joe just shrugged and resumed writing. He suspected that Shorty and Ronnie were already hungry when they decided to move on, but it didn't matter. He needed to finish his report and enter the incidents in the logbook.

―――

Sheriff Fulmer returned just before noon without the canvas sack, took off his hat then stepped past the front desk and stopped before the cell.

Shorty and Ronnie left their cots and approached the bars before Tap said, "I just talked to the county prosecutor. You boys are gonna get off lucky 'cause of all the legal hoops he woulda had to jump through. So, all you gotta do is make restitution to Mister Walker for the damage you caused to his door and for what you took. Then you'll leave town and never come back."

Shorty said, "I know we're lucky, but we don't have any way to make restitution."

Sheriff Fulmer said, "I'll tell you what I'll do. I'll pay you sixty dollars for your buckboard and horse and make restitution to Mister Walker."

Shorty glanced at Ronnie before replying, "We'll take it. We'll grab our clothes then you can have the trunk, too. But can we take some of those tins of food?"

"Sure. Now let's get you outta my cell, outta my jail and outta my town."

As Tap unlocked the cell, Joe pulled Ronnie's Colt from the drawer and handed it to him as the sheriff escorted them past the desk and out of the jail.

When the door closed, Rocky grinned and said, "I reckon Tap had his eye on that buckboard right off."

Joe smiled as he said, "It sure looks like it. He must have withdrawn the money from his account on his way back from Walker's."

Rocky stood and said, "I've gotta get to the boarding house if I wanna get fed."

When Rocky walked by, Joe gave him a one-fingered salute using his index finger to avoid insulting him.

After Rocky left, Joe leaned back with his hand's locked behind his neck and imagined the discussion between Tap and Mister Blanton. He started smiling then continued his mental journey to the sheriff's visit with Mayor Williams at The Idaho City Bank. He soon left the image of the very happy banker and moved to Tap's explanation to Mister Walker. When his mind returned to the jail, Joe again reminded himself to stop by Faircloth's Jewelry to pick up Faith's necklace and drop off the uncut garnet.

Joe was sure that Faith would like it, but he was curious what the six-star garnet would look like after it was mounted. If she had visitors when he returned home, he'd wait until they were alone to give it to her. Doctor Taylor was going to visit her today, but he should already have returned to his office.

―――――

Joe was a bit surprised when Sheriff Fulmer was the first to return.

Tap closed the door then grinned as he said, "Those boys are probably halfway to Boise City already."

Joe stood and asked, "Did you already move the buckboard to your place?"

"Yup. Mary was really pleased to have it, too. Joey wanted to drive it around the block, but I told him we'd do that on Sunday."

They met at the peg wall, and as Tap hung his hat and coat, Joe pulled his hat and coat on then left the jail.

He walked quickly along the boardwalk and when the street traffic cleared, he angled across to the other side and a minute later, entered Faircloth's Jewelry.

As soon as Joe stepped inside, he found George Faircloth smiling at him then took off his hat as he stepped to the counter.

George opened a drawer behind him and took out a long, blue velvet box and set it on the counter before saying, "I hope you like the necklace, Joe."

Joe smiled and said, "It's more important for Faith to like it, George. And I'm sure she will."

Despite having already seen the other polished garnets, when Joe slowly opened the lid and saw the necklace, he was stunned by what his eyes revealed. He expected it to be mounted in gold, but Mister Faircloth had used silver. He thought it enhanced the natural beauty of the deep purple gem much better than yellow gold would.

He looked up at Mister Faircloth and said, "It's perfect, George. I thought you'd mount it in gold because we have so much of it around here, but I'm really happy that you used silver."

"It's not silver, Joe. It's white gold which is an alloy of 90% gold and 10% nickel."

"Pardon my ignorance, but it's absolutely perfect."

SPRING SURPRISES

Joe closed the lid and slipped the box into his coat's right pocket before taking out the unpolished garnet from his left pocket.

After Joe handed it to him, George looked at the stone and asked, "How long did it take for you to find this one?"

"Not long. I was with Faith when a hungry black bear made his appearance, so we cut our visit short."

"That was a wise decision. This one may be another six-star, but I'll see how it turns out when it's cut."

Joe shook his hand and said, "Thank you, George. Now I'm going home for lunch and surprise Faith."

George replied, "In her condition, don't surprise her too much."

Joe chuckled as he waved then headed to the door. He soon turned onto Third Street and smiled when he saw his house knowing that Faith was waiting for him. He wasn't concerned about surprising her with the necklace, not after all the other surprises she'd endured over the past few days. First there was the bear, then the arrival of the Fergusons and the Boones who brought the news about Chuck and Marigold. He hoped the necklace would be her last surprise before Kathleen Maureen arrived.

When Joe entered the foyer, he didn't see Faith in the parlor and didn't hear her announce her location, so he assumed she was already napping. He hung his hat on the coat rack then crossed the parlor and soon found her curled up on their bed. He stood in the doorway just watching her and was about to walk to the kitchen when Faith rolled onto her back and smiled at him.

"I was just resting until you came home."

Joe stepped close to the bed and asked, "Haven't you eaten yet?"

"I was going to have lunch if you hadn't returned in another ten minutes."

Joe sat beside her then leaned over and gently kissed her before saying, "I'll fix lunch, sweetheart. But before I do, I have something for you."

Faith kept her blue eyes focused on his as Joe slid the blue jewelry box from his coat pocket and said, "I asked Mister Faircloth to use the small six-star garnet to make this for you."

SPRING SURPRISES

Faith looked at the box then said, "I think I should sit up before opening it."

Joe helped her to a sitting position and once her feet were on the floor, he gave her the slim box.

Faith glanced at Joe before she slowly lifted the lid.

She gasped when she saw the necklace and after a short pause, she quietly exclaimed, "I can't believe this is one of the rocks we found in our canyon! It's stunning!"

"Do you want to put it on?"

Faith hesitated before asking, "Can I wait until I can show it to Kathleen Maureen?"

"Of course. But she won't appreciate it until she's much older."

Faith smiled then closed the box and returned it to Joe who set it on the side table.

As they walked to the kitchen, Joe asked, "Did Doctor Taylor already visit?"

"Yes. He and Mrs. Taylor arrived around ten o'clock."

When she didn't mention what the doctor said after his examination, Joe wondered if he'd expressed a measure of concern. It would explain why Faith decided to postpone wearing the necklace.

After Faith sat down at the kitchen table, Joe walked to the cold room to gather ingredients for their noon meal. As he prepared their lunch, he told her about the theft of the tins of food from Walker's. He went on to tell her how it led to the discovery of the counterfeiters who were already on their way to Boise City.

He was still telling the story as he and Faith began to eat.

When he finished, Faith said, "Doctor Taylor told me that I'm doing well but when I start having contractions, you need to let him know."

Joe asked, "He doesn't think Sister M.C. is a good midwife?"

"No, he thinks very highly of Sister Mary Catherine and wants her to be notified as well."

Joe nodded as he took a big bite of his salted pork sandwich. He was concerned that Doctor Taylor felt it was necessary he had to be notified when Faith went into labor.

SPRING SURPRISES

And he had no doubt that Faith was much more concerned than he was. If he had an opportunity to talk to the doctor privately, he'd ask if there was any reason for concern. It would have to be soon because he felt Kathleen Maureen wouldn't wait much longer.

The afternoon was uneventful except for a short visit by Will and Bo who gave them an update on their status. They'd moved everything from their wagons into their new homes and did some shopping to fully stock their pantries. They'd just returned from C&L Shipping where they arranged to sell their wagons and teams to Charlie Grossman. They said they might be reporting to work in the morning, but their boss told them there was no rush. They didn't expect the hoards to descend on Idaho City for a few more days.

When Joe returned home, Faith had supper waiting and after he'd disarmed himself, she embraced him and said, "Welcome home, Deputy."

Joe kissed her and asked, "What inspired such an enthusiastic welcome?"

"I'm just expressing my appreciation, husband."

"You didn't need to go to such lengths, my love. I knew how happy and grateful you were when you saw the necklace."

"It's not the necklace that I'm grateful for having. It's you, my wonderful husband."

Joe kissed her again before saying, "Now I imagine you expect me to say how grateful I am for having you, too. But I'm not going to say that. You already know you're not just a part of my life, Faith. You are my life."

Faith sighed then rested her blonde head on his shoulder and tears began to flow from her blue eyes. For more than two silent minutes, the young couple stood in the center of the kitchen simply sharing their emotional warmth.

It was Faith who finally broke the silence when she sniffed, then wiped her wet cheeks and said, "Our supper is getting cold."

Joe smiled, then kissed her once more before they walked to the cookstove and began filling their dinner plates.

The subject of Doctor Taylor's visit didn't enter any of their conversations for the rest of the night, and Faith appeared to be her normal, cheerful self. But before he succumbed to slumber, Joe watched his sleeping wife and could almost feel the tumult in her soul. As he'd done almost every night before he closed his eyes, he asked God to protect and soothe His perfect creation.

CHAPTER 12

Wednesday began normally until midmorning when Will and Bo reported for duty. When they arrived, Sheriff Fulmer shifted into his role as teacher and led them both into his private office.

For the rest of the day, Joe and Rocky handled the complaints and the routine administrative tasks without any serious incidents. At the end of the day, Tap announced a sheriff's office gathering Sunday afternoon at his home. Everyone hoped it would be a quiet Easter Sunday, but they'd settle for a few peaceful hours.

That night, when Joe made his whiskey walk, he was accompanied by Bo and Will. Each of the new deputies carried a shotgun while Joe was only armed with his Remington which was hidden beneath his coat. For once, Joe hoped it wasn't a peaceful stroll past the saloons.

Since they left the jail, Bo and Will talked about how happy their new families were. When they decided to make the journey, they didn't know what to expect, so there was a fair amount of trepidation. But not even in their most optimistic dreams could they have imagined such an amazing outcome.

When they started down the row of saloons, Joe was flanked with Bo on his left and Will on his right. As they walked along the boardwalk, Joe provided a brief description of each barroom and the likelihood of finding trouble.

SPRING SURPRISES

The three deputies passed eight saloons without any problems and Joe was beginning to believe they'd have no incidents at all when they approached The Rich Raccoon. It was not only the place with the strangest name but was also frequented by some of the town's least reputable citizens.

Just as they reached the large front window, they heard shouting followed by the sound of glass shattering. In unison, they turned their heads to look through the stenciled glass.

Bo and Will brought their shotguns level before Joe said, "Hold up. Let's see what happens."

As the three lawmen peered into the smoke-filled barroom, the large room erupted in laughter when two men dropped to their hands and knees to slurp the spilled whiskey from the dirty floor.

Bo said, "I reckon the barkeep musta been yellin' at some drunk and knocked over a bottle."

Joe grinned and said, "Yup. Let's check on the other ones."

Just after they began walking, Will said, "Nora is excited about the big get-together on Sunday. She hopes that it stays nice and quiet, so none of us have to leave."

Bo said, "It's Easter Sunday, so it oughta be peaceful."

Joe glanced through the window of Pete Parker's Palace as he said, "The kind of men who start trouble won't care if it's Easter. I just hope we don't have any surprises during those few hours we're visiting the Fulmers."

Bo nodded as he said, "Amen to that."

———

Joe entered their dark kitchen twenty minutes later and hung his outerwear and gunbelt on their hooks. He softly walked down the hall and entered their bedroom where he found Faith already asleep under the blankets.

He quietly undressed and managed to slip beneath the covers without disturbing Faith. He studied her peaceful face for a few minutes before closing his eyes and offering his nightly prayer for her and their unborn child.

―――

Thursday morning, Joe was still the first one to arrive in the office, but Sheriff Fulmer showed up just as Joe sat behind the desk.

Tap was hanging his coat as he asked, "How'd things go last night?"

"It was one of those rare times when we didn't need to visit a single saloon."

Tap grinned and said, "I hope Bo and Will don't expect it to always be that way."

"I told them it didn't happen very often."

The sheriff sat down and asked, "How's Faith doin'?"

"She's doing well. I think she's a little worried after Doctor Taylor asked to be notified when she went into labor. And to be honest, I'm a bit concerned myself. If I get a chance, I'm going to ask him if he thinks there's a problem."

"I reckon if he found somethin' wrong, he'd tell ya."

"I hope so."

SPRING SURPRISES

Rocky stepped into the jail, yanked off his hat and asked, "Where are the new boys?"

Tap replied, "They oughta be here soon, but you won't be seein' 'em very long. I'll be takin' 'em to Centreville and Placerville today, so you and Joe will be the only law in Idaho City for most of the day."

Joe said, "While you get to meet your pal Marshal Elrod Jefferson's upstanding deputies."

Tap rolled his eyes as he said, "Don't remind me."

Bo and Will arrived a few minutes later but didn't stay long enough to have a cup of coffee before they followed Sheriff Fulmer out the door.

After they were gone, Rocky asked, "I reckon Faith is pretty excited about the big gathering at Tap's house."

"She was happy when I told her about it, but I'll just have to make sure she doesn't overdo it."

"She was getting pretty big the last time I saw her, Joe. Are you sure she's not supposed to have the baby for two more weeks?"

Joe grinned as he replied, "That's what everyone asks her, so I suppose our arithmetic could be off by a few days."

Rocky smiled and said, "As long as she waits 'til Monday."

Joe nodded but almost wished she went into labor today as long as Faith was able to hold their healthy baby in her arms.

———

When Joe entered the kitchen for lunch, he found Faith sitting at the table with Nora.

As he took off his hat, Joe smiled and asked, "Are you all settled in, Nora?"

Nora replied, "Almost. I brought over a pan of hash, so Faith wouldn't have to cook."

Joe hung his coat and said, "That was very kind of you. After my poor offerings, I'm sure Faith will appreciate eating something edible."

Faith laughed and said, "You may not be a chef, Mister Beck, but you cook better than most men. But I can't say the same about your baking ability."

"That's why we have a bakery in town, Mrs. Beck."

Joe stepped to the table, kissed his wife, then asked, "Have you had your lunch yet?"

"I have, but only because I was about to leave to see Nora and Mary's houses. I was waiting to let you know."

"I hope you weren't planning on walking that far. I'll get the buggy ready for you."

"It's not even a half a mile, Joe. I'll be fine and need to stretch my legs."

Joe glanced at Nora who nodded before he said, "Be sure to wear your heavy coat to hide your condition so the old biddies don't faint when they see you parading along the boardwalk."

Faith smiled as she and Nora stood and left the kitchen.

SPRING SURPRISES

Joe snatched a plate from the shelf then walked to the cold room and started grabbing a few loose edibles including an enormous sour pickle.

As he ate his thrown-together lunch, he heard the front door close and felt a bit uneasy letting Faith walk to Nora's house. He knew he was probably being unreasonably protective. But it was partly because of Doctor Taylor's request to be notified immediately when Faith entered labor.

Joe quickly cleared his plate then washed and placed it in the drying rack. He pulled on his hat and was buttoning his coat as he opened the door and left the house.

―――

Joe had to intervene in two minor squabbles that afternoon and Rocky needed to conduct an extensive search to find where Teddy Pollard and Arnie Bishop decided to play hooky. When he found the boys, he escorted them home to face a very short trial before their father-jury-judges administered punishment.

The sheriff and his two new deputies had just returned before it was time to lock up. After Tap provided a brief but harsh description of the men occupying the new Placerville town jail, the five lawmen abandoned their own jail for the night.

Joe walked faster than usual on his way home even though he knew Faith had no difficulties walking to Nora's house and back. When he turned to cross the empty lot east of St. Joseph's school, he was relieved to see smoke floating out of the cookstove pipe.

Joe shook his head and said, "If you keep this up, Beck, you'll be crying like a baby when Faith goes into labor."

After chastising himself, Joe admitted why he was so nervous. He'd calmly faced death many times, from fighting off Confederate soldiers to outrunning an avalanche. But dying was easier than living without Faith. What made it even worse was that it was out of his control.

When Joe entered the kitchen, he saw Faith at the cookstove then took off his hat waved it three times overhead, but just barely or his hat wouldn't clear the ceiling.

Faith laughed and asked, "May I assume you had a quiet afternoon?"

Joe grinned as he hung his hat and replied, "Yes, ma'am. I had a couple of minor incidents, but Rocky hunted down and caught two escapees."

Joe was hanging his coat when Faith asked, "Is he all right? Are they in your jail now?"

Joe unbuckled his gunbelt, slipped the buckle over a brass hook then stepped close to Faith and lassoed her with his long arms.

He kissed her then smiled and said, "They didn't put up a fight, so Rocky's fine. But they aren't in jail. I imagine that Teddy Pollard and Arnie Bishop won't be able to sit down comfortably for a while. They decided to skip school and do some prospecting."

Faith laughed then said, "Maybe they found some gold and bribed the judge."

Joe chuckled then released her and asked, "What did you think of Nora's house?"

SPRING SURPRISES

"It's a nice house, and so is Mary's. They're both very happy and are busy turning them into homes. Nora's further ahead because her children are older, but she sends Jack and Carl to Mary's house to help."

"How was the walk?"

"I'll admit it was fatiguing, but I'm glad I decided to walk."

Joe nodded then left Faith at the cookstove and began setting the table.

―――

Joe handled the cleanup before they adjourned to the couch. After an hour or so, it was obvious that Faith needed to rest, so Joe escorted her to their bedroom. He waited until she was tucked beneath the blankets before kissing her gently, then leaving the room and closing the door behind him.

He was going to return to the kitchen to have some coffee when he changed his mind and headed to his office. After Joe sat behind the desk, he pulled out the new ledgers to see how current Faith was in her entries. He flipped to the last written page and smiled when he found her description of their visit to the canyon. She wrote about the surprise visit by the bear followed by the bigger surprise meeting the Boones and Fergusons. He noticed that she hadn't written a word about Chuck or Marigold.

As he stared at the page, Joe found it hard to believe that just a year ago, Faith couldn't read or write. Now her use of the language and penmanship would put many a schoolmarm to shame. He smiled, closed the journal, and was about to return them to the drawer when he noticed a small ink stain on the edge of the unused ledger.

Joe set aside the journal and opened the second ledger. The first page was blank, but after flipping two more pages, he found one filled with Faith's writing. It wasn't so much a journal. It was a personal diary. Joe was hesitant to read Faith's inner thoughts, but wanted to know if she was troubled, so he turned to the last page with entries.

On the same date she'd entered the journal description of their visit to the canyon, Faith wrote:

March 21

I was overjoyed when we were reunited with the Fergusons and Boones but was filled with grief when Nora told me about Marigold. I was sad for her family, too. The Smiths were all good people. Yet despite my happiness for their unexpected arrival, the news about Marigold is beginning to fill my soul with dread of my own death once again.

I know there is no rational reason for my fear, but it is there. I must learn to live with it and not let it interfere with my life. I pray often to lift this unnecessary fear from my heart, but I don't believe my prayers will be answered. I try to keep my distress from Joe because I cannot add to his burden. At least my fears are most intense at night.

But if I am taken while giving birth, I hope that God will at least grant me a final moment to embrace our child. I only ask for one more heartbeat so I may kiss her forehead.

I will miss nurturing Kathleen Maureen, but even more, I will miss my beloved husband. Heaven cannot be heaven without Joe. I know he will be heartbroken if I die, but I hope he can find another woman to love. I can't imagine any woman could ever love him as much as I do, but Joe needs love.

SPRING SURPRISES

Joe slowly closed the ledger, then returned it and the journal to the drawer. He'd eased her fears before but knew the only thing that could eliminate them completely was when she held Kathleen Maureen in her arms. Until then, he believed the best he could do would be to hide his concerns just as she was disguising her anxiety.

He sighed, then blew out the lamp and left the office. He undressed in the bathroom then tiptoed across the hall and silently entered their bedroom. Joe lifted the blankets and slid onto the bed without waking Faith. After pulling the covers over his shoulders, Joe studied his troubled wife's face for a few minutes before closing his eyes.

Joe and Faith began their Friday as any other weekday, but after Joe left the house, he decided to saddle Duke instead of walking to the office. While he was preparing his stallion, he checked the condition of the mares. They could begin dropping their loads soon and the question of mule or horse foal would be answered. He needed to give all of them, including Bernie more exercise, too.

He mounted Duke and headed down the gravel drive then turned onto Third Street. Even though it was still early, when he swung onto Main Street, he could already see the anticipated increase in traffic. The stream of newcomers was growing each day, and he doubted if even an early spring blizzard would slow it down.

Joe soon entered the jail and after taking off his hat and coat, he started a fire in the heat stove then walked to the back room to fill the coffeepot.

By the time the water had been converted to coffee, Rocky had arrived and was soon followed by Sheriff Fulmer. Will and Bo walked in the door just a minute or so after Tap.

The five lawmen shared coffee and family news for a few minutes before they needed to get to work. Now that he had four deputies, Sheriff Fulmer handed out assignments before heading to his private office. Rocky was given the boring job of minding the desk, and Joe's assignment was to evict a squatter.

He'd established residence in the barn loft of the Putz farm, which was about a mile west of the town. When Amos Putz tried to convince him to move elsewhere, the man had claimed to be a Flathead chief and Amos and his family were the squatters. Amos wasn't sure if he was armed but didn't want to risk getting into a gunfight. What made it more troublesome was that the self-proclaimed Indian was eating their chickens and eggs.

After mounting Duke, Joe turned north on Main Street, then after a short stop at the house, he rode west along A Street. When he passed the abandoned cabin, he wondered if Shorty Griswold and Ronnie Oglesby still had some of those bad five-dollar banknotes in their pockets when they left town. They probably could have spent them in Boise City before dipping into the money that Tap had paid for their buckboard.

Joe left the roadway and began following the ruts that would lead him to the Putz farm. It wasn't so long ago that he followed much deeper ruts left by the wagon train, but this time, he'd only need to be concerned with one Indian. But Joe doubted if the man in the Putz' barn was a Flathead at all, much less a chief.

When he spotted the barn and farmhouse at his ten o'clock, he focused on the open loft doors. As Duke carried him closer,

SPRING SURPRISES

he saw occasional flashes of motion. He suspected that the squatter would spot him soon and notice the shiny badge pinned to his dark coat. Although Mister Putz didn't know if the squatter had a rifle, Joe had to assume that he did.

But Joe didn't pull his Henry or his Sharps as he rode beside the ruts because he didn't want to spook the man. He was still more than four hundred yards away, so he'd have time to move if he saw a muzzle flash.

When Duke carried him past the two-hundred-yard mark, the squatter appeared from the loft's shadows and just stood there looking at him. He didn't have anything in his hands, but if he made a sudden move, Joe would start Duke at a gallop and pull his Henry.

Joe turned his black stallion onto the farm and kept his eyes focused on the squatter who was watching him with his arms folded. His stance seemed to indicate that he was prepared to state his prior claim to the Putz farm to Joe as well, but Joe had already prepared his rebuttal if he tried.

Joe pulled up about a hundred feet from the barn and looked up at the man who looked nothing like an Indian except for his black hair and brown eyes. He even had a thick stubble covering his face.

"I'm Deputy Sheriff Joe Beck. What's your name?"

The squatter replied, "I am Chief Big Bear. This is my land, and you must leave and take those other white eyes with you."

Joe asked, "Are you prepared to fight to make me leave?"

The man slid a large knife from under his belt and exclaimed, "I will fight you like a man without your white man's guns!"

Joe snapped, "You dare to challenge me? A war chief of the great Blackfeet!"

The squatter laughed then shouted, "You are no war chief! You are a white eyed devil!"

Joe took off his hat then hooked it over his saddle horn before he twisted in his saddle and carefully slid his war bonnet from his saddlebag.

He pulled it on then pointed at the amazed squatter and using some of the Lakota he'd learned from Hanepi Wi, he said, "I am a man who fishes."

The squatter silently stared at Joe as he returned the headdress to his saddlebag then put his hat back where it belonged.

With his head recovered, Joe said, "I want you to come down out of there right now, and we'll talk."

The squatter slid his knife into its sheath then turned and walked away. Joe wasn't sure if he went to retrieve his rifle, so he pulled his Henry then dismounted and moved to the side of the barn doors to wait for the man to appear. As he stood beside Duke, he wondered where the Putz family was but didn't take his eyes off the barn.

The squatter soon stepped into the sunlight with a stuffed burlap sack over his shoulder before he spotted Joe and walked towards him.

He stopped a few feet away and asked, "Are you really a Blackfoot war chief?"

"No, I'm not. But a real Blackfoot war chief gave me the headdress as a token of respect. I've met a lot of different

SPRING SURPRISES

tribes, and you're not from any of them. So, what's your real name?"

"Dell Finley."

"Why did you turn these folks' barn into your private hotel and then tell them you were a Flathead war chief?"

Dell shrugged then said, "Me and my brother worked our claim for a whole year without findin' a speck of gold. When I woke up three days ago, our camp was as naked as a tadpole. He took our mules and everything else, even my rifle. I knew about this place and figgered they wouldn't care if I stayed in their loft.

"But I was hungry and there were a lotta eggs just layin' around, so I ate a few then, well…there were a lotta chickens, too. When the farmer spotted me, I didn't wanna leave, so I told him I was a Flathead war chief. It just kinda popped into my head."

Joe glanced at the farmhouse and spotted Amos Putz standing on the front steps before he looked back at Dell and said, "Well, you can't stay here, Mister Finley. After I talk to Mister Putz, I'll walk with you to an abandoned cabin near town. You can stay there and I'm sure you'll be able to find work to fill your belly."

Dell nodded and said, "Okay, I guess that's better."

Joe returned his Henry to its scabbard then took Duke's reins and led him to the farmhouse to explain what had just happened. After telling him of his unwanted guest's situation, Amos agreed with Joe's decision not to jail Dell as long as he didn't return. He was also very grateful for Joe's peaceful resolution of his problem.

After leaving the farm, Joe walked with Dell alongside the ruts and after Dell asked, Joe explained why the Blackfoot war chief had given him the headdress.

When Joe finished his story, Dell asked, "If you was livin' in Missouri, how come you ain't in the army?"

"I wasn't old enough to be conscripted."

Dell quickly turned to look at him before he asked, "How old are you, anyway?"

Joe grinned and replied, "I haven't been asked that in a while, but I just turned seventeen in February."

Dell's eyebrows rose as he exclaimed, "You're joshin' me!"

"No, sir."

"Well, I'll be snookered! I figgered you were a lot older than that. I can't see how a kid your age coulda faced a Blackfoot war party. How long you been a deputy?"

"Six months."

Dell shook his head in disbelief and asked, "I reckon you're lucky you ain't got into any gunfights."

Joe smiled as he answered, "I have a guardian angel."

Dell snickered then pointed and asked, "Is that the cabin you were tellin' me about?"

"Yup. I haven't looked inside, but I don't think you'll find any food. I'll give you some money to keep you fed for a few days before you find a job. Just don't return to the Putz farm and stay out of trouble. If you need help, you can find me at the sheriff's office."

SPRING SURPRISES

As Joe slid his wallet from his inner coat pocket, Dell looked at him and asked, "How come you're bein' so generous?"

Joe pulled a five-dollar bill from the wallet, handed it to Dell and as he slipped his wallet back into his pocket, he replied, "It's Good Friday, Dell."

Dell accepted the banknote and was surprised to see the number five printed on its face. He quickly stuffed it in his pants pocket then offered Joe his hand.

As they shook, Dell said, "I won't give you or anybody else any trouble, Deputy. I promise."

Joe grinned and said, "I appreciate it, Dell. By the way, what is your brother's name and what does he look like?"

"His name's Montgomery, but we call him Monty. He's my older brother and looks a lot like me, but he's a bit taller and heavier. If you run across him, I'd appreciate it if you could make him give me back my rifle. I don't care about the rest of my stuff, but I really liked my rifle."

"What kind of rifle was it?"

"It was a Remington Mississippi, and I kept it a lot cleaner than Monty kept his Springfield. I reckon that's why he stole it."

They stopped before the cabin and Joe said, "Go ahead and check out the cabin. Don't leave until I come back. Okay?"

Dell nodded then watched Joe mount his tall black stallion before he turned and walked to the cabin to inspect his new lodgings.

Joe rode down A Street and soon turned onto Main Street. Two minutes later, he pulled up in front of his house, dismounted and tied off Duke. He bounded up the front porch steps and entered the foyer.

Faith had been sweeping the parlor floor when she heard Joe's hurried entrance and as soon as he stepped into the room, she asked, "Is something wrong, Joe?"

Joe smiled as he took off his hat then walked close and kissed her before saying, "No, sweetheart. Nothing's wrong. I'll tell you all about it when I return."

"I'm sure it'll be interesting."

Joe said, "Not so much this time," then trotted up the stairs.

After grabbing his Mississippi rifle and hanging its ammunition pouch over his shoulder, he hurried down the stairs and smiled at Faith before leaving the house.

Joe slid the Mississippi into his bedroll then released Duke's reins and put his foot into his stirrup. He lifted his right leg as high as he could before he swung it over the long rifle and settled in the saddle seat.

As he rode away from his house, Joe imagined he'd left Faith puzzled when he walked by with his Mississippi rifle. It wasn't his father's rifle, and he hadn't fired it in almost a year, so he had no problem with giving it to Dell. He sounded like a man who would appreciate the gun and care for it properly.

Dell stepped out of the cabin just as Joe pulled up.

Joe didn't dismount and as he slid the ammunition pouch from his shoulder, he said, "I brought you a Mississippi rifle and an ammunition pouch. Take the rifle out of my bedroll, so I don't have to dislocate my hip trying to swing my leg over it again."

SPRING SURPRISES

Dell grinned as he quickly stepped away from the cabin and slid the long rifle from the bedroll while Joe lowered the ammunition pouch to the ground.

Dell was admiring the Remington as he said, "This one's even better than mine. Where'd you get it?"

Joe didn't want to spend the time explaining how he'd acquired the rifle, so he replied, "I had it when I first started out but haven't fired it in almost a year. And a good rifle isn't much use just hanging on a wall."

Dell looked up at Joe and said, "I really appreciate your help, Deputy. And I reckon it's not just 'cause it's Good Friday, either."

Joe smiled, tipped his hat and said, "Call me Joe," then wheeled Duke around and headed back to the road.

When he returned to the jail, he found Sheriff Fulmer alone in the office. Rocky had returned then gone to lunch while Will and Bo had been dispatched to Bill Hedge's ranch. The rancher had sent one of his cowhands to report that someone had stolen his prize bull.

After Joe sat down, Tap asked, "Did you get rid of Amos' squatter?"

"Yes, sir. His name is Dell Finley. He and his older brother were prospecting but had no luck. When Dell woke up a few days ago, he found his loving older brother had taken everything and disappeared. So, he decided to hang his hat in the Putz' barn and enjoy some eggs and a chicken dinner."

Tap snickered then asked, "So, where is he?"

"I gave him new accommodations in that abandoned cabin at the end of A Street. I don't think he'll be a problem."

"Do you mind if I go get some chow before you?"

"No, sir. Besides, you're the boss and you could have just ordered me to stay at the desk."

Sheriff Fulmer was grinning as he stood then walked to the peg wall.

Once he was alone, Joe pulled out the logbook and entered the basic information of his solution to the sad squatter situation. After returning the ledger to the drawer, he wondered how Bo and Will were doing. He began tapping the pencil on the desk as he stared at the door and thought about locking up and riding out to the Hedge ranch.

Joe stopped after seventeen seconds of pencil tapping and laughed. He had just turned seventeen and here he was worrying about two older, more experienced men who would have no problem dealing with the rustlers. Joe returned the abused pencil to the cup and leaned back as he waited for someone to return. Then he'd head home for lunch and explain the missing Mississippi mystery to Faith.

———

Will and Bo were the first to return from what turned out to be a wasted ride as the prize bull had already been found when they arrived. After Joe gave them a very succinct explanation of his visit to the Putz farm, he quickly left the jail, mounted Duke and headed home.

When Joe entered the kitchen, he was appalled to find Faith scooping ashes from the cookstove and exclaimed, "I'll do that!"

SPRING SURPRISES

Faith let him take the shovel before she leaned back and placed her hands on her lower spine and replied, "I just feel so useless these days."

Joe leaned the shovel against the cookstove then took off his hat and kissed her before saying, "You'll never be useless, Faith."

Faith walked to the table, sat down and said, "You work all day and then when you come home, you do most of the cooking and my chores. It just isn't right, Joe."

Joe tossed his hat onto the table then took off his coat and draped it over a chair before sitting down and saying, "You're going to be pretty busy after Kathleen Maureen arrives, Mrs. Beck. I'm just practicing my homemaking skills."

Faith smiled and said, "I am very grateful for your help, but it's so frustrating. I'm even looking forward to being able to cook and clean again. I'll be happy when I can walk like a human again, too."

Joe said, "You'll be light on your feet when you do, ma'am. Now I'll fix lunch and tell you why I needed my Mississippi rifle."

As Joe walked to the cold room, Faith said, "I was wondering why you took it, but now I'm even more curious that you didn't bring it back."

Joe began telling her about Dell the Squatter while he selected lunch items. He kept her entertained with a humorous telling of the unusual situation while he prepared their noon meal. Faith was impressed with his use of the Blackfoot headdress and laughed when he told her what he'd said in Lakota to convince Dell of his bona fides. By the time he described his Good Friday solution to the issue, they'd finished eating.

Joe had cleared the table and was washing the dishes when Faith asked, "How long do we need to stay at the shindig on Sunday?"

Joe placed the last clean plate into the drying rack as he replied, "We'll stay as long or as short as you want. We don't even have to go if you'll be uncomfortable. Tap decided to have it so the families could meet each other, but we already know everyone."

"Let me see how I feel on Sunday."

Joe was sliding his right arm through his coat sleeve as he grinned and replied, "Maybe you'll be too busy feeding Kathleen Maureen."

Faith smiled and rubbed her swollen middle as she said, "It would be a little early, but I won't complain."

Joe snatched his hat from the table, kissed Faith then said, "Remind me to return the headdress to the closet when I get back."

"Yes, sir."

Joe pulled on his hat then waved before opening the door and leaving the house. As he trotted down the porch steps, he glanced at the bullet wedged into the board then shook his head and mumbled, "You're getting forgetful in your old age, Beck."

SPRING SURPRISES

Friday afternoon was hectic, but each of the situations was more annoyingly time-consuming than dangerous. Before they closed shop, Joe told Tap that there was a chance he and Faith might not be at the gathering because of Faith's burden. Sheriff Fulmer said he'd tell Mary and was sure she would understand as most mothers would.

After the short ride home, Joe walked Duke into his barn and dismounted. As he unsaddled his tall stallion, he was proud of himself for remembering to remove the headdress from his saddlebag. While Duke was greedily emptying his full sack of oats, Joe slipped the war bonnet from his saddlebag and was about to leave the barn when he smiled and took off his hat. He laid the hat on a shelf, donned the headdress then retrieved his hat and left the barn.

He was grinning as he opened the kitchen door expecting to hear Faith's laugh but was disappointed when she wasn't there to witness his impressive entrance.

He hung his hat and was taking off his coat when Faith called, "I'm in the parlor with Sister Mary Catherine, Joe."

Joe hung his gunbelt and debated whether or not to remove the headdress. He didn't take long to decide to make Sister M.C. laugh as well. So, he adjusted his feathered headpiece then squared his shoulders and strutted down the hallway.

He stepped into the parlor then stopped and solemnly faced Faith and Sister Mary Catherine before saying the same Lakota words he'd spoken to Dell Finley.

Sister Mary Catherine was momentarily stunned, but Faith immediately burst into laughter before she was joined by the unstartled nun.

Joe grinned, removed the headdress and said, "I'll be right back," then crossed the parlor and bounded up the stairs.

Less than a minute later, he returned bareheaded and sat down on the couch beside Faith.

Faith smiled and said, "That was a spectacular entrance, Chief Silly Surprise."

Sister Mary Catherine said, "Faith told me how you handled the squatter, and I was very impressed with your compassion. When I asked her where you'd gotten the headdress, she told me the story about your confrontation with the Blackfoot war party. I can't imagine how frightening that must have been."

Joe shrugged then replied, "I really didn't have another choice, Sister. If I'd turned and rode away, they would have caught up with me then attacked the wagon train."

"I still can't believe you just sat on your horse and waited for them."

"I knew they wouldn't bother me because I didn't matter. When they saw the other scout riding back to warn the folks, the chief knew they'd lost their element of surprise. So, if they pressed their attack, he'd lose too many warriors."

Faith said, "My husband is being too modest, Sister. He probably saved everyone in the wagon train at least three times. He even stopped a dozen rebel soldiers from killing a Union captain when he was just fifteen."

Sister Mary Catherine stood then said, "You'll have to tell me those stories tomorrow, Faith. I'll be here just after noon."

SPRING SURPRISES

Joe and Faith both rose and walked with the good sister down the hallway to the kitchen. Faith took a seat at the table and Joe hurried to open the back door.

As Sister Mary Catherine passed through the doorway, she glanced at Joe and smiled before stepping onto the porch.

After closing the door, Joe said, "Did Sister M.C. check on Katie, or was this a social call?"

Faith replied, "She always gives me an examination, but most of the time, we just talk. So, is it just Katie now?"

Joe opened the cookstove's firebox door and said, "I'm just practicing. When I greet her, I don't want to confuse her by using Katherine Maureen."

Faith laughed then said, "I don't think she'll be able to understand what you're saying, Mister Beck."

Joe lit the kindling then closed the door before stepping to the table, taking a seat and kissing his wife before he said, "With such a smart mother, I wouldn't be surprised if she looks at me and tells me I need to shave."

Faith ran her fingertips across his cheek then smiled and said, "You do need to shave. But if she does notice, it'll be because she has such a remarkable father."

Joe gazed into her deep blue eyes for a few seconds before he stood and started preparing their supper.

As the light waned, so did Faith's cheerful mood. By the time she slid beneath the covers, the feeling of morbid fate was creeping back into her mind and soul. She lay on her side watching Joe strip off his britches and felt a powerful urge to confess her worries.

Faith had just dismissed the idea when Joe sat on the bed and smiled at her. And even though she returned his smile, Joe could almost feel her anxiety.

He wasn't sure if it was her familiar demons that had returned to haunt her, but as he leaned over to blow out the lamp, he had a revelation when he saw the blue jewelry box sitting on the table beside it.

Joe opened the lid of the velvet case and carefully lifted the necklace from the box.

Faith quietly asked, "Why are you taking it out now, Joe?"

Joe smiled as he dangled the garnet before her blue eyes and replied, "I know you told me that you didn't want to wear it until you could show it to Kathleen Maureen. But when you're holding her, it would be awkward for you to reach to the side table and put it on, wouldn't it? So, I think you should already be wearing it when Doctor Taylor places her in your arms."

Faith was staring at the necklace when Joe said, "Then as you look at your infant's face for the first time, you can just lift the garnet and show it to her. And you can tell her that when she's older, she'll be wearing one, too."

Faith looked at Joe and whispered, "She'll be perfect, won't she?"

Joe kissed her on the forehead then said, "She has to be perfect because she'll have a perfect mother."

Faith smiled and rolled onto her back before Joe carefully fastened the white gold necklace around her throat. She then

SPRING SURPRISES

took the garnet in her fingers and looked at it in the dim lamplight for a few seconds before rolling back onto her left side.

Joe blew out the lamp then slipped under the blankets and wrapped Faith in his arms. He kissed her softly then heard her sigh before she closed her eyes. He wasn't sure if the necklace would serve as a barrier to her fears but still asked God to put an end to her mind's torture.

His prayer would soon be answered but not as he hoped or expected.

Joe was preparing breakfast when Faith stepped into the kitchen and took a seat at the table. He was pleased when he saw her wearing a smile as well as the necklace.

He stepped away from the cookstove, kissed her and said, "Good morning, sweetheart."

Faith lifted the garnet and said, "Good morning, my love. And thank you for changing my mind about the necklace. When I finally got out of bed, I walked to the window and held the garnet in the sunlight. It's very beautiful, but it means much more than a pretty gemstone."

Joe hurried back to the cookstove and flipped the slab of ham over before he said, "I'll stop by Faircloth's and see if he's finished with the small one that we found during our interrupted visit to our canyon. He thought it was another six-star, and if it is, I'll have him make it into a necklace for Katie."

Faith smiled and asked, "What will you do with it if Sam arrives instead?"

Joe stuck a fork in the ham, transferred it to a plate then replied, "If Katie turns out to be Sam, maybe we should give it to Grace. After all, Miss Fulmer does bear your overlooked name, Faith Hope Charity Virtue Goodchild Beck."

Joe began cracking eggs and dumping them into the frypan's sizzling grease as Faith said, "You'll never stop reminding me of my thirty-five-letter name, will you?"

Joe was scrambling the eggs as he answered, "No, ma'am. I'm acting out of jealousy because mine has just a fifth as many letters. At least I only appended four letters to your already lengthy appellation when we were married."

Faith laughed and watched her husband continue to scrape and flip the eggs until he pulled the frypan from the hot plate and scooped them onto their plates.

As they shared their morning meal, Faith asked, "Do you have the walk tonight?"

"Yes, ma'am. At least now it's only once every five days."

"For which I am very grateful. Are you riding Duke to work?"

"I'll probably use Porch today. He needs the exercise and so do the mares and Bernie. Before I leave, I'll move them all to the corral where they have more room."

"I imagine Bessie will foal Bernie's offspring, and Duchess will deliver Duke's foal, but Betty and Nellie could go either way."

Joe said, "Personally, I'd prefer that Betty and Nellie both foal either jennies or jacks. They're more useful than horses and live longer. But I'm sure Duchess' foal was sired by Duke and should be very handsome."

SPRING SURPRISES

"Are we going to keep them?"

"It depends on what they are and what we need. But we're not going to sell Duchess' foal. We'll keep their firstborn for our firstborn. When Katie is old enough, she'll learn to ride on the horse she grew up with."

Faith patted her bump and said, "Did you hear your father's promise, Katie? But you won't ride your tall horse until you're seven."

Joe chuckled then quickly cleared his plate before taking it and his empty cup to the sink.

―――

Twenty minutes later, Joe pulled Porch to a stop before the jail and dismounted. When he entered the office, he was almost embarrassed when he realized he was the last one to arrive.

As he took off his hat, Sheriff Fulmer grinned and said, "We were beginnin' to wonder if Faith was in labor already."

Joe laughed then hung his hat and was unbuttoning his coat when he said, "I'm sure she wished that was true, but after I saddled Porch, I moved the mares, Duke and Bernie to the corral."

Rocky asked, "How long before those mares start dropping foals?"

"They should start arriving next month, but Duchess won't foal until June."

Bo smiled and said, "And I guess you'll be expectin' Bessie and Betty to give you mules, too."

"That's what we think, too. But if Duchess drops a jack or a jenny, Duke might have a word or two with Bernie."

The sheriff and three deputies laughed as Joe stepped to the heat stove hoping that Rocky hadn't made the coffee.

Shortly after finishing his coffee, Joe donned his hat and coat and left the jail. He mounted Porch and headed south to John Griffith's lumber mill. It was just two miles north of Fort Boise, so it would be a long ride. His assignment was to investigate the death of a lumberjack. They'd found a note on the floor from a lumberjack who claimed a friend of his had been murdered by the foreman.

The army usually handled any trouble in the local area, but this was out of their scope. Joe hoped it wouldn't be long before Boise City hired a town marshal as they'd probably have a larger population than Placerville within a year.

Joe soon passed their canyon and planned to pay a short visit to the pool on his way back if he had the time. He only hoped the bear had filled his belly by now.

He had Porch moving at a fast trot and soon began passing traffic on its way to Idaho City. There were groups of riders, and some were leading pack animals. He greeted three freight wagons and when he was around halfway to Boise City, he waved to the driver of the Coleman Line's new stagecoach.

As Joe acknowledged each group of riders, he checked their weapons and their overall appearance before making a quick evaluation of which ones might cause trouble. Most were making the journey in hope of discovering riches, but there was one pair of men he marked as a potential problem.

SPRING SURPRISES

It was midmorning when Joe turned Porch to the west and entered the extensive lumber operation. He headed to the large building where the logs were turned into boards, posts and columns then stacked to dry.

Joe wanted to talk to the lumberjack without the foreman being present and assumed he was still on the job because it was difficult to find men willing to do the dangerous work rather than ride north to hunt for gold. But he wasn't sure where to find him, so he'd probably need to talk to the foreman first.

Joe pulled Porch to a stop before the mill then dismounted and tied off the gelding before walking to the wide doorway. The sound of one large circular saw cutting boards and another turning long logs into short logs was almost deafening as he headed to the small, enclosed office.

He opened the door and looked inside, but the room was empty, so he turned around and walked towards a man he assumed was the foreman. He was talking to a worker who was sharpening a dull circular blade when he turned and spotted the tall young man wearing the silver badge. He quickly ended the conversation and walked to meet Joe.

When the foreman was close, he pointed and yelled, "We can talk in my office, Deputy."

Joe nodded then walked beside the foreman and soon entered the relative quiet of the small office.

The foreman sat behind his ugly cluttered desk and Joe took a seat on one of the three chairs scattered around the small space.

The foreman said, "My name's Paul Brown, and I reckon you're here about Cody Anderson's death."

Joe studied the foreman's eyes as he replied, "Yes, sir. I'm Deputy Joe Beck and the only reason I had to ride down here is one of his friends claimed he had been murdered."

Paul leaned forward and said, "That's what I heard from some of the men this morning. So, I reckon you'll want to talk to Bill Roberts after we're finished. He's working on the northwest section right now."

"I'll do that. But tell me what happened. All I know is what was written on the short note that was left under our door."

"Cody was a high climber, the most dangerous job for a lumberman. It's why they get paid more than those fellers out in the cutting room. Anyway, he was at near the top of a ninety-foot spruce when his rope snapped. Nobody survives a fall like that."

"So, why did Mister Roberts accuse you of murdering him?"

"When I got there, he blamed me for his pal's death 'cause I wouldn't give him new rope. I told him if Cody wanted a new rope, he just needed to see Ed Smith in supply. We aren't going to risk losing a high climber for a few cents' worth of rope."

Joe nodded then stood and said, "I'll go talk to Mister Roberts and then I'll return and tell you what I'll write in my report."

The foreman replied, "I'll stay in the cutting room until you get back."

As Joe mounted Porch, he was reasonably convinced that the foreman was telling the truth. He suspected that Bill

SPRING SURPRISES

Roberts was just looking for someone to blame for his friend's death and didn't like the foreman.

He headed northwest through the acres of stumps until he found the work crews bringing down the tall pines. He had to angle more to the north to avoid falling trees but soon approached the closest lumbermen. He dismounted and tied off Porch to a small oak before he approached the clump of workers.

Joe stopped and asked, "Where can I find Bill Roberts?"

The lumberman just pointed at a stocky man swinging a double-edged axe into the thick trunk of a nearby pine. Joe nodded but as he started walking, he was surprised when his sense of danger arrived. He didn't know why it did, but he wasn't about to ignore it, so he unbuttoned his coat and released his Remington's hammer loop.

Joe halted about ten feet from Bill Roberts who seemed to ignore him as he vigorously attacked the defenseless pine. He waited for almost thirty seconds expecting the lumberjack to stop working and acknowledge him, but he kept slamming the sharp axe into the trunk.

Joe finally shouted, "Mister Roberts? I'm Deputy Joe Beck. Could I talk to you about Cody Anderson?"

Bill focused on the tree and kept cutting as if Joe didn't exist. The deep wedge he'd created was almost halfway into the trunk and Joe thought he wanted to finish the job before talking to him. But his sense of danger told him that Mister Roberts had a very different reason for ignoring him.

As Bill's axe cut even deeper into the tree, Joe quickly calculated the arc of the axe if the lumberjack tried to swing it in his direction and took a step backwards. It wasn't a moment too soon.

The tall tree began to tip before the remaining trunk gave way with a loud crack and it crashed to the ground. If Joe's danger sense hadn't warned him, he probably would have watched the tree fall. But almost immediately after the crack, Bill turned, took one step and swung his axe at Joe.

Joe watched the axe's sharp blade as it curved through the air and still had to lean back to avoid being sliced open like a fish.

Bill was surprised when his axe whooshed past without stopping, but the momentum of the heavy tool spun him off balance.

Before the lumberjack could regain his footing, Joe pulled his Remington, cocked the hammer and shouted, "Drop the axe! Now!"

Joe would never know what had motivated Bill to take the killing swing, but it seemed to drive all rational behavior from his mind.

As soon as he regained his balance, Bill raised the axe above his head and shouted, "I didn't kill him!"

In his enhanced mode, Joe waited until Bill began to step forward and the axe started its downward arc before he fired. But even after his Remington's .44 slammed into Bill's chest, Joe had to jump aside as the dying lumberjack finished his last swing. Bill's axe head punched into the ground before he fell onto the handle with his face narrowly missing the back edge.

Joe holstered his pistol then stepped to Bill and rolled him onto his back.

SPRING SURPRISES

He was still breathing when Joe angrily exclaimed, "I only wanted to talk to you! *Why didn't you just drop the axe? Why did you make me shoot you?*"

Bill's mouth opened and closed three times, but no words escaped his lips before he stopped breathing.

Joe stood then took a deep breath before he turned to the small crowd of startled lumbermen and loudly asked, "Do any of you know why he acted that way?"

Among the murmuring negative responses, one of them said, "They were havin' words yesterday before Cody fell, but I don't know what it was about."

Joe said, "I guess it doesn't matter. I've got to tell Mister Brown what happened. Can you bring his body?"

The same lumberjack replied, "We'll take care of it, Deputy. There wasn't anything you coulda done different."

Joe nodded then walked to Porch, untied his reins and mounted. As he rode back to the cutting building, Joe wondered if there hadn't been a better way of handling the situation. Maybe he could have stepped aside and knocked him in the head with his pistol's barrel. Before he reached the large, noisy building, Joe decided that there was no purpose to dwelling on what he could have done. But he still felt guilty for having to shoot the lumberman.

After he told Mister Brown what had happened, the foreman wasn't able to explain why Bill had acted that way, either. Paul said he'd notify his boss, so Joe left the building just five minutes later.

When Joe turned onto the road, it was already around eleven o'clock, so he pushed Porch to a fast trot. He'd need to tell Tap about the incident and write his report, so he probably wouldn't make it home until mid-afternoon. He definitely wouldn't have time to visit the canyon, either.

Ninety minutes later, Joe stopped in the middle of the creek that crossed the road to let Porch drink. He was quenching his own thirst from his canteen when he spotted a fast-moving rider in the distance. He capped his canteen and hung it from his saddle horn then tapped his heels into Porch's flanks to get him moving.

Porch had just stepped onto dry land when Joe identified the rider. He nudged his gelding to a faster pace to find out why Bo was rushing to meet him.

Bo was fifty yards away when he pulled up then wheeled Ranger around and just before Joe reached him, he started his gelding forward.

When Joe pulled up alongside, Bo exclaimed, "Faith is gonna have her baby!"

Joe was stunned by the early news and excitedly asked, "*When did she start having contractions? Is Doctor Taylor with her? Is she all right?*"

"When I left, the doc and the nun were with her, and so was Nora. But I reckon by the time you get home the doc might be back in his office. And Faith is doin' fine."

Joe knew Kathleen Maureen wouldn't arrive for hours, but still was still anxious to be with Faith. So much so, that he didn't give a thought to what had happened less than an hour earlier. But when Bo asked, Joe described the strange confrontation in detail to fill the time for the rest of the ride.

SPRING SURPRISES

The landscape seemed to pass by in slow motion, but when they reached his canyon, Joe knew he'd see Faith in just a few more minutes.

Just as they entered Idaho City, Bo said, "Tap ain't expectin' you back, so I'll tell him what happened. I reckon he'll be payin' you a visit later, too."

Joe nodded but kept his eyes focused ahead as Bo pulled up in front of the jail. He soon turned right onto Third Street and finally slowed Porch just before he swung onto his graveled drive. Despite his anxiety, after he dismounted, he led his exhausted horse into the barn and quickly unsaddled him before hurrying to the house.

He leapt up the back steps then bounded across the porch and burst into the kitchen.

Nora was at the sink filling a pitcher when she heard Joe's thunderous arrival, so when he flew into the kitchen, she said, "Slow down, Joe. It's going to be a long time before you meet your child, and Faith is doing fine."

Joe ripped off his hat, hung it and was popping his coat's buttons as he asked, "Can I go see her?"

"Of course, you can. Wait until I finish filling the pitcher."

Joe hung his coat then took off his gunbelt and slid the buckle over a hook before he stepped to the sink and said, "I'll take that for you, Nora."

As Joe picked up the large pitcher, he asked, "How long ago did she go into labor?"

Nora replied, "Shortly after noontime, just as Sister Mary Catherine arrived," then she and Joe walked to the hallway.

After passing their bedroom, Joe entered their nursery just as Faith grunted.

Before he could ask how she was doing, Faith smiled and said, "I was surprised when Katie decided she wanted to see the outside world, and I imagine you were just as surprised when Bo told you."

Joe stepped past Sister Mary Catherine, set the pitcher on the side table then leaned down and kissed Faith before sitting on the chair next to the head of the bed.

"I was more than just surprised, sweetheart. I only wish I hadn't been so far away when it started."

"Doctor Taylor said Katie might not arrive until after midnight because she's my first baby. So, she'll be born on Easter Sunday."

Joe took her hand and said, "Whenever she arrives, I know she'll be as beautiful as her mother."

Faith laughed lightly before saying, "You're getting even more maudlin than usual, Mister Beck."

Joe asked, "Is there anything I can do for you?"

"No. But pretty soon, you'll be banned from the room. And I want you to behave like a normal husband and stay in the kitchen drinking gallons of coffee."

He smiled then turned to Sister Mary Catherine and asked, "Is Doctor Taylor going to return?"

"When Faith's contractions get closer, I'll have someone fetch him."

SPRING SURPRISES

Joe nodded then Faith asked, "Did anything happen at the lumber camp?"

Joe said, "I expected it to be just a matter of talking to the man who left the note claiming his foreman had killed his friend, but it turned out much differently. When I arrived…"

As Joe told the story, he watched Faith, but not for her reaction to what he was saying. He could already see the strain on her face and knew she would suffer for hours. Knowing that that all mothers endured the pain of labor and childbirth didn't diminish his strong compassion for Faith. He also felt a deep sense of guilt knowing that he was the cause of her suffering.

When he finished his story, Faith said, "You couldn't have done anything different, Joe. You might have missed if you tried to hit him in the head and then he would have been angrier."

Joe nodded then said, "I know. But it was just so unnecessary."

Sister Mary Catherine said, "I agree with Faith, Joe. You did nothing wrong. But I'm afraid I need you to leave for a while. I'll let you know when you can return."

Joe nodded, said, "Yes, ma'am," then stood, kissed Faith and stepped past Sister M.C. and left the room.

After Nora closed the door, he walked to the kitchen then entered the cold room to pick out his lunch's ingredients. After selecting a choice sour pickle and clenching it between his teeth, he began gathering the rest of his selections.

He was sitting at the table eating his thick ham and cheese sandwich when he heard footsteps on the porch. When the door opened, Sheriff Fulmer and Rocky stepped inside.

Tap took off his hat and said, "Bo told me what happened, Joe. That musta been one helluva surprise when that feller took a swing at ya."

"I almost expected him to do something rash when he acted as if I wasn't even there. But after I told him to drop the axe, I was surprised when decided to take another swing at me."

Rocky grinned and said, "I reckon your day is full of surprises, Joe. And it ain't over yet."

Joe said, "There's a reasonably fresh pot of coffee on the cookstove if you're going to stick around."

Tap said, "I never turn down a cup of coffee," then he and Rocky stepped to the shelf to grab a mug.

After their cups were full of hot, black brew, they sat at the table and Tap said, "I'm goin' back to the jail shortly, but Rocky's gonna stick around 'til he heads to the boarding house for supper. Mary is gonna stop by later to spell Nora for a while, and I'll come along to keep you from goin' crazy. Bo and Will are gonna show up, too. I reckon we can play poker most of the night."

Joe said, "I appreciate it, boss. But I'll be all right."

Tap smiled and said, "It's not about you, Joe. Our wives kinda ordered us to keep you from bustin' in while Faith's havin' the baby."

Joe grinned as he said, "And here I thought you were in charge, Sheriff."

SPRING SURPRISES

Rocky laughed before Tap gulped down his coffee, stood then said, "I'll see you later, Joe. Don't worry about writin' your report 'til Monday."

Joe said, "Thanks, Tap," then watched Sheriff Fulmer pull on his hat and leave the kitchen.

Joe finished eating as he and Rocky talked about the strange lumber yard confrontation and other work-related topics. As he was washing his plate, Joe looked down the hall and wondered why he hadn't been granted permission to enter the room yet.

When Joe returned to his seat, Rocky surprised him when he started talking about Chen Ai, Mister Chen's oldest daughter. It seemed that Rocky had been the laundry's best customer since Sarah married Jim Pritchard. He had even learned that her parents wouldn't object if Chen Ai married a white man. After his initial astonishment, Joe was able to let Rocky ramble on about Chen Ai as he waited to hear Nora open the nursery door.

Rocky was still expressing his admiration for the diminutive Oriental woman when Joe heard Nora announce that he was being allowed to visit Faith.

He bolted from the chair and hurried down the hall before swinging into the room and stepped to the head of the bed. When he looked at Faith, she was smiling but already seemed exhausted.

After he sat down, he took her hand then kissed her softly and asked, "How are you, sweetheart?"

She replied, "I'm okay. The contractions are getting…"

As Faith gripped his hand like a vise, Joe watched her face scrunch in pain.

After the contraction ended, Faith released her grip, took a deep breath and said, "They're getting stronger and more frequent."

Joe asked, "How frequent?"

"I'm not sure. But Sister Mary Catherine said they aren't close enough to call Doctor Taylor."

"As soon as he's needed, I'll ride Duke to his house to let him know."

Faith smiled and said, "Don't turn Main Street into a race course, Joe."

Joe managed to create a reasonable smile before saying, "I promise to be reasonable. Maybe I'll harness the buggy so I can bring the doctor back with me."

"That's much more reasonable."

Joe felt his allotted time was close to an end, so he said, "The next time I visit, I'll bring our Bible, a pen and a bottle of ink. I'll trust you not to misspell Kathleen Maureen."

Faith laughed then said, "I think I can manage to get it right."

Joe nodded then he and Faith gazed into each other's eyes for almost thirty seconds before Sister Mary Catherine laid her hand on Joe's left shoulder.

SPRING SURPRISES

Joe said, "I'll be back whenever Sister M.C. gives me permission," the kissed her once more before standing and leaving the nursery.

After the door closed behind him, Joe didn't return to the kitchen, but turned right and headed to the office. He entered the dimly lit room and took a seat behind the desk. The Bible was on the corner of the desk, and a bottle of ink and a narrow box with pens and nibs were on the desktop as well. He'd bring them to the kitchen when he left the office.

Joe slowly opened the middle drawer and took out a small leather pouch and set it on the desktop. He pulled open the top then slid his father's watch and the winding key into his hand. He'd only wound the watch once to check its condition, but now he wanted to use it to mark the time of Kathleen Maureen's birth. He didn't know the current time but could make a reasonable estimate.

Joe opened the lid and when he looked at his mother's lock of hair resting on the inside of the gold cover, he quietly said, "Faith is going to have your first grandchild soon, Mama. You and papa would be so proud of her and would love her almost as much as I do.

"Before I wind papa's watch, I have an indulgence to ask of you. Could you and papa add your voices to mine in beseeching Our Lord to protect Faith? I want to hear her singing Kathleen Mavourneen to Katie just as you sang it to me. And I want you both to know that I am forever grateful for having you and papa to guide me and teach me what matters in this world."

Joe wound the watch and after the second hand began to move, he set the time 5:20 and closed the lid. He slipped the watch into his pocket then stood, picked up the Bible, the bottle of ink and the pen before leaving the office.

When he returned to the kitchen, Rocky stood and said, "I gotta get to the boarding house for supper, Joe."

Joe set the Good Book, ink and pen on the table and said, "There's no need for you to return, Rocky. It's going to be a long night and I'll be okay."

Rocky was pulling on his coat as he replied, "Okay. I reckon Tap, Will and Bo will be able to keep you company."

After Rocky left, Joe added wood to the cookstove's fire, then began preparing a large pot of stew to keep everyone fed.

Joe's stomach was already rumbling as he tasted the thick stew then slid the pot from the hot plate and walked to the shelf to take down three bowls. He was setting the table when he heard the nursery door open and close.

Nora soon stepped into the kitchen and said, "I was going to prepare supper when the aroma of whatever you're cooking reached my nose."

"I made a large pot of stew and was just about to fill my bowl. How is Faith doing?"

"She's progressing nicely. Sister Mary Catherine estimated that she has at least six more hours to go."

Joe nodded then said, "Have a seat, Nora, and I'll bring your dinner."

Nora sat at the table and said, "Thank you, Joe. I'm not accustomed to being served."

SPRING SURPRISES

Joe replied, "Don't thank me until you taste my creation, Nora," then walked to the cookstove and began scooping the stew into two bowls.

After he set the bowls on the table, he sat in his usual chair and said grace before he and Nora started eating.

Nora swallowed her first bite and said, "This is very good, Joe."

"You're just being considerate, Nora. When can I see Faith again?"

"You can ask Sister Mary Catherine when I take her place so she can enjoy your marvelous stew."

As Joe buttered his biscuit, Nora asked, "Where is Bo? I thought he was going to stay with you."

"I imagine he's having supper with the children. Tap and Will are probably sharing dinner with their families as well. Will has tonight's saloon stroll, too. But now that we have four deputies, our boss wants Rocky to go along because it's a Saturday."

"Even on Holy Saturday?"

"The men who frequent those saloons and bawdy houses aren't worried about their souls, Nora."

"I'm sure you're right. But if any men need to worry about their mortal souls, they should."

Joe smiled, said, "Amen to that," then took a big bite of his biscuit.

As Joe and Nora shared supper, Nora tried to ease Joe's anxiety by talking about her experience in giving birth to her four children. She spoke as if it was nothing more than having a long bellyache but emphasized the joy of holding each of her newborns.

Joe understood why she described her four long labors in that manner and appreciated her thoughtfulness. But even as he listened to Nora, he could hear Faith's muffled cries of pain emanating from the nursery.

When they were almost finished eating, Joe said, "I'll clean up, Nora."

Nora stood and said, "You're spoiling me, Joe. I'll relieve Sister, so you can spoil her."

Joe smiled as Nora disappeared into the dark hallway then picked up their empty bowls and set them in the sink. He pumped some water onto the bowls before he walked to the cookstove to fill a bowl for Sister Mary Catherine.

He had just set the steaming bowl onto the table when he heard Sister M.C.'s footsteps.

When she floated into the kitchen, Joe said, "Have a seat, Sister, and I'll bring you a cup of hot coffee. How are you holding up?"

Sister Mary Catherine took Nora's seat before replying, "I'm doing very well, Joe, and so is Faith. Nora told me you made a very good stew."

Joe was pouring coffee as he said, "She was just being considerate. But you can judge for yourself, Sister."

SPRING SURPRISES

After he set the coffee onto the table, Joe sat down and waited for Sister Mary Catherine to say grace before taking another biscuit from the small pile.

Sister M.C. tasted the stew and said, "I agree with Nora's assessment of your cooking skills. And I noticed that you didn't add any sour pickles to the stew."

Joe grinned as he said, "I knew I forgot something."

After Sister Mary Catherine laughed, she surprised Joe when began to devour the stew like a half-starved prospector.

He took a bite of his biscuit and washed it down with some coffee before asking, "When can I visit Faith again?"

The nun swallowed then replied, "You can come along with me after I've finished all of your marvelous stew."

"Thank you, Sister. Is there anything I can do to help her?"

"No. I'm afraid it's all up to Faith and your child now. Did you harness the buggy yet?"

"No, ma'am. I'll do that after I see her."

"I glad that you remembered to bring your Bible as you promised as this will probably be your last visit."

Joe nodded then sipped his coffee and wondered if Faith had explained why he wanted to leave it with her.

Then the good sister said, "Oh. And I need to tell you one more thing. When you see her, don't be alarmed if she seems angry for putting her through this. She will probably insult you and call you despicable names, too. I have never attended a birthing when the mother didn't lash out at her husband."

"I wouldn't blame her if she tried to shoot me, Sister."

Sister M.C. laughed then said, "Then I guess you're lucky there isn't a pistol in the nursery."

Joe grinned then swallowed the last of his coffee.

When Sister Mary Catherine finished, she stood and took her bowl, spoon and cup to the sink while Joe picked up their Bible, the bottle of ink and the pen.

When he entered the dimly lit nursery, he was shaken when he saw Faith. Her face looked drawn and was bathed in perspiration. But she still smiled as he sat down, set the Bible on the side table then carefully aligned the pen and ink bottle.

He took her sweaty hand and kissed her before saying, "Sister told me this is probably the last time I'll be allowed in the nursery until you have Kathleen Maureen in your arms."

"That may be a while. Do you have any male visitors to keep you company?"

"Not at the moment. But I'm sure one or more of them will show up soon."

Faith touched the garnet and said, "Thank you for making me wear my necklace, Joe. It's…"

Joe felt her tight grip and wanted to turn his eyes away to avoid witnessing her pain but forced himself to watch her grimace as a small penance for causing it.

When the contraction ended, Faith breathed deeply for a few seconds before she looked into Joe's eyes and softly said, "I hope Katie has your green eyes, Joe."

SPRING SURPRISES

Joe kissed her again before saying, "You know I want her to have your blue eyes and be just as pretty as her beautiful mother."

Faith smiled and said, "I thought you were done with maudlin."

Joe grinned and replied, "I'm only maudlin with you, my love, and I'm not about to stop."

When the sound of the kitchen door being slammed shut reached the nursery, Nora stood and said, "I think Tap and Mary are here," then left the nursery.

Joe looked at Sister M.C. and asked, "Can Faith have some stew?"

"I think she can have some gravy, but nothing solid."

Joe nodded then said, "After I leave, I'll give it to Nora or Mary if she's taking over."

Faith very quietly said, "Joe, I need to tell you something."

When Joe leaned close to her lips, Faith whispered, "I won't tattle if I find a small piece of beef or potato in the gravy."

Joe managed to keep from laughing by kissing her before he leaned back and said, "You know I always do whatever you ask of me, Mrs. Beck."

"I know you do, even when it's a silly request."

Sister Mary Catherine had a pretty good idea of what Faith had whispered to Joe but didn't object. But the time between contractions was growing short enough for her to end Joe's visit. So, she laid her hand on his shoulder again to let him know it was time to leave.

Joe smiled at Faith as he said, "I'm being ordered to vacate the nursery, sweetheart. So, I'll kiss you once more. When I see you again, I'll kiss you first before I kiss Kathleen Maureen."

Joe leaned across the bed and shared a long, loving kiss before he stood, smiled at Faith then took off his imaginary hat and waved it three times overhead. He tugged it back on then left the nursery.

He soon entered the kitchen and greeted Tap, Mary and Bo.

He smiled and said, "It looks like I'll have to make another pot of coffee."

Bo said, "You might need another coffee pot, Joe. Rocky and Will are makin' the whiskey walk, but they might stop by later."

Nora said, "Mary hasn't been a midwife before, so I'll return after I put the children to bed."

Joe had snatched a clean bowl and was walking to the cookstove when he said, "If you'll wait for a few minutes, I'll drive you home in the buggy. I want to have it ready when I need to fetch Doctor Taylor."

Nora said, "Thank you, Joe."

Joe used the ladle to spoon Faith's gravy into the bowl and was sure to include small pieces of beef, potato, onion and carrots.

SPRING SURPRISES

When the bowl was a little more than half full, he grabbed a spoon and asked, "Mary, could you bring this to Faith?"

Mary nodded, took the bowl of warm stew then walked down the hallway.

Joe said, "I'll be right back after I get the buggy ready," then grabbed his hat, pulled it on then snatched his coat from its hook and left the kitchen without putting it on.

He waited until he was on the ground before he slid his right arm through his coat's sleeve and entered the barn before he had it buttoned. Joe felt rushed even though he knew it would be at least another four hours before Kathleen Maureen arrived.

When he drove the buggy out of the barn, Joe didn't need to leave his seat as Nora was already waiting at the bottom of the porch steps.

After he turned onto Third Street, Nora asked, "Can you wait for me, Joe? After I check on the children, I need to grab some things, but it will only be a few minutes."

Despite his anxiety, Joe replied, "That's not a problem. I'd just be sitting in the kitchen, anyway."

"It's only a few more hours, but I'm sure it will seem much longer to you."

Joe turned onto Main Street then said, "But it will seem even longer for Faith."

"It will. But it will be well worth the wait."

Joe nodded as they passed the string of saloons. He looked for Will and Rocky but didn't spot them before they turned right onto B Street. He pulled up in front of the Fergusons' home and set the handbrake before Nora left the buggy.

After she'd disappeared through the doorway, Joe pulled out his father's watch then turned to block the southern breeze before opening the lid. The hour and minute hand told him it was 7:47 before he quickly closed the cover to keep his mother's lock of hair from floated away. When he slipped the watch back into his pocket, he decided to purchase a grandfather clock for the parlor.

Joe avoided fidgeting while waiting for Nora to return by revisiting the morning's confrontation. What struck him the most were the only words Bill Roberts had spoken. He'd shouted that he hadn't killed his friend. *Did he think that he was about to be arrested?* He was the one who'd left the note claiming the foreman had murdered Cody Anderson, *so why did he deny his guilt?* Maybe Bill Roberts had seen Joe enter the cutting building and suspected the foreman had accused the lumberjack of murder. There was also the possibility that Roberts had murdered his friend and left the note to deflect blame. Joe knew that he'd never know what happened but would include his suspicions when he wrote his report on Monday.

He was writing his report in his mind when Nora stepped onto their porch and hurried down the short walkway carrying a small bag.

She climbed into the buggy and said, "Jack surprised me. When I entered the house, he had just put his brothers and Anna into their beds and even washed their faces and had them say their prayers."

Joe released the handbrake and snapped the reins before saying, "You shouldn't have been surprised at all. You're a very good mother, Nora."

SPRING SURPRISES

As he turned onto a side street, Nora said, "Thank you, Joe. But I think Jack was just trying to impress Bo. When I praised him for taking care of his brothers and sister, he asked me to tell his papa, too."

"I can understand why Jack would admire him. Bo is one of the finest men I've ever met."

"I agree with you, Joe. I'm very fortunate to have him as my husband and father to our children."

"He says the same thing about you, Nora."

Nora smiled and hugged her bag as Joe drove the buggy through the dark streets. He soon pulled up near the back porch, set the handbrake then climbed out and took Nora's bag before assisting her out of the buggy. After giving Nora her bag, they stepped onto the porch and Joe opened the door.

Bo was holding a full house when he heard Joe and Nora climb the porch steps but tossed his cards onto the table and met his wife as she and Joe entered.

As Bo gave Nora a quick kiss, Tap grinned and said, "I was bluffin', Bo," then scooped up the eleven-cent pot.

Nora soon disappeared into the hallway and her husband returned to the kitchen/poker table.

Joe hung his hat and was quickly popping his coat's buttons when he asked, "How is Faith doing?"

Bo said, "All that's happened since you've been gone is that Mary returned the empty bowl and said Faith was very grateful for the gravy."

Joe was hanging his coat when Mary entered the kitchen, so Tap stood and said, "I reckon Will and Rocky will be here shortly, Joe."

Joe said, "I didn't hear any gunfire when I drove past the saloons, so I'm sure they'll be here shortly."

As the sheriff and Mary donned their coats, Joe took Tap's place at the table. He wasn't in the mood to play poker, but it was better than just sitting around letting time pass.

After he and Bo were alone in the kitchen, Bo said, "I'll take the first deal, so do you wanna ante up, Joe?"

Joe said, "I'll get some change and be right back," then stood and walked down the hallway.

After entering their bedroom, he listened for any sounds coming from the nursery but all he heard were muffled women's voices. He picked up the small dish on their dresser and dumped the coins into his large palm then headed back to the kitchen.

He set his stacks of pennies, nickels and dimes on the table and watched Bo shuffle and deal the cards. As they played their hands and wagered their pennies, Joe found it difficult to concentrate on the game.

Joe folded his first two hands and was shuffling the deck when Rocky arrived.

As he hung his hat, he said, "Will said to tell you he was sorry he couldn't make it because he was needed at home."

Joe said, "That's okay. It's going to be a long night."

SPRING SURPRISES

Rocky joined the game and the minutes continued to crawl by, at least for Joe.

Joe had to fill both kerosene lamps before Rocky left for the night. After he was gone, Bo called an end to the game because he knew Joe was distracted, so he and Joe simply shared coffee and a broad conversation that didn't include babies.

Nora or Sister Mary Catherine made occasional visits to the kitchen to give Joe updates on Faith's progress and to reassure him that she was doing well.

Joe tried not to look at his watch too often, but as the night dragged on, he started checking the time once every five or six minutes.

It was 11:41 when Nora hurried out of the nursery and said, "It's time to fetch Doctor Taylor, Joe."

Joe shot to his feet, snatched his hat from its hook then grabbed his coat and rushed out the door. He bounded into the buggy and snapped the reins to wake Porch before he remembered to release the handbrake. As the buggy rolled down the gravel drive, Joe began tugging on his coat and let Porch navigate the turn onto Third Street.

As soon as he pulled up in front of Doctor Taylor's house, Joe leapt from the buggy and jogged up the walk. He hurried onto the front porch steps then knocked loudly on the door. Joe tried to calm his nerves as he waited anxiously for the doctor, but it was almost impossible. It seemed like hours but was probably less than three minutes before Doctor Taylor opened the door.

Before Joe could say a word, the doctor said, "I'll be there in a few minutes. There's no need to panic, Joe."

"I'll wait in my buggy, Doc."

Doctor Taylor nodded then said, "Alright," and closed the door.

Joe trotted back to the buggy, and after climbing aboard, he grabbed the reins and gave them a sharp snap. Porch pulled the buggy for fifty feet before Joe made a U-turn. Now when the doctor boarded, Joe would be able to save a few seconds on the return trip. He knew it was a silly thing to do, but he was almost terrified that something might happen to Faith before the doctor arrived.

As he sat waiting for the doctor to appear, Joe finally shared the same fears Faith had endured since they'd been married. While his life wasn't at risk, he would have willingly offered it in exchange for hers.

He began tapping his right foot as he focused on the doctor's front door and could feel that he was sliding into panic. So, he stopped his rhythmic toe tapping and softly began to hum Kathleen Mavourneen. As he did, his mind added the lyrics and a translucent image of his mother's face. The ballad soothed him just as it had when his mother sang it to him when he was a small boy.

Joe felt his spirit calm and when he finished, he whispered, "Thank you, Mama."

Less than a minute later, the front door opened, and Doctor Taylor hurried onto the porch carrying his black bag. He quickly stepped along his walkway then climbed in beside Joe. After he settled into the seat, Joe snapped the reins, and the buggy began rolling.

SPRING SURPRISES

Before he turned onto Main Street, the doctor asked, "Did Sister tell you how far apart her contractions were?"

"No, sir. Nora just told me it was time."

Doctor Taylor nodded then said, "Thank you for not driving like a madman, Joe."

Joe smiled as he replied, "You should thank my mother, Doc."

"I'll ask you why you believe I should after I've delivered your baby."

Joe soon turned onto Third Street and then down his drive. He pulled up near the back of the house to let Doctor Taylor exit then drove to the barn to free Porch of his leather shackles. He owed the exhausted gelding for his day-long service, so after he was out of the harness, he'd give him a large helping of oats. He knew he was of no use in the house, so while Porch filled his belly, Joe would give his coat a good brushing.

Twenty minutes later, as he briskly walked to the house, he noticed the smoke drifting out of the cookstove pipe and assumed the doctor had asked to keep a pot of boiling water ready. He hoped that someone made a fresh pot of coffee as well.

When he entered the kitchen, he found a large pot of water on the cookstove and Bo sitting at the table drinking a cup of his freshly brewed coffee and playing solitaire.

As Joe hung his hat, Bo said, "I figgered you'd come rushin' in just a minute after the doc."

Joe replied, "I felt obligated to take care of Porch after riding him most of the day then making him pull the buggy. Did Nora or Sister M.C. tell you anything while I was gone?"

"Nope. They didn't even leave the room."

Joe hung his coat and after filling a large mug with coffee, he took a seat at the table.

Before he took a sip, he pulled out his watch, flipped open the cover and said, "It's 12:37, Bo. So, Kathleen Maureen will be born on Easter Sunday."

He snapped the lid closed and as he was sliding it back into his pocket, Bo said, "You could still be wrong, Joe. Sam Grant might be arriving instead."

Joe smiled then took his first sip of coffee before saying, "I'll be just as happy with a son, Bo. I just want to see Faith's smile when she proves how wrong I was."

Bo grinned and gathered the loose cards into a deck and set it aside before saying, "You don't seem as high strung as you were when you left, Joe."

"It didn't serve any purpose, but I still feel useless."

Bo was about to ask Joe if he wanted to play poker when a bone-chilling scream echoed from the nursery.

Joe leapt to his feet and hurried away from the table but stopped at the hallway entrance. As he stared down the dark hall, he heard Doctor Taylor telling Faith to push followed by her loud wail. It wasn't as frightening as the first, and Joe hoped it would be her last. But it wasn't.

SPRING SURPRISES

Bo stepped beside him as Joe listened to Faith's cries of pain and Doctor Taylor's loud commands to keep pushing. He wished he could do something to help her but knew there was only one way available to him. So, he closed his eyes and prayed for Faith's ordeal to end.

Joe's eyes were still closed when he heard the miraculous sound of a baby's wailing entrance into the cold outside world.

He opened his eyes just before Bo pounded him on the back and said, "Congratulations, Papa Joe."

Joe smiled but didn't reply as stared at the nursery door. He knew that Doctor Taylor and Sister M.C. would be busy for a few minutes. But he hoped to see Nora to leave the nursery soon to tell him that Faith was all right.

The baby was still crying when the door opened, and Nora stepped into the hallway wearing a big smile as she said, "Sorry, Joe. You were wrong. You may not be meeting Kathleen Maureen, but you have a beautiful son."

Joe quickly asked, "How is Faith? Is she all right?"

Nora replied, "She's doing fine. You'll be able to see her in a…"

Nora's answer was interrupted when Faith screamed and Doctor Taylor exclaimed, "Close the door! We need you!"

Joe took a long step into the hallway before Nora slammed the door shut and Bo grabbed his arm to keep him from barging into the nursery.

Joe was closer to panic than he'd ever been in his entire life as he listened to Faith's loud cries, the baby's wails, and Doctor Taylor giving loud instructions to Sister Mary Catherine and Nora. The mixed sounds behind the walls made it impossible for him to understand what was happening in the nursery. All he knew was that there was an unexpected complication and could only hope that Doctor Taylor would save his beloved Faith.

The terrifying sounds continued for another six minutes before Faith released her last shriek and then all he heard were the loud voices and Sam's constant crying. He desperately wanted to rush down the hallway but was held back by the fear of what he might find if he entered the nursery.

Bo quietly said, "I'm sure everything's all right, Joe."

Joe nodded but knew that Bo was just trying to keep him from losing his mind and barging into the nursery. He strained to listen to what was happening, but all he heard were low voices and Sam's wails. He couldn't hear Faith but hoped it was just because she was exhausted.

He silently prayed as he waited for the door to open. As he strained to listen for Faith's voice, he drew comfort from Sam's crying. It meant that even if he lost Faith, she would still live in their child. But then he noticed that Sam's wailing sounded different somehow and feared that his newborn son might be taken from him before he even met him.

Joe felt a surge of anger at the thought and was ready to explode when he heard his mother's voice whisper, "There is no need to fear, my son. Faith is still with you."

Joe knew it was just his mind using his mother's voice to tell him what he wanted to hear, but it still gave him a surge of hope. He was still anxious but was no longer angry or despondent.

SPRING SURPRISES

He didn't know how long he'd waited but it seemed like hours before the door opened and Doctor Taylor stepped into view. He just beckoned to Joe before disappearing back into the nursery. Joe hadn't been able to read the doctor's expression during his brief appearance in the shadowed hall but remained hopeful that Faith and Sam were all right.

Joe glanced at Bo before slowly stepping down the hallway. He took a deep breath before he passed through the open doorway then quickly looked at the bed. What his eyes revealed was the biggest surprise of his young life.

Faith's blonde hair was soaked in perspiration, but her deep blue eyes sparkled in the lamplight. She didn't speak but just smiled at him as she held a tiny, bundled baby in each arm.

A smile slowly grew on his face as he quietly asked, "Are you all right, Faith?"

"I'm tired but so very happy. Aren't you going to say hello to Sam and Kathleen Maureen?"

Joe slowly stepped past a grinning Sister Mary Catherine and when he reached the head of the bed, he leaned down and gently kissed Faith.

Then he asked, "Which one is Kathleen Maureen?"

"She's closer to you."

Joe kissed Katie on her forehead then carefully leaned across Faith and kissed Sam.

He was going to sit down when Doctor Taylor said, "You need to leave, Joe. We need to clean up, and Faith needs to rest and feed the babies."

Joe nodded then smiled at his perfect wife and said, "I guess I'll have to buy another cradle."

As he stepped away, he received the precious gift of hearing Faith's gentle laugh. When he closed the door, he took a moment to thank God before he slowly walked to the kitchen while quietly singing Kathleen Mavourneen.

TRANSITION

Easter Sunday had begun in an enormously happy fashion and while the rest of the holy day was not as spectacular, it was equally joyous. Father Burns arrived early to say Mass and give communion. He blessed Sam and Katie then said he'd baptize the babies on Saturday.

The Beck home rarely had fewer than six visitors as friends arrived with food and to admire Sam and Katie. After her much-needed rest, Faith was the center of attention.

Joe didn't need to make a run to Walker's on Monday to make his emergency cradle purchase, either. Tap had rummaged through his storeroom, found their unused boxy baby bed and happily donated it to the new parents.

After Joe cleared the nursery of visitors, he closed the door then sat on the bed beside Faith.

She smiled and said, "I hope you aren't expecting me to fulfill my wifely duties now that we no longer have an impediment."

Joe kissed her before saying, "No, ma'am. I have another duty for you."

He took their Bible from the side table and gave it to her before he opened the bottle of ink. As he dipped the nib into the black liquid, Faith opened the Good Book to the page with the entry of their marriage.

Joe smiled as he handed her the pen and watched as she entered Sam Grant Beck born March 27, 1864. She skipped a line for Sam's baptism before writing Kathleen Maureen Beck followed by the same date. She smiled at Joe as he took the pen from her fingers and set it on the table.

As they waited for the ink to dry, Joe looked at their babies sleeping in their cradles and said, "They're both perfect just like their mother. They even have blue eyes."

Faith said, "They are beautiful, aren't they? It was a painful experience, but now I finally understand how Becky felt when she rocked her imaginary baby. When Doctor Taylor placed Sam and Katie in my arms, I was filled with a joy beyond my imagination. The love I feel for our children is so powerful, I know that my fears will never return."

Faith gave the Bible to Joe before he said, "Friday night, I asked God to help you overcome your demons but was surprised by how He chose to answer my prayer."

Faith said, "I was surprised, too."

Joe set the Bible on the table then took Faith's hand and said, "Even if we only have happy surprises in our future, none will ever be as wonderful."

SPRING SURPRISES

BOOK LIST

1	Rock Creek	12/26/2016
2	North of Denton	01/02/2017
3	Fort Selden	01/07/2017
4	Scotts Bluff	01/14/2017
5	South of Denver	01/22/2017
6	Miles City	01/28/2017
7	Hopewell	02/04/2017
8	Nueva Luz	02/12/2017
9	The Witch of Dakota	02/19/2017
10	Baker City	03/13/2017
11	The Gun Smith	03/21/2017
12	Gus	03/24/2017
13	Wilmore	04/06/2017
14	Mister Thor	04/20/2017
15	Nora	04/26/2017
16	Max	05/09/2017
17	Hunting Pearl	05/14/2017
18	Bessie	05/25/2017
19	The Last Four	05/29/2017
20	Zack	06/12/2017
21	Finding Bucky	06/21/2017
22	The Debt	06/30/2017
23	The Scalawags	07/11/2017
24	The Stampede	08/23/2017
25	The Wake of the Bertrand	07/31/2017
26	Cole	08/09/2017
27	Luke	09/05/2017
28	The Eclipse	09/21/2017
29	A.J. Smith	10/03/2017
30	Slow John	11/05/2017
31	The Second Star	11/15/2017
32	Tate	12/03/2017
33	Virgil's Herd	12/14/2017
34	Marsh's Valley	01/01/2018

35	Alex Paine	01/18/2018
36	Ben Gray	02/05/2018
37	War Adams	03/05/2018
38	Mac's Cabin	03/21/2018
39	Will Scott	04/13/2018
40	Sheriff Joe	04/22/2018
41	Chance	05/17/2018
42	Doc Holt	06/17/2018
43	Ted Shepard	07/16/2018
44	Haven	07/30/2018
45	Sam's County	08/19/2018
46	Matt Dunne	09/07/2018
47	Conn Jackson	10/06/2018
48	Gabe Owens	10/27/2018
49	Abandoned	11/18/2018
50	Retribution	12/21/2018
51	Inevitable	02/04/2019
52	Scandal in Topeka	03/18/2019
53	Return to Hardeman County	04/10/2019
54	Deception	06/02.2019
55	The Silver Widows	06/27/2019
56	Hitch	08/22/2019
57	Dylan's Journey	10/10/2019
58	Bryn's War	11/05/2019
59	Huw's Legacy	11/30/2019
60	Lynn's Search	12/24/2019
61	Bethan's Choice	02/12/2020
62	Rhody Jones	03/11/2020
63	Alwen's Dream	06/14/2020
64	The Nothing Man	06/30/2020
65	Cy Page	07/19/2020
66	Tabby Hayes	09/04/2020
67	Dylan's Memories	09/20/2020
68	Letter for Gene	09/09/2020
69	Grip Taylor	10/10/2020
70	Garrett's Duty	11/09/2020

SPRING SURPRISES

71	East of the Cascades	12/02/2020
72	The Iron Wolfe	12/23/2020
73	Wade Rivers	01/09/2021
74	Ghost Train	01/27/2021
75	The Inheritance	02/26/2021
76	Cap Tyler	03/26/2021
77	The Photographer	04/10/2021
78	Jake	05/06/2021
79	Riding Shotgun	06/03/2021
80	The Saloon Lawyer	07/04/2021
81	Unwanted	09/21/2021
82	reunion	11/26/2021
83	The Divide	12/28/2021
84	Rusty & Bug	01/21/2022
85	The Laramie Plains	02/15/2022
86	Idaho City	03/16/2022
87	Poole's Gold	05/06/2022
88	Spring Surprises	06/30/2022

C.J. PETIT

Made in the USA
Columbia, SC
26 July 2022